Drowning in Amber

a Marie Jenner
mystery

E. C. Bell

Drowning in Amber

a Marie Jenner mystery

E. C. Bell

TYCHE BOOKS LTD.

Drowning in Amber
Published by Tyche Books Ltd.
www.TycheBooks.com

Copyright © 2015 E.C. Bell
First Tyche Books Ltd Edition 2015

Print ISBN: 978-1-928025-37-5
Ebook ISBN: 978-1-928025-38-2

Cover Art by Guillem Marí
Cover Layout by Lucia Starkey
Interior Layout by Ryah Deines
Editorial by Allison Campbell

Author photograph: Shelby Deep Photography

This book was funded in part by a grant from the Alberta Media Fund.

Alberta ▆
Government

Contents

Dedication

To Bear, the best dog ever...but don't tell Buddy and Millie. I don't want to hurt their feelings.

Prologue:
"Brown Eddie" Hansen:
The Kicking and What Came After

UNDERSTAND NOW, I'VE taken a kicking or two in my life. I have. That's part of living on the streets. But these three guys in Donald Duck masks—which made me half laugh and think, "What the hell?" just before they caught me—put the boots to me good.

I curled into a ball, felt my kidneys turn to mush, and knew I'd be pissing blood for days as I waited for them to stop. Ribs broke—snap snap snap—the pain a distant burr, thank God. They'd caught me just after I'd smoked, and I wasn't feeling much. But I was going to. Like I said, I've taken a kicking or two in my life. I knew what was coming. Another visit to the Royal Alex Emerg.

"Please stop." My voice sounded funny, whiny and high. "Please. I won't do it again."

Had no idea what I'd done, but I was ready to admit to just about anything to get them to stop. Really, just about anything. My pathetic-sounding voice must've touched a chord in one of them, because the boots laid off and the voices started, and so I did what I always do when I get a small break in a beating. I tried to run.

Didn't go so good, I must admit. I crawled about a foot and a

1

half. They grabbed me again, and as they hauled me to my feet, I heard screaming. Took me a second to realize it was me.

Stop the noise. Just stop the noise and maybe they'll leave you alone, I thought. But it didn't stop. Just gouted out of me like it was my lifeblood. Like if I stopped that, I'd stop everything.

Through my high, I started to feel afraid. No. That word's not big enough for what I was starting to feel. Not by a long shot.

They dragged me across the Holy Trinity Church front yard where I'd been sitting, peddling my wares. Scruffy grass, mostly dirt. I watched my feet kick up dust as I tried to run, but the hold on my arms didn't loosen, and then they had me under the only tree left.

They pushed me up against it, face first. The bark bit into my bloody cheek and the screaming went up in pitch. I sounded like a girl—why wasn't anybody helping? There had to be someone around. They flipped me so I was looking out at them. Their masks didn't look so fucking funny anymore, and I tried to stop screaming so I could talk them into letting me go but my voice just wound up and up to soprano registers as they held my arms out, touching the branches of that fucking tree, and I felt the broken bones grinding in one of them. I was broken everywhere.

"Please!" I screeched, blood spewing from my mouth like a fucking fountain, and then even my screams got small and thread, and I couldn't catch my breath.

One of the ducks looked at the leader. "Isn't this enough?" he asked. At least I think it was a he.

"No," the leader said. "We have to make an example of him. These pieces of shit have to understand—"

And then he pulled a hammer out of somewhere, and with it long spikes, and I found the strength to fight against the hands holding me, and almost made it, almost fell out of their grasp, but not quite. Oh god. Not quite.

"We have to make them all understand that nobody can do what this shit bird did and expect to live."

He held one spike to my mostly open left palm and smacked it a good one with the hammer. And again I found my voice.

The last thing I remember seeing, after he nailed me to that fucking tree, was the hammer swinging up in the full moon light. I watched the blood—my blood, my god that was my blood, there was so much of it—arc away, black against the grey of the rest of the world. Then the hammer came down and hit me on the forehead.

My last thought as the world went black was, "I'm in real trouble here."

Truer fucking words were never spoken.

STAGE ONE
GETTING TO WHY

Marie:
Looking for Another Ghost,
Like I Have Nothing Better to Do

I WENT LOOKING for Brown Eddie one day after he died. I wasn't happy about this particular meeting, because to that point, dealing with ghosts hadn't helped me further my life goals one iota.

I thought I'd have a career by now, know what I mean? That I'd never wear mismatched socks, my hair would always look good, and I wouldn't have to worry about paying my rent again.

Not a very long list, but the only thing I could definitely check off was not having to worry about paying my rent, because technically, I was homeless. (That's what happens when your ex-boyfriend burns down your apartment building in a city with a zero vacancy rate.) My best friend, Jasmine, was letting me couch-surf at her place, but still. Not good.

On the plus side, I did have a job—sort of. I was working as a secretary for James Lavall, who'd inherited a ramshackle private investigation business from his recently deceased uncle.

The big problem was, James wasn't even a real private eye, yet. He'd inherited his dead uncle's licence with the business, so he had a month to either wind up the old man's affairs and close the office, or get his own licence and carry on.

The fact that he was suffering from a concussion—due to our last, and only, case—was making him think very hard about whether he wanted to do this private eye thing. Which meant, well, I had a job, but only sort of.

In short, I felt like a fly trapped in amber or something. My life wouldn't get better no matter how hard I tried. But there I was, trudging toward the Holy Trinity Church near downtown Edmonton, preparing to talk to another ghost like I thought it was actually going to help my situation at all.

My cell phone chirped. James Lavall's name showed on the display, and I sighed, deeply. He might be my boss, sort of, and gorgeous, definitely. But I didn't want to talk to him, because I hadn't yet told him about the new case I'd taken in his name. I stared down at the phone and decided that since this job was one of the only things I *did* have going for me, I didn't want to screw it up. So I slapped a big, fake smile on my face and answered his call.

"Hi, James. How's your head?"

"Not great." He sounded terrible, like he was recovering from a concussion, which he was. "Somebody named Honoria Lowe called. She told me to tell you the dead guy's name is Brown Eddie and that she wants her appointment moved to two o'clock."

Oops.

"Who is she," he asked. "And *why* does she think she has an appointment?"

"Because she does," I said. "She wants to hire us."

"Why?"

"The cops think she had something to do with a murder. She didn't, of course, so—"

"A what?" His voice went from impatient to angry. "A murder?"

"I'll explain everything when I get back to the office," I said and crossed my fingers.

He was silent for a long time, and when he spoke, he sounded even more tired than he had moments before.

"I thought we were going to make some decisions before we took another case," he finally said.

"Decisions?" I asked, weakly.

"About this place," he replied. "This business. Us. You know, decisions."

Us. There it was. The thing I didn't want to deal with. The possibility of us. Chicken that I am, I decided to ignore that and concentrate on the business.

"I know we haven't had a chance to talk, James, but here's the thing. You still have a month to use your uncle's private investigator's licence. That's the reason I told Honoria to come in for a meeting. I think we should take her case. Why not have some money coming in while you're deciding. You know?"

"Twenty days," he replied. "I have twenty days."

"All right, twenty days," I repeated, trying to keep the crankiness, which was really bubbling to the surface by that time, at bay. "I don't know about you, but I could use some cash."

He was silent for so long I wondered if we'd lost our connection.

"Do you honestly have a lead?" he finally asked.

"Yes." And I held my breath.

"Then go," he said. "I gotta lie down."

I put the phone away and picked up my pace. I had to get to the Holy Trinity Church, find the dead guy—who I now knew was called Brown Eddie—and convince him to tell me, clearly and without a doubt, who had killed him, so I'd have good news to take back to James.

Technically, things like "who killed you" didn't matter when it came to moving a ghost to the next plane of existence, but it would help Honoria, and that would help the Jimmy Lavall Detective Agency, which would in turn help me.

All right, so I wasn't going to see the ghost for any altruistic reason. I was doing it for a paycheque. My mom would have never done anything like that. She saw our gift as a calling, not a career. But I wanted a career.

Forget career—I wanted a life. And not the same as my mother's, that's for sure. All that gift gave her was a broken marriage, screwed-up kids, and cancer.

Okay, so maybe it didn't give her cancer, but it sure gave her the rest. Why would I want that? Why would I ever willingly accept that as a viable life choice? It never paid. It's not like I could invoice ghosts. Could I?

No. Trust me. I couldn't.

Now, I didn't feel particularly good about trying to get information from this Brown Eddie guy without offering to help move him on to the next plane of existence, but I'd decided I wasn't going to volunteer. I was still exhausted—and dehydrated—from the last ghost I'd moved on. If Eddie didn't ask for help, he'd just have to find his own way.

Usually, they move on without help, I told myself as I trudged down the street toward the church where the dead guy had been killed. Usually.

But not always. Sometimes they needed help from people like my mother. Like me. So if Eddie asked, I'd probably feel compelled to help, which was just about the last thing I wanted to do.

It wasn't just because I didn't want to interact with ghosts anymore, though that was a big part of it. It was because I'd have to lie to James Lavall about any and all information Eddie gave me. You see, he didn't know a thing about my ghost-seeing abilities, and that's the way it had to stay.

For about a second, I wished I could just come clean to James about being able to interact with ghosts. It would have made it all so much easier. But I knew I wasn't going to do that. Normal people like James don't want to know about this kind of stuff. They live on the surface of the world. And they always—always—think that people who live any deeper are crazy.

Just ask my dad.

Thinking about the way he'd treated my mother girded my loins, so to speak. Nope. James didn't need to know about the ghost. James just had to be massively impressed when I walked in with all the answers, solved the case, and brought in a quick—and real—paycheque for both of us.

I hoped.

I HAD TO push through a large crowd to get to the big tree in the dusty front yard of the Holy Trinity Church. Nothing draws the crowds like death, I guess. I couldn't really see anything until I got to the yellow police tape draped around the tree. Then I saw the blood.

The front of the tree looked as though it had been drenched in it. Two branches, reaching out from the trunk about four feet up, looked as though they had been attacked with an axe. I felt sick and turned away, nearly stepping on a frighteningly skinny woman about my age, squatting in the grass by the yellow tape.

She was trying to light a candle that she'd set by a grocery store bouquet of white daisies.

"Watch it," she said, without looking up. She sounded exhausted, as the lighter in her hand spewed hugely ineffectual sparks all around the candle and the daisies. She rubbed her eyes distractedly, smearing her mascara. "I can't make the stupid thing light."

"Want me to try?"

She stared at me for a second, then handed me the lighter. It took a couple of tries, then the candle was lit, and I handed it back to her. "Thanks," she said.

"You knew Brown Eddie?" I asked. "The guy who died?"

"He didn't like being called that." Her eyes narrowed, and she clutched her purse. "You a reporter or something?"

"No. I work for a detective agency," I said. "And I want to help. What was his name?"

I will never know why she told me, but she did. Her bottom lip quivered, and she turned back to the tree. "His name is—was—Hansen. Eddie Hansen."

"Thank you." I turned, but her voice brought me up short.

"I wish I could be the one to tell his mother what happened to him," she whispered. "She needs to know."

"The police will do that," I said.

"Yeah," she said, and shook her head. "But I'd like to be the one to look her in the eye and say, 'You did this to Eddie, you bitch.'"

Her mouth pulled into a thin, tight line in her pocked face. I didn't know what to say, but for once did the smart thing and kept my mouth shut.

"If she'd only let him back home, maybe none of this would have happened." Her lips quivered. "I mean, she lived in the city and everything. And he was only a kid."

She turned toward me as though she was going to say more, then her eyes iced, and she shook her head. "I shouldn't be talking to you. I don't even know who you are."

Before I could speak, she turned on her heel and walked away, letting me know without a shadow of a doubt that our interview was over.

So I looked around the rest of the church yard for a dead guy named Eddie Hansen. What I found was nothing. Absolutely nothing.

I kept looking at the tree as I searched in vain for the ghost. He should have been here. The violence to that tree told me he'd have questions—a boatload of them was my guess—before he made his decision and moved on. So, where was he?

Nowhere I could see.

I left the churchyard and headed back to the office, not completely depressed, but close. I had Eddie's last name and knew that his mother lived in the city. Somewhere.

I hoped I could turn those bits of information into something concrete before James and I had our meeting with Honoria Lowe, our almost client, since I had no idea where Dead Eddie Hansen was, and my hour was up.

Darn it anyhow.

Marie:
Honoria Lowe's Not Crazy.
She's Special

I WASN'T FEELING fantastic as I walked back to Dead Uncle Jimmy's office, where James Lavall was waiting for me. I was supposed to be bringing back all sorts of information that would help us quickly wind up the case I'd taken.

However, Dead Eddie hadn't been where he should have been, which was close to his place of death.

Typical. Never a ghost around when you really need one.

I briefly wondered if he'd moved on to the next plane of existence all on his own. It was unusual, but not out of the question. The big problem was, if he'd moved on, I'd have to actually do some detective work if I wanted to figure out who killed him. Since I had no idea how to do that, Honoria Lowe would probably have to find someone else to save her from the police. Which meant no paycheque for us.

James was sitting at his dead uncle's desk, reading a book, with a pizza box and two cans of soda sitting in front of him. He looked up and smiled as I walked in, gesturing at the pizza box, which I could see had been opened.

"Want some?"

"Thanks," I said. I was starving, and the cooling cheese and pepperoni smelled divine.

He handed me the unopened can of soda, then leaned back, watching me as I mashed the slice into my mouth. I realized I was not being very ladylike and tried to slow down, but my starving stomach said no-go to that idea, and I swallowed and rammed more in, grinning at him.

"Just a teeny bit hungry," I said. I was going to get embarrassed, which would have made me say something mean, I'm sure, but he shrugged.

"I was starving, too. When was the last time we had a decent meal?"

"I don't remember," I mumbled.

"Neither do I," he said. "Things got a little exciting. Couldn't seem to work it in."

"Yeah." I sipped the soda and took another big bite of the pizza, sighing deeply. It felt like a little bit of heaven, and James was good enough to let me finish eating before he grilled me.

"So, tell me about this meeting we are supposed to have," he said, as I swallowed my last bite.

"Yes," I said. "The meeting."

"Yes," he replied, and smiled at me encouragingly. He sounded nothing like the angry man I'd spoken to an hour before. "Tell me all about it."

"Did you take a painkiller?" I asked.

"Yep." He grinned even more broadly. "Those are good pills."

Ah. Drugged. Explained just about everything.

"Okay, the meeting. Honoria Lowe is the cousin of one of your Dead Uncle Jimmy's old clients."

"Don't call him that," James said.

"Sorry." I shrugged, and continued, "She wants us to help her cousin Honoria prove she had nothing to do with the death of Eddie. I thought I'd gather some intel while you were asleep—"

"Intel?" He snickered.

"Yeah," I said, bristling. "I can gather intel as well as anyone else. Can't I?"

"Yes," he said, and luckily for him, the snickering subsided. "You're actually quite good at it. Were you successful?"

I thought about not finding Eddie and shook my head. "Not really. I figured out the dead guy's name. Eddie Hansen—"

"I knew that, too. It was announced on TV just before you got back."

Of course it was. Which meant Eddie's next of kin had been informed. "All right, fine," I sighed. "I met one of his friends, but she didn't give me much more than his name. Not yet."

"In other words, we have nothing."

"Not right now."

"So we should probably tell this Honoria person we can't take the case," he said.

"It's a job, James." The words rushed out of me before I could stop them. "I don't know about you, but I could use some extra cash, even if it is only for a couple of days' work. At the very least, let's talk to her. If she can give us some clues, maybe we can figure out who killed Eddie and get her off the hook."

"Clues. Intel." He grinned again and walked slowly over to the door. "You're starting to sound like a detective, or something."

I tried to grin back. "I'm just the secretary," I said.

"Like fun you are," he replied. Then he leaned heavily against the door jamb and thought.

"All right," he finally said. "We'll talk to her. Maybe there's a way we can help her prove to the police she wasn't involved."

"Thanks," I whispered.

"But if she doesn't give us any good 'clues'"—and he grinned again—"then we'll send her on her way. Right?"

"Right," I said.

I wondered why the cops saw her as a potential suspect. Then I shuddered, remembering all the blood around that tree. What if she actually was the one who killed Eddie Hansen? And what if we figured it out?

"Would she still pay us?" I muttered.

"What did you say?" James asked.

"Nothing," I said. "I didn't say anything."

HONORIA LOWE CAME to the office at two o'clock on the dot.

I was sitting behind my desk in the reception area, trying to look busy. James was back in his dead uncle's office, doing whatever.

Honoria walked into the room so quietly I did a double take. She could have been one of the dead. Even her footsteps were silent. She stood, staring at the top of my desk.

"My name is Honoria," she finally said. "Honoria Lowe."

Then she smiled and literally lit up the room. I could have worked up a big case of "I hate you" right there, if she hadn't also looked like she'd been psychically beaten to a bloody pulp. I've never seen anyone who looked so haunted in my whole life.

And I see ghosts, for heaven's sake.

"You mentioned on the phone that you're having trouble with the police. What's going on?" I asked.

Honoria frowned. "I thought I was supposed to have a meeting with the owner. James Lavall."

She was making it much easier for me to hate her.

"Yes, you're absolutely right. My apologies."

She didn't acknowledge my existence after that. Nice. She didn't want to talk to the hired help, obviously. I pushed myself out of my chair and walked to the closed door of the inner office. James could deal with her.

I knocked twice, then stuck my head into the office. "She's here."

James looked up from the book he was reading and closed it softly. I didn't understand his fascination with books. They just made my head hurt. "I'm ready," he said. "Send her in."

Honoria smoothly walked past me and up to James's desk. "Honoria Lowe," she said, and held her hand out to him. "My cousin says good things about this agency."

Her cousin knew James's Uncle Jimmy. James's very recently dead Uncle Jimmy. The actual private investigator. I hoped Honoria didn't know about that. No need to worry her with our lack of expertise.

She sat in the chair opposite James's, then stared at the top of his desk as though she'd been struck mute.

James glanced over at me, his eyes wide. I shrugged, letting him know I had no clue what our potential client's damage was. He shrugged back and looked at Honoria. "Tell me what happened."

She seemed to thaw. "All right," she said softly, and smiled. "If you want."

"I do," James replied, and almost batted his eyes at her. He was basking in the glow of her fantastic smile, for heaven's sake! I felt an ugly prick of jealousy, knowing for a fact that I'd never smiled that beautifully in my whole life.

"Just don't judge me, until I'm done," she said. "Please."

Now, that was just a little bit strange. I looked at James, but he ignored me.

"Consider it a judge-free zone," he said, then glanced in my direction. "Take notes?"

I nodded, grabbed some paper and a pen, and settled in a chair next to James's desk.

"How do you know the man who was murdered?" James asked. "I believe you said his name was Brown Eddie?"

"I've never actually met him in person," Honoria replied. "He comes to me in my dreams."

"What?" James asked.

"What?" My pen stutter-stepped across the page. Had she actually said, out loud, that a dead guy came to her in her dreams?

Honoria looked down at the floor. "I'm not crazy," she finally said. "No matter what my family thinks. I-I see Brown Eddie in my dreams." She put her hands to her face, briefly. "I watch him die. And I keep watching him die."

She opened her eyes, and looked at James, fiercely. "You have to help me," she said. "I can't get the dreams to stop, this time. He won't get out of my head!"

James didn't say anything, but I did.

"Oh my God," I muttered.

She dreams of the dead. She's a frigging clairvoyant.

THAT'S WHAT MY mother called them. She'd told me about them, before I moved away from home. I always thought they were urban legends or something. Even Mom had never actually met one. Just heard about them.

"The poor dears can't even communicate with the dead," she said. "They are condemned to a life of trying to piece together clues about the dead from their dreams. No way to help, no way to stop it, so I've heard."

"We can't stop seeing the dead, either," I'd whispered.

She'd reached out and patted my hand gently. She did things like that when I got worked up about our "gift," which meant she patted my hand a lot.

"Dear, we are nothing like those poor creatures! With just a little training, we can do wondrous things for the spirits of the dead. Help them move on. Help them understand what's tying them to this earth, what lessons they need to learn from their time among the living, what they would like to do next—we can help them with all of that."

"And those other people? The clairvoyants?"

"They can only watch." My mother shuddered. "What a terrible life it would be."

Looking at Honoria, I thought that my mother was on to something.

Honoria stared between her feet as she droned out her life story. She'd been able to see visions most of her life. She wasn't sure what made it start, but when it did, it was like a flood. Every night she was bombarded with visions of death and dying. Her mother had had her hospitalized and drugged to the eyeballs. The drugs she was given helped for a while.

"Then they lost their effectiveness," Honoria said. "I was almost glad, because they made me feel—disconnected. Disjointed. Horrible. But they let me pull it together enough to go home again. There, I was able to come up with some strategies that seemed to work. Until now."

James stared at Honoria. He seemed hypnotized by her story. "So, what happened this time?"

"I don't know," she said. "Brown Eddie—I think he's a drug addict who hangs around Needle Park, across the street from my apartment—popped into my dreams a couple of days ago. Horrible, what happened to him."

She shuddered, and I didn't blame her. The tree Eddie had been hung on was going to feature in my nightmares for a while, and I hadn't even seen the actual murder.

James didn't move, so, after an awkward moment, I spoke. "What did you do?"

"I went to the police." She shook her head. "Bit of an error, there."

No kidding, I thought as I scribbled feverishly on the pad of paper. First lesson my mother taught me was to never go to the police. They do not handle people like us very well at all.

"Why was it an error?" James asked.

"Because now they think I was involved in the murder," she said. "They held me for eighteen hours. I just got out. Didn't even have time to get home and clean up, or anything." She looked down at herself, then up, apologetically, at James.

"I'm sorry," she whispered. "I must look a wreck."

"You look fine," James said.

"Thank you." And then, she practically batted *her* eyes at *him* as she smiled that fantastic smile again.

Good grief.

"You must have known the police would think you were involved if you went and talked to them," I said, a little nastily. "So why did you do it?"

"I told you. Eddie won't stop coming to me." Honoria said. She sobbed, a strangled sound, and I passed her a tissue. "And he dies—so badly."

"You said he hung around Needle Park," James said. "How did you know that if you never met him?"

"I think he tried to panhandle from me once or twice, but . . . There's so many of them around the park, I can't be sure."

"And now you're dreaming about him?"

Honoria nodded.

"Who did you speak to? At the police station?"

I heard strangeness in James's voice and glanced up from my scribbled notes. He still looked attentive enough, and nodded encouragingly, but I was certain I'd heard something off in his tone. Reminded me of people back home and the way they'd sometimes spoken to my mother.

"A Detective Rumsfeld," Honoria said. "And later, someone named Stewart."

Her voice sounded stiff, and I would have been willing to bet large amounts of money that she'd picked up the same tone in James's voice as I had. After all, if a person had to live with this kind of disability, a person could get pretty tuned in when it came to disbelief.

James was going to blow this, if I didn't do something. So, I did what I usually do. I barged right in.

"What information did you give to them?"

She turned to me, relief on her face. "I told them what I'd remembered from my dreams, and I showed them my sketches."

"Sketches?"

"What I draw, to stop the visions. Sometimes words don't do it." She blew out a shaky breath. "Often words won't do it."

I thought about the way the crucifixion tree looked, even without the dead guy attached to it, and suppressed a shudder.

Those would have been some horrible drawings. No wonder the cops were interested in her.

"Did you leave them with the police?" I asked.

"Yes," Honoria said. "They wanted them, and I thought they would help." She snorted derisively. "I think those drawings are the reason the police believe I'm involved."

"Is that what they told you? That they think you're involved?" James finally spoke. I noticed the tone was gone.

Honoria looked at him. "Before they let me go, they called me a 'person of interest.' Said they'd have some more questions for me later. Told me not to leave town." She sniffed and looked like she was going to burst into tears again.

"And you are absolutely sure you don't know this man—" James started to speak, and I could tell it was a stupid question, a question that meant nothing, so I rode right over it with my own.

"Do you have copies of your drawings? Or maybe some others, that you didn't take to the police? Anything like that at all?"

I didn't even look at James when I heard him slump back in his chair with a huff. He'd get over it. I—we—needed to see those drawings.

"Yes."

"Any chance we can see them? Soon?"

"How about now?" She reached into her purse and pulled out a handful of wrinkled sheets of paper. "Here are some that I drew on my way here. You can have them if you want."

"Hey, wait—" James started, but I glared him into quiet, and took the proffered pages from Honoria's hand. I put them on the desk top. Then I stared, hard.

"What am I looking at?" I finally asked. This wasn't the crucifixion tree, or anything like it.

"I don't know," Honoria said.

James stood and looked at the topmost sheet. "Looks like the front of a house."

"I get that," I said. "But why?" I glanced at Honoria. "I thought you said all you saw was his murder. That was at the church, wasn't it?"

Honoria shrugged. "It comes to me and I draw it," she said. "I have no control." She pointed at a small figure hastily penciled into one of the windows of the house. "That's him," she said. "In that house. For some reason."

I looked at the sketch again and blinked. The address of the house was etched above the hastily sketched door. If Eddie had somehow figured out a way to go to this house, maybe he was still there. Maybe I could catch him . . .

"I have an idea," I said.

"I don't know how much help we'll be," James said over my words, glaring at me when I turned and stared at him. "We don't have much to go on."

Actually, we did. If I hurried and got to the address on the sketch, I was certain I could catch Eddie there and then talk to him. We'd have the case sewn up in no time. This was going to be a cake walk.

"I think we should take the case, James." I smiled, hoping I sounded businesslike and not like I was begging. "I have a few ideas—"

"No doubt you do," Honoria said, and then she gave me an appraising look that brought my smile down a few lumens, I have to tell you. "I think *you* will be able to clear up this misunderstanding that I have with the police in no time at all." She glanced at James again, a strange half-smile on her face. "Make sure you listen to her," she said. "She has—skills in this area, I think."

"See?" I looked at James so I didn't have to look at Honoria anymore, suddenly afraid she knew more about me than I was willing to admit to anyone else in the room. Namely James. "We can do this."

He stared at me for a long moment, until I silently mouthed, "Please" at him. He shrugged and then turned back to Honoria. "I'll give you a call and let you know what we decide. Tonight."

"Why don't you come to my place," she said. "I've got more sketches there. You can look at them, too, before you make your decision." She grabbed a pen and scribbled on the edge of one of her sketches. "Here's my address," she said. "Come by about nine."

"Nine?" James said.

"Nine," Honoria repeated. "I have to work."

She reached her hand over the desk. James stared, and then slowly took it, and shook it, once. And then, she was gone.

"Can you explain to me why we should take that case?" James

asked, almost before the door closed on our newest almost client.

"Shhh. She might hear you."

We sat in silence for what felt like enough time to let Honoria trundle down the stairs and out the front door to the street. Then I turned to him and tried to explain, in my overwhelmingly unhelpful way.

"We need the money, James. And I don't think she did it."

Short, sweet, and to the point. Though I wasn't really too sure about the last bit. She could have done it, for all I knew. But I wanted to hear who had done it, from the ghost's mouth, and it looked like Honoria was going to be able to help me find him.

"Do you really think she's innocent?" James asked, looking about as unsure as I felt. "The cops—they have instincts about things like this. There has to be a reason she's a person of interest."

"For heaven's sake, she can't weigh more than 100 pounds! How could she have hung that guy in the tree?"

He shook his head. "I don't know. All that talk about visions and things. That all sounds crazy. Right?"

"Yeah, right," I snapped, sudden anger flooding through me. I'd heard those words all my life. Those words were the reason I'd moved away from home and to Edmonton, and they were the last words in the world I wanted to hear coming out of his mouth. "Anyone you don't understand must be crazy."

"Well, what do you think's going on with her?" he asked, and I could hear anger in his voice. If I didn't get off this track, we were going to fight again, and I didn't want to fight.

"I think there's more out there in the world than we know," I replied, doing my level best to drive the emotion from my voice. "And maybe we need to just believe her, for the moment."

"Seriously?" He laughed, and it bumped up against the anger still rolling through my veins until I thought I'd blow a gasket. "She's been in and out of mental institutions all her life. *That* doesn't make you think she's crazy?"

"No." I stared down at the top of the desk, at the sketches Honoria had left. "There's something else going on here. Just call it a feeling."

I picked up the sketches with shaking fingers and rolled them into a tube. "I'm going to go and check this place out," I said. "Maybe there's someone there who can tell me something."

"This is the definition of a wild goose chase, you know," he said.

"I don't care what you think," I said. "I told her we'd help, and we're going to help. At least, I am."

I whirled and headed for the door. His voice stopped me.

"So you really think we can figure this out?"

I shrugged. "Honestly? I don't know. But I have to try."

"Want me to come with?"

The last thing in the world I needed was James watching me interact with a ghost. "Why don't you just rest? It won't take me long."

He looked relieved. "But you'll get back in time for our next meeting with our client, right?"

I looked at my watch. "Just about," I said. "If the buses are running on time."

"Do you want to take the car?"

"What?"

I was surprised. That Volvo—which his dead Uncle Jimmy had left him in his will—was his pride and joy.

"I asked if you wanted to use the car."

"Well, yeah." Then I frowned. "Are you sure?"

"Will it get you back here quicker than the bus?"

I grinned in spite of myself. "Absolutely."

"Then yes, I'm sure."

He smiled crookedly, looking all cute and vulnerable, with the white bandages wrapped around his head and his blue eyes looking deeply into mine—and I realized that if I didn't move immediately, I wasn't going to move at all. And that would not pay the bills.

Getting information about Dead Eddie would. Maybe.

I pulled the keychain from his fingers without touching him.

"Thanks," I whispered, and headed for the door.

I decided to ignore his nervous voice yelling, "Hey! You know how to drive a standard, don't you? Jeepers, do you even have a driver's licence?" and let the door slam shut behind me.

No reason for him to get too comfortable, no matter how nice he was being.

Eddie:
I Wish I'd Stayed Asleep

I SHOULD HAVE realized something wasn't right with me, because the plastic on my mom's couch didn't make a sound as I twisted and turned, trying to stay asleep. I didn't want to open my eyes, even though my dreams had been more of the nightmare variety—something about ducks, which was weird, because I've never been afraid of ducks before—until the doorbell chimed.

That brought me to attention, even though this wasn't my place. All right, so my place doesn't have a doorbell, but anybody knocking on the door was usually somebody wanting money I owed them, or somebody wanting to arrest me.

"Don't answer it," I said, before I was really, truly awake.

My mother, who I could hear shuffling toward the door, ignored me as usual. Before I could even move, she threw open the door.

Two police officers stood on the step, looking shocked stupid. They blinked, glanced at each other, and blinked again. Finally, one of them spoke.

"Are you Mrs. Naomi Hansen?"

"Yes," Mom said. "What do you want?"

"Edward Nathaniel Hansen is your son?"

That brought me to attention. I scrabbled off the couch and up to her, looking past her at the two uniformed cops on the doorstep.

"Don't let them in, Mom," I said. "They cannot find what's in my top drawer." Crack pipe, well used. "Seriously. Tell them to leave."

Her manufactured smile did not hold, and her face went paper white. Her long-fingered hand clutched the door jamb as though she would collapse if she didn't.

"Yes, I am," she said. "Why?"

The cops looked at each other, just a quick glance, but that told me everything. It was bad news. Bad bad news.

"Don't listen to them, Mom," I said. "Whatever they're gonna tell you about me, it's all lies."

"I'm afraid I have some news for you, ma'am," the tall cop said. "May we come in?"

"I only have a minute," Mom said, her tight white lips barely moving. "My book club—"

"I'm sorry, ma'am," the smaller of the two said, and stepped up into the house. "We need to speak to you, now."

Mom stepped back, and the larger cop stepped into the front foyer, pushing all the light and air out with his bulk.

"Don't listen to them," I whispered.

But she did. Oh God, she did.

And so did I.

NOT MUCH WENT through my mind after the cops left my mom's place other than, "Oh my God, I'm dead. I'm dead. I'm fucking dead."

I realized I was screaming it and tried to stop. No go. Still screaming, and then I was crying. And all through it, my mother cleaned her house.

I couldn't believe it. She'd just been told her son—her only son—was dead, but after the cops left, all she could do was wash the walls, and the windows, and vacuum the rug.

She didn't call anyone. She didn't throw herself to the floor and cry. She didn't even scream, past the one time when the cop told her the news. Just the one. Then she hustled them out of the house and kicked cleaning into high gear.

I dropped back onto the couch, on my back, with one arm over my eyes. I felt as though I'd just run a marathon or some shit. I didn't want to listen to my mother, and I didn't want to hear my occasional moans. I just wanted everything to go back exactly the way it was before the cops showed up at my mother's door.

Nobody could hear me or see me. I was dead, and nobody could see me.

I heard a noise and looked over at my mother.

She was vacuuming the floor. And she was singing. Happy as a clam, doing what she loved.

Marie:
Meeting the Book Club

TO BE HONEST, I was feeling a little bit nervous about the whole driving thing. I hadn't driven in three years. Ever since my cute little 1980 Honda Civic, which I'd paid for with my own hard-earned cash, had an unfortunate meeting with a deer.

That happened when I was still living up in Fort Mac, and I was almost over the horror, but still felt a teeny bit uneasy as I started the motor of James's Volvo and listened to it gently purr.

"The good thing is, there aren't many deer running across the streets of Edmonton," I muttered to myself as I checked my seatbelt twice, and then shoulder-checked about ten times before getting the guts up to actually pull into traffic.

All things considered, the drive went smoothly. I only had to stop once due to hysteria. And it only took me twenty minutes to drive all the way out to the north end of town, to a nice little suburb that looked about as normal as anything you'd ever see.

Hard to believe somebody named Brown Eddie lived here. But, you can't often tell what goes on inside a house by looking at the outside. I'd lived in a pretty nice house up in Fort Mac before Mom and Dad split up—and next to Mom, I was one of the weirdest people I knew.

I pulled the parking brake, wiped the sweat from my palms on the thighs of my black jeans, and took a quick look in the mirror.

I'd forgotten to brush my hair. It looked like a fuzzy rat's nest piled on top of my head.

I tried to do some reconstructive surgery right there, but my 'do didn't look much better by the time I dragged myself out of the car and up the walk of the house.

I rang the doorbell and then had an attack of the jitters. Whoever lived here might not want to talk to me. Jeepers, maybe it was that woman with the candle at the church. She would definitely not want to talk to me. I'd alienated the crap out of her.

No answer, no matter who lived here. Which meant there was no one home, and I needed to break in to see if Eddie was actually in the house. If I could.

I pulled a dead credit card from my wallet and attempted to unlock the door with it. Stupid idea, I know, but it was all I had. It wouldn't run between the door and the jamb, and I grunted as I tried to push it a little further up in the jamb—and nearly crapped my drawers when I heard a man's voice.

"Why are you trying to break into my mom's house?"

The voice wafted around me, through me. I was hearing Eddie, the dead guy. I was sure of it. I whirled, but could not see him anywhere.

"Where are you?" I whispered.

"You can hear me?" he asked. He sounded less snippy, and more nervous.

"Yes, I can," I repeated. "Where are you?"

"Living room window," he replied. I glanced at the picture window to my left. Dead Eddie was standing there, staring at me, and I weakly waved. "Now, tell me why you're trying to break into my mom's house?"

"I was looking for you," I said. "Come out and talk to me. Please."

He materialized in front of me before I'd finished speaking.

"Who are you?" he asked.

"Marie," I said. "Marie Jenner." I glanced around, hoping no one was walking by the house. I didn't need anyone seeing me carrying on a conversation with thin air. Coast was clear, but I didn't know how long it would last. I needed to get into that house.

"Do I know you?" he asked.

"Nope. But we need to talk."

He nodded and absently scratched his scalp with one of his horribly mangled hands. "I'm dead. You know that?"

I nodded.

"So how—"

"Long story." I cut him off before he started with all the usual "why can you talk to ghosts" questions. "We need to talk, Eddie. Inside, if possible."

"About what?" he asked, and I blinked. Really? He finally found someone to talk to and he didn't want to talk about his murder? This was a first for me.

"About who killed you." I pointed at the front door. "Do—did you live here?"

"Used to," he said. "Like I said, it's my mom's."

Questions boiled up in my brain, not the least of which was, "How did you get here?" but I pushed them all aside. I needed to get inside so he and I could have a decent conversation, face to dead face. "I take it she's not home. Any way for me to get inside so we can talk?"

"Oh, she's home."

"But she didn't answer the doorbell." Then I had a horrible thought. The cops had just been here, told her her son was dead. She hadn't done anything to herself, had she? "Is she all right?"

"She's fine. Happy as a clam, since her book club showed up. That might be why she didn't answer the door," he said. "Did I tell you I think I know who killed me?"

That pulled me off the "Why didn't Mom answer the door" jag. He knew who killed him. Maybe I could finish this business without getting into the house.

"And I want you to help me get revenge."

Revenge? Not so good . . . But wait—what did he mean by "I *think* I know?"

"Who did it?" I asked.

"My mother's fucking book club," Eddie said, hooking his thumb at the front door of his mother's house. "They're in there right now, talking shit about me, just like they always do—"

"Your mother's what?" I asked. "Did you say—"

"Book club," Eddie repeated. "Those bitches always had it in for me."

Any of the good I was feeling oozed out of me. "Book club?" I asked.

"Yeah." Eddie frowned. "You deaf or something?"

"No." I closed my eyes briefly, in a futile attempt to compose myself. "So, those are the people you saw—when you died?"

"No." Eddie shook his head, frustrated. "No, I just saw ducks. But—"

"Ducks?" Jesus, how messed up was this guy's head?

"They were wearing duck masks," he said. "But I'm pretty sure that it was my mother's fucking book club."

I bit my lips, to keep from screaming. "So, you're not absolutely certain who did this to you?"

Eddie's face took on a petulant sneer. "I told you," he said. "It's the book club."

"In duck masks."

"Yep."

"You're serious."

Right at that moment, the front door clicked open, and I jumped just about a mile straight into the air. As I tried desperately to pull myself together, Dead Eddie glared at the older, heavyset woman who had opened the door.

"Naomi's not taking visitors," she said.

"That's the ringleader. Bea Winterburn," Eddie said. "Make a citizen's arrest or something. Bitch killed me."

I ignored Eddie and concentrated on Bea, smiling like there was no tomorrow. "When will she be taking visitors?" I asked. Now, I didn't care what the answer was. I needed Bea to close the door, so I could continue talking to Eddie before he disappeared. "I have a couple of questions for her, when she has the time."

Eddie decided at that moment to start chanting, "Citizen's arrest," over and over, while dancing on his butchered feet. I took a step closer to the door and put a hand on the knob.

"Just tell me a better time," I said, trying to keep my voice low, even though it felt like I had to yell over Eddie's increasingly panicky chant.

Bea sighed as though I'd asked her an impossible question and turned away from the door, her hand still firmly on the door knob. "Naomi!" she called. "There's a girl here. She won't leave."

"Marie Jenner," I said. "But really, I can come back—"

"A Mary Jenner," Bea called. "She said she needs to talk to you."

There was a commotion from somewhere inside the house and

Bea frowned just before she was rather unceremoniously pushed away from the door by a slight woman with a hairdo that seemed far too tightly pulled back and a ferocious expression on her face.

"Where is she?" she cried, as she pushed past the older woman. Trying to get to me.

"Good luck," Dead Eddie whispered. "You're about to meet my mom. She seems pissed." He grinned. "Does she seem pissed to you?"

Yes, she did. I took a tiny step back, teetering on the very edge of the topmost step.

"You!" Eddie's mom cried. "Are you one of those drug fiends? Like that Luke Stewart! Are you?"

Her voice wound up to a scream, and she fought Bea, who was trying to pull her back into the house.

"My name is Marie Jenner," I said, grubbing in my purse for a business card. I could not believe I was now face to face with Eddie's mom. I just wanted to get as far away from this place as I could. No way I was going to be able to be alone with Eddie after this.

"I suppose you're here for money or something," Eddie's mom snarled. "That's all you drug fiends want, isn't it? Showing up at my house. Demanding money . . ."

She sobbed, then pulled her hand back and swung at me. If I hadn't moved my head, she'd have slapped me across the face.

"I am not a drug fiend," I said, waving the business card in the air like a pathetic flag of surrender. "I'm just trying to figure out what happened to your son."

"My son is dead!" she screeched, tears and mascara flooding her cheeks. "Why can't you fiends leave me alone?"

"I'm sorry," I whispered.

"Tell her that those bitches did it," Eddie said, quite conversationally for someone watching his mother have a full core meltdown. "Queen Bea and her mob. Tell her that. She deserves to know."

I ignored him because he was definitely not being helpful.

"Don't you want to know what happened to your son?" I asked.

"Of course I do!" Eddie's mother screamed. She took another small step forward and then sank to her knees, sobbing uncontrollably. Bea caught her before she collapsed completely.

"Let's get you inside," she said, soothingly. She turned her head and bellowed, "I need some help here!" A thundering herd of middle-aged women appeared in the foyer and scooped up Eddie's sobbing mom, pulling her away from my line of sight and back into the house.

"I told you she wasn't ready for visitors," Bea said, smugly.

"I didn't want to upset her," I said. "I was just looking for—"

"She has every reason to be upset." Bea rode roughshod over my words. "Even though I think that it's better, in the long run, that her boy is dead."

"What?" I gasped, barely able to believe what I had just heard.

"What?!" Eddie was having even more trouble with what the big woman said. He turned to me. "Do you have a gun?" he asked. "Shoot her right now. No one would ever blame you."

I shook my head, then turned back to the woman at the door.

"You can't mean that," I said.

"I absolutely do," the woman replied. "In fact, I thank the good Lord he's finally dead. What his mother has gone through."

I tried to think of something to say, but couldn't manage anything past blinking, repeatedly.

"I'm just speaking the truth," she said. "That boy was a millstone around poor Naomi's neck since the day he was born. This is a blessing."

"A blessing?" I whispered.

"It wasn't a blessing, you cow," Eddie muttered. "Shut your mouth."

"And it was inevitable," the woman continued. "Someone was going to put that dog down, eventually."

"Dog," Eddie whispered. "She's calling me a dog."

I glanced over at him and was horrified to see that his light had all but extinguished. This woman's words were destroying him, right in front of me.

"Mom," Eddie gasped. "Make her stop."

A swirl of ice cold hit me as he staggered up to the door and into me. He started screaming again, and for a few horrifying seconds, I was caught inside him and could feel all his fear, and self-loathing, and sickness. And something else. Something that instantly ate away my stomach, but made me ache with hunger at the same time.

I couldn't take it anymore, and flailed my way out of him, then stood, gasping for air.

"Is there something wrong with you, girl?" Bea asked, as Eddie disappeared back inside the house.

"No," I said shortly, as I waited for my eyesight to clear.

I couldn't exactly call out to Eddie to get him to come back and talk to me, ghost to living, but I had to give him a way to find me.

"Give this to Mrs. Hansen," I said, holding the business card out to Bea. "And ask her to call me."

She didn't answer me. Just took the card between two fingers, as though it was covered with dirt or something. Then she sneered and slammed the door.

"Well," I muttered. "That could have gone better."

Truer words, and all that. I crept back to the Volvo, and with one last look at the front of that house, I drove away.

No wonder Eddie did drugs. With people like that around, how could he have done anything but?

I was pretty sure he was wrong about that bunch of women having anything to do with his death, but I knew that if I didn't prove to him that they weren't involved, he'd never get off that tack. And he needed to, if he was going to be able to help me find out who really killed him.

I needed to talk to him again, but not in that house. I hoped that he'd see the business card and the address on the front.

"Please, Eddie," I muttered, as I white-knuckled it back to James's office. "Please come to me, so we can talk. For real, this time."

Eddie:
I Gotta Remember That Address

HERE'S THE ONLY cool thing that happened in a day otherwise filled to the brim with warm shit. Queen Bea gave my mother the business card from that crazy girl. Marie. Marie Jenner, from the Jimmy Lavall Detective Agency.

I stared at the card, attempting to commit the address to a memory that was notoriously bad. Hoped I'd hang onto it as Mom scooped up the card and stared at it, hard.

"What do you think I should do about this?" she asked the cackling old crows. They all thought about it for a minute, then told her to let it go.

"You have enough on your plate right now, dear," Bea said. "You don't need to deal with anything more. Don't you think so, girls?"

The "girls" all agreed, so enthusiastically I thought I'd puke.

And then that old bitch plucked the business card from my mom's hand and dropped it in her huge purse. "Why don't you let me deal with little Mary Jenner?"

"All right," Mom whispered, and my heart wrenched. She sounded so hurt. So lost. And it was my fault. I couldn't stay there and see that look on her face. Not for one more moment.

As I left my mother's house, I heard Mom thank them for all their help and for being such good and loyal friends.

Yeah, Mom. You got some great friends there, I thought.

Then everything went grey, and I guess I lost it again because when I came to, I was back at the tree where I'd been crucified.

This must be what hell is like.

Marie:
James Wasn't Going to Be Happy

I DROVE BACK to the office with no problem at all, even though I was in a particularly foul mood.

I'd found Brown Eddie, but hadn't been able to convince him to give me any useful information about the people who killed him. All he'd done was blame his mother's book club.

I mean, really. A book club?

I realized I'd probably have to go back to that horrible tree if I wanted to talk to him again, because it looked like he was ping-ponging back and forth between those two places. I shuddered, hating the thought of seeing that tree again.

However, our potential client, Honoria Lowe, had given me a really decent clue. She'd led me right to Dead Eddie's mom's place with that sketch she'd made. Maybe I'd be able to figure out who killed Eddie without having to deal with him again at all. Maybe she'd just draw it all for me.

Wouldn't that be nice? Solving a murder without dealing with the dead guy? Just dealing with someone who dreamed about the dead.

I sighed deeply as I parked the car and trudged up the stairs to James's office. I couldn't seem to get away from the dead, no matter how hard I tried.

I GLANCED AT my watch and was surprised to see only an hour and a half had gone by. *Having a vehicle certainly cuts down on the away time*, I thought as I let myself into the office proper. *I could get used to that.*

James looked up from one of his books and smiled.

"My car all right?" he asked.

"Absolutely," I replied. "Hardly hit anything."

His face whitened at my pathetic excuse for a joke, and I mentally kicked myself. He'd been through enough, lately.

"It's all good, James," I said, hastily. "Didn't have one problem. Thanks for letting me use it."

As I handed him the keys and he pocketed them, I was relieved to see the colour come back to his face.

"Glad it helped," he said. "So, how went the wild goose chase?"

"Very well," I replied, trying to keep my smile from disappearing, even though his words instantly ticked me off. "I ended up at the dead guy's house. Well, not his house, exactly. His mom's house."

"Seriously?"

"Seriously."

"Huh."

He looked suspicious. Like maybe he thought I was lying to him. Which, of course, ticked me off even more.

"I'm telling you the truth," I bristled, like a stupid cat ready to do battle. "That address on the sketch took me right to her house. I even talked to her." Sort of.

"I didn't think you were lying," he said, but something in his tone still sounded off. "But maybe Honoria knows Eddie's mom. Maybe she knows Eddie."

"She said she didn't." I frowned. "If she knows them, why wouldn't she tell us? The cops will figure that out quickly enough. Won't they?"

"They should," James said. "That murder was messy enough, and public enough, that they'll want to catch the people responsible. For the media, if nothing else."

"Well, then, why would Honoria lie to us about knowing Eddie?"

"People say a lot of things to protect themselves," he replied. "Maybe she figures that going back to the nuthouse would be better than going to jail for murder. If she has us following her 'vision' leads, this might convince the cops that she's gone crazy again."

This took me aback. I never once thought that Honoria was lying about being a clairvoyant. But what if she was? What if she was playing us—me?

"Did you ask Mrs. Hansen if she knew Honoria?" James asked.

"I didn't even think of it," I admitted. "She'd just found out about Eddie being dead." I shrugged. "Probably not the best time for me to drop by for a chat. She was sure I was one of Eddie's 'drug fiend' friends. She mentioned someone named Luke. Luke Stewart. She called him another drug fiend. Maybe he's someone we can check out?"

"Maybe," James said. He glanced at the bare desk top, and sighed. "If we had our computers, this would be so easy," he said. The police had taken them both, as evidence from our last—and only—case, and it looked like we weren't going to get them back for a while. If ever. "We need to get a replacement. You know, something cheap, just for searches and stuff, until we get ours back."

"Sounds like a plan," I said, and then burst out with, "Can you afford that?" without thinking.

"Yes," he said, with that superior smile all those people with a bank account that doesn't hover around zero use that drives the rest of us crazy. "Let's go tomorrow."

We. This meant vicarious shopping, which took the sting out of the superior smile I'd probably imagined. "I love that idea," I said.

After that, we settled into a tiny, comfortable bit of silence. I would have thankfully stayed there for a long time—like a cat in a sunbeam or something—but James snapped the moment.

"Have you called your mother lately?"

I blinked.

"No," I finally said, looking out the far window, even though there was nothing much to see.

"You should," he said. "She's probably worried."

"Probably," I mumbled. I walked over to the window and stared out, willing James to shut his mouth about Mom.

"We have time before the meeting with Honoria," he

continued. "You could touch base now. If you want."

The last thing I wanted to do was talk to my mother. She'd ask me hard questions—about my finances (nonexistent), my prospects for the future (equally nonexistent), and my love life (abysmal). And then she'd ask me if I'd met any good ghosts lately, and because James would be listening to everything I said, I'd have to lie. And she'd know I lied. That would probably lead to a fight, and I didn't feel right about sparring with a woman who was fighting for her life.

"I'll call her when I get to Jasmine's," I said, still staring for all I was worth out the window at nothing.

"Up to you," he said, and I heard the rustle of pages as he reached for the book he'd been reading.

I felt the tightness in my chest ease. I was off the hook for the moment. Time to keep the searchlight away from me and my family stuff.

"Have you found out when you can move back into your apartment?" I asked, turning away from the window.

"It's almost repaired," he mumbled, without looking up from his book.

"Glad to hear that," I said. His apartment had been damaged by the same freak who had burnt down *my* apartment building. That freak, unfortunately, was my ex-boyfriend Arnie—may he rot in jail for the rest of his unfortunate life—Stillwell.

I wandered back in James's direction, running my fingers over the spines of the books that filled the bookcases covering nearly every bit of wall space in that office.

"When can you move back in?" I asked.

James closed his book, carefully keeping his finger between the pages to mark his spot. "In a couple of days," he said. "Why? You tired of staying with Jasmine? Want to move back in with me for a while?"

I'd stayed at his apartment for a few days after my apartment had been torched.

I laughed halfheartedly. "Thanks for the offer, but no," I said. "Staying with Jasmine's not so bad. Most of the time."

"She's got a lot of kids, doesn't she?"

"If three is a lot then, yeah." I shrugged. "Most of the time it's all right, but sometimes they're so loud—"

"You could stay here," he said. "If you want."

"Maybe I should," I said. "Just until I get my own place—"

My stupid throat tightened up, because there was no way in the world I was ever going to get my own place. Not until money started flowing in my direction.

"We have to take that job, James," I said. "You might have enough money to ride out this—"

"Series of unfortunate events?" he said.

I shrugged.

"Close enough. I can't, though. I need money coming in. Even if it is to build an alibi for Honoria."

"I could lend you some," he said.

"No." I tried to keep my voice from quavering like a little kid's. "Thanks, but no. Let's just take the job. It could be profitable. For both of us."

"Like I said, I want to think about it," he said. He picked up his book. Conversation was nearly over. "I get this feeling she's lying, and I don't want to be used by a liar. You do understand, don't you?"

"I understand," I said. "But you have to understand that if we don't take this job, I'll have to find something that pays. I'm talking about another job, somewhere else."

That got his attention. He put the book down with a thump, all thoughts of keeping his place marked obviously forgotten. "You're not serious, are you?"

"I don't have the luxury of time the way you do. I'm sorry."

James stared at me for a long, measured moment. "I'd prefer that you worked here," he finally said. "So, how about this? I'll hire you officially, starting today. Pay you, no matter what work we do. It won't be much, but it'll be something." He smiled, but it looked sad. "Even if I decide not to keep Uncle's office open, I'll still need help dismantling everything. Won't I?"

Good grief. In my big rush to get us involved in another stupid case, I'd forgotten that James was trying to decide whether or not he even wanted to keep this business running. This was big, and I wasn't giving him time to really think it through.

"Would that help your situation?" he asked.

"It wouldn't hurt," I said. And by that I meant it would help immensely.

"And if we take Honoria as a client, I'll split whatever we make with you fifty-fifty, just like the first case we took."

"You mean the one we didn't get paid for?"

"That's the one."

I considered. His offer was a good one. At least I'd have something coming in. I might even be able to keep body and soul together, for a while.

"All right," I said.

He stuck out his hand. I blinked and took it. Felt my cheeks heat as his hand enveloped mine. I shook his hand, once, and then pulled free.

"My hand's sweating," I said, and wiped my hand on my sweater. "Sorry."

"Just as long as we have a deal."

"We do," I said. "We do indeed."

I just hoped he didn't do something stupid and wreck it for both of us. And I doubly hoped I didn't do anything stupid and wreck it for myself.

Eddie:
Watching the Cat

I SAT BY the tree for a while, watched the flies buzz around the blood, which was dark and starting to crack, and wondered why no one had washed it off yet. Ripped ends of the yellow police tape flapped in the breeze.

I was dead. The cops had said so, and much as I hated them, I believed them. Explained a lot, actually. Why I didn't hurt much, even though I could now see that my hands and feet were ripped to shit. The only pain I felt was a gnawing in my gut. That old familiar pain. Jonesing for my own particular drug of choice. That was a bitch, because I had no idea how I was going to score, being dead and all.

I was really dead.

This sucked shit in a big way. And the only person who even acted like she could see me was that weird chick from Jimmy Lavall's detective agency. Marie. Marie Jenner.

Even though I'd told her I thought my mother's book club killed me—I didn't know if I believed it. They were a nasty bunch, but they were also weak-assed women, no matter what they thought of me. It would have taken somebody strong to hang me in that tree. Hammer those nails through my hands and feet . . .

Thinking about it made me feel sick to my stomach. Jesus, that was a terrible way to die.

A cat slipped out from beneath a bush near the steps of the church, and snaked its way over to the tree. It looked like it was stalking something, but hard as I looked, I couldn't see anything that looked like a mouse or whatever the hell else a cat would chase.

It walked up on delicate feet, ears twitching as though it was listening for danger. Closer and closer to the tree, stepping on the green, then dyed brown sticky grass. One more look around, and then that son of a bitch began to lick my blood off the bottom of the trunk of that tree.

I yelled at it, but its ears didn't even flicker, so I knew it couldn't hear me either, so I stopped that shit quick. No point. And hey, somebody had to clean up that tree. Why the hell not a cat?

As I turned away from the tree and back onto the street, one more time with feeling, the sun dipped behind the tall buildings, and the churchyard was covered in instant dusk.

The gnawing in my gut picked up so it was almost all I could think about, but I did my best to ignore it as I carefully walked in the direction of Jimmy Lavall's Detective Agency, so I could talk to that Marie chick again. Even though it was only ten blocks away, I honestly didn't know if I could make it or not, because it seemed the only places I'd managed to get to were that damned tree and my mother's house.

So I wasn't really that surprised when I turned a corner, and there was my old neighbourhood. Again. And my mom's house. Again.

Marie:
Isn't a Park Supposed to Be Fun?

JAMES OFFERING TO pay me made me feel better, and I was ready to settle in, maybe even have a nap or something, until our meeting with our potential client, Honoria Lowe, but James shook his head when I suggested it and grabbed his coat.

"We're going to Needle Park," he said.

I frowned. "Needle Park? Didn't Honoria mention Needle Park?"

"Yeah," he said. "She said it's right by her place. It's also where a lot of people go to make drug deals."

He picked at the white bandages covering his head. "Help me get these off. I want to talk to the locals about Edward Hansen. And Honoria. Maybe someone saw them together. If they did, a big hole is blown in her story, and we can turn her down."

Going to that park actually sounded like a pretty good idea. Not to try to blow a hole in Honoria's story, but because there was a small chance that Eddie might be able to get there, too. For some reason he was bopping back and forth between his mother's house and his place of death. I'd hoped that he would have seen the business card and tried to get to me, but he hadn't shown up. However, maybe he'd tried to get to the park. If he managed it, we could still have a talk, living to dead.

But I couldn't do that with James hanging around. I needed to go alone.

I watched him pick rather ineffectually at his bandaged head. "That's a good idea," I said. "But maybe I should go by myself."

"What?" His hand stilled. "Why?"

"Because you look just terrible and should probably rest."

"But—"

"But nothing." I grinned, and hoped it looked convincing. "Does your head hurt?"

"Yes," he admitted. "It really does."

"So let me go. After all, it's just a park, right? I'll chat up whoever's there and get back in time for us both to go to Honoria's place. If I find out she's been lying about knowing Eddie, we'll dump her as a client, and then we can go out for a meal. A real meal, in a sit-down restaurant. What do you say?"

"I don't think you should go there by yourself," he said, but I noticed he'd stopped trying to remove the bandages. "It's not safe—"

"I'll be fine," I said breezily, and walked to the door before he had a chance to say anything more. "You nap. I"ll be back before you know it."

"I don't need to nap," James said. He sat on the edge of the cot, and then reclined until his head was on the old, flat pillow, and he sighed. "Other than the headache, I'm fine. Really."

"Yeah, I can tell," I said. "Now, tell me the address so I can go."

Even as he told me the address, his eyes slid shut. "Want to use the car again?"

I said no, because I didn't even have the money for parking.

"All right," he whispered. "Be safe."

"I will," I said, and left.

I'd be fine. It's just a park, after all. How bad could it be?

ONE OF THE greatest things about living in Edmonton in the summer is that the sun doesn't set until ten o'clock in the evening. Since it was not quite eight o'clock, the sun was still well above the horizon, bathing the city in pink and gold. When I got to Needle Park, I was really glad. There was no way in the world I would have walked into that place without the sun. No way at all.

The park wasn't actually a park, just a bit of green space crammed up against a couple of old buildings in downtown Edmonton. Even in the soft pink glow of the slowly setting sun, it looked decidedly sinister to me.

I glanced across the street, at the building where Honoria probably lived. Low-rent businesses on the main floor, and what looked like apartments on the second and third. If she lived there, and if Eddie had frequented this park, there was a chance they'd seen each other. Maybe even knew each other.

James might be on to something. I hoped not. But I had to find out.

I turned back to the park, with its scruffy grass and dusty trees and sad-looking park benches that had been placed there, so hopefully, some years before. They were covered in graffiti and had been desecrated by so many knives over the years that I could barely believe they were still holding together.

Could this actually be the right place?

I glanced at the street signs, hoping against hope that I had it wrong. But I didn't. Corner of 104th and Jasper. Just like James had told me.

Now I needed a plan.

I know, I'd walked ten blocks and should have had plenty of time to come up with something, but mostly I had avoided eye contact with anyone on the streets and not really thought about what I was going to do once I found the park.

I spied two men sitting on a park bench and decided I'd start with them. I'd ask them if they knew Eddie. And if they did, if they ever saw him hanging around with Honoria of the beautiful smile.

Easy peasy.

As I stepped onto the grass, I looked past the two men and was genuinely surprised to see more people in the park. I hadn't seen them before. They'd blended with the background so that all I'd seen was the scruffy grass and the dusty trees. And those pathetic park benches.

Most of the people—who actually looked more like ghosts than living humans, which gave me a real jolt—didn't fit anywhere in the daytime downtown Edmonton I knew, and I wished the sun was even higher in the sky.

I headed toward the two men on the bench. The other people saw me, of course, and a ripple of unease went through them all.

I had a sudden attack of nerves and shuffled to a stop. I opened my purse, as though I was looking for something, and tried to regroup. What the hell was I doing?

I honestly had no clue, but closed my purse, slapped a smile on my face, walked up to the two guys on the bench, and tried to act like I knew what I was doing.

"Can I talk to you?" I asked.

Most of the people around the park bench melted away when I opened my mouth. The two men sitting on the bench glared at me, mightily.

"Are you a cop?" the bigger of them asked.

"No," I replied. God forbid! "I just have a couple of questions about someone I think you might know."

The two men continued to stare at me, without even blinking or anything. My heart quickened, and I reached into my purse again, digging out one of James's business cards.

"I'm with the Jimmy Lavall Detective agency," I said, and held it out. I was distantly pleased that my hand wasn't shaking. It should have been, but it wasn't.

The big guy leaned forward and grabbed it from my hand. I just wanted to run, but didn't. Just stood, trying to look taller and more confident than I had mere moments before.

"I just have a couple of questions for you," I said. "You answer, and I'll leave. Promise."

The bigger guy glanced back at the small thin man sprawled across one end of the bench. He tilted his head, just a tad, in a "what the heck" move. The bigger guy shrugged, handed him the card, and stepped aside.

"What do you want to know?" the thin man asked.

"Do you know Edward Hansen?" I asked.

"Who?"

"Brown Eddie," I said. The thin man's eyes crawled all over me, and I felt sick. A drug dealer was mentally undressing me. I grabbed my sweater and closed it. Then I crossed my arms over my chest, and the thin guy laughed.

"Do I make you nervous?" he asked.

"No," I said. "Not at all." I uncrossed my arms, but pulled my purse from my side and held it in front of me like a shield. "Did you know Eddie?"

"That's the guy who got himself killed, over at the church. Right?" He grinned lazily, stretching like a cat. "I don't know him."

"But you know he was killed."

The thin guy snorted laughter, and the bigger guy, who had been standing still as a mountain, echoed the scoffing tone. "Everybody knows that. It was even on the news."

"So, if you don't know him, maybe you know someone who does?" I asked. And I took a small step forward.

I could feel the big guy come to attention when I did that. Like a guard dog. I smiled, trying to look small and not dangerous at all, and was relieved when he relaxed. Just a titch, mind you, but I didn't feel like he was going to beat me to death with my own arms or anything. Not at that moment, anyhow.

"I just want to talk to people who knew him. I'm trying to figure out what happened to him."

"Now, aren't we supposed to let the cops work out that shit?" the small man asked, and smiled. It was a teeny bit like watching a snake smile, and I slid back a step.

"Yeah," I said. "I'm sure they will figure it out, eventually. But I have a friend who's been implicated—"

The big guy looked massively confused, so I decided to be helpful.

"The police think my friend's involved somehow."

"I know what implicated means," the big guy snarled. "I'm not stupid."

"Sorry."

"Relax, R," the smaller guy said. "The puss was just trying to give you your word for the day."

I bristled. "What did you call me?"

The little guy stood, glowering. "I called you a puss. You know, like—"

"I know what you meant," I said, and glared at him. "I don't appreciate being called names."

"Oh," the thin guy said, and took another step toward me. He was definitely menacing me, but at that moment, I didn't care. Because I hate someone calling me names. Even a drug dealer in the scariest park in Edmonton. "Is that right?"

"Yes," I snapped. "That's exactly right. Apologize."

The small part of my brain that tries to keep me safe screamed, "Have you lost your mind? Run away!" but I wasn't listening. That piece of crap was going to apologize to me.

The thin guy blinked.

"Are you serious?" He looked at the big guy. "Is she serious?"

"Seems to be." The big guy flexed everything he had to flex, and my mouth dried in belated fear. "Want me to straighten her out?"

I pretended to ignore the big guy even though I was so certain he was going to grab me that I could almost feel his hands on my arm.

"I am absolutely serious," I said. I hoped the thin guy couldn't see the way my lips were sticking to my suddenly completely dry teeth. "You shouldn't talk to me like that. You don't even know me."

The thin guy stared at me a moment more, and I stared back, just as hard. Then he laughed.

"I guess I owe the lady an apology," he said. He laughed delightedly, as though he was watching a kitten stand up to a pit bull. "I'm sorry. Didn't mean to hurt your feelings."

"Thank you," I said primly, and he laughed again, shaking his head.

"All right, what do you want to know?"

"Who knows Eddie?"

He shrugged. "I don't know." He turned to the big guy. "Who knows the dead guy, R?"

"No clue," the big guy said. He hadn't moved. Just stared at me like a huge scary statue.

"See?" the thin guy said. "We don't know anything about that piece of shit." His smile fell away, and I knew my time was absolutely up. "I think it's time for you to go back to the suburbs, where you belong."

"Thanks for your time," I said, trying to keep the snottiness in my voice down to a dull roar. I was still afraid, but I was angrier at being dismissed by this piece of garbage. "I guess I'll have to talk to someone else." I pointed to a clot of humanity clinging to the brick wall of the building adjacent to the park. "Maybe them."

The small guy didn't move a muscle. "I don't think so," he said. "I think it would be better if you leave."

"I'm just here to ask some questions," I said. "What's the problem?"

"The problem is I don't need you upsetting my people," the small guy said. "They might decide that this isn't a safe place to be. And *that* would be bad. For everyone."

My inner voice began chanting, "Run away, run away, run away" in a terrified monotone, but I continued to ignore it. I was getting really tired of being told what I could or could not do on this horrible little piece of real estate.

"I don't care if it's good for business," I said. "I just want to ask them some questions. Last time I checked, we lived in a free country."

The last of the thin guy's smile disappeared, and all that was left was threat. "This isn't any part of *your* country," he said.

And then R, the big guy, walked up and gave me the hairy eyeball, just to set me straight. "Get out of here, little girl, and don't come back."

"Fine," I replied. Honestly, I think that's all I could have said, because staring into R's eyes was like looking into a cold, dark version of hell. "I'll go."

I walked out of the park and back to the sidewalk, and then down the street, and finally out of sight of the two men. I collapsed against a wall and tried to keep from throwing up. Slowly, the feeling of abject fear eased, but the anger remained.

Stupid, stupid anger.

I'd risked my life—kind of—and had absolutely nothing to show for it. And that couldn't stand. I had to find out if Eddie had ever been to this stupid park.

At the very least.

I went around the block and entered the other end of the alley that backed onto the park. I'd ask a couple more people about Eddie, and with any luck at all I'd have something to take back to James.

The alley was packed with people. I was really quite surprised. And none of them even gave me a second look. I was pretty surprised about that, too.

I walked up to the first group and asked them if anyone knew Brown Eddie. They all shook their heads, avoiding eye contact, so I walked on. Same thing happened with the second group, and with the third.

This wasn't working, and I was getting seriously depressed. Maybe they'd seen me over at the other side of the park. Maybe they knew the thin guy had thrown me out. Told me to go home—

"Well, if it isn't the little rubbernecker!" A woman's voice called from the shadows. "Still rubbernecking?"

I stared, hard, but didn't recognize the woman who had left the flowers and candle by the crucifixion tree until she stepped out into the dying sunlight.

"Hi!" I said. I was almost happy to see her. A familiar face, in that crowd of strangeness. "You're Eddie's friend, right?"

"Right," the woman said. "What are you doing here?"

"Still trying to figure out what happened to Eddie."

"Hmm."

"Have you heard anything?" I asked. "Anything at all?"

The woman gave her tight faux leather skirt a tug, to settle it on her bony hips. "I've heard some things. But my time's not free, you know." She smiled. "You know?"

"Yes. Absolutely." I reached for my purse, hoping that by some miracle, I'd find a bill in it, even though I was fairly certain I didn't have a dime to my name. I dug, and dug, and felt my face grow hot.

"I'm sorry," I said. "I don't have any money."

"Jesus, girl." She stared, and when I finally had the courage to look her in the eye, all I saw was sympathy. Seriously. Sympathy from a prostitute. "You don't have no money at all?"

"It's been a tough month," I whispered.

"Fine," she said. "I'll give you a minute free, but that's all. And if Romeo comes up, you get the hell out of here."

"Romeo?"

"My pimp, sweetie."

"Oh."

"So, what do you want to know?"

"Did Eddie ever come to this park?"

She laughed. "Of course he did. All the time."

"And did those guys I talked to know him?" I jerked my head in the direction of the park bench, and she nodded.

"So why would they lie to me?"

"Because they don't know you," she scoffed. "Now hurry up. Your time's almost up."

I thought furiously. I was probably only going to be able to ask one more question before she told me to leave. Now, did I want to waste my time trying to explain to her who Honoria was, or did I want to ask the obvious question. Which was—

"Any idea who killed Eddie?"

She looked around, to see if anyone was listening to our

conversation. "Some say it was Ambrose," she whispered.

"Ambrose?"

"Ambrose Welch. Yeah." She stared. "The guys you were talking to? Out by the benches?"

"Oh," I whispered, and felt a thrill of fear course down my spine. "Was one of them Ambrose?"

"No!" she scoffed. "He doesn't come to the park. Those were his lieutenants."

Then she smiled, and I was shocked to see warmth. "Some say Ambrose finally got tired of Eddie. It could be the truth, because Eddie could be aggravating. But I don't think so."

"Oh?" I said. Seemed to be the only thing I could think to say, but it was enough.

"Yeah. I think it's that cop. Angus the Asshole Stewart. That son of bitch hated Eddie with a passion."

"You think a policeman killed Eddie?" I asked.

"Stewart's no 'policeman,'" she snapped. "He's a drug cop. Through and through. Different breed, them. And he hated Eddie."

"With a passion."

"Yeah," she said. "With a fucking passion."

She didn't tell me to leave, so I thought I'd try asking her one more question.

"Do you know someone named Honoria Lowe?" I asked.

Her face twisted. "Who?"

"Honoria Lowe. She lives around here and says she knows Eddie. The cops think she might be involved in his death."

Not quite the truth, but whatever.

"Never heard of her," she said. "And I know everybody Eddie knows." Her face spasmed. "Knew." She looked around as though suddenly afraid someone else in the alley had heard her. "Your minute is up. I got work."

She turned on her heel and started to walk away from me.

"Hey!" I called. "What's your name?"

She stopped and lowered her head for a second, then shrugged.

"I'm Noreen," she said. "And who are you?"

"Marie." I thought about giving her a business card, but realized, belatedly, that maybe these weren't the kind of people James wanted as potential clients. "Thanks for your help,

Noreen."

She waved briefly, then turned and walked to the street without looking at me again.

If I needed to talk to Noreen, I'd know where to find her. Besides, she hadn't looked like she'd ever heard Honoria's name before. If she truly was as close to Eddie as she said, then I guess we'd call that confirmation that Honoria wasn't lying about knowing Eddie before his death.

I glanced down at my watch and gasped. I had to leave, immediately, if I wanted to go with James for his meeting with Honoria.

I turned, preparing to walk back down the alley and to the street without being seen by Ambrose's lieutenants, so I could head back to the office and tell James all my news. That was the plan, anyhow.

Two cop cars, lights flashing, slewed off the street and onto the dusty grey grass of the park, spreading panic through the multitude in the alley and changing my plans, just a bit.

"Five O!" someone yelled, and everyone stampeded back into the alley, away from the cop cars. I ran too, just like all the rest of the frightened, panicky sheep, and I honestly thought I was going to make it until two more vehicles careened down the alley toward us, effectively blocking our escape.

"Dammit." I straggled to a stop in the middle of the stampeding addicts. I was going to miss the meeting. I could just tell.

Marie:
Oh Yay! Cops!

SOONER THAN I would have believed possible, we were up against the wall, faces pressed into the disgusting bricks, as the cops went up and down the line, frisking us and asking us for our IDs.

"Never seen you before," one of the cops breathed into my hair as he grabbed way too much of me, making sure I didn't have a bomb in my bra. "What brings you to this little playground?"

"I was just out for a walk," I said.

"Really?"

"Yep." He glared at me until I turned my eyes down and stared at my shoes. "Sorry," I whispered. "Yes, sir."

"Better," he said. "So, you're trying to tell me you were alone? In this park? Just out for a stroll?"

"Yes."

"And you somehow end up in this alley. That's what you're trying to tell me?"

I didn't blame him for sounding the way he did, even though I was pretty desperate for him to believe me and let me go. "Yeah," I said. "There were no signs."

"What?" Sharp tone in his voice—that probably meant things were about to get bad for me. "What did you say?"

"Nothing," I whispered. "I didn't know. Really."

"So, you're just an innocent bystander, out for a stroll." The sarcasm dripped from the cop's voice, and again I didn't blame him. It sounded more stupid every time he repeated it.

The problem was it was also pretty close to the truth. So I thought I'd try again. "It's the truth."

The cop's eyes went cold. "Enough. Shut your mouth and get back in line. Now."

"Please let me go," I said. "I haven't done anything—"

The cop didn't give me time to finish. He grabbed me by the sweater and threw me at the wall. I hit it hard and briefly saw stars. "I said back in line!"

"You got a problem, Stew?" another cop called from further down the line of the unluckiest people in Edmonton. My ears perked up at the name. Could this be Stewart, the drug officer Noreen had mentioned?

Stew leaned in on me. Hard. "No," he replied. "No problem here."

He put his face next to mine, and I could smell his coffee breath. "I don't have a problem, do I?"

"No," I grunted. He had me pinned to the wall so hard, I was having trouble catching my breath. "No problem at all."

"I didn't think so," the cop said, and walked to the next group of unfortunates.

I really didn't want to go to the police station, but I for one didn't want to attract any more attention from that particular police officer. What the heck was I going to do?

I glanced up and down the line of people hugging the wall. The cops were nearly finished going through pockets and harassing us. If I didn't do something quick, I was going to be in the back of a paddy wagon or whatever, and I would definitely be late for our meeting with Honoria.

"Back in line, sweetheart." The cop named Stew had somehow snuck up behind me without me noticing. He pushed me back against the wall.

I thought about saying, "I'm not your sweetheart," for about a microsecond and decided against it. "Please let me go, sir," I said instead. "I haven't done anything wrong. Seriously."

Stew laughed. "Sorry, sweetheart. You're going downtown with the rest of your friends. If you were just out for a stroll, like you say, downtown will work it out." He leaned back in, crushing the breath from me. "Consider it a lesson, from me to you. So you remember to stay away from this particular park."

I closed my eyes and tried not to attract his attention any longer. Lesson learned, El Creepo. Lesson definitely learned.

In no time at all, we were being loaded into a bunch of vehicles so they could haul us to the downtown police station and process us.

As I was getting into the back of a van, I saw Stew yelling at another cop. He looked furious.

"What do you mean he's not here?" His face was a dangerous purple as he stood nose to nose with the unfortunate police officer who'd given him the bad news. "He was here. They said he was here!"

I didn't hear any more, because I was rather unceremoniously tossed into the rear of the van at that time, but I wondered, as I tried not to touch any of the great unwashed in the back, who they'd missed in their sweep.

Someone important, if Stew's purple face was any indication.

Now, that was interesting.

GETTING PROCESSED IS nothing I want to talk about. Ever. But after, we were allowed to make our phone call—well, I was, because I got really loud about it all—so I called James.

What can I say? He wasn't impressed.

"You were just supposed to talk to people. Marie. Just talk."

"That's all I did," I protested. "I walked into the middle of a drug sweep. I think they thought they were going to catch someone important, but it looks like they missed him." I shrugged. "Whatever. I just want out of here, and I really don't want to wait until I'm arraigned. This wasn't my fault, James."

"I know." He snapped back to attention. "I think I can get you out. But it'll mean we owe Sergeant Worth, big time."

"Is that the only way?" I whined. I really didn't want to owe Sergeant Worth anything. Or anything more. She'd already saved my butt once, after all, and it was never good to owe the police too much. Besides, I was pretty sure she knew all about my mom and her ability to see ghosts. Worse, I think she suspected I had the same ability.

"Yes," he said. "I think it is."

"Are we going to miss our meeting with Honoria?" I personally saw the potential paycheque flying out the window, but he chuckled.

"Don't worry about the meeting," he said. "I'll call her and let her know we're going to be late."

"Good," I said. "Now, please, get me out of here. It really stinks."

Eddie:
So, Who Is Jimmy Lavall, and Why Should I Care?

I KINDA WONDERED if I could even go to that detective agency place. I'd been in some kind of weird loop since—well, since my death, I guess—that had me going from the tree where I died to my mom's and back again. Didn't want to be stuck like that forever. I needed something to change. Well, what I really needed was a quick fix to put my head back on straight. I was starting to hurt something fierce.

I caught the LRT back downtown and got off near Chinatown. So far so good.

I walked the few blocks it took to get to the address I'd seen on the business card. I'd made certain to remember it, didn't need my spotty memory screwing this up for me. I needed to talk to Marie. She'd seen me—actually seen me. Only person so far. I had the feeling she knew something that might help me.

THE OFFICE, WHEN I finally found it, was in a nothing kind of a building. Just a street-level door opening onto a set of stairs. No elevator or entryway or anything.

Great. The only one who could see me, and she worked for a loser. Sounded like my kind of luck, still running the way it always did.

I went up to the second floor. Dark, dingy, dirty. Yeah. Of course. Finally found the door. "Jimmy Lavall, Private Investigator" painted on the glass. Looked legit enough, so I pushed through and into the office proper.

No one there. Luckily, light from the street flooded through the window at the far end of the office, so I could see well enough to have a look around.

Small desk, sitting in the middle of the room. No computer. No nothing. And it was dark and empty. I thought private eyes worked all night and stuff.

I took a look through both of the other doors in the room, hoping that the Marie chick was behind one or the other. One led to a closet, and the other one led to another office. The chick wasn't in either one.

There was a cot and a neat pile of men's clothes in a suitcase in that second office. Somebody was living here. Man. These people were losers. And I needed their help. Help from losers. Again. Batting a thousand.

I was trying to decide whether to wait for the losers to come back or head to the park and figure out a way to get high, when the front door burst in, small bits of smashed-to-shit wood and glass flying everywhere.

I ducked behind the desk—force of habit, what can I say—and heard a couple of guys walk through the hole that used to be the door.

"What are we looking for?" one of them asked. My ears perked up at that voice. Man, I knew who it was.

It was Crank. A two-bit hood who would do anything for a buck, and also somebody I called a friend. Sort of. Why the hell was he here?

I glanced over the desk, saw who he was talking to, and shuddered. Full body shake. It was R. R for Rage. Or Ronald, or something. Ambrose Welch's man. Big as fuck and twice as scary.

"What the hell?" I breathed. When did Crank move so far up the food chain? He never got to hang around with people like R before.

"I said, what are we looking for?" Crank asked again.

R turned on him, and Crank flinched, which was a smart thing to do with R. I'd seen him kick a guy raw just for breathing wrong.

That was a butt ugly thing to watch.

"We need to find out what these people were really looking for," R said. He held out a business card, and Crank squinted at it. So I did too.

"Jimmy Lavall, Private Detective." It looked like the card Marie had given my mother. Man, whoever this Jimmy guy was, he sure knew how to kick a hornet's nest. Handing out business cards to Ambrose Welch's crew? What was he, nuts?

"Right," Crank said. He glanced at the desk and frowned. "No computer."

"Check around," R replied. "There has to be one somewhere."

He and Crank made short work of the room, then kicked in the two remaining doors. Guess they'd never heard of just turning the knob. I listened to them tear apart the inside office, tipping over file cabinets and the like.

"Son of a bitch!" R cried, when the smashing stopped. They came back out soon enough, and R went through the desk again, more thoroughly this time.

"There has to be something here," he grunted, working his way through each drawer. He came up with nothing past pencils and paperclips.

Then he grunted, sounding almost pleased, when he focused on the daytimer, still sitting on the desk. He flipped pages and then stopped, pointing.

"Honoria Lowe," he read, and turned to Crank. "Ever heard of her?"

"No," Crank said, staring at the page as though hoping he could somehow read more into the name than R could. "Who is she?"

"How the hell would I know?" R said, instant anger tingeing his voice. "But they got a meeting with her, tonight. Somewhere."

He looked through the rest of the pages, slammed the book shut, and then, for good measure, swept everything off the desk. The coffee cup smashed, joining the paper and glass and wood that littered the floor.

Then and only then did he look satisfied.

"Let's go," he said.

"But Ambrose is expecting us to find something," Crank said, looking all jittery and scared, which is his usual M.O. "We can't go back with nothing."

"Did we find anything?" R asked.

"No. Well, we got the name of that chick. Honoria whatever."

"Then that's what we'll take back to him."

"Do you think it will be enough?"

R laughed. "If it isn't, I'll tell him it was your fault we couldn't find more."

"R, you wouldn't do that," Crank gasped, the fear that lived just under his skin all the time oozing from him like sweat. He looked like he was going to piss himself until R cuffed him and turned to the wrecked door.

"We got everything there is. If he wants us to come back and do more, we will."

He grabbed Crank and hauled him through the open doorway. A few moments later, I heard the downstairs door wheeze shut, and then I was alone again.

I looked around at the train wreck that Crank and R had left and decided to leave, myself. Maybe this Marie chick *could* see me, but if she was stupid enough to bring Ambrose down on her, she wouldn't have the time to figure out who killed me. She'd be trying to figure out who killed her.

Marie:
James Breaks In, and All Hell Breaks Loose

"I CAN'T BELIEVE it took that long for the police to let me go." I straggled morosely along beside James as we finally left the cop shop. It was nearly ten o'clock. We were an hour late for our meeting with Honoria Lowe.

"That wasn't long," James said. "You're lucky they didn't hold you overnight."

"Even with Sergeant Worth's help?"

"Even with." He pulled out his cell phone to call Honoria and let her know we were on our way. There was no answer, and he frowned.

"Do you think she gave up on us?" I asked.

"I called her before I came to get you. She knew we were going to be late. I wonder where she is?"

He walked quickly, forcing me to occasionally do that awkward skip-step to keep pace with him. Damn men and their long legs!

He'd parked on the street in front of the cop shop, and I was seriously glad to see the car there. My feet were starting to hurt. Terribly. The shoes I'd picked up at the Sally Ann when I was replacing my wardrobe were starting to pinch in all the bad spots, and all I wanted to do was take them off. I minced up to the car, and as soon as I was sitting in the passenger's seat, I tore them off and rubbed furiously.

"Your feet hurt?" James asked. Talk about stating the obvious.

"I kind of wish I'd picked runners instead of shoes with heels," I said.

"So, why did you?"

"Why did I what?"

"Pick shoes with heels?" He put the car into gear and pulled into traffic. "I've never seen you wear heels before."

I looked down at the shoes, so I didn't have to look at him. I'd picked the stupid shoes because I thought they made my legs look nice. But there was no way in the world I was telling him that. I just rubbed out the cramps and ignored the heck out of him.

"Tell me what you found out," he said, as he turned onto Jasper Avenue and headed west. "You did get to talk to some people before you were arrested. Didn't you?"

"A couple," I said. "But they didn't tell me anything. Wouldn't even tell me if they knew Eddie." I sighed. "I did talk to one of Eddie's friends, but she said she didn't think Eddie knew anybody named Honoria." I shrugged. "Doesn't mean Eddie doesn't know her. Just means he didn't tell Noreen."

"Noreen?" he asked. "Eddie's friend?"

"Yep." I shrugged again. "Sorry. I didn't get much."

It felt like I got nothing, to be honest, but James just took note, without any comment. I didn't know what to make of that. He usually had a comment.

We made it to 104th in excellent time and parked on the street next to the park. Being that close to the park again made me seriously twitchy and jumpy.

"Can't we park somewhere else?" I said, as I pulled my stupid shoes back on my feet and tried not to groan in pain. "I don't want any of them to see me."

He didn't argue. Just put the vehicle back into gear, pulled down the street, and around the corner.

"Is this good?" he asked.

I looked around and could see no one I recognized. "I think so," I said, and we got out of the car and walked back to Honoria's apartment door.

I kept James between me and the park side, feeling ever so happy that I could use him to hide me from whoever was in the park. It looked pretty empty, but that didn't mean there was no one there. It just meant I couldn't see them.

As James studied the bank of names below the intercom, I pulled off the shoe that was pinching the worst and rubbed my poor poor toes, one last time.

"Let's get you some sneakers tomorrow," he said. "Heels really aren't your style, are they?"

"All right," I replied, trying to keep the anger out of my voice. "Fine. But you don't need to act like that."

"Like what?" he asked. He pressed a button a third of the way down the list of names.

"Like a smart ass," I said. I stretched my toes and sighed.

"I'm not," he said. Then he grinned. "Well, maybe. Just a bit."

"Yeah, you were," I said, ramming the shoe back on, and trying to ignore my screeching toes. Then I frowned. "Why isn't she answering?"

"I don't know."

"Did you push the right button?"

"Yes!"

He gave me a look that told *me* not to be a smart ass, and I shrugged. Two can play that game. He pressed the right button on the intercom—even I could see he'd chosen the right one—again.

It crackled to life, and a man's voice answered. It didn't sound happy. "Yeah?"

"I'm looking for Honoria Lowe," James said.

"You got Joey," the man wheezed.

"Is this Honoria Lowe's apartment?"

"No!" The wheezing voice took on a peeved tone. "I told you, you got Joey."

James shook his head. "Can you tell me—"

"Screw this," the guy said, and then surprised us both by unlocking the front door.

"Good enough," James said, and pulled it open.

I personally didn't think it was so good. Anybody could get in. Anybody at all.

We walked through the front foyer, and James headed for the stairs. I followed, trying not to groan about my feet.

On the second floor, we found her door, and James knocked. No answer. Knocked again.

"Maybe she's out," I said, not very helpfully.

James growled, pulled his cell out, and dialed her number. After a moment, a cell phone rang inside the apartment.

James frowned. "She didn't take her cell."

"Nobody leaves their cell," I replied, and felt a flutter of nerves.

"She said she'd be here," James muttered, pulling a small ring of something that didn't quite look like keys from his pocket. He played around with the lock on her door. After a very short time, it clicked open.

"I think we should make sure she's all right," he said.

I stared at the door, and then at him. "How did you do that?"

"Just something I picked up," he muttered, having the good grace to look embarrassed.

"You picked her lock."

"Yes," he said. "Can we just go in, please? Make sure she's really not here?"

"I'm impressed." I gave him a soft punch on the arm. "You got skills."

"Thanks," he said, and looked around the empty hallway as though afraid the police would dive out and arrest us. Again. "Now, get in."

I stepped inside and James followed, gently shutting the door.

We skittered down the short hallway into the apartment proper. It was a tiny affair, not much bigger than my apartment was before it burned down. The kitchen was nothing more than a short line of appliances set against the far wall, with a sink and teeny cupboards. Dirty dishes mouldered in the sink. The rest of the kitchen looked clean enough, though a small TV took up most of the counter space.

A small table and two chairs sat a few feet away from the line of cupboards. The table was piled high with old mail. A few feet past that was the living area, no couch or arm chairs. Just a motley collection of bookshelves piled high with books and paper. Another television sat in front of them, and in front of it was a desk. On the desk were pens and pencils and stacks of paper. I glanced at the top sheet. It was a pencil sketch of a man's face.

"Hmm," I said. "This looks like you."

James glanced at it and shrugged. "Could be."

I pointed at two doors in the far wall. "Shall we check?"

"Yeah." He walked up to the first one, swung it open, and took a quick glance inside. "Bathroom," he said. "Empty."

Beyond the other door was a small neat bedroom. On the bureau sat another television. Honoria was not in this room, either.

"Okay, so she's officially not here," I said. "What do we do now?"

"I think we should look around," James replied, walking up to the kitchen table. He began going through the pile of mail. examining every unopened envelope before turning to the next.

"We came in here to snoop on her, didn't we?" I asked. "You were counting on her not being here, weren't you?"

"Let's just say an opportunity presented itself," James replied. "Shouldn't let one of those go by."

"Why?" I turned over a couple more of the sketches on the desk and looked at them. Both were of James, and they were pretty good. I held one up. "I think she has a crush on you."

James pointedly ignored the sketch. He walked over to the bookshelf and pulled out a pile of paper bound with a large elastic band. "We need to know more about her, don't we?"

"I guess." I turned over a couple more sketches. More buildings. Or, to be more exact, one building. A two-story house, looked like it was in one of the older rundown areas of Edmonton. The windows looked boarded-up. "But I don't know why we just didn't wait until—"

"Until what? She tells us everything? Do you really think she's going to do that?"

I stopped looking at the pictures and looked at him instead. "You don't trust her?"

"No." He shook his head, still going through the papers. Looked like bank statements. "I really don't. Saying she dreams the murder. I mean, that's just too strange."

"Yeah. Maybe." I set down the sketches. I didn't feel like digging around in her life anymore. "I don't feel very good about going through her stuff like this—"

"Why?" he asked. "You've done this before, haven't you?"

"Well, yeah," I replied, feeling trapped. He was right. I'd gone through my old boss's office—and from the information I'd gathered, James and I had been able to prove that my boss was truly a bad man and deserved to go to jail.

But this didn't feel the same. Honoria was—different.

"So what's the difference?" he asked, and I jumped like he'd read my mind.

"Nothing, I guess. However, she is our client."

"That decision hasn't been made yet."

"Oh come on!" I cried. "We already said yes, mostly! And Noreen said Eddie didn't know her—"

"And like you said, Eddie might not have told Noreen," he said. "I still have no reason to trust her."

"Oh, so you have to trust someone before you take their case for real?" I asked, walking over to a bookshelf as far from him as I could get. I pulled out a book and glanced at it. Some kind of horror thing. Wouldn't be my cup of tea, if I read. A sheaf of papers that had been tucked in beside it slithered off the shelf in a papery waterfall.

"Crap!" I bent down and tried to pick them up in order.

"I don't need to trust them," he replied. "But I have to be able to get a read on them. I can't with her. There's something about her that's—off."

"Yeah, well, there is the fact that she's been hospitalized and drugged most of her life," I said.

I'd managed to get everything that I'd knocked to the floor more or less back in order, and looked at the top page. It had the same title as the book. The only difference was, on the typed pages, Honoria's name appeared below the title. On the book—a different name.

"There is that," James replied. "I don't know if I can trust someone who's certifiable."

I glared at him. "You know, there is a possibility she actually has visions or whatever."

"I doubt that," James replied, putting back the bank statements and pulling out another pile of papers. "I think her 'visions' are a scam."

"Fine. Whatever." I looked back down at the sheets and read the first few lines, then looked inside the book. Exactly the same lines.

I looked back at the typewritten sheets and read a bit more. Then back at the book. Same words.

"Hmm," I said. "Maybe she's not crazy. Maybe she's just a writer."

"You find something?"

"Looks like she wrote a book."

"Really?" he asked.

"Really, book boy," I scoffed. "You ever heard of this one? Maybe she's somebody."

I held up the book, and his eyebrows raised.

"She wrote that?" He walked over and took it from me. "That was on the *New York Times* bestseller list three years ago."

"You remember stuff like that?" I asked, and laughed. "Man, you gotta get a life."

He didn't answer, because he was looking at the shelf where I'd pulled out the book and the sheaf of paper. There was a line of books, with sheafs of paper tucked in beside each of them.

He pulled out another book, with a different writer's name on the cover, and frowned. "This guy died last year."

He looked at the typewritten pages, then opened the book and looked at the date it was published.

"She wrote a date on the front—it was three months before this book came out."

"Huh," I said. "She writes fast."

"No," he replied. "Something's not right. This guy has written twenty-three books. And he's dead."

He pulled out another and then another, and his frown grew. "What is going on here?" he finally asked.

"What do you mean?"

"All these different authors—and the dates on the manuscripts all read a few months to a year before the books were published."

I found a DVD tucked in behind the line of books and manuscripts. It had its own sheaf of paper, and when I opened it, I could see it was a screenplay. I recognized the name of the movie—had actually gone to see it. I looked at the date scrawled across the top of the manuscript, then at the release date. Four months separated them.

"So, what? She's copying these things word for word?" I asked.

"Looks like it," he replied. "But why would she do that? And what's with the date?"

"I don't know," I replied. "Weird."

"What the hell are you doing in my apartment?"

As I squawked and jumped about a foot and a half straight up, I was almost happy to see James do the same thing. Then we whirled around and faced an absolutely furious Honoria Lowe.

Her arms were full of plastic bags of fast food, which she tossed on the kitchen counter by the television. I watched the huge plastic Slurpee cup tip over and disgorge its contents onto the counter, and then onto the floor. But I didn't say a word. Like I said, she was furious.

"Tell me! What are you doing in my place?"

My mind was absolutely frozen. I could not think of one thing to say that would not at the very best get us kicked out after being fired, and at the very worst get us both jailed, this time for a long time.

I glanced at James, hoping to see inspiration on his face. I was disappointed. I saw only shock. But luckily, it thawed.

He put down the manuscript he was holding and took a tentative step toward her.

"Sorry, Ms. Lowe," he said, his voice a soothing rumble. "We became concerned when you didn't answer your door."

"How did you get in the building?" Honoria asked. Then she sighed. "Joey let you in, didn't he?"

"Yes." This was James again. I was still feeling fairly frozen.

She shook her head. "He always does that. I wish they'd fix the intercom."

"Oh." James frowned. "That's fairly inconvenient."

"Yeah." Honoria almost smiled, then remembered that she'd caught us in her apartment going through her stuff, and frowned again, ferociously. "You didn't answer my question. What are you doing in here?"

"Like I said," James said, taking another hesitant step in her direction. "We were concerned for your safety."

"My safety?"

"We called your cell and heard it ringing in your apartment," James said. "That's the reason I let us in. We thought—"

"Oh." Honoria patted her pockets. "I was sure—" She looked at the kitchen table and saw the cell phone sitting amongst the unopened mail. "Oh. Well, shit."

She shook her head. "I'm always forgetting that stupid thing. You were late—I figured you weren't going to show up, so I went to get myself something to eat."

I finally felt like I could say something. "Your Slurpee," I said, pointing.

She followed my finger, saw the tipped cup, and hissed, jumping for it and holding it up, staring at the little bit left in the bottom dejectedly. "Crap."

She tossed the cup into the sink with the dirty dishes and took some halfhearted swipes at the soda dripping from the counter to the floor, before throwing the sopping cloth in the sink with the rest of the mess.

"Whatever. I didn't need it." She turned back to us and frowned again. "What are you doing with those?" she asked, pointing at the manuscripts we were holding.

James and I both looked down, and then back at her, but before either of us could come up with anything, she shook her head.

"I don't care what you were doing. Just put them back."

James and I glanced at each other, and I did my best to signal that I would be more than happy to put everything away if he'd just go and make up with our furious almost-client. He seemed to catch my frantic thoughts and handed me the pile of paper he was holding, then turned back to Honoria.

"Like I said, we were afraid that something happened to you," he said. "We were just looking for—"

"Clues!" I called from the bookshelf, as I stuffed the manuscripts back as quickly and tidily as I could.

"Yeah." James sighed. "Clues."

"Clues?" Honoria asked, looking skeptical. I didn't blame her. As soon as the word was out of my mouth I thought it sounded pretty stupid.

"We were worried," James said hastily. "We're sorry. We shouldn't have touched your—"

"Writing," Honoria said. "It's my writing."

"Those books—Did you write them?"

"Kind of."

James frowned. "Kind of?"

"Well, I did write them." Honoria said. "I just wasn't the only one."

"I don't understand," James said. Honoria ignored him and pushed the pile of mail on the kitchen table to the floor.

"I'm hungry," she said. "You want some?"

Without waiting for us to answer, she pulled the various boxes from the plastic bag and set them on the table.

"Sure," I said, and sat down across from her. James didn't answer, but eventually took the last chair.

She ate silently, offering us something every time she opened another box, merely shrugging and digging in when we shook our heads. Finally, when she was finished, she pushed all the empty boxes into the bag and tossed the whole mess in the garbage can in the corner.

"So, you want to know about me, do you?" she asked. "About the writing, and all the rest?"

"Yes," James said.

"It's all part of the deal," Honoria said.

She laughed shortly and pulled out a cigarette. She shook her head when James offered her a light and tucked it behind her ear.

"I quit," she said. "Just feels good to hold the thing for a second."

"The writing?" James prompted.

Honoria sighed. "I channel—things. Like that guy who died. Brown Eddie. I channeled his death. It comes to me in pictures."

"But that doesn't explain the writing," James said. "All those manuscripts. And the books."

Honoria snorted soft laughter. "It's a little side benefit. Sometimes I don't channel murder victims. Sometimes, I channel writers."

She walked over to the shelf and pulled out the manuscript closest to her. "This is the first one. I'd never written a thing before."

She laughed, but it sounded like a sob. "I honestly thought this was me, this time. I finished the thing in weeks, and gave it to a buddy to read. He got real excited. Said I should try to get it published. So I did. Picked a publisher out of a hat, basically, and sent it in. Thought I'd lose my mind when I heard from them, a couple of weeks later." She shook her head.

"I guess my manuscript was word-for-word the same as a book that they'd just sent to press. Their lawyers talked about plagiarism being a crime, among other things. I guess I really shook them up."

She picked up the hardcover book. "This came out two months later. Then I wrote fourteen more of the things. Knew enough not to let anyone see them. Just started looking for the novels a few months after I'd finished. And I found them all." She pointed.

"Almost all of them are *New York Times* bestsellers. A couple won awards."

"Holy crap," James whispered. He looked shocked.

"Yeah," Honoria replied. "I'm glad it finally stopped."

James frowned and looked at the fifteen novels on the shelf. "You mean to tell me you wrote—"

"That's right, big guy," Honoria replied. "I wrote fifteen novels in three years. Like I said, would've been nice if any of it had been my own, but whatever. Now I'm back to my 'artwork.'"

She carefully replaced the novel with the others and then went through the pile of sketches on her desk. She found one near the bottom and held it out so we could see it. "Ain't it grand?"

I don't know much about art, but I know what I like. I did not like this. Not at all.

It wasn't because it was bad. Honoria obviously had some real talent. She was able to put detail, emotion, and intensity into just a few strokes of the pen, or pencil, or whatever, it seemed, she had in her hand when the visions struck.

It was her choice of topic. Not that choice had a thing to do with it, if she was telling the truth. The sketch showed Brown Eddie being beaten and then being hung in a tree.

"Crucifixion," she said. "I thought that had gone out of vogue."

"What's the deal with the ducks?" James asked.

"Ducks?" I asked. Eddie had talked about ducks. "What ducks?"

"These." He pointed, and I finally saw the duck. Not a real duck. Donald Duck, the Disney character. And, Donald Duck was killing Brown Eddie.

Holy crap. Eddie had been telling me the truth.

I glanced over at Honoria, but her face was blank.

"I just draws 'em like I sees 'em," she finally said. "I'll leave the detective work up to you. If you're going to take my case."

She looked at James, her eyes bright and sharp. Not missing a thing.

"So, what about it? You going to? Even though you think I'm either bug shit crazy or the biggest conman alive?"

"I didn't—I never—I—" James stammered, then, finally, his words stopped. "I don't know," he whispered.

"Fair enough," she said. "At least you're honest. You'll save me a few bucks, anyhow."

"I didn't say I *wasn't* going to take the case," James said. "I just have to give it a bit more thought."

"Whatever," she said. "You can get back to me, when you finally decide. Call, though, okay? Don't just break in."

"Okay." James pointed at the sketches. "Can we take some of these?"

"Sure," she said. "Hope you can decipher them. I can't. Just understand, I'm not going to be a scapegoat for the cops. And I'm done with going to the nuthouse. They might not let me out if I'm committed again. So, decide quick, all right? Because, if you're not going to help me, I have to find someone else."

"I will," James said. "I promise."

He reached over and shook her hand, then headed for the door. I grabbed his sleeve and stopped him.

"I have one more question, Honoria," I said.

"What?" she asked.

"Why so many TVs?"

She snorted soft laughter. "I use them to drown out the visions. So I can sleep."

"Does it work?"

"Sometimes."

James and I left her apartment and walked down to the street without saying anything. I was boiling over with questions, the biggest being, "Why didn't we take her case?" but I let him set the pace, and soon we were on our way to the car. He didn't speak until he'd plucked the parking ticket off the windshield and we were both inside and buckled up.

"Park's full again," he said.

Life had indeed returned to the park.

For a second, I thought I saw the light of a spirit floating around amongst the addicts, but gave my head a great big mental shake. Much as I'd hoped that Eddie would've shown up at the park, my guess was it wasn't him. It was probably some other dead person, and that was the last thing I needed in my life at that moment.

"Why didn't we say we'd take her case?" I asked James. "All we have to do is—"

"Is what? Prove she didn't kill him? How are we going to do that?" James shook his head impatiently. "Marie, I don't have a clue how to proceed—and I still don't know anything about her.

Not really."

"So she was right," I said, softly. "Wasn't she?"

"What do you mean?"

"You still think she's either crazy or trying to con us. Don't you?"

James looked at me, surprise on his face. "Don't you? What about the fact she's been in and out of mental hospitals most of her life? And she thinks she's having visions? Hey, and don't forget her saying she channeled writers for two years . . ."

"She explained that," I said, talking over his voice and wishing he'd just shut up about everything she'd told us. Mostly because it *did* sound crazy, and I didn't know how to convince him otherwise.

"Some explanation," he said shortly.

"She isn't calling herself crazy, James. She's calling herself a clairvoyant."

"Same, same," he said dismissively. "But what if it is all a con? What if she's trying to use us to throw the cops off her trail?"

"Why would she do that?" I asked.

"I don't know," he snapped. "Maybe because we're desperate for money and would do just about anything for it."

"And by 'we' you mean 'me,'" I said. "Right?"

"Well, you are quite motivated," he replied. "What I don't get is why you're buying into any of her craziness at all."

"Well, there are these," I said, holding out the sheaf of sketches we'd taken from Honoria's apartment. "Don't you think they're something?"

"Yeah," he said. "Something."

That horrible tone was back in his voice. He didn't believe. I looked at the sketches clutched in my hand and tried one more time. "Maybe it's like she said. Maybe everything we need to know is here. All we have to do is decipher them."

"You're kidding, right?" James said. "They prove nothing."

"But what about Eddie's mom's place?" I asked. "Honoria drew it, and I drove right there. I met her."

"And you didn't ask if Eddie's mom knew her. Because you believe her," he said. "Even through all the crazy talk. You still believe her. But we have to do the right thing, Marie. We have to check everything out."

"You mean we have to prove she's either crazy or conning us."

"Yes."

"Because she says she sees the dead?"

"For one thing. Come on, Marie, only a crazy person would—"

"Screw you, James!" He pushed the biggest button I have, and my rage was instant and complete. "Do you honestly believe you know everything? That you have some kind of special power that allows you to determine the insane from the sane, just by looking at them? Don't you think that maybe—just maybe—there are a couple of things you don't know? That maybe you haven't seen everything there is to see?"

"Marie, relax," James said. "She was in a mental hospital, for goodness' sake! Everybody knows she's nuts! She might even be dangerous—"

And then, I lost it.

"Dangerous? *Dangerous*? She's not crazy, and she's not a danger to us! And you are being a great huge steaming pile of assholes about this whole thing! She needs our help. She doesn't need us being all judgey and jerky. I'm betting she has enough of that in her life already! And if you won't take her case, James, well, maybe I'll take it all on my own! Can't you see she just wants help?"

"Whoa!" James cried. "A steaming pile of what?"

"Assholes," I said, but without much enthusiasm. I felt kind of bad for calling him that. Felt that maybe, just maybe, I'd overreacted just a tad.

"Sorry," I said. "I shouldn't have said any of that. Seeing her—it upset me."

"I see that."

"Can we just go back to the office, please?"

"All right," he said, but the look he gave me was not a good one. The "steaming pile of assholes" conversation wasn't over yet. I could just tell.

Eddie:
What a High's Like When You're Dead

I WAS SURPRISED to see Needle Park was nearly empty. Almost as surprised as I was at not bouncing back to the crucifixion tree. I *had* concentrated all the way to the park, but I didn't think that would make such a big difference. Apparently it did.

I wasn't hurting as much as I had been earlier in the day. This also surprised me. This is not the way it normally works. It had been days since I got high. Normally by this time I'm puking my guts out and screaming for help.

Actually, since the tree, I hadn't hurt much at all. Some, yeah. Coulda used a hit, no doubt about it, but nowhere near as bad as it has been.

I wouldn't have minded a little something, though. And that was the truth.

So I was pretty happy to see my street sister, Noreen, when I got to the edge of the park. I had been looking for Crank, even though I didn't know what he could have done for me. That son of a bitch never helped me much—without money—even when I was alive, but I could count on him. His stuff was always clean. Well, cleaner than most.

My mind dove away from that thought, because it reminded me of Luke, and I didn't want to think about him. Because of me, he was dead.

Hell, because of me, *I* was dead. But as I walked through the small groups of people standing around talking about the latest bust—looked like I just missed it, lucky me—I couldn't keep my thoughts from Luke Stewart.

Growing up, he'd been my best friend in the whole world. Poor son of a bitch, his dad was a cop, and that had been pretty hard on him. He'd tried to do right by that asshole, but it was like nothing he did was good enough. Guess I was half lucky that my dad hadn't stuck around. At least I hadn't had to go through what Luke did.

Luke never took drugs. That was the funny thing about him. Me? Man, started as soon as I could, and never let it go. But Luke tried to do life on the straight and narrow for his old man. And I think if his old man had ever let up on him, even for a minute, he would have done all right. Got married, house with the white picket fence, all that. But his old man was always on his back. Until one day, Luke just couldn't take it anymore.

He'd watched me get high, lots of times. I wasn't shy about it, and he didn't seem to mind. Until that last time, six months ago. Six months ago, almost to the day.

Thinking about that started the pangs until I was jonesing something fierce.

That's when I saw Noreen coming back out of the alley, and I could tell by that blank, orgasmic look that I'd caught her moments after smoking. I walked up to her, and I actually started to drool. Like I was starving and could see a steak.

Don't know what made me do it, but I reached my hand out to her arm, through her arm, and for a second I could feel the blood pulsing in her veins, could almost feel the warmth, and there was something else, a tingle. A hint of her high transferred to me. When she shuffled past me, the feeling was gone.

Almost made me cry, being that close to getting high and then having it walk on like that.

"Stop!" I cried. Or some such shit. Who really knows what I said? I was crying—don't know when that started, could have been when I thought about Luke, or when I felt that ghost of a high through Noreen's scarred-up skin—and I ran after her. "Wait, Noreen! Please wait!"

It was like she heard me. Stopped short and looked around. And I ran right into her.

When I say I ran into her, I'm not kidding. I ran right into her body. Felt her heart beat in my chest—hers was pounding like a racehorse's run close to death, I recognized the feeling—and felt her warmth. And then her high hit me full-bore, and I knew if I'd seen my face in a mirror, I would have had exactly the same blank look that she had on hers.

She stood still for about five seconds, then moved on, but five seconds was enough. I was flying, flying, flying, and didn't even care that she'd walked away.

My knees buckled, and I ended up on my ass on the ground. Still didn't care. Felt good. Felt great. Felt my mind slip away, so I didn't notice the garbage or the dirt or the fight that broke out next to me. Didn't notice anything at all. Just felt at peace. That peace you feel for those three seconds after climaxing. All thoughts gone, and every good hormone in your body running through your system congratulating the hell out of you for doing your best to keep the human race going. That one. You know that one. But it went on and on, and just before I slipped onto my side and closed my eyes, I felt as good as I ever had before. Living or dead.

OPENED MY EYES. The screaming good part of the high was just about gone. All that was left was the capacity to deal with life for a few hours. Looked around and groaned.

"Dammit."

I was back at the crucifixion tree.

I pulled myself upright, and almost without thinking, hit the sidewalk. Took ten steps, then stopped and thought. Where was I going? Realized I'd been thinking of going to my mom's, and I stopped in my tracks. There was someplace else. Someplace better.

That girl. Marie Jenner. I needed to see her.

So I headed back to the Jimmy Lavall Detective Agency, over in Chinatown.

"This is the last time, girl," I muttered under my breath as I stumbled along the sidewalks, but I knew I was lying. Even if she wasn't there, I'd wait.

Whatever it took. I needed her. She could help me.

Somehow, I knew that.

Marie:
This Night Just Goes On and On and On . . .

JAMES BARELY SPOKE a word to me the whole way back to the office, and I was getting as jumpy as a cat. Under normal circumstances that can make me mean, but I did my best to keep it under control. It was now nearly 12:30, and I was really tired. Didn't want another long-winded discussion about me and my stupid ideas and my overreacting. I just wanted to be able to lie down for a little while, then head back out with the sketches, find Dead Eddie, and get him to explain them to me.

He was the key to the whole thing, darn it anyhow.

James stopped, and I nearly ran into him. "So, are you going to stay here tonight?" he asked.

"If you don't mind," I said, primly. I felt my face heat, and then felt ridiculous.

"You can stay here anytime," he said. "You know that."

"I know." I was even more uncomfortable and skipped ahead of him so I could be the one to open the door.

The building was quiet and a little bit creepy. The only time I ever felt that way was when a ghost was around. I frowned, wondering if maybe Eddie had finally figured out where I was. Maybe I wasn't going to have to look for him after all. That would have been a massive break. But I didn't see him anywhere.

Nope, something else was giving me the creepy feeling, and it didn't take long for me to figure out what it was.

We came out of the stairwell and walked down the short hallway to the door of the office. Except the door to the office had been kicked in.

"What's going on here?" James breathed, stepping through the open doorway.

"Wait," I whispered. But it was too late.

He was already well into the office, and I could hear his shoes crunching on glass and debris. Debris in our nice little office. I sighed and stepped through the door myself.

Someone had certainly done a number on the place. Everything was pulled apart and broken. All the drawers of my desk hung open, and everything that had been sitting on it was now scattered all over the floor.

"Shit," I whispered. "Shit shit shit . . ."

I crept toward the door that led to the inner office. James was already in there, and I could hear him. I didn't want to look, but I had to.

It too was a wreck. James had picked up a book that had been ripped in half, and I thought he was going to cry.

"Why would someone do such a thing?" he asked.

"I don't know," I said, and walked closer to him. The place still felt massively creepy, even though I could see that no one was here but us. Living or dead.

He gently put the ripped book on the empty desk. "Who would have done this?"

I felt a flutter of something close to guilt. "Maybe I rattled a cage or two at the park."

"But—"

"Or maybe it was that cop, trying to figure out what I was doing there."

"The cop?" James looked confused. "Why would either a cop or someone from the park have showed up here? At my office?"

I heard the "my", and my face warmed. "It might have been because I gave a guy at the park one of your business cards," I whispered. "And I used this address when I was arrested."

His face showed no emotion, but his eyebrows raised until I was afraid they were going to get lost in his hairline. "You were handing out business cards at the park?"

"Just one, but yeah."

"Maybe don't do that again." He still looked relatively calm, but his eyebrows hadn't dropped back to their usual place on his forehead.

"All right." I looked around so I didn't have to look at him. "It could have been the cop, though. The cop that busted me. Stew, I think his name was."

"Oh." He shrugged. "Maybe." Then he frowned again. "But why?"

"I don't know!" I cried, then shook my head, and tried to calm down. "I don't know." I looked around at the mess. "We going to call the cops?"

"Let's see if they took anything first," James said. "Might give us a clue who did this."

We looked around, but could see nothing missing. Just stuff wrecked. As though someone had come in looking for—something—and then had a temper tantrum when they couldn't find it.

"I think I'm glad the cops still have our computers," I said. "Maybe this didn't have anything to do with the park. Maybe somebody decided to rob you. You think?"

"I guess," he replied, but didn't sound convinced. "There's nothing missing though, is there?"

I went back out and looked around the outer office, but still could see nothing missing. My daytimer was lying facedown on the floor. I picked it up and looked at the page to which it had been opened. Bits and pieces of my day written down on nearly every page—and Honoria's name and the time of our initial meeting. Under that I had written "Eddie Hansen."

I was relieved to see I'd forgotten to write down our meeting with Honoria that evening. I would have written in her address, and I had a feeling that would have been a very bad thing.

I carried the daytimer into James's office, and held it out. "It was turned to this page," I said.

He looked at it. Shook his head. "I knew that woman was going to be trouble."

"Or maybe we're bringing trouble to her," I replied.

"Yeah," he said, and pulled his cell from his pocket.

"It's James," he said after quite a long pause. "I'm sorry I woke you, Honoria, but I wanted to make sure you were all right." He leaned over and plucked a piece of wood from the cuff of his jeans, tossing it to the floor with the rest of the garbage.

"We had a break-in here," he said. "And I just wanted to make sure— No. I don't think so. Yes, I probably will." He rolled his eyes at me, then, when I giggled—and why did I giggle like a kid at him? It was so embarrassing!—he turned his back to me and continued to answer her obviously panicky questions.

"So, who's he talking to?"

The voice was right behind me. I whirled, ready to do battle, scared almost out of my mind, and faced Dead Eddie Hansen. Face to dead face.

"How ya doin'?" he asked, and grinned, his teeth black, broken, and really quite horrible. They looked way too old for his young face. "I didn't think I'd ever catch up with you."

He'd found me. Finally! He'd look at the sketches, tell me who had really killed him, I'd tell James—making up some suitably plausible lie concerning how I found this information out—and we'd be done.

I glanced at James. He was still standing with his back to me with his cell phone pressed to his ear, so I turned to Eddie and pointed through the open door to the other room.

He shrugged and led the way. I followed him, trying to figure out the best way to get the information out of him without him getting upset. Upset ghosts were always more trouble than they were worth.

He watched me, a fuzzy smile on his face. I think he was pleasant-looking at one time, but not anymore. He looked used-up. Paper-thin, his hands and face covered with old scabs and scratches that hadn't healed before his death. Plus the big new ones, of course. The great huge holes where the spikes had gone through both hands, and a bashed-in bit on his forehead. I glanced down at his feet and could see carpet through a hole in one foot. The other one wasn't quite as bad, but close enough. I felt sick and pulled my line of sight back up to his face. His teeth might be bad, but at least I could stand looking at them.

"Look pretty bad, don't I?" he asked.

"You don't look too good."

"Haven't for a while." He grinned. "But I'm feeling good now."

"Oh?"

"Yeah." He smiled even more broadly, and stretched both arms above his head, looking like a beat-up alley cat. "My buddy

Noreen—she hooked me up."

Before I could ask him what he meant, he leaned in, hard. "Why were you at my mom's?"

"A friend—a friend of mine told me you might be there." Close enough to the truth.

"Who told you that?"

"Her name is Honoria Lowe."

He frowned. "Don't think I know the chick," he finally said.

"You're sure?" I asked.

"Pretty sure." The frown stayed. "You gotta leave my mother out of this. She doesn't know anything."

"I will. I promise," I whispered, to make absolutely certain James in the next room heard nothing. "Honoria is our client." I blinked. "Mostly our client. The cops think she's involved in your murder, and we're trying to prove that she isn't."

I grabbed a couple of the sketches off the desk and held them out. "She drew these. Plus one that was of your mother's house. She said you were there. That's why I went. I was just trying to find you."

"Huh." The frown was gone, thank goodness, but the suspicious look still hung on his face. Then he blinked twice, rapidly, and half-smiled. "So she sees ghosts, too?"

I nodded. "Yes. But not the way I do."

"Huh." He glanced down at the sketches in my hand, and his light dimmed appreciably. "I told you there were ducks," he finally muttered.

"Yeah, I saw that." I held the sketches out. "Please look at them, closely. I think everything we need to know is in them."

He glanced at them, then closed his eyes. "Those are horrible," he whispered, and turned away. "I don't want to look at them anymore."

I closed my eyes, to calm myself. James was still talking to Honoria in the other room. I still had time. All I had to do was get Eddie to really look at the sketches—but he'd wandered away from me, and was staring out the window.

"So, how come I don't see no more ghosts hanging around?" he asked. "This part of town, there should be lots of us."

"Most of them move on."

"Where to?" Gave a small laugh, but it sounded more frightened than amused. "Calgary?"

"God forbid!" I whispered, and he laughed again. "No. They move to the next plane of existence. Sometimes, if they need it, I help them."

What was wrong with me? All I'd wanted to do with this particular ghost was get the information about his death—specifically, who had brutally killed him. Why had I even put the thought of moving him on in his head?

"Oh." His face went back to a frown. "You're not going to do that to me, are you?"

"No," I finally said. "I wasn't really thinking of it."

"Good," he replied, and the easygoing grin was back. "I have business to attend to, after all."

"Yeah." I walked up behind him, staying just out of his crazy-making aura. "About that, Eddie. Why are you so sure that your mom's book club had anything to do with your death?"

He didn't answer me for a long moment. "You met 'em," he finally muttered. "They wanted me dead. They said so."

He wasn't going to be easy to convince.

I heard James put down his phone and walk toward the door. "We'll finish this conversation later," I whispered, just as he walked into the reception area.

"What are you doing out here?" he asked.

"I thought I heard someone," I said.

Eddie stared at James for a second, then smiled. "He doesn't know you can see me, does he?"

"Who were you talking to?" James asked.

"Does he?" Eddie repeated.

"I wasn't talking to anyone," I replied, trying to ignore Eddie.

"It sure sounded like you were," James said.

"Well," Eddie muttered, chuckling. "This oughta be interesting."

You said a mouthful, Eddie.

"OKAY, FINE," JAMES said for the third time, and for the third time didn't believe one word I was saying. "So you were just talking to yourself."

"Yes," I said. Again.

"And you just wanted me to have a little privacy."

"Yep. That's it, exactly."

"Is this the way you guys communicate all the time?" Eddie asked. "My guess, you ain't gonna make it."

I ignored him, or tried to. "We should call the police. Report the break-in."

"Break-in?" Eddie asked, and looked around the wrecked room. "Oh. Yeah. That was R and Crank."

I almost whirled and screamed, "R and Crank? Who are they?" But I didn't. I needed to keep up stupid appearances, after all.

James righted the chair, then sat at the desk and pulled the old-fashioned phone up by the cord, reconnected it to the wall, pressed a button or two, listened, seemed satisfied, and set it on the desk. "I already did."

"When?"

"After I talked to Honoria."

"Did they say when they'd get here?"

"Probably never," Eddie said. "Not with this address."

"They didn't say," James said. "But it's probably going to take them a while in this area of town."

"Well, what do we do, then?" I asked. Both of them, apparently.

"We wait," James said.

"We could get high," Eddie suggested. I decided to ignore Eddie.

"What if whoever did this comes back while we're waiting?"

"Then we protect ourselves," James said.

"They probably *will* come back," Eddie said. "Didn't look like they found what they were looking for."

"And what were they looking for?" I asked. James gave me a strange look, and Eddie cackled out laughter, so I asked, "Do you have any ideas?"

Weak, I know, but it was all I had. This three-way conversation was beginning to make my head ache.

"I think you were right. I think you probably rattled some cages at the park," James said.

"You went to the park? My park?" Eddie cried. "No wonder they were here."

"So, if the druggies—"

"Druggies!" Eddie laughed. I shot him a quick look, even though, to James, it would look like I was glaring at an empty corner of the room. Luckily, though, he had leaned over to pick some broken stuff off the floor.

"You shouldn't touch anything," I said. "The cops will want to check for fingerprints or something. Won't they?"

"You're right," he said, and pulled his hand back. "So, if it was those guys from the park that did this, they came here looking for information . . ."

"The only real information they could get would be Honoria's address, and since I hadn't written it down, she should be safe," I said. "Right?"

"Right."

"But what about us?" I asked. "We could be in danger, or something."

"Don't worry," James said, and smiled at me. "I'll protect you."

"Thanks," I said, hoping I didn't sound too sarcastic. He didn't respond well to sarcasm.

"You're welcome." He favoured me with another smile. Then we all jumped about a foot when someone hammered on the door. Through the broken window I could see two blue uniforms.

"Well, look at that," James said. "The police."

I really hoped neither of the cops standing at our door had been involved in the drug bust earlier that evening. That would be just too embarrassing.

As James let them in, Eddie skittered over to me. "I'm not sticking around," he said. "I personally hate cops."

"Come back, though," I whispered. "I want to know more."

"All right. Tomorrow." And in a swirl of light, he was gone. I was surprised and then angry. No walking? Swirling light and disappearing? Where did that come from? Ghosts always seemed to be doing things I'd never seen before. What was the deal with that?

TWO HOURS LATER, the police were gone, and James and I were alone in the wrecked office.

"Let's board up the window and get some rest. We can decide next steps tomorrow."

He yawned, a jaw-cracking affair, and then we quickly picked up as much of the wreckage as we could and found some cardboard in the overstuffed closet. James duct-taped it in place over the broken window in the door.

"This won't keep anyone out," I said. I felt nervous. These guys, whoever they were, could get back in here, easily. "Maybe we could go to Jasmine's."

"Marie, it's three in the morning."

"Oh."

"Trust me, if they come back, we'll hear them and deal with them," James replied, and yawned again. He didn't seem the least bit nervous, and I decided I was being a real girl about everything.

"All right."

I looked around for something else to clean, and realized we'd finished the worst of it. I was going to offer to make tea or something, and then realized I was trying to put off actually going to sleep. I was being ridiculous.

"You take the cot," James said. "I'll be okay on the floor."

Sometimes he took this being a gentleman thing way too far. "You're still pretty banged up," I said. "You use the cot. I'll be fine out here. I'll keep watch, just in case we have any more visitors."

"You sure?"

"Yes."

He pulled a blanket from the closet, handed it to me, then walked into the inner office. "Wake me in a couple of hours. I'll spell you off," he said, and I nodded.

Moments later, I heard the springs of the cot creak as he rolled onto it, and then, very quickly, all was silent.

I pulled the big chair over by the office door and settled into it, pulling the blanket over my shoulders. Heard a creak and jumped up to check if someone was coming up the stairs. Nothing. Settled back down, and tried to relax. Another creak, and I jumped up again. Didn't remember this building making quite that much noise before. Looked around, even going so far as opening the front door a crack. Nothing.

Settled down, and was instantly up again, this time because I couldn't hear anything and was certain that the silence meant someone was creeping up the stairs.

"Good grief!"

I pulled the blankets back over me, but didn't even bother closing my eyes this time. Wished that Dead Eddie would come back, so at least someone was in the room with me. But he'd said he would come back the next day. I was alone for the rest of the night. Heard a cat yowl somewhere close by, and jumped up, heart pounding.

"Marie?"

"What!" I screamed, my heart hitting that ultra-high range

that meant either I was about to have a heart attack or I was scared out of my tree.

"Come here."

It was James, in the other room. I pulled the blanket closely around me and skittered in.

"What?"

"You want to stay in here with me?" he asked.

I honestly thought I was going to say, "No, it's all right, I'll just keep watch out there, everything's fine." What came out of my mouth was a strangled, "Yes."

"Come on, then." He pulled the covers open.

"Just a sec."

I grabbed a wooden chair and stuck the back of it under the doorknob of the front door. I'd seen this done in the movies, and hoped it would work to keep the door jammed shut. Then I skittered over to the cot and crawled in beside James.

Under normal circumstances, I never would have done anything like that. The cot was small, and he is a large man. And there was the whole "this is a business arrangement" thing. Crawling into bed with him did not really send that message. But these were not normal circumstances. I snuggled into his arms and instantly felt safer.

"You're shivering," he whispered. His breath touched my ear, and I shivered even harder.

"I'm cold."

"Want another blanket?"

"No." Like a cat, I snuggled further into his arms, against his chest, pulling the warmth from him to me. "No, this is good. You're sure I'm not taking too much space?"

"No," he murmured, and wrapped his arms around me. "Lots of room."

So I did the only thing I could do. As I felt him relax and ease into sleep, I followed him, feeling safer than I had in a long time.

Maybe my whole life.

Eddie:
Seeing the Girl of Your Dreams,
After You're Dead

I BOPPED BACK to the crucifixion tree again, but I wasn't surprised this time.

I didn't want to hang around, but didn't know where to go. It was too late to go to the park and get another hit, because I was certain that even Noreen would have called it a day by that time. Everyone who had a home would have gone to it. The only ones left would have been the truly homeless, and I didn't need or want their kind of high. Nope, it was time to settle in for the night.

I was wandering around the churchyard looking for a spot when I heard someone call me.

No. That's not right. That's not what it was. No one was actually calling my name, even though I looked around and said, "Who is that?" like they had. No, it was more like someone reached into my brain and whispered something only I could hear.

I recognized the voice. A girl who lived by the park. I'd run into her a few times, when I was alive. And she'd talked to me, if you could call, "No I don't have any spare change" a conversation. But I was certain it was her voice I was hearing. And it sounded like she was looking for me.

I looked around the churchyard, thinking she was there, mourning my loss or something. Yeah. Right. But there was something compelling about her tone. Like she really needed to see me.

Who am I to turn down a woman? Especially a cute one with blonde hair. Those kind of women usually never notice me, so when her voice tickled my brain, I decided to follow it.

The further west I walked, the stronger the connection became. Her voice didn't get louder or anything. I just felt like I was more connected to her.

I ended up at the park, and I almost stopped, but by that time the compulsion to follow her voice was overwhelming. Like I was jonesing, but in a good way. One more step, my head kept saying, and I'll find her. Wasn't quite sure what would happen then, but knew I couldn't stop.

Walked around the figures sleeping on the grass, to the far sidewalk, and then across the street in front of a three-story building. Bottom floor was commercial, and not the good commercial, either. Between a pawn shop and a payday loanshark place was a scratched-up door with a bank of beat-up buttons beside it. Checked the names—force of habit from life, I guess—but most of them were Smith and Jones, so I closed my eyes, and let her voice pull me through the door and up the stairs to the second floor.

Dark dingy hallway, most of the lights burnt out or knocked out, but it didn't stop me. Her voice was like a beacon pulling me to the third door on the right.

I hesitated at the front of that door. I didn't walk in on women, when I was alive. That type of behaviour could bring much unwanted police attention—but her voice in my brain was like an itch that desperately needed to be scratched.

So, I walked through the door of the girl of my dreams.

It wasn't quite like I'd imagined. I thought it would have been cleaner, and more feminine. There was a big pile of mail—most of it fliers—on her kitchen table. Books everywhere. On the kitchen counter a TV was on, and I could tell by the snow she didn't have cable. I could barely see the show, and the voices were muffled, as though the two guys on the screen were talking through mouths full of cotton.

"Eddie."

I looked around, wondering as I did so if I'd heard the name on the television and mistaken it for the blonde calling my name.

"Dead guy."

No mistake that time. It was the blonde. Wasn't too taken with her calling me "dead guy," and I didn't see her anywhere in the room. She had to be there somewhere though, because what I was hearing was not in my head this time. She was talking out loud. To me.

Two doors leading out of the messy main room. Stuck my head through one, and could tell it was the bathroom, and empty. Backed out and tried the other door.

This one led to the bedroom. This room was as stark and clean as the other was messy. Just two pieces of furniture—a bed and a dresser—and nothing else. By the light of another television—this one sitting on the top of the dresser, tuned to a different, but equally snowy, channel—I could see a form in the bed. It was the blonde.

She was so slight she barely made a mound under the blankets. She muttered something and clutched at the blankets desperately, as though she didn't quite have the strength to pull them up over her face.

"Eddie," she moaned. In spite of myself, I smiled. Nice hearing her say my name, even if it did sound like she was having a bad dream.

"Yeah?" I said. Hoped I'd be able to pull her out of the dream. Maybe she'd sit up and see me. Talk to me. That would have been cool. "I'm right here. What do you want?"

"Eddie," she said again, but her voice didn't sound like she'd heard me. Still sounded like she was caught in the dream, and whatever was going on in there, it didn't sound good. "Run."

I frowned. Not so much because she'd suggested I run from whatever she saw in the dream, but because it looked like she couldn't hear me. I'd hoped she would have—hoped she was like that Marie chick and would be able to talk to me, even though I was dead.

Maybe I wasn't talking loud enough. It wasn't like I could shake her awake or anything.

"Hey, chick!" I called. "Wake up!"

Still nothing, past her frowning and clutching her blanket even more desperately.

"Come on, chick, open your eyes!" I cried. "I'm right here!"
Nothing.

"Come on!" I yelled. "Open your eyes!"

I got more reaction than I ever thought I would.

Her eyes popped open, and she looked around the room like she was looking for me. But there was something about her eyes that let me know that even though they were open, she wasn't seeing anything in that room, including me. She sat up, clutching the blankets to her chest, as she gasped in air like she was drowning. Then she opened her mouth and started to scream.

That scream drove me to my knees, because she wasn't just screaming out loud, she was screaming in her head, and then she was screaming in my head, and with the screams came pictures, not pictures but a movie—a silent movie with only her screams punctuating the horror that was being shown on the screen of my mind.

I started screaming too. I couldn't help it. The jerky, shadowy, snowy images drove it out of me as surely as if I was being beaten to death. Again.

I could see my face. My screaming face. And I screamed, matching the image. Watched me as I begged for my life, among the rain of blows. Then I was being dragged to the tree, and I could see the hammer, and I watched the blood, and it all came back to me, the way I had died came back to me, a rain of blows hitting me so hard I curled into a ball on the floor by her bed.

"Stop it!" I cried. I was yelling it at her, even though I knew she couldn't hear me. Because I knew the images of my death—and that's what I was watching, a frigging movie of my death—were coming from her. And I couldn't stand it anymore. "Stop it! Stop it! Stop it!"

But she didn't. Or couldn't. Just sat upright in her bed, screaming her own ghastly screams at the visions we were both seeing.

I crawled to the door and through to the other room. The visions were not as clear there, but I could still see them, and I could definitely still hear her. So I crawled out of her apartment and into the dark, dank hallway.

Better. Mostly snow, and my eyesight had cleared so I could see where I was going. I pulled myself to my feet, shakily, feeling like I was going to puke. And then, I heard her voice, clear as a

E.C. Bell

bell.

"Trust Marie," she said in a singsong voice. "She'll save you. She'll save us both."

That's when I ran to the park and rolled into the first guy I found, taking as much of his high as I could stand. Finally, that voice in my head faded away to grey.

I pulled away from the guy, and stood, shakily, then walked east.

East. Away from the blonde. I was going to get as far away from the blonde as I could. I never wanted to see any of that again. Never wanted to see her again.

Ever.

STAGE TWO
AVOIDANCE, TO THE EXTREME

Marie:
The Next Day Brings More Crap

I THOUGHT I heard the phone ring, but didn't want to move. I was warm, lying in James's arms, and I wanted to stay there forever.

James groaned in his sleep, and pulled me closer. My body tingled, that good tingle, and as I snuggled into him, he murmured something, possibly my name—I hoped it was my name—and wrapped his hand in my hair, gently pulling my face close to his.

The phone rang again. I groaned and disengaged myself from James's warmth, reaching the desk before the phone had a chance to ring a third time. Way deep inside, I was hoping to get rid of whoever it was and sneak back into bed. With James. To hell with normal. Being with him, lying in that bed with him, felt absolutely right.

"What?" I barked.

"Marie?" It was Honoria. Calling the office phone. What was going on?

"Yes," I said shortly, "I'll get James."

"No. I want to talk to you."

I glanced at the clock. 4:30 in the morning.

"Do you know what time it is?"

"No."

"Are you in trouble?"

"No."

I frowned and looked at James, who was moving restively, as though he was waking up. "Can't this wait until morning?"

"We need to talk. Now."

I sighed, and grabbed a pad of paper and a pen. My feet were starting to get cold, and I wished I'd grabbed my socks. "All right. Tell me what I need to know."

"No," she replied. "Not over the phone. You have to come here."

"What?"

"Please."

I looked back at the bed, and the man, once more. "Why?"

"Because I had another dream." She sniffed, and I almost imagined her crying, distraught.

"Don't you have sketches or something I could pick up tomorrow?" Please?

"No." She sniveled, and it was all I could do not to roll my eyes. "This was different. He was here. In my place. I could feel him."

"Who?" I asked, a jolt of fear running through me. "Who was in your apartment?"

"It was Eddie," she said.

"The dead guy."

"Yes. He wanted to talk to me—or something. I tried, but he ran away." She sobbed. "Please," she said. "Please come over. By yourself. James wouldn't understand any of this. You know?"

"I know," I said. He'd continue to think she was crazy—or worse, he'd think she was trying to make us believe she was crazy, to keep out of jail. "What did Eddie say to you?"

"Please," she pleaded. "Just come over. I'll tell you everything. Everything."

"All right," I muttered. If this could get me some real information and help me figure out who killed Eddie, I'd do it. "I'll be there soon."

"Thanks," she said. "Hope you weren't sleeping."

I looked at the man in the bed, regretfully. So much for my grab at normal.

"No problem," I whispered, and hung up the phone. "No problem at all."

I LEFT JAMES a note telling him where I was and crept out of the office. I almost knocked down the chair I'd set under the door handle and froze as it clattered and banged, but James didn't move.

I walked the fourteen blocks on my own. Surprisingly, it wasn't as frightening as I thought it was going to be.

It was so late that it was early. The streets had that cold grey look, as though everything in the world were holding its breath, waiting to see if the miracle that was the sun rising would actually happen again. The still air felt cold, and only a couple of cars crept along the streets. Even they were quiet.

I got to Honoria's apartment building and saw her through the scratched plexiglass of the front door. She let me in.

"Thank you for doing this," she said.

"You're welcome." I tried to keep the aggravation out of my voice, because she really looked spooked. "So, what happened?"

She gestured toward the stairs. "Not here. Let's talk upstairs."

I followed her up the flight of stairs to her apartment, where the smell of freshly brewed coffee put me in a better mood almost immediately. Honestly, it was like walking into heaven.

"Want some?" she asked.

"That would be wonderful." Truly wonderful.

As she poured the coffee, I looked around. The tiny kitchen table was empty of the mound of mail, and her desk was tidy. All the books were back on the shelves, and the air smelled fresher. Less like a cave where someone had hidden out for the past few years. The window in the kitchen was open, and a gentle breeze made the old curtains wave. "Looks nice."

"Thanks," she said. "Cleaning helps with the dreams, sometimes."

I sat down as Honoria brought two steaming cups to the table. I grabbed one and took a sip. It tasted as good as it smelled.

"So, tell me," I said. "Why did you want to talk to me? James is the private detective, you know. I'm just the—"

"I think we both know you're more than just a secretary," Honoria said. "You understand me, better than James does. Don't you?"

I stared down at my coffee cup as I considered whether I wanted to know what the hell she actually meant by that. Decided I didn't, and smiled disarmingly. I hoped.

"You said that Eddie came to you in another dream," I said.

"Why don't you tell me about that?"

"Yeah, okay," she said. "It started the way all the dreams about him start. At that horrible tree."

"And you saw the crucifixion?"

"Yes."

"You see ducks again?"

She blinked, but did not speak, so I tried again.

"You saw the people wearing duck masks?"

She nodded, once.

I sighed, knowing the next words out of my mouth would sound stupid, but I wanted to eliminate Eddie's book club foolishness as quickly as possible. "Any old women behind those duck masks?"

"Old women?" Honoria looked surprised, then amused. "No old women. That I'm sure of."

"I knew it," I said, feeling quite vindicated. I was good at this detective thing. One question to the right person, and I had the answer Eddie was seeking. "What *did* you see?"

"Men," she said shortly. "I saw men doing—that." She stared again, but this time it was at me. Directly at me. "Why would you ask about women being there?"

"Just trying to eliminate all the possibilities," I said, studiously ignoring her oh-so-sharp eyes. "What happened next?"

"It moved past the tree pretty quickly, this time," she said. "But then—"

"What?" I took another sip of coffee and wished she'd get to the point.

"He showed up. Here. In my apartment."

What?

"You mean, he showed up in your dream. Right?"

"No." Her voice sharpened, and she frowned. "He was here. Really. I tried to wake up, tried to talk to him, but he freaked out and left." She laughed, her voice quivering. "This has never happened to me before."

"Are you telling me Dead Eddie was in your apartment? For real?"

"Yes."

I wondered, briefly, how Eddie was moving from place to place so effortlessly. This was not usual for a spirit—which was, unfortunately, pretty usual for me. Then, I quit worrying about Eddie, because Honoria said something that freaked me out to the extreme.

"I told him to trust you," she said.

I blinked. "Why would you tell him to trust me?"

"Because you can see ghosts, too. Can't you?"

"Huh?"

All right, not the best reaction, but wow, she caught me off-guard.

"That's your deal, isn't it? You see ghosts."

I couldn't answer her. Just stared, doing my oh-so-famous "deer in the headlights" imitation.

That damned fantastic smile lit up her face. "I knew it," she said. "I was getting a vibe from you. We have the same gift!"

None of this was going the way it was supposed to. I had come here expecting to have to comfort someone being plagued by her gift, but here she was, happy as a clam, it seemed, and trying to figure out what *my* deal was. Because she got a vibe from me. A vibe. I was giving off a vibe!

"Don't you want to talk about your dreams anymore?" I could hear panic in my voice and hated myself for it. "I mean, that's what I came here for. Because you called."

"We can talk about that later or you can take the sketches." She pointed over at her drawing table, and I saw that the stack of drawings was half again as high as it had been when James and I were here before. "Do you get visions, the way I do? Or, is it different?"

"Um." I tried to figure out a quick and easy way out of both the conversation and the apartment. "I would feel much more comfortable talking about your dreams," I finally said, stiffly. "Really."

"I'm sure you would," she replied. "But . . ."

"But nothing." This had to stop. "Just leave it alone."

She stared at me for a long moment, and I felt my face heat. It felt like she could read right through into my soul.

"Have you ever talked to anyone about this?" she asked. "Maybe it would help."

"I'm normal," I said.

"Normal. Yeah, I got that." She stood up and put her mug in the sink. "How's that working out for you?"

I glared at her, hating her. "It's working out fine."

"Yeah, sure. I bet you don't have many friends in your normal little life, do you? Relationships are hard when you're lying about yourself all the time."

"I'm not lying!" I cried. I stood up, so I could get away from her. I didn't want to hear anything more she had to say. "I just don't tell everybody everything. That's all."

"Lying by omission. Still lying," she said. "Does *anybody* know everything about you?"

"My mother," I whispered.

"And how is she with your everything?"

"She's fine with it," I said. "Hey, but why not? She's the reason—" I cut off my words. What was I doing? Why was I saying anything to her? Had I lost my mind? "Forget it."

"Ah. So, you have a bit of the love-hate thing going on with her—"

"I love my mother!" I snapped.

She laughed. "And your dad? How does he feel?"

"I don't know," I said. "He left, years ago. I don't have much to do with him anymore."

"Oh. So you have abandonment issues too."

"Too? What do you mean by that?" I shook my head, suddenly furious. "I do not have abandonment issues! What are you, a freaking psychiatrist?"

"No." She laughed. "But I've definitely been around them enough to know a few of their favourite theories about why people act the way they do."

"Well, you're wrong," I snapped. "I don't have abandonment issues, or a love-hate relationship with my mother."

"Let's say you're right," she replied. "What about relationships with men? Had any good ones? Had any?"

"I've had relationships with men!" I barked. Creep Arnie popped into my head, and I did my best to exorcise him. Hoped he was still in jail, for what he'd done to me. Realized that he was the only long-term relationship I'd ever had with a man besides my father.

"What about James?" Honoria asked.

I thought about the cot, and snuggling into James's warmth, and how right it felt. My face grew hot, and I shook my head.

"What about James?" I snapped. "I have a business

arrangement with him, and that's all. And you know he thinks you're crazy, don't you? Absolutely loony. I defended you! If it hadn't been for me, he wouldn't even be considering your case! Why would I want to hook up with someone who—"

"Could think that people like us are crazy?"

"Yes." I grabbed my coat, feeling angry, and stupid, and frightened. All at the same time. And I hated it. "This was a mistake. I shouldn't have come here."

"Oh, calm down!" Honoria said, a tinge of anger colouring her voice for the first time. "I understand completely why he thinks I'm crazy. Doesn't surprise me a bit."

"Well, I don't," I replied. "He should be—"

"What? More understanding? Why?"

"Well, because—" Then I really thought about it and didn't actually have a good answer for that one. "I don't really know," I finally said. "It just feels like he should."

"If you let him in, just a little bit, he probably would be more open to the idea that people like you and me are not crazy, just different," Honoria said. "You know?"

"I can't do that," I said. "Because—"

"Because then he'd leave?" she asked. "Abandonment issues, I—"

"No!" I cried. The fear and anger and stupidity were boiling up in me so I could barely contain myself. I wanted to run away from this woman and her words that were making me feel this way. I wanted her to just shut up. "Because I'm afraid he wouldn't!"

"Oh."

She stared at me for a long moment, and I finally had the silence I was hoping for. But in that silence, I had to listen to my own brain trying to make sense of what I had just said.

Was that really it? Was I afraid that he *wouldn't* be driven off by my ability? Was I actually afraid that he'd stay—and that I would have to live with my gift, out in the open in front of everybody? Was that really the way I felt?

"I gotta go," I muttered. "Things to do, and all that."

"Thanks for coming over," she said. "I feel better, knowing I have you in my corner."

"Oh, I don't think James is going to take your case," I said. "I think it would be better if you find someone else. I really do."

Honoria's eyes narrowed. "Seriously? You're going to

abandon me just because I guessed your stupid secret? You promised—"

"I don't care what I promised!" I yelled. "He won't help you! I won't help you!"

"But you have to," she said. Her voice turned brittle, angry. "If you don't, I'll tell James everything."

"What?" I swung around, fear making my heart pound so hard I was pretty sure she'd be able to see it through my tee shirt. "You wouldn't do that!"

"Yes," she said. "I would."

I glared at her, feeling sick, and frightened, and angry. Definitely angry. And I believed her. "Fine," I said. "I'll convince James to stay on the case. But you say nothing to him about me. Absolutely nothing. Got it?"

"Got it," she said. Through my haze of fear, I could hear relief in her voice. "Don't worry. It'll be our little secret."

Fantastic.

I grabbed the pile of sketches and left. As I walked the fourteen blocks back to the office, I tried to convince myself that a little bit of blackmail wasn't going to do anything to wreck what was left of my life.

I just wanted normal. And I knew that James—especially a James who knew my secret—would never fit in that life. Ever.

So I picked up a morning paper. I would scour the want ads, find another job, and get the heck away from stupid James and the ghosts that seemed to haunt everywhere that he was.

Yeah. I even tried to blame him for the ghosts. What kind of a person was I, anyhow?

I was one scared person, that's what I was. But as I searched those want ads, found a job at the Leary Millworks Inc., and faxed a copy of my resume, I never admitted it to myself, even once.

He could deal with Honoria the frigging clairvoyant. I was done.

Eddie:
Make It Stop

AFTER I GOT high, I hung around the park, waiting.

What was I waiting for? No clue. Just knew I didn't want to move. Didn't want to hit the streets. I was tired, and that was a surprise. I didn't often feel the need for sleep when I was high. Maybe it was the kind of high I was on, but beggars can't be choosers. The homeless guy was high on Lysol, so I was, too.

Thinking about that started me thinking about being alive and getting high. That was the one thing I'd been good at, most of my life. Where to score the next fix. I wished, sometimes, that I hadn't even tried crystal meth once. That stuff—it eats into your soul. And quick, too. You can't ever get that first high back, but that's what you're looking for. Ever after, that's what you're looking for.

Heroin addicts call it chasing the dragon. For us meth heads, it's nothing so romantic.

That's what I was looking for. And I didn't care who I hurt to do it. My friends—like Luke—my mom. I'd do anything, hurt them all, for that next high. That wasn't quite as good as the last one. Not even close to the first one. Mostly, just trying to keep from going into withdrawal. Just trying to keep from crashing.

My whole life was that. Just trying to keep from crashing. What a waste.

I felt my throat close up painfully, and I almost started to cry—but then felt myself slip. Like the biggest case of vertigo I'd ever felt in my life. If I didn't do something, I was going to end up back at that tree. I knew it.

The feeling scared me, I don't mind telling you. As a matter of fact, everything was starting to scare me.

I decided to go see that Marie chick again. The blonde had said she could save me, and she seemed to know about this stuff. Maybe she could tell me what was going on. Make it stop. Something.

Anything.

Marie:
Overreact Much? Thank You, I Will

ALL RIGHT, SO I felt like a perfect fool microseconds after I faxed my resume to Leary Millworks Inc. I shouldn't have done that. I didn't want to leave this job. I just didn't want James to know my every secret.

All I had to do was figure out how to get the police to leave Honoria alone, and I'd be safe. I hoped.

I should have called and told whoever answered at Leary that I'd sent the resume in error and to take me out of contention, but I didn't. I decided to assume I wouldn't even get a call for an interview, and basically, put the whole thing out of my mind.

Avoidance *is* my middle name, after all.

Then, as James slept the morning away, I made a file for Honoria and her case. I even went to the Stanley Milner Library, to see if I could find anything about her. All I found was a small article from a few years before (looked like it was the last time she'd gone off her meds, and it hadn't gone well) and there was a photo, too. Quite possibly the worst photo I'd ever seen. She looked three-quarters high, and her hair was standing out from her head as though she was having the worst hair day of her life. And she was definitely not smiling.

Made me feel a little bit better about not having to deal with her any longer than I had to, to be honest.

As I shoved a copy of a contract in the mostly empty file folder, Eddie pushed through the door and into the room.

"You all right?" I asked.

"Why?"

"You look like crap."

"Right back atcha."

"Thanks." I imagined I did look terrible. "I didn't get much sleep. What's your excuse?"

"I'm dead."

He made me laugh with that one.

"So, how come not much sleep?" Eddie asked.

"I had to sit with our client," I said. "She was having nightmares, and—"

"Are you talking about the blonde chick?"

"Blonde chick?"

He looked down at the front of the file, at the positively wretched photo I'd stapled to the front. "That chick," he said. "I've seen her look better."

"That's Honoria Lowe. Our client."

Had Honoria been telling the truth about Eddie acting like he'd seen her in her dream? "Why?"

"Just wondered."

"BS," I snapped. "Fear factor way up there, buddy. What's going on?"

"You'd asked me about her before, and I told you I didn't know her," he said. "Here's the thing, though. I didn't know her name. But I know her—knew her—to see her." His face twisted. "I kind of saw her dreams."

Oh wow. "You saw her dreams?"

"Yeah." He shuddered. "I heard her calling my name, so I went to her, and got caught in her dreams or something. Scary as shit, I must say."

"I wouldn't doubt it," I said, then shook my head. I needed facts. "She told me about that."

"So, she saw me, too?"

"Yeah, she did." I sighed, then dove in. I needed to tell him this bit of business as quickly and painlessly as possible. Like pulling a bandage off a seeping sore. "She told me she saw no old women at your crucifixion."

"So Mom's book club didn't kill me." He sighed. "Didn't really think they did, to be honest. Just hoped, you know? But if it wasn't them, who was it?"

"She couldn't tell."

"Oh." His face froze. "So, what happens next?"

"Well," I said, "since neither you nor Honoria can identify who was behind the duck masks, I guess this means we're going to have to do this the hard way."

I picked up a pad of paper and a pen. "Tell me who would want to hurt you."

"You mean, like, enemies?"

"Yes."

"Really?" His face closed as he stared toward the ceiling and thought, hard.

"You really can't think of anyone past your mother's book club?" I asked, impatiently. "No one at all?"

"Not really the problem," he replied. "It's just, who did I piss off lately?"

"Oh." That surprised me, but it shouldn't have. He could be a real pain. "Oh. Well. Maybe think about the park." Had he ever mentioned being at the park? I couldn't remember. "You *did* hang out at Needle Park, didn't you?"

"Oh yeah!" he said, nodding enthusiastically. "Didn't go even a day without showing up there. Hell, I was there just last night."

I looked at him. "You were at the park last night?"

"Yep."

So, it had been his glow I saw at the park when James and I had left Honoria's apartment. All I could say was, this boy sure could get around. But I left it alone for the moment. I had to get a list of suspects, and he had to give them to me.

"Can you think of anything that's happened there lately? Anything at all. Doesn't matter how insignificant—"

"Well, there was the turf war."

Did he actually say a war? I goggled at him, and he laughed. "What? Did you actually want me to start on the small stuff and work up to the war?"

"No, no!" I said, and flipped to a fresh page in the notebook. I wrote "Turf War" across the top in block letters, and Eddie smiled.

"What?" I asked. He pointed.

"Takes me back to grade school. But I guess I'm the teacher, this time."

"Guess so," I said. "So, tell me about this—war."

"It started five months ago. Maybe longer. There was a—vacancy created at the top of the food chain, and a couple of guys decided to take over the park for their own."

"Food chain?"

"I'm talking about selling drugs," he said.

"Oh." I felt momentarily foolish. Of course he was talking about drugs. "Why a vacancy?"

"Maxie Lewis got offed. He owned the park." Eddie frowned. "How come I haven't seen him if he got killed there?"

"He might have already moved on," I said absently, still writing.

"But his murder—" He shuddered. "It was a bad one, and in my neck of the woods, that was going some."

"That doesn't necessarily mean the spirit sticks around," I said, putting down the pen. "If he was prepared for death, he could have moved on right away. Or maybe he's gone somewhere else." I smiled. "After all, you haven't exactly been stuck like glue to the place where you were killed, now have you?"

Eddie looked confused. "Why? Should I be?"

"Yeah. Usually."

"Why is that?"

"I'm not sure, exactly," I replied.

"I thought you were the expert about all this stuff," he said.

"Well, I'm not," I said, rather stiffly. I picked up the pen and poised it over the notebook. "Tell me more about the turf war," I said. "And how you were involved."

Eddie closed his eyes, as though he was trying to remember.

"After Maxie was offed," he started, "there was nobody supplying the place regular. So this brought a few gangs into the area. That's really when the war started." He shook his head. "I really should be seeing a bunch of dead guys there. Lots of people got gacked this past while."

"Lots?" I stared at him. "Why hasn't this been in the news?"

"Some of them have. The drive-bys, and the stuff that happened out in the 'burbs. Those made the news. The rest—well, some of them got dumped, lots of them, actually. And as for the rest, well, if it doesn't happen close to civilians—"

"Civilians?"

"People not involved in drugs. People like you."

"Oh." Made sense. I wrote it all down, and when I underlined "like me," Eddie laughed, but it didn't sound real. Not in the least.

"Nobody cares if we kill each other off," he said. "Less of us to put in jail, less cop time taken up with our BS. Nobody cares. Just as long as we stay away from your kind."

I couldn't think of a thing to say. Was he telling me the truth?

"This is where I got involved," he said. "Even though it looked like Ambrose Welch was going to win the war and take over the park, I decided to try my hand at dealing in the park. Like I said, there was still room—and I figured what the hell. My buddy—Crank—fronted me enough to get me started. And people—my people, anyhow—bought enough that it looked like maybe I was going to be able to do some business. But then R showed up, and suggested strongly that I not come back the next night. If I wanted to keep my head."

"R?" I asked. "I think I know that name."

"He's one of Ambrose Welch's enforcers." Eddie stood up and paced. "Man! R came and talked to me four nights before I was killed. I feel sick."

I almost said, "Take a deep breath," but stopped myself before that bit of foolishness left my mouth. "Then what happened?"

"I listened to him," Eddie said. "I did. In fact, didn't go back to the park for a few nights after that. Didn't want to get in their line of sight. Plus I owed Crank money, and I didn't want to see him before I had it. So I went to the churchyard."

He paced, harder, and I wished there was something I could do for him. He looked distraught.

"The night before—you know—I went and paid back Crank everything I owed him." He almost smiled. "That was the high point of my week. I honestly thought I was going to do okay after that. Crank was happy. I was happy. And I was out of Ambrose's territory. Thought I was going to do all right. But the next night. Well."

He rubbed his hands together, as though trying to warm them. "The next night I met the Donald Ducks. And you know the rest."

"Could it have been this Ambrose fellow?" I asked.

"Don't know why it would have been," he replied. "I did what he told me to do. Moved on. He was left with his territory. Shouldn't have been a problem."

"Do you know who owns the church territory?"

Eddie laughed. "God?"

Seriously, Eddie? Jokes? I glared at him until his laughter stopped.

"I don't know," he said. "Never saw anybody there, selling. Not before me, anyhow." He shrugged. "Not too many to sell to, to be honest. Enough for a guy like me, maybe."

"Okay." I frowned and looked over my notes, touching the point of my pen to something Eddie'd said, close to the beginning. "So, who killed Maxie?" I asked. "Was it Ambrose Welch?"

"I don't think so. Like I said, Ambrose showed up after." Eddie started pacing again, like he couldn't stop himself.

"So, who did it?"

"There were rumours." Eddie stood by the window and looked out. I could see past him. The sun was up, and the streets were starting to come alive. People, going to work or whatever. He sighed, deeply. "I don't want to talk about it anymore."

"Why not?"

He sighed again, and it sounded like it was coming from the bottom of his soul. "I think it was because of me."

"How?" I asked. He didn't turn around, and he didn't answer me, so I tried again. "Tell me, Eddie. How do you think—"

"I had a friend," he said, the words jerking out of him like they were being pulled, like rotten teeth, out of his mouth. "I had a friend, and he came to me to buy drugs. This was just before the war."

"And?"

"I sent him to Maxie."

"And?"

"He died."

"Oh."

"Yeah. His name was Luke Stewart. His dad didn't take it so good."

"Stewart?" I asked, and my heart rate spiked. "Is he related to that police officer, Angus Stewart? The one they call Stew?"

"Stay away from him," he said, and he looked terrified. "He's dangerous."

"Oh my God, Eddie," I whispered. "What did you do?"

Eddie:
I'm Outta Here

I COULDN'T TELL if there was accusation in Marie's voice. Didn't care. Didn't matter if she accused me or not. I was doing enough accusing for both of us. Wished I could get high—high enough so that it didn't hurt—but knew there wasn't enough high in the world to wash that one away. I'd killed my friend. My best friend.

I looked out the window, and the sun looked warm. I wished I was out in it, and suddenly the wishing won. There was a soft grey swirl around me, and I didn't even hear her reply before I was gone.

Marie:
Maybe Mom Will Know . . .

ANOTHER COLOURFUL SWIRL, this time a little more grey than blue, but whatever. He was gone, again.

I looked at what I'd written down on the pad of paper and tried to keep from shuddering. How could stuff like this be going on in a sleepy little city like Edmonton?

Worse than that, it looked like Eddie had been right in the middle of it all when he died.

Even though he couldn't—or wouldn't—talk about who he thought killed him, I was pretty sure if I could figure out a way to keep him in the room with me and keep him talking, he would probably lead me right to the people who killed him. He knew a lot, and I got the feeling we were just touching the surface.

But he kept disappearing. What should I do?

Call my mother. That's what.

I looked at the phone for a long time, not wanting to make that phone call.

"Just get it over with," I whispered. So I did. Look at me being all brave. Almost put the receiver back down and disconnected when I heard the voice on the other end, though, because it wasn't my mother. It was my sister, Rhonda.

"Yes?" she snapped. I sat, frozen, long enough for her to bark, "Is anyone there? I'm hanging up if you don't answer immediately!"

"Hi, Rhonda, it's me."

My voice sounded all weak and whiny, the last thing I wanted. I had to sound strong with her. After all, she was the successful one of the family. Meaning she'd found a guy who could actually provide for her. "I need to speak to Mom. Is she there?"

"Oh. Marie. Nice to hear your voice." She was lying. She had not been pleased when I'd left town because that left her with Mom. After all, she had that successful life of her own.

I felt the anger quotient jump up a few degrees, but did my best to cool it. I didn't need to fight with her. I needed to talk to Mom.

Then I did a stupid thing. I asked, "How are things?"

"As good as can be expected." She sighed. Darn it. I'd given her the opening she always looked for. The "oh poor me, my life is crap" opening. Even though it wasn't. Her husband, Jasper, was a nice enough guy and did seem to love her, though I didn't quite understand why. And her kids were well-mannered—another surprise, but hey, I guess a person can be a good mom and a bitch all at the same time. But I didn't want to hear her complain. I just wanted to talk to Mom.

"That's great!" I said, as enthusiastically as I could, hoping it would shut her up. "Can I talk to Mom?"

"She's sleeping," Rhonda snipped.

"Oh." I didn't want to wake Mom up, but I really didn't want to listen to Rhonda anymore. "When do you think she'll—"

Then I heard Mom's voice before Rhonda slapped her hand over the receiver. There was muffled two-way bickering for a moment, then Rhonda came back.

"She's here."

The phone clattered as she dropped the receiver. There was scrabbling, and then I heard Mom's voice. Breathless as always, but she sounded in a much better mood than Rhonda, thank goodness.

"Marie!" she cried. "How are ya, girl?"

"All right, Mom. You?"

"I'm good. Good." I could hear Rhonda yelling something about not lying to me, but Mom talked over her words. "The medication I'm on seems to be helping a bit, so . . . I'm doing good."

"I'm glad."

I stopped talking for a moment, unsure how to proceed. If Mom was sick enough for Rhonda to be there, I needed to know that. But I didn't feel strong enough to push through her well-intentioned lies. I had a problem, and only she could help me with it, and I think Mom knew that.

"Can you wait one moment before we talk?" she asked. "I want to move to another room. For a little privacy."

"Okay." I could hear Rhonda's outraged voice fade as Mom walked to her bedroom. It disappeared when she closed the door.

"That's better."

I laughed. "That's going to piss her off, you know."

"Ah probably," Mom replied. "She'll get over it. She doesn't like to hear me talk about the other side, and I'm assuming that's why you're calling. Right?"

"Right."

"I thought you moved on the gentleman you were working with."

I laughed. "Farley wasn't really a gentleman, Mom. And yes, I moved him on. But I've met someone else."

"Another spirit?"

"Yes."

"Interesting."

"Yeah." Interesting was never good. I knew enough to know that. "He's a drug addict."

"Oh! I'm so sorry! They're so hard to work with!" Meaning, I knew, it usually took them forever to realize they were even dead. How I wished that was my problem.

"No. He knows he's dead. It's just that—"

"What? Most of the hard work is done. You just have to help him understand what's holding him here and—"

"I know that, Mom. But he told me he doesn't want to move on."

That, at least, was the truth, but I could hear her frown in her voice. "Then what are you doing with him?"

"I'm—trying to solve his murder."

"You know that doesn't matter . . ." Her voice faded, and I wished I could tell her something, anything, that she'd actually want to hear from me.

"I met a clairvoyant, Mom," I said, hoping that meeting an

urban legend might put her off the whole "solving the murder doesn't matter in the grand scheme of things" issue.

"Really," she said. She didn't sound impressed. "Does she have anything to do with this case you're working on?"

"Yes. She's a person of interest in Eddie's murder."

"Eddie's the spirit?"

"Yes."

There was silence for a growing number of increasingly uncomfortable moments. Finally she asked, "Why did you call me?"

"I need to know how to get him to cooperate with me."

"To figure out who killed him?"

"Yes."

"Even though it doesn't matter."

That one stung. "Yes."

"Are you planning on helping this spirit?"

"Helping? You mean move him on? Mom, he said he didn't want to. I should respect his wishes, shouldn't I?"

"Girl, they all must move on. Eventually. You know that as well as I do." She shuffled, and I heard the springs of her old-fashioned bed ping as she sat down. "What are you playing at?"

"I'm not playing at anything, Mom."

I was lying to my mother. This made me feel even sicker.

"I'm working for James now—I told you about that—and the clairvoyant came to us so we could help her prove she wasn't involved in Eddie's death. So, Eddie isn't our client, Honoria is." I shuffled my feet, feeling increasingly terrible. "I just want to know what to do next. To get him to help me figure this all out."

"Huh," Mom said. "That is a bit of a pickle."

"I'm sorry," I whispered. I hated hearing that tone in her voice. That tone let me know that I was letting the side down. "I just—"

"I know!" Mom's voice turned sharp, angry. "You want a normal life. You've told me that a number of times."

I felt a spike of anger and knew if I didn't calm myself, I'd end up fighting with her, and that wouldn't do anyone any good.

"So what should I do?" I asked.

"Perhaps get another job?" she said, sarcasm dripping through her words. "Something that doesn't put you in touch with the dead quite so often. I mean, if you aren't going to help them—"

"I'm trying to help someone living, Mom!" I cried. "Isn't that good? I thought that was a good thing."

"Yes. Helping the living is fine. But you have the capacity to help the dead." She sighed, and then coughed, and I flinched. Waited for the coughing to continue, even as I hoped it wouldn't. I hated hearing her like that. Absolutely hated it. After a moment, the coughing stopped.

"All right. If you're determined to follow this course of action, then I would advise you to forget the spirit. Focus on the clairvoyant's dreams. I believe everything you need to know will be found there."

"Are you sure?" I whispered the words, wishing I didn't sound like I didn't believe her—but I knew she'd never met one before. "Are you absolutely sure she'll have everything I need? After all, I have the dead guy—"

"He's a spirit. The least you can do is call him by the proper name," she said, sharply. "And it would be best if you left him alone, if you aren't going to help him. You are leading him on—and that is just cruel."

She was right. Absolutely right. I was being cruel.

"I gotta go," I muttered. "Thanks for the info."

"Tell me one thing before you go."

"What?"

"How is James? He seemed very nice on the phone, and I thought—"

"You thought what, Mom?"

"I hoped that maybe—"

"Maybe what?" Please don't say it. Please don't say it.

"I hoped that maybe you two would date," she said. "You could do worse."

"I *have* done worse," I whispered.

"I know," she said.

"I don't want to talk about this," I said. "Not now."

I heard a noise behind me and whirled. James was standing in the doorway, looking tousled and suspicious.

"Who's that?" he mouthed.

"My mother," I mouthed back, then turned away from him.

"Gotta go," I said, hoping Mom would let me off the hook quickly. "James is here, and we have work to do."

I put down the receiver and tried to compose myself before

facing James. I felt like he'd be able to read the whole conversation on my face, and I didn't want that.

"How's your mom?" he asked.

"She's good," I said. "Coffee? It's fresh."

"Thanks." He grabbed a cup and poured. "So where'd you go?" he asked. "I woke up, and you were gone."

I felt my face heat. "When did you wake up?"

"Oh, about five minutes ago," he said, and I felt a thrill of relief. I didn't have to mention my visit to Honoria. "But I missed you. It was nice, sleeping with you. You know?"

"I know." I was blushing so hard, I was pretty sure my head was going to start sweating. "But I had work to do."

"Work?" He sipped his coffee. "What couldn't have waited?"

Now we were dangerously close to me telling him a lie about going to see Honoria, and I didn't want to do that.

Oh yeah, the file. The file on Honoria.

"I started Honoria's file. And a contract for her to sign, if you decide she can be our client."

"Ah," he said. "Bet that makes interesting reading, but I can't do it now. I gotta head out. We need a computer, so I'm going to buy one." He smiled. "Maybe two. Want to come?"

"Shopping?" I grinned. Shopping therapy. The best kind. "Do I ever!"

I put on my sweater and grabbed my purse, and then we headed out the door.

I didn't care what either Honoria the Clairvoyant or my mother said. I loved doing normal. I really really did.

Eddie:
Getting the Cold Shoulder Is a Real Bitch

I ENDED UP by the tree, again. Thinking about Luke had done it, I was pretty sure of that. Luke and his asshole father, Angus Stewart.

I guess that was the ultimate joke in all of this. My best friend's dad was a cop. He was also a terrible father. He made Luke feel like he never measured up, because his old man always did the, "98 percent, huh? What happened to that other 2 percent?" kind of a guy. The kind you wanted to crotch-kick, when you got tall enough.

I often wondered if Luke hung around with me just to get back at his old man. Even asked him a couple of times, but he just gave me the smile that told me everything was A-okay, and said no. He liked me because he liked me. Didn't have anything to do with his old man. And I believed him, right up until the end.

He'd found me in the park, hanging with Crank. I'd come into some cash—thanks, Mom—and looked all right. New clothes, and I'd eaten some. I was also just at the good part of my high. I could carry on a conversation, act like a human being, shit like that. So, it was nice to see him. I was pretty sure we were going to eventually have a "why don't you get out of this life" talk. Most everybody I knew in my other life tried to have this talk with me, if they ran into me. And we did, but it didn't go the way I thought it would. Not at all.

We talked about the good old days, and then I blew it by asking him how his old man was.

"That son of a bitch is killing me," he'd said, rubbing his hands together as though he was suddenly all-over cold. "I don't think I can take it much more."

"You still at home?" I asked. "Maybe you need to move out. You know, be on your own."

"He won't let me do that," Luke said, shaking his head like he'd never spoken a truer word in his life. "I'm never going to get out of there."

"Hell, he can't make you stay." I laughed. "Just move out. What's he going to do, arrest you?"

"Huh. Like I don't think about that every day," he muttered, and sat down at the end of Crank's bench.

Crank gave him a glare, but I told him to lighten up, we'd be done in a bit.

"So why don't you just do it?"

"I don't know." He shook his head. "I don't think I could do that."

"Why not?"

"Because he's got friends everywhere. He'd find me and bring me back. I'll never get away from him." Luke closed his eyes, and I shuddered. He was so pale, he almost looked dead.

Then he opened his eyes and stared at me, and the pleading look on his face screamed junkie. "I just need something," he said. "Something to take the edge off."

"Something?" I asked, even though I knew what he meant. I didn't want to hear it, though. He was the good one.

"Yeah."

The need was so naked in his eyes that I looked away from him, out over the park and the rest of the junkies, all with that look. You get that look, and you're never getting out.

"I can't help you, man."

"Why not?" He sounded devastated. As though I'd just stabbed him in the back or something.

I stood up. I had to walk away from him, because I wanted to hit him as hard as I could—and I was afraid it wouldn't be hard enough. Nothing stops you, once you start down that road. "Just go home."

"I can't," he whined. "He's out of his mind! I can't take it anymore!"

"Yeah, right," I said. "It's just terrible, your old man giving you everything you want, so you can have a great life. That's real shitty of him." I felt a piece of a cracked tooth fall onto my tongue, and I spat. As I watched the decayed bit fly off and roll in the dusty grey grass of the park, I felt more anger at him than I ever had in my whole life. He was the good one!

"I got something for you, man," Crank said, obviously thinking he could at least make some money as a reward for giving up part of his bench for so long.

"Fuck off, Crank," I growled, pushing him away from Luke.

"Then get off my bench," Crank growled back, glaring hard at me. "And take your friend with you."

He said "friend" like it was a curse, and for a moment, it felt like it.

I grabbed Luke's arm to pull him to the street, but he wrenched away from me. "I thought you were my friend, Eddie."

"I am," I said. "Just go home."

He stared at me for a long time, his eyes pleading until I thought I'd scream. Then he left. That was the last time I saw him.

I STARED AT the tree where I'd died and wondered. Really wondered, for the first time, if Luke's dad had done this to me. Thinking about it made me tired. What difference did it make if he killed me or not? Knowing might bring closure or some such shit for my mother, and that would be a good thing, but for me— not so much.

I'd lived badly and died worse. It didn't really matter who had done the final deed to me. That was beside the point. I was starting to understand that.

For a moment, I thought about going and getting high, but realized that getting high wasn't what I needed. I needed something else. It wasn't at the park. It was with Marie. She had the answers, no matter how bad she made me feel.

But when I got to the corner where I had to turn right to get to her office, I turned left instead and walked to the park.

Old habits die extremely hard. Being dead won't stop them. I didn't know what could.

Marie:
Connected with the Wonderful Web, Again

SHOPPING WAS SO nice, I can't begin to explain just how nice it all was. We went to not one, but three different computer stores, and ended up with two nice little portables with all the bells and whistles. Then James took me out for lunch, and that was wonderful too.

Normal. All wonderfully normal. Exactly what I needed.

He dropped me off at the office. When I asked him where he was going, he mumbled something about paying bills.

"I thought you paid them already," I replied.

"Not this one," he said. "Don't worry about it. I'll be back in a couple of hours." He pointed at the computer boxes in my arms. "Are you going to need help setting those up?"

"Are you kidding?" I laughed. "I can do this in my sleep."

He drove away, and I spent the next couple of hours hooking everything up and reveling in the sound the computer made as it reconnected me with the outside world.

The first thing I did was check my email, to see if there was anything from Leary Millworks Inc., and felt a thrill of relief run down my back when I saw a big fat zero in the inbox.

That proved they hadn't taken my resume seriously. Right?

And Honoria had not been in contact with either James or me since my late night visit, so I was almost certain she was going to keep her word about not saying anything to James about me. If I could just figure out who had really killed Eddie, she'd be off the hook, and then, so would I.

Then I called Jasmine. I hadn't been home—if you can call couch surfing at a friend's place home—in a couple of days, and I wanted to touch base. My life had been fairly exciting of late, and I didn't want her afraid that I'd ended up back at the hospital or something. She had three kids and her own life. She didn't need to worry about me, too.

She was happy to hear from me, which was nice, too.

"Glad you'll be home," she said. "I'll make popcorn, and we can watch my show tonight. Does that sound good, or what?"

More normal. A quick painful lump formed in my throat. "Want me to bring anything?"

"Maybe some chocolate? To offset the saltiness of the popcorn?"

"Sounds great." The lump was still there, making it hard to speak.

"Are you all right?" Her voice went a teeny bit hard. "You sound strange."

"Oh, it's just the idea of having a nice quiet night. I haven't done that in a while."

"Oh. James keeping you jumping?"

"Well, we have a new case—"

"Is this one going to pay?"

"I hope so!"

"Got it down in writing?"

"Just about."

She chuckled. "You two need a secretary to keep you straight about that kind of stuff."

I felt my face heat. Our first official case, which should have paid a whole pile of money, had fallen through because we hadn't gotten the paperwork signed. Jasmine was right. James needed a real secretary. Not someone with as much baggage as me. "You're right."

"Of course I am. Now, tell me about James. Still as dreamy as always?"

"There's nothing much to tell," I muttered, hoping she'd let it go. "Both of us, just working. You know. Working on the case."

"Yeah. Sure. I believe you." She laughed, and after a second, I joined her, hoping it sounded real. "You can tell me all the juicy details tonight."

"There aren't any."

"Sure. Like I said, I believe you." She laughed again, harder this time. I did not join in. "I'll see you tonight," she finally said. "Remember the chocolate."

She hung up, and I went to double-check the paperwork on our only case, just to make sure I hadn't screwed it up. I felt relief when I pulled out the contract. All legal, no loopholes. James just had to get Honoria to sign it, and he would be paid for this one.

But that was if we could pull some actual evidence together. I turned to the computer with a small sigh of satisfaction. This was something I could do. I could check out the people that we knew were involved. That might give us a lead.

I stared at the screen, then punched in the name "Angus Stewart."

"I'll start with him," I muttered. "Just to eliminate him."

No matter what I said, I had the feeling he would not be so easily eliminated. He creeped me out. And as I plowed through all the information I found on him, I realized there was a reason I was creeped out. He was one creepy guy.

Elimination was not an option. He was in this. Up to his neck.

JAMES CAME BACK two hours later, just as I was printing out the last of my research on Angus Stewart, the drug cop who scared the heck out of Dead Eddie.

"Find anything interesting?" he asked. "I'm assuming you jumped on the research wagon as soon as you had the computer set up."

"You know me too well," I said. "Give me a second, and I'll print it out for you."

"Great," he replied, and grabbed a cup of coffee. He grimaced when he tasted it. "How old is this?"

"A couple of hours," I replied. "Want me to make more?"

"No. I'll do it."

As he made a fresh pot, I re-checked my email to see if I had received any reply about the job inquiry with Leary Millworks.

I'd been checking every fifteen minutes, compulsively, and knew what I should be doing was letting them know I was no longer looking for a job. But for some reason, I didn't do that. It was like I thought that if I actually reached out and contacted them, it would make what I'd done to James that much more real.

"So what are you looking for?" I jumped almost out of my skin when I realized James was looking over my shoulder at my email account.

"Nothing," I said, and clicked it closed. "Just some information I thought would be in. It's not."

He walked back to the front of the desk, and sat down opposite me. "So, tell me what you found out about Honoria Lowe," he said.

"I—this isn't about Honoria," I stuttered.

James frowned. "Why not? We need to know she's telling the truth. Don't we?"

"I didn't mean I won't check her out," I said quickly. "I just meant this report isn't about her."

"Why isn't it?" James's mouth was set in a tight line, and I had this horrible feeling we were going to argue. Again.

"Because I decided to start with someone else." I pulled the sheets of paper from the printer, and held them out to him.

"This is more important, I think. It's about the cop, Angus Stewart. Want to read it?"

James said something, but just at that moment, I was distracted by a leg materializing through the door. It was quickly followed by a body, and then Eddie's head popped into view. I stared at him as he walked up behind James, and pointed at him.

"Your buddy here is a fucking moron," he said.

"What?" The word escaped my mouth before I could stop it.

"What what?" James replied. "I said, 'Why Angus Stewart?'"

"Moron," Eddie said again, shaking his head. "Ask him where he went. I dare you."

"Ah, yes, Angus Stewart," I replied, trying to ignore Eddie and focus on James. But it was hard. "I decided to check him out, just to eliminate him, know what I mean? Because he creeped me out at the park. But I don't think we can. Eliminate him, I mean. I think he's in this, up to his neck."

"Why?" James asked, then shook his head. "Give me the gist."

"Angus Stewart. Married, with one kid. Wife dead. He was on track to take a big chair—maybe even Chief of Police, until six months ago. Then his kid died. As far as I can tell, it was a drug overdose—but it could have been bad drugs. Nothing in the newspaper articles ever actually cleared that up. After that, he transferred out of Economic Crimes to Drugs. That's when the suspicious deaths started on the street, but nothing that could ever be linked to him, exactly. Just a lot of talk about the cops using way too much force. A couple of guys even said they'd been tortured for information—but they disappeared before they could actually give a formal complaint."

"I told you," Eddie said. "That guy is evil."

I tried not to stare at him, because at the same time he made that announcement, James frowned and asked, "And how does this tie into Edward Hansen's death?"

Now, I couldn't tell him that Eddie had told me about being best friends with Stewart's son, could I?

"I told you before, I had a feeling about the guy," I muttered. "I wanted to check him out."

"Best plan you've had," Eddie said.

"I think you're going in the wrong direction," James said.

"What the hell do you know?" Eddie cried.

"Well, who do you think is responsible?" I spoke calmly, even though I wanted desperately to echo Eddie's words. "And why do you think I'm wrong?"

James shrugged. "I think it's the drug dealer, Ambrose Welch."

"Yeah, you would pick on the drug dealer," Eddie said sarcastically. Then he turned to me. "Ask him what he did. Where he went, before he showed up here."

"Why do you think it was him?" I asked, desperately wanting to ask Eddie's question.

"Because he was the one who got those thugs to break into our office—"

"Thugs! What a fucking word!" Eddie cried.

"—and I think his cohorts know a lot more about what happened to Edward than they will admit."

"Why would you think that?" I asked.

"Because of what they said to me at the park."

I frowned. "But you weren't at the park."

"Here it comes," Eddie said. "Now you're going to see just what a moron you are hooked up with."

"I went there," James said.

"Why?"

"Because those guys can't get away with wrecking our place, and I could tell that the police were going to do nothing about it," he replied.

"See? Moron!" Eddie yelled. "Absolute moron. He's going to bring them down on you so hard, you'll think the devil sucked you into hell."

Then he said something that should have scared me, but didn't.

"Oh my God," he muttered. "Hell." And then he got really quiet.

I ignored his whispered words and turned on James.

"Tell me why you thought going and talking to the people who probably wrecked this place just last night was a good idea," I said, probably more snippily than I should have, but good old anger was bubbling to the surface. Again.

James's smile faltered. "I wanted to let them know we are on to them," he said. "They need to be put in their place."

Why did I always feel angry with everything he did? Either angry, or absolutely safe and warm. There didn't seem to be any middle ground.

"This is a macho boy thing, isn't it?" I snapped.

"A macho boy what?" he asked. I could see he'd swung over to angry himself. Another stupid boy trick. "I don't know what you're talking about."

"It's like two dogs vying for the same bone," I replied. "He comes over here to your territory, so you go back to his. Just to get in his face. Stupid macho boy stuff."

"That's not what I was doing," James said. "Not at all."

"Well, what did I get wrong?" I asked. "What happened with letting the police do their jobs? Going there could have been really dangerous, James."

He stared at me for a long time, then sighed explosively. "I didn't like how that whole situation made you feel," he said. "You were so frightened—"

"Weren't you?" I exclaimed.

"No. Kind of angry that they'd wrecked the place, but not scared. Not the way you were."

"So, you did that for me," I said incredulously.

"Yes."

"And did you think it would make me feel better?"

"Well, maybe." He looked at me. "Does it?"

"No!" I said. "My God, you're probably going to bring those idiots back down on us. And they won't just wreck the place, this time!"

"Oh, they won't be back," James said, sounding confident.

"I'm going to hell," Eddie said, much louder this time. He sounded frightened.

I frowned. Hell? Why was Eddie talking about hell?

"Yes, they will," I said to James. "That was a foolish thing to do."

"A foolish thing?" James sneered. "Foolish? Really?"

"Yes. Really." I closed my eyes and tried to think.

The phone rang, and we both stared at it.

"Expecting a call?" I asked.

"No."

He glanced down at the view screen on the phone, and his face blanched. "It's Sergeant Worth."

"Answer it."

"No." He shook his head. "You."

The phone rang again, impatiently.

"You're the receptionist," he said, churlishly. "Answer the phone."

"And you're a chicken," I replied, just as churlishly. I picked up the receiver and took a deep breath. I hated talking to the police, and I especially hated talking to Sergeant Worth.

"Jimmy Lavall Detective Agency," I chirped. "How may I direct your call?"

"Let me talk to James. Now."

I smiled and held the receiver out to James. "She wants to talk to you," I whispered. "I think you're in trouble."

"Good grief," he sighed, and put the receiver to his ear. "James Lavall here."

Those were the last words he spoke in that telephone conversation. He nodded a couple of times, true, but he didn't speak again until he gently put the receiver back in the cradle.

"She wants to see me," he said. "Now."

"Why?"

"She didn't say, but I'm pretty sure it's nothing good." He glanced at me. "Want to come with?"

My stomach clenched at the thought of facing that woman.

"Did she ask for me?"

"No."

"Then I'm not going." I shook my head vehemently. "You're on your own."

"But you should thank her for getting you out of jail," he said. He sounded desperate, and I almost felt sorry for him. Almost.

"Nope. I'll send her flowers, or something. Deal with her yourself."

"Aren't you worried about the drug dealer's buddies coming back?" he asked.

I was less worried about them than I was about talking to Sergeant Worth again. Our last meeting had convinced me that she knew something about my mother and her abilities. I was afraid she suspected something about me, too. I did *not* want to have a conversation with her about any of that. James was on his own.

"I'll keep the door locked, I promise."

He looked over at the door, which still had only cardboard covering the broken window, and then back at me. "Please come with me," he pleaded.

"No, James." I said the words as firmly as I could, so he'd believe I was completely all right with being here by myself. "Go on. I'll be fine."

He grabbed his coat and headed for the door. "Any problems, give me a call," he said.

"Will do." And I smiled in spite of myself. His wanting to protect me suddenly gave me warm, fuzzy feelings. See? One or the other. Nothing in the middle. I make myself crazy, sometimes. "How about if I call you in a half hour? Save you from her?"

"Maybe," he replied, and smiled back. Then he left, and I was alone.

Well, mostly alone. Eddie was still there, and he looked panicky. Past panicky, if I was going to be honest. He looked terrified.

"What's wrong?" I asked, and tried not to roll my eyes. I failed, but I did try.

"Hell!" he squeaked. "Is that an option for me? If I—move on?"

That brought me up short. Why was he talking about moving on? "Hell?"

"Yes," he said, his voice sounding shuddery and frightened. "My God—going to hell . . ."

"Why are you worried about this, Eddie? You told me you don't want to move on."

"Yeah, I know I said that," he said. "But, what if I decide to move on? I could go to hell. Right?"

This was definitely a turn. What had made him even think about moving on?

"If you think you deserve it. But just as long as you don't feel you deserve to go to hell, you won't. It's your choice."

I hoped. I'd never dealt with anyone absolutely evil, who deserved to go to a place like hell, even if they didn't think they deserved it. Had never asked my mom about those types of people either. Much as the TV shows like to pretend there are serial killers and the like around every corner, I knew from experience that most people are generally decent, even if their specific code of conduct or honour isn't the same as mine. Just depended on where and how they were brought up. A guy raised on the streets lives—and dies—by a different set of rules than a guy raised in middle class suburbia. Different cultures, different skill sets, and different rules. Doesn't make one good and one bad. Just makes them different.

The truly evil are harder to find. My mom had never run into a truly evil spirit. At least, she never told me if she had, and I think she would have told me.

Eddie was not evil. He was just a messed-up guy who died a drug addict. He didn't even need to think about hell, or any variation of it, as far as I was concerned.

The look on his face wasn't one of relief, though. If anything, he looked more frightened than before.

"I've done things," he whispered. "Bad things. Really shitty things. To people who cared about me. Who I was supposed to care about."

"Eddie, everybody's done things they are ashamed of," I said shortly. "Try to get past it."

As soon as the words were out of my mouth, I could have kicked myself.

"Try to get past it?" he said. "And how exactly do I do that? I hurt my mother so many times. I let my best friend—my best friend in the whole world—die. I should have known he was going to do something—but all I did was tell him what a lucky bastard he was. Didn't listen to him, didn't try to help him."

"Are you talking about Luke Stewart?" I asked.

"Yes." He sniveled and then started to cry. "How do you get past something like that?"

"I don't know," I whispered. I could see that he would do one of two things, if I did not get involved. He would stay on this plane, doing exactly what he had done before he died, or he would send himself to hell. His own special form of hell.

From what I knew of him, he was not an idiot. I could help him pick a better direction than either choice he felt he had right now. He just needed to be nudged in the right direction, and he would finally make a good choice for himself.

But this meant *me* making a decision. All I had to do was make the right choice, the right choice for Eddie, which meant me helping him move on.

"Eddie, it doesn't have to be this way for you," I said, hoping I wasn't going to regret the decision I was about to make. "If you let me help you, you can move on to the next plane of existence with no regrets, and no reason to punish yourself."

"Are you talking about no hell?"

"Yes. That's exactly what I'm talking about."

"I can't believe you can pull that off," he said, wiping his eyes. "But if you think you can, I'm in. I don't want to go to hell."

"Good," I said, even though I was sighing like crazy inside. Mom better be impressed. I was doing the right thing, even though I really didn't want to.

"So what do I have to do?" Eddie asked.

"Tell me about your life."

"Everything?"

"Yes. Everything."

"I think I need something to clear my head first. I'm kind of hurting," he said. "Mind if I get another fix before I tell you my deepest and darkest secrets?"

"What are you talking about?"

"Going and getting high." He snorted laughter. "Never underestimate the ability of a meth head to get high."

I should have said, "Get a grip. You're dead," or something, but what popped out was, "So, how do you do it?"

Maybe I was going to have to write a book about this stuff.

Ghosts never ceased to amaze me.

"I walk through somebody who's already high."

"That's all?"

"Yep. Works like a charm." He turned to the window. "Wish I could pick the high, though. The last guy—it wasn't the best in the world."

"There are different kinds of high?" A book about drug-addicted ghosts—I bet people would buy it.

"Yep. As many different kinds as there are drugs—"

We both jumped when someone hammered on the door.

"Got a gun?" Eddie asked.

"No," I breathed, and looked around for something with which to protect myself. "Don't have one of those. Go out there and find out who it is."

"No," Eddie said. And he cowered against the window sill, like a great big chicken, as whoever it was hammered on the door again. Hard.

"Go away!" I squealed. "Or I'll call the police!"

"Oh, you don't need the police," a woman's voice called. "We're here to help you."

I frowned. Felt like I recognized the woman's voice, but couldn't place it. I didn't need to. Eddie knew.

"Son of a bitch!" he cried. "What are they doing here?"

"Who is it?" I asked. A bit too loudly, obviously, because the woman behind the door answered me.

"It's Bea Winterburn! And the rest. Let us in!"

"Who?"

"It's my mother's book club," Eddie said.

Good grief, I thought. What now?

Marie:
The Book Club, Redux

I OPENED THE door, and Queen Bea and the rest filled the front office with their noise and old lady perfume.

"How can I help you?" I asked. Queen Bea looked around the reception area and sniffed imperiously, as though the furniture—indeed, the whole office—was beneath her contempt.

"We need to sit," she said.

So, I helped everyone get settled. But, as I found enough chairs—or at least sitting spaces—for everyone to get off their feet, I thought that perhaps it would have been smarter to keep them standing. They probably would have been easier to move out if I had.

"Coffee," Bea said.

I blinked and looked around the room. Every one of the women smiled or nodded, or waved enthusiastically.

Coffee for everyone, it seemed.

Most of them made happy old lady sounds as they settled in their chairs. One of them even pulled off a shoe and rubbed her instep as I brought everybody a coffee.

Then I walked back behind my desk and sat down. The twittering slowed, and then stopped.

"So, how can I help you?" I asked.

"We have a few questions, young lady," Bea said, after sipping the coffee and nodding her head, once, like she was giving it her approval.

"What kind of questions?" I asked.

The Queen didn't answer. Just narrowed her eyes in an uniquely infuriating way. "What were you doing at Naomi's? You upset her, with all your questions about her son, Edward."

I glanced around. Eddie's mom, Naomi, wasn't in the room.

"It's Eddie, you old cow!" Eddie yelled.

I glanced over at him, and he shut his mouth, but I could tell by the look on his face that he wasn't going to keep control for long. I hoped he would, because I had to find out why they were here.

"You mean Eddie?" I asked, and saw Eddie relax, a little bit.

"Yes," Bea said. "I suppose. Though I never understood his need to use a contraction of his name. Seemed so—boyish. Don't you think so, girls?"

The rest of the women nodded, agreeing wholeheartedly with Queen Bea, and obviously not seeing the irony of her calling Eddie's name boyish, and then calling them girls.

"I'm sorry I upset Eddie's mother, but it was important that I speak to her about her son," I said. "We're trying to solve his murder—"

"Aren't the police doing that?" one of the other women asked. Bea gave her a "you stole my line" look that could probably wither corn on the stalk, and the woman shut her mouth with a small snap. I tried to hide the nasty little smile that came over me, even though it was really nice to see that Bea could be rattled.

"Yes, of course they're doing what they can," I said. "But we've been hired to exonerate a person of interest—and if we can solve the murder at the same time, then that will help the police. Won't it?"

"Yes, yes, those poor dears, run off their feet the way they are, any help is good, I'm sure," Bea said. She looked like she thought she was back in control, just where she liked it. "And who are you trying to exonerate, dear?"

I smiled at her, wishing my lips didn't feel quite so angry tight. The old woman was getting under my skin, darn it, anyhow. "I'm afraid I can't tell you that."

Bea smiled. It wasn't pleasant to see. Felt a bit like watching a shark smile. "I'm afraid I don't understand," she said, and settled back in her chair, clutching her oversized purse in her hands like she was settling in for a really long talk, one that would probably last until she got the information she wanted.

"I'm afraid it's a matter of client confidentiality," I said. I smiled even harder, letting the old woman know I wasn't going to let her push me around.

Eddie whispered, "You go, girl!" and pumped his arm in the air a couple of times. I ignored him, concentrating on the smiling old woman sitting before me.

"But you're not a doctor, dear," she said. "Or a lawyer." She looked around the office again, and clucked. "Doesn't even look like you're much of a private investigator. You do have a licence, don't you?"

"I am not the private investigator," I said, and stopped with the smiling. She was really starting to bug me. The rest of the old biddies leaned back in their chairs, but Bea leaned forward, ready to do battle.

"So who is?"

"James Lavall."

"And why wasn't he conducting the investigation?"

"That is none of your business." I opened a small pad of paper, and picked up my pen. "I'll need your names, please."

"Why?" Finally, Bea looked taken aback. I liked to see that look on her face. I really did.

"You'll have to be checked out," I said. "You've decided to become involved in an ongoing investigation, for some reason. I believe it goes past just being Eddie's mother's friend." I glared at the woman sitting to Bea's right. "Name and address, please."

The woman opened her mouth as if she was about to give me everything I'd asked for. This brought Bea back to attention.

"Shut your mouth, Edna. You don't need to tell this young woman anything." She stared at me, obviously hoping to break my will down with a look.

Not a chance.

"If you have nothing to hide, why wouldn't you tell me your names?" I asked, pen still poised over the paper. "Not telling me makes you look guilty, you know."

"Oh Bea, maybe we should tell her," a woman sitting near the door said. "We have nothing to hide—"

"Fine," Bea snapped. "If you need our names and addresses so you can check us all out, we'll give them to you. We have nothing at all to hide, do we, girls?"

"No," the woman to the right of Bea said, and I swore I heard a hint of "I told you so" in her voice.

Looks like a bit of a mutiny there, Queen Bea.

In five minutes, I had all their contact information written down. I closed the pad of paper and put down the pen.

"Thank you for your cooperation," I said. "And now, if there isn't anything else, perhaps you should be on your way. I have a very full day, and—"

"Oh no," Bea said, shaking her head vigorously. "We came here for some answers, missy. We are not leaving until we get them. We gave you everything you wanted. Turnabout is fair play."

There was some additional grumbling from the other women, and it looked like I was going to be stuck with an old lady sit-in if I wasn't careful.

Darn it. I'd thought it would work.

I plastered the smile back on my face. "What information are you looking for?"

"Are you absolutely certain Eddie was murdered?" Bea asked the question quickly, as if afraid that if she wasn't fast, I'd reconsider, and they'd be left sitting there drinking cold coffee and getting nothing more.

"Yes, ma'am," I replied. That much information they could have gleaned from the morning news.

"Do you have any idea at all who could have done it?"

"I am not at liberty—"

"Yes, yes, fine," Bea snapped. Her lips thinned as she thought, hard. "Would you like some help?"

What?

"What kind of help?" I asked. Had these old women actually figured something out about Eddie's murder? "Do you know something—"

"Oh no, nothing like that," Bea replied, shaking her head. "However, we have some—expertise in solving crimes of this sort, don't we, girls?"

Assenting noises from the other old women, and I stared. What were they talking about? What kind of expertise could they have?

"We've studied under the masters," Bea said. "For years."

"The masters?" I asked.

"Doyle, Patterson, Christie, Roberts. You know. The best the literary world has to offer."

"The literary—" I blinked. "You're talking about mystery writers. Right?"

"Of course," Bea replied. "We've studied them extensively and understand exactly how to run an investigation. Don't we, girls?"

More rumblings of assent from the rest. Oh, my. I had to nip this in the bud.

"I don't think—" I started, but Bea cut me off. Again. It was getting tiresome; it really was.

"As a matter of fact, we only came here as a courtesy," she said. "To find out who you were and why you were bothering Naomi. However, I like your face and believe you are trustworthy."

"Well, thank you," I said.

"We've already started our investigation. When it's complete, we'll bring you our findings, gratis."

"Gratis?" I tried to keep smiling, but it was starting to hurt. What I wanted to do was laugh, but I guessed that would probably be a bad thing to do. I imagined Bea could get vicious if someone laughed at her.

"That means for free, girl," Bea snapped. "We'll go out and solve this mystery. Not for you, of course. We're doing it for Naomi. But we will share our findings with you. So you can find out if your secret client is guilty or not."

Bea grabbed her huge handbag and hitched the straps over her shoulder, then hauled herself upright. The rest of the women took it as the signal that they were finally leaving, and all stood.

"Oh," I said, and belatedly stood, too. I *had* to put a stop to this before they left. "Thanks, but I don't think—"

"We are doing this for Naomi, girl," Bea repeated, her eyes glittering dangerously. "For you, we'll call this a test. If we do a good job, we *will* expect you to consider us for your other endeavours. And we will expect to be paid."

"Oh." I glanced around the room, hoping against hope that the rest of the women—or maybe one of them—thought this was a bad idea. But no, all heads were bobbing enthusiastically. Eddie wasn't even any help, because he was laughing his butt off in the corner of the room. I took a deep breath and blew it out slowly, to get myself back under control. "Oh. Well. Thank you. I will definitely keep that in mind."

"See that you do," Bea replied. She dug in her voluminous bag and pulled out a business card, which she dropped on the desk in front of me. "You can reach me there."

"Thanks."

"And you?" Bea asked.

"Me what?"

"Give me your card, girl," Bea snapped.

Seriously? Handing out that stupid business card had brought me nothing but trouble so far, but Bea's hand stayed outstretched. I had this horrible feeling that she could stand there, like a statue, forever, if I didn't give her what she wanted.

I opened a drawer, and stared into the huge mess of stuff I'd dumped in there after the break-in. I shifted some stuff, and one popped into view. I pulled the card from the mess and handed it to Bea.

"The number's on the front," I said. "Call if you have any information."

"Oh no, this is not the way this is done, girl," Bea replied. She turned to the rest of the women and snorted indignant laughter. "As if we'd do this over the telephone." The rest obediently tittered, and Bea turned back to me, staring with her shark-cold eyes.

"No. The only reason we'd call would be to set up a meeting. To discuss our findings and so forth."

She dropped the card in her purse and led the way out of the office, the rest of the women bobbing along in her wake like a handful of dinghies following an ocean liner.

I didn't move until I heard the downstairs door slap shut. Then I dropped Bea's business card in the garbage.

"Where did your mother find those women, Eddie?" I asked.

"No idea," Eddie replied. "No idea at all."

But he was lying to me. I could tell.

I sighed, and sat down at my desk. Time to check out these women and find out what their secrets were. If Eddie wouldn't tell me, I'd find out myself.

Eddie:
No Confession for Me

ACTUALLY, I KNEW exactly where my mother had found the women from her book club, but Marie didn't need to know that Bea Winterburn had been running the local "Tough Love" group, and my mother had joined when I first got in trouble with the law.

After a few months, Bea and Mom had figured out that they both liked to read mysteries, and Bea invited her to join the book club she'd organized. All the women were old and cranky, like Bea, but even though Mom was at least twenty years younger, she fit right in.

And between the stupid mysteries, Bea kept telling Mom to get me out of her life. For her own good.

No. Marie didn't need to know any of that.

"No idea," I said. "No idea at all."

Marie glanced at me, and I could tell she knew I was lying. More lying. I felt exhausted. I also felt like I needed to get high and let it all drift away.

"I gotta go."

"Eddie?" she asked. "Are you all right?"

"I'm dead. I'm as far from all right as I can get." I didn't turn around or anything. I just wanted to get out. "I gotta go."

I didn't want to talk about this anymore. I knew the book club hadn't killed me. I knew I'd picked them to blame because it felt like they'd made my life miserable for almost as long as I could remember. I just wanted a little payback. At least, I had. Now I didn't know. It seemed stupid, and childish, and pointless. I was dead. I needed to let this stuff go. "I'll be back."

"When?"

"Later!" I snapped, then closed my eyes. I remembered saying the same thing to my mom, when she'd asked me that question. "Later," I said, trying to make my voice sound more reasonable. "After I—"

"Get high?"

That stopped me. "Maybe."

"It'd be better if you didn't do that, Eddie," she said.

"Why?"

"Because, if you want to move on, you need to feel the feelings and really understand. You can't do that high. You're hiding behind the drugs. You get that, don't you?"

"Yeah, sure. I'll think about it." Then I left, before she could say anything more, and hit the sidewalk almost running.

No matter what she said, I needed to clear my head. And the only way I knew to do that was to get high.

I desperately needed to get high. More than that, I needed to get away from her. She made me think about shit I really did not want to think about.

So I ran to the park, found the first junkie I could, and stepped in.

Marie:
Should You Drink Something Blue?
Sure. Why Not?

I HAD JUST finished checking up on Naomi Hansen's book club members when James came back, looking like he had been beaten with a large mental stick. I decided not to mention a thing about the book club dropping in on us, because he didn't look like he could take any more foolishness. A book club helping us figure our case out—for a fee—was about as foolish a thing as I could think of.

"I take it things did not go well with the sergeant," I said instead, and pointed at the coffee machine. "Want some?"

He shook his head and threw himself into a chair. "Do we have anything stronger?"

"I think so."

I went into the other office, to the bottom right drawer of James's dead uncle's desk. There were a few fingers of some really decent scotch left, so I brought it out with two glasses. I poured him a little more than half and emptied the rest of the bottle into a glass for me. He took the glass and managed a smile.

"So, what happened?" I asked. He held up his hand, then tossed the drink back in one shot.

"Want mine?"

"If you don't mind." He took my proffered glass, and finished it almost as quickly as he had the first one. Then he leaned back and covered his eyes with one of his hands. "This has turned into a really bad day," he muttered.

"What happened?"

"The cop who ran the sting you got caught in has decided that you tipped off the big guys, just by showing up. And apparently I didn't help things at all by going there today."

"They knew you went down to the park today?"

"Yes. Apparently, there's surveillance everywhere down there." His face closed. "I tried to tell them you weren't involved. That you'd gone down on my order."

"Stewart?"

"That's the one. He wants our hides, he really does."

"So what happens next?"

"We have another meeting scheduled with the good sergeant tomorrow morning. 9:00 a.m. Sharp."

"What for?" Suddenly I wished I hadn't given James my drink. I could have used it myself.

"She says we have to give all the information we've gathered to Stewart."

"But James, this is our case! She can't expect us to just hand over everything we've found out—"

"What have we found out, Marie? Really, what have we found out? We know that our client has visions. Or pretends she does. We know she lives right by the park where a lot of drug addicts— including the murder victim—hang out. The police already know all of this. What else do we know for sure?"

"I—I don't know," I muttered. He was right. We didn't have much more. Not on the surface. Heck, not even when I took into account the little Eddie had told me about the turf war.

"I really could use another drink."

He stalked over to the closet. It was still filled with his dead uncle's stuff, and he began pulling apart the boxes, one by one. I left him to it, secretly hoping that he'd find something, so we could both have a drink.

He was absolutely right. We had no case. Nothing at all. And if Stewart was telling the truth, I'd wrecked his big sting operation just by wandering into the park on that particular night. Maybe we were idiots.

"Yahoo!" he cried, and backed out of the closet with a bottle of something blue in his hand.

"What is that?" I asked.

"No clue," he said.

He poured a liberal dollop for me, and then another for himself. Then he knocked it back, shuddered, and poured himself another. He looked over at me as he put down the bottle and picked up his glass once more.

"Go ahead," he said.

"Are you sure it's something we should be drinking?" I had never seen a bottle of alcohol that colour blue before. "Maybe your uncle filled it with—"

"No, it's actually pretty good. A little sweet, but you'll get used to it," he said. "Try it."

I touched the drink to my lips and tasted. He was right. It was sweet, but seemed drinkable, so I took a big sip and swallowed. It warmed me all the way down. I sipped some more as James poured himself another big glass.

"To the two biggest idiots in the world!" he said, holding his glass up. I laughed and touched the edge of my glass to his, then we both drank to ourselves.

"Maybe we just need to learn how to do this right," I said. "I mean, there are courses we could take, aren't there?"

"I suppose," he muttered, burying his face in his glass again. "It's just so embarrassing, having my ineptitude thrown in my face like that." He held up the nearly empty bottle. "More?"

"No, I'm good."

As he poured the rest into his glass, I sipped a little more from mine and savoured the warmth as it slid down my throat.

"So she wants to see us tomorrow."

"Yep."

"Bright and early."

"That's right."

"And we don't really have anything much to say to her at all, do we? Clue-wise, I mean."

"That's exactly right."

"Oh, what the hell," I said, and slammed back the rest of my drink. "We'll go tell her we don't know a darned thing, then go for breakfast."

"If she doesn't lock us up for messing with a police

investigation," James said gloomily.

"We didn't know, James. She can't lock us up for that!"

"I believe her exact words were, 'Ignorance of the law is no excuse,'" he said morosely. "She was really mad. Especially about *me* going to the park."

"Oh." I'd forgotten about that.

"She said that she thought I at least had a brain in my head. Thought I knew enough to stay away from dangerous people. Called it stepping on a hornet's nest." He shook his head. "I have to tell you, I would have paid a fee not to hear her call me stupid one more time."

"She actually called you stupid to your face?"

James sighed and tipped his empty glass up, then set it back down and sighed again. "Not exactly. But she could have. And I would have deserved it." He turned to me. "Want to go out and have some supper, then head back here and bunk for the night? We could pick up another bottle. Maybe not that blue stuff, but something. What do you say?"

It would have been so wonderful to stay and have a few more drinks, and then some food, and then see what happened, but I knew I couldn't do that to Jasmine. She was expecting me.

"Sorry, James, I told Jasmine I'd be home tonight. She's expecting me."

"Oh." He shrugged and grinned. "No chance of another cuddle, then."

I felt my face heat. "No," I said shortly, and grabbed my sweater. It was definitely time to go.

"Don't forget we have to be at the police station at quarter to nine," he said.

"I won't." I turned back to him, hand on the doorknob. "Are you staying here tonight? I thought your place was fixed."

"Yeah, got the go-ahead to move back in, but I've decided to stay here tonight. Just to make sure that nothing more happens to the place. Just in case the dear sergeant is right, and I was stupid for going down to the park. I might figure out a way to get something more to drink, and maybe something to eat, but here is where I'll stay."

He grinned at me, warmly, and I smiled back.

"Make sure you lock the door," I said, and headed for the door.

"Will do," he replied. "Be safe, Marie."

"You too, James. I'll see you tomorrow."

IT TOOK ME an hour by bus to get to Jasmine's place. By that time the bit of alcohol I'd had to drink was gone, leaving me with a dirty little headache and an oogey stomach. I couldn't tell if it was because of the alcohol or because I hadn't had anything decent to eat, but as I jumped off the bus and walked up to her neat little bungalow, I decided to try eating something decent first. I wasn't quite ready to give up alcohol full-time. I had this sneaking suspicion I'd need it.

Two of Jasmine's three kids were already in bed. Ella, her oldest daughter, was sitting at the table, doing homework. She always seemed to be doing homework. She smiled at me and wriggled her fingers in a quick hello before bending back over her books. I glanced at what she was poring over. Physics. Good luck, I thought, and turned away before she asked me for help.

Jasmine walked into the kitchen and gave me a quick hug. I hugged back. It was hard not to.

"You hungry?" she asked.

"Starving."

"Sit," she said, and turned to the refrigerator. "Ella, take that to your room. Marie needs space."

Ella smiled at me again, gathered her books, and left.

"She's really smart," I said when I heard her door shut.

"I know," Jasmine replied as she tossed chicken, rice, and vegetables into a saucepan and turned the heat up on the stove. "Much smarter than I was, at that age."

"Yeah, I saw—she's taking physics. What, she want to be a scientist, or something?"

"I think so, but that's not what I mean," Jasmine replied. She turned the food expertly in the saucepan, then went to the cupboard and pulled out a plate. "She understands that now is her time. She's decided she doesn't need a boyfriend. She's concentrating on her studies. Wants to establish herself before she commits to a relationship."

"Really?" I was surprised. I thought all girls between the ages of fifteen and thirty were in it for the relationships. "Did she say that?"

"I paraphrased for brevity," Jasmine said, placing the heaping plate of steaming food before me. "She has told me, repeatedly, that she feels I wasted the best years of my life looking for the right mate."

"Mate?" I giggled, then picked up the fork and tasted. Mouthwatering, as always. "She actually said that?"

"Among other things," Jasmine said. She placed the pan in the sink and ran water into it. It hissed, and steam billowed up, touching Jasmine's hair. Curls started almost immediately, and she frowned, pulling back. She hates her curly hair. "I don't think she realizes that if I had done that, she would not be around to harass me about my life choices."

She went to the cupboard above the sink and pulled out a bottle of scotch. "After you finish eating, we can toast bad life choices. Or maybe friendship." She shrugged. "One or the other."

"I don't know if I should drink any more tonight," I mumbled around a mouthful of truly exquisite chicken. "James and I had a couple before I left tonight."

"Ah, one more won't kill you," she said. "I don't often get to use my good crystal." She opened a cupboard above the sink and, standing on tiptoe, fished out two etched glasses. They chimed like bells when she touched them together. "One more thing I wouldn't have if I hadn't been so determined for that perfect relationship."

"Oh, you'd probably have crystal glasses," I said. "Think of all the extra money you'd have if you hadn't gotten married."

"Probably," she replied, and held one of the glasses up, so I could see the intricate floral pattern etched into it. "But I never in a million years would have picked something that looks like this."

She poured two liberal scotches as I finished the last of the food. I thought for a second about licking the plate clean, but decided against it and grabbed the glass instead. Jasmine was right. One drink wouldn't kill me.

"Here's to all the men we've loved and, thank God, have lost."

Jasmine laughed, and we chimed the glasses together, then drank, deeply. The scotch was good. Dark sweetness on the edges of the tongue and smoky warmth all the way down the throat.

"Speaking of men," she said, reaching for the bottle and refilling our glasses. "What's going on with Cutie Pie?"

"You mean James?" I knew she meant James. I picked up my glass and drank again. "Nothing much."

"Oh really," she said. I could tell by the look on her face she didn't believe a word.

"Really." I buried my face in my drink, one more time. Just to avoid her smirk. "I even applied for a different job."

Her smile faded. "Why did you do that?"

"Because I'm stupid," I said. "I thought the job might pay more. I can't live here forever, you know."

"I love having you here. You know that, don't you?"

"I know. And I like working for James, I really do. But I'm afraid he expects more. And what was it that Ella said? I shouldn't be wasting the best years of my life looking for a mate."

Jasmine laughed and took another sip of her drink. "Ella doesn't know everything. You two seem pretty right together."

"Now, that's not the truth, and you know it." I took another drink myself. "Since I've known him, I've been caught in explosions, beaten up, in the hospital . . ."

"But he didn't do any of that stuff to you. And he saved you from the explosion. Didn't he?"

"Yes. He did." I shook my head. "He's a great guy, Jasmine. He really is. I just can't see a relationship with him working out."

"Sounds to me like that would be because of you, and not him."

I took another drink, then held out my glass for a refill. "Probably."

"So why wouldn't it work?" She poured me another drink. "What big secret do you have? He already knows about the crazy ex-boyfriend. What else do you have hidden away that you're not telling him?"

"Nothing." I sipped and grimaced. I was drinking too fast. "Well, not much. Everybody's got stuff they'd rather not talk about. Don't they?"

"Not me," Jasmine replied. "My life's an open book. You want to hear about my past relationships—no problem. I can talk about them for hours."

I grinned. She was right. She could.

"My kids?" she continued. "I'll talk about them for hours more. My scrapes with the law?"

"You've had scrapes with the law?" This was news to me. "What happened?"

She thought for a long moment, then took another sip. "You're right. Everybody's got something in their past they'd rather not talk about," she finally replied.

"Oh, come on! You can't leave me hanging like this! What did you do?"

She looked around the kitchen, as though checking to make certain her children hadn't materialized around us. I didn't blame her. I'd seen them pull that trick before. We'd be right in the middle of some juicy bit of gossip, and suddenly the room would be full of children all asking for details. I glanced down the hallway, but it appeared all bedroom doors were still securely shut.

"It's safe," I whispered. "What did you do?"

"I shouldn't be telling you this." She giggled. "You'll laugh at me."

So it wasn't murder, then. A person didn't laugh at confessions of murder. Or drugs either. Drugs weren't funny. I sipped a bit more scotch, thinking that perhaps I'd had just about enough.

"So what did you do?"

"I—I was involved with a group. That group got in a bit of trouble." She shook her head. "Man, that was a long time ago."

"So spill," I said. "I'm dying here."

"All right, but you have to promise you won't laugh."

"I promise."

"You have to say it like you actually mean it."

I held my hand over what I hoped was my heart. "I promise."

"Heart's on the other side."

Oops. Changed position and tried again, hoping I looked sincere. "So what did you do?"

"Broke into a lab and stole rabbits."

"What?" I decided I had had more than enough to drink. It sounded like my friend had said—

"I broke into a lab on the south side of town and freed all the rabbits they were using for testing."

"Rabbits?"

"Yes. Rabbits."

I felt the smirk begin to form and tried valiantly to make it go away. I could tell by the look on Jasmine's face that I was completely unsuccessful.

"You promised you wouldn't laugh," she said.

"Rabbits?"

"Yes." Her jaw set. "They were doing unspeakable things to them—"

I took another big drink, just to compose myself. I looked at Jasmine over the rim of my glass and laughed out loud at the thunderous look on her face.

Laughing with my face buried in a glass of scotch was a mistake. I managed to breath in, not out, and sucked some scotch, which caused me to choke. That led to me blowing alcohol all over the table. Some of it came out through my nose, which was both extremely painful and in terrible form.

Jasmine stared at me as I choked and slobbered all over the place, then burst out laughing herself.

"Serves you right, you wretch," she said, reaching behind her for a dishcloth and handing it to me. "I told you not to laugh."

I grabbed the cloth and wiped my face and my streaming eyes, as I tried to stop choking. It took a minute, and brought Ella from her room.

"Is everything all right?" she called from the safety of her doorway.

"Absolutely," Jasmine said. "Don't worry about a thing, girl. Marie just had a karma attack is all. She'll be fine as soon as she apologizes to me."

"Good grief," Ella said, disdain dripping from her fifteen-year-old voice. "Well, keep it down, please. I'm trying to get my homework done here."

Jasmine and I both burst into gales of laughter as her door clicked shut. "Good thing there's someone mature in this house," Jasmine said. "Otherwise, it would all fall to ruin, I'm sure."

"Probably. Oh, and Jasmine?"

"Yes?"

"Sorry about laughing." If there was such a thing as karma, I didn't need to get on its wrong side.

"That's all right," Jasmine replied. "Are you ready to share your big secret?"

"What? What secret?"

"Well, when we were talking about James, you said something about everybody having secrets. So, what secret do you have?"

I stared at her.

"Do you want another drink?"

"God, no," I gasped. "That was more than enough."

"Good," she replied. "You're not going to tell me, are you?"

"No." I stared down into my glass. "I just can't."

"Some day you'll have to," Jasmine said. "You know that, don't you?"

I didn't answer, but all she did was smile. "You're lucky. No more interrogation. It's time for my show. Come on, I'll catch you up."

I wiped up the last of the scotch off the table, then followed her to the front room, to watch her favorite nighttime medical drama. And for that hour, I was able to forget my own drama.

I wished it had lasted longer. Drama on TV is—dramatic. Drama in real life is messy. And painful, usually.

Just like nostril scotch.

Eddie:
Crank! Buddy! Tell Me Everything

I STEPPED OUT of the drunk—yeah, picked a drunk—and just felt, well, drunk. That was definitely not what I was going for, but it did take the edge off, a bit. I decided to go find Crank and hang out with him. Even though he couldn't see me.

Hell, it would almost be like old times. Crank wasn't exactly my friend. He was more of a business acquaintance. He supplied me with drugs, and I supplied him with money. It was a pretty good system, all things considered. Unless I didn't have enough money. Then he turned mean. Hey, but that's business, right?

He worked for Ambrose Welch. Barely above street level, so he didn't get all the news right from the horse's mouth. But he knew the guys that knew—and that was almost as good. When he was in a giving mood, he'd tell a guy some of what was going on. He wasn't supposed to. He was supposed to keep his mouth absolutely shut around us addicts. But he liked to talk, and I was always ready to listen. Sometimes what fell out of his mouth was pure gold.

True, the son of a bitch hadn't warned me that by going to the churchyard, I was stepping on somebody else's toes, but I guess that was my own fault as much as his.

I got lazy, believed what he said, and went on my merry way. That way led to the tree.

159

So, this time, I was going to listen to what he said, and then get it checked out. By that Marie chick. She could do the leg work, since she was the one who thought this all meant something.

Yeah, look at me being lazy again. Screw it. I got a real good excuse. I'm dead.

CRANK WAS AT his usual table, with his buddy. I didn't recognize him, but it didn't surprise me. Crank's buddies were transient and unremarkable. I sat down beside him and laughed when he shuddered and rubbed his arm, like he'd suddenly felt a chill.

Yeah man, the dead are haunting you . . .

"So, what's your problem?" Crank asked. "You'll scare the freaks away, acting like that."

I laughed out loud. Nothing would scare the freaks away but the cops, or Crank being out of product. Looked to me like he had lots, and I didn't see the cops anywhere for the moment, so—no problem, Crank. You fuck.

"Nothin'," his buddy answered. He stood and walked a couple of feet away from the table. Could have been to get away from me, or from Crank. Didn't blame him, for either of the choices.

I watched them do business—and a brisk business it was, too—for a little while, and was just about ready to go find Noreen just for a change of pace, when Buddy decided to come back and huddle up with Crank.

"I got news," he whispered. "About Ambrose."

Rumours—that's what Buddy called "news"—especially about the top dogs, were always interesting, so I eased closer to Crank.

"What about him?" Crank asked. Although he wasn't acting too interested, I knew he was. Because he always had been.

"He's getting a hunting party together."

Crank frowned. "Who's he after?"

Buddy shook his head. "Jerry didn't say. But he thinks it has to do with the shakedown here the other night. Jerry says that Mike said that Joey thought that Ambrose knew who brought that bit of shit down on us."

"Really?" Crank pointed at a girl, couldn't have been over fourteen, who looked like she was hurting real bad. Buddy ran off, did business, and when the girl scurried away, came back.

"So who?" Crank asked.

"Apparently Mike thought it probably had to do with that do-gooder who showed up just before the raid."

My ears pricked up at that. Do-gooder—had to be Marie.

"Didn't she get picked up too?" Crank asked.

"Yeah, but she was out fast. Ambrose sent a couple of guys over to her office, to find out why she'd been to the park. Who she was connected to. You know. And then, after, that guy showed up here. In R's face about wrecking his office and scaring his bitch. Even if he didn't have anything to do with the raid, he disrespected R. And that disrespected Ambrose, on his own turf."

"That's enough for a hunting party, right there." Crank looked around, to see if anyone was listening. It was disconcerting when he looked right at me. Right through me. I almost flinched away, then remembered I was dead. "So, they're gonna get gacked?"

"Sounds like Ambrose wants to know what they know first. Joey said that the do-gooder talked to Noreen, just before the raid. Noreen told Joey—to his face— that the girl was asking if Brown Eddie knew somebody named Honoria. Honoria Lowe, I think that's her name, anyhow. She lives around here, somewhere. That's what Noreen said that the do-gooder said, anyhow. So, Ambrose wants to know who the chick is, and why the little do-gooder was trying to connect her to Brown Eddie." Buddy shrugged. "Then, I guess they all get gacked."

"You didn't say anything to Joey about joining the hunting party, did you?"

"It was Jerry I was talking to, and no." Buddy shook his head vigorously. "Wouldn't say anything like that, unless you were interested." He frowned. "You want to?"

"No," Crank mumbled. "I got a business to run here. I don't need that kind of trouble, unless I have to go. Jerry didn't ask for me, did he?"

"No. I guess it's Sonny, R, and a couple other guys."

"Good." Crank leaned back and relaxed. "We're businessmen. Don't need to be involved."

Crank might be all right with what Buddy said to him, but I wasn't. This wasn't good. Marie was in trouble. She needed to be warned.

I BLASTED BACK to the office, but it was dark and quiet. Well, not completely quiet. There was that James guy, sitting in a chair close to the front door with a baseball bat over his lap and his head thrown back, snoring. But no Marie. I didn't know where she'd gone, but felt scared for her. She didn't know what she had stepped into, going to that park. And she wouldn't, if I couldn't find her.

So, I tried focusing on her. You know, picking up her vibes, or something. I got nothing, though. Absolutely nothing.

What was the point being a ghost if you got no special powers with the whole deal?

So I did the only thing I could think to do. I sat down, listened to the idiot snoring for all he was worth, and waited for Marie to come back so I could save her life.

Marie:
I Wasn't Even Drinking Anything Blue! Why Do I Feel so Horrible?

I STROLLED INTO the office at just after eight in the morning.

All right, I didn't stroll, I dragged my carcass through the door, hoping against hope that James had coffee on. My mouth felt moon-dust dry, and my head spun every time I closed my eyes.

The office was quiet, thank goodness. I carefully walked over to the coffee machine, to see if the coffee in the pot was drinkable. I couldn't remember shutting it off the night before, and my stomach didn't feel strong enough to deal with coffee over ten hours old.

I took a shallow, cautious sniff and was rewarded with a freshly brewed scent. Thanking whatever Gods there were looking after foolish women who drink too much on a work night, I poured myself a cup and carefully carried it over to my desk, but almost dropped it when I heard groaning. I couldn't tell where it was coming from—sounded like everywhere and nowhere at the same time. I slopped coffee as I slammed the cup down and threw the door to the other office open.

"James!" I cried, looking around frantically. "Are you all right?"

He wasn't there. I ran back to the other room, and looked in corners, and in the overstuffed closet—everywhere I could think of. Nothing.

I heard another groan, this one long, drawn-out, as though someone was screaming in his sleep. But I still couldn't see anyone, anywhere.

"Eddie?" I called cautiously. "Eddie, is that you?"

He came into view as he slowly woke up. He was curled in a ball by the window and kicked out frantically with one wrecked foot as he pulled himself out of whatever nightmare place he was in, and back to reality.

"Eddie!" I called again. Louder this time. "Wake up!"

He popped into full view as he jerked awake. Then he stretched and opened his eyes, smiling when he noticed me.

"Hey there," he said.

"Hey yourself." I went back to my desk and tried to clean up the spilt coffee with the last of the tissue from the box on my desk, then gave it all up and sat down. "Were you having a nightmare?"

"Don't think so," he said, stretching again, then pulling himself upright. I could see ribs through his thin tee shirt. "I can't remember."

"Is James here?"

"He was." He frowned. "I didn't hear him leave."

That spiked my heart rate. I put down my cup again, though more carefully this time. "The coffee tastes fresh. How long were you asleep?"

"I dunno. Not too long."

I went to the washrooms in the hallway and punched the door to the men's open, calling James's name as I did so. When I was certain there was no one there, I went back to the office. Where could he have gone?

Ignoring Eddie, I walked back into the inner office and checked the desk. Saw James's coffee cup sitting there, half-full of coffee. I touched it. Still warm. He hadn't been gone long at all.

I walked around the desk and knocked over a baseball bat that had been leaning against the desk.

"What the hell?" I asked, and bent down to pick the thing up. Was hit with an attack of vertigo, and grabbed for the desk. I hadn't had that much to drink the night before. Had I?

"Your buddy was using it for protection last night," Eddie said.

Then he frowned. "You all right?"

"Not so much." I stood stock-still until I was certain I was not going to embarrass myself by falling down in front of the ghost.

"Hungover or sick?"

"Apparently, hungover." Didn't like admitting it, and hated hearing him chuckle the way he did. "It's not funny."

"Yeah, actually it is."

"Where would he have gone?" I asked the question, not because I expected an answer, but because I didn't want to talk about being hungover any longer.

"I don't know," Eddie said, again. "Hope Ambrose didn't get him."

"What?" I swung around, and stared at him. "Who?"

"Ambrose Welch. That's why I came back. It looks like you shook him up some when you were down at the park, before the raid. He wants to find out what your deal is." He shrugged. "Maybe that's what happened to your boyfriend."

"He's not my boyfriend, and this isn't funny! Do you think they grabbed him? Where would they have taken him?"

"Dumpster, maybe?" Eddie shrugged, and I wanted to smack him. "I dunno."

"Jesus." I ran my hands through my hair and tried to think. James and I were supposed to go meet Sergeant Worth in—I checked my watch—thirty-five minutes. Which meant she'd be at her desk.

"Maybe she can help me," I muttered, and ran back out to the reception area. Eddie followed me out, then planted himself by the front door.

"Where are you going?" he asked.

"I have to go see—I have an appointment." I edged past him to get to the door, not wanting to go through any part of him. Drugs plus hangover. No thanks.

"But what about your guy? Don't you want to find him?"

"The appointment—she can help me. I hope."

I touched the doorknob, then shrieked when it turned of its own volition.

I scrabbled back, wishing for all I was worth that I had the capacity to make myself vanish the way Eddie could, or I was so far away from this office that whoever was on the other side of that door and coming in would never find me. At the very least, I wished I'd picked up the bat.

I scrambled to get it as the door opened, but shambled to a stop with a rush of relief as pure as anything I have ever felt in my life as James came into view with a brown paper bag in his teeth and the keys to the front door in his hand.

"James!" I ran to him, and threw my arms around him enthusiastically. More than that, actually. "Thank God you're all right!"

"And why wouldn't I be?" he asked, rather mushily around the bag. He hugged me back and took the bag from his teeth. "What did you think happened?"

"Well, I thought—" I pushed out of his arms a little, trying to get a coherent thought going. Nothing. "I was just worried," I finally muttered. "You didn't leave me a note."

"Oh." He grinned and tossed the bag on my desk. "Doughnuts. I figured we'd need breakfast before the meeting. And sorry about no note. I didn't think of it."

"Well, you should have," I said, but smiled anyhow. "I was scared."

"I saw that. Anything in particular you're afraid of—or just life in general?"

"Tell him about Ambrose," Eddie said. "That'll shut him the hell up."

But I couldn't do that.

"I guess—it was the bat," I blurted out, pointing at the inner office. "I saw it—"

"Oh yeah." James opened the bag and pulled out a chocolate doughnut. "I forgot about that."

"So why was it out?"

"I didn't want to be surprised by anyone last night." He gestured to the open bag. "Have one. They're fresh."

I glanced inside. The doughnuts looked good, so I took a chance, pulled one out, and bit into it. He was right. They were fresh, and the sweet doughnut goodness miraculously eased some of the pain in my brain.

"Thanks," I muttered.

"Told you so." He popped the rest of his into his mouth and chewed enthusiastically. "You almost ready? We have to go soon."

Oh yeah. The meeting with Sergeant Worth. Now that I knew

James was safe, I didn't feel as enthusiastic about going and seeing her. The last time we'd spoken, she'd hinted that she knew about my background. Where I'd come from. Who my mother was. What she was. I didn't want to face her again, because I was not prepared to tell her anything more about myself than I had to. Especially not in front of James.

"Any chance I can bow out of this?" I asked. "Maybe just stay here and get some of the paperwork in order or something?" I looked over at my desk and the remains of the coffee spill. "See? The place is a wreck."

James glanced at the desk and laughed. "No," he said. "She specifically asked for both of us—and she was pretty angry yesterday. So we're both going to be there."

"But the mess—" I pointed at the desk again, but less hopefully this time. "It really needs to be cleaned up."

"Tough," he replied. "We're going. Finish your doughnut."

"No thanks." I dropped the unfinished pastry on the desk beside the puddle of coffee and pulled in a deep breath. "If we're going to do this, let's get it over with."

"Good girl," he said, and, gentleman that he is, held the door open for me, then linked his arm in mine when we were both out in the hallway.

"Afraid I'll run?"

"Not really," he replied, then laughed. "Maybe."

"I'm coming, too," Eddie said, and jogged up behind us. I guess I made a noise, because James stopped and looked at me, concern on his face.

"Are you all right?"

"I'm fine. Really, I'm great." I smiled, hoping it looked right, even though the last thing in the world I felt like doing was smiling, or even walking another step. I did not need to have the diversion of a ghost in that office while we were talking to Sergeant Worth. I really didn't. "We'd better get going."

James held my arm even more tightly, and when I looked over at him, his smile was gone.

That look meant he was watching me closely. If I didn't want to give everything away, I had to be very careful.

Eddie followed us down the stairs and out into the street, looking both ways, and then shrugging. "Looks like you're safe for now," he said. "But I bet that your place is pulled to shit again when you get back." And then he laughed. "Maybe it'll be the cops this time."

SERGEANT WORTH, AS usual, looked like she hadn't slept much the night before. She waved to the two chairs in front of her paper-covered desk as she finished a phone call on her cell, and then one on her landline.

"She's too busy to see us," I muttered to James, hopefully. "We should go."

James didn't answer, but Worth pointed at the chairs again, as she blathered police jargon into the phone.

Eddie, luckily, hadn't shown up yet. He'd somehow missed the elevator, and the maze that was the downtown police department headquarters would probably keep him away from us for the entire meeting. I hoped so, anyhow.

We sat down, James looking like he belonged, and me sitting gingerly on the edge of my seat, wishing I was just about anywhere but there.

"Give me five minutes," Sergeant Worth said into the phone. She was only giving us five minutes? Excellent. This would not turn into an investigation of my past. Heck, five minutes was barely long enough to give us a hard time for the trouble we'd gotten into—check that, the trouble James got us into—the day before. I felt my gut loosen, and the headache, which had been threatening since we arrived at the police station, magically disappeared.

When she put the receiver down and turned her chair to face us, I was even able to manage a smile. She did not smile in return, but I still felt all right. James was the one in trouble here, not me. I just had to pretend to be invisible and—

"So Marie, what's your involvement in all this?"

Stomach tightened. Invisibility wasn't working worth a darn. I tried smiling harder, but that didn't take the ice off the look the woman was giving me.

"What do you mean?" I asked.

"I mean exactly what I said," Worth replied. "Tell me what you did to get James involved in the drug trade."

"The drug—" I stared at her, then decided that the best defence was to get angry. "What do you mean, how did *I* get him involved? I didn't do anything! He's an adult. He decided to go there—"

"That's not what I mean," Worth said, and leaned forward like she'd caught me in a lie or something. "I get that he decided to go to the park—and I can understand why, even though I did express to him yesterday just how foolish I thought he'd been. But what I need to understand is why you showed up there in the first place. Just in time for a drug sweep. Can you explain that to me?"

My mind froze. I couldn't even remember why I'd gone there. Had Eddie said something to me—or had it been our client? Our client. We had a client.

"I think it was our client that told us about the place," I said quickly, then glanced over at James, hoping he would confirm.

"I told you this yesterday, sergeant," he said. "I don't think you need to interrogate her—"

"I'm just trying to figure out her involvement in all this, James," Worth replied. "She does seem to show up just in time for the fireworks, now doesn't she?"

"I do too," James replied. I snuck another glance at him, but he still seemed relaxed, at ease. I could barely believe it. How could he be so calm? Sergeant Worth was one of the scariest women I knew, but he looked like he was chatting with his nice little old aunt, the one who sent him socks every year for Christmas.

"And I think you're there because of her," Worth replied, and turned back to me. "So? Am I right? Does he show up because of you?"

Mostly. I looked down at the floor.

"It's like I told you yesterday," James said. "I'm running my uncle's detective agency now." Still calm, still completely in control. Amazing. "And Marie works for me. So, I'd say I am the one to answer these questions."

"Ah yes, your detective agency," Worth said, flipping open a file on her desk and peering at it. "I decided to check it out. Found some interesting stuff, I did."

"Yes?" James said, but didn't look quite as confident as he had mere moments before. "What did you find?"

"I found that the only one who had a licence was your uncle," she said. "And now that he's dead, that leaves no one qualified to run that office. Unless you're applying for one?"

"I'm going to," James replied, and I knew, even without looking at him, that his calm had disappeared, replaced with anxiety just like mine. I felt like I was going to turn into a screeching pile of jello in seconds, and wondered if he felt the same way. "But I do have—"

"Seventeen more days to use your uncle's licence," Worth finished his sentence for him, and slapped the file shut. "You see, I know the law too. When do you expect to have yours?"

"In two weeks?" More a question than an answer, and I wondered if he even knew how long it took to get an investigator's licence. Looked like he'd either done some research, or he'd made an extremely lucky guess.

"Ah, you're taking the high road and doing it online," she said, a sneer pulling her lips down. "Excellent. If and when you pass, I will expect you to give me a copy. For your file."

"Yes," he muttered. I suspected he was now looking at his shoes. I didn't know for sure, because my eyes were firmly glued to mine.

"You two are making me crazy," Worth said. "I do not have time to pull your fat out of any other fires—"

"I understand," James began.

"You understand nothing," Worth said through gritted teeth. That brought James's explanation to a grinding halt, and since I had my mouth clamped shut, the silence was nearly complete. The only noise was the small clock sitting on Worth's bookshelf behind her head, ticking the agonizing seconds away.

"Sorry," James finally muttered.

"As long as we understand each other," Worth replied. Knuckles rapped sharply on the door, and she turned her attention to it. Thank God.

"Enter," she said.

Eddie chose that moment to burst through the door. "He's coming! He's coming!" he screamed. "Get out!"

Unfortunately, there was nowhere I could run, though I really wished I could have when the door swung open, and I saw who "he" was.

Angus Stewart. The police officer who had arrested me at the park. The father of Eddie's best friend, who had died of a drug overdose, who was now waging his own personal war on drugs in the city of Edmonton.

He looked just as angry as Worth, and my anxiety level spiked again. I wondered briefly if a person could actually die from too much adrenaline.

"So, these are the two idiots," he said.

My first impulse was to say, "Nope, you have the wrong two idiots," but luckily, I continued to keep my head down and my mouth shut.

James, not so much.

"I don't think we did anything to—" he started, stopping when Worth snapped her fingers in front of his face.

"Yes," she said, as though James hadn't spoken.

"You guys gotta get outta here," Eddie whispered. I didn't even venture a glance in his direction, but could feel the fear and anger wafting off him in waves.

"Aren't you listening?" Eddie cried. I kept staring at my feet, hoping he'd shut up. He didn't.

"You have to listen to me! This is one dangerous guy! You can't—"

"My name is Marie Jenner," I said, and stood, reaching mostly through Eddie, in a futile attempt to shut him up. He shuddered and moved away.

"Don't do that," he said. "You're messing with my high."

"Tell her to sit down," Stewart said to Worth, ignoring my outstretched hand.

Before she had a chance to speak, I sat and held one hand down by my side, attempting to signal to Eddie to shut the hell up. James glanced in my direction.

"Are you all right?" he whispered.

"Yes, fine," I whispered back. "We just have to be quiet while the officer tells us how we wrecked his operation."

James nodded, but it was Eddie I was trying to make understand. He stared at me for a moment, then nodded his head, indicating that he got it. Finally!

"Exactly," Worth said. "So shut up, both of you."

We both stared back down at our shoes.

"Do you two have any idea what you did?" Stewart asked, his voice rough with badly suppressed anger.

I snuck a glance at James, wondering how we were going to get out of this nasty catch-22 situation. He looked as trapped as I felt. Surprisingly, Worth saved us.

"No," she said. "They have no idea."

"You blew our best chance to clean up this city," Stewart said.

"The top dog was there—at the park—just before the raid. We finally had a shot at him." He glared at both of us. "Then you—" He pointed at me, and I felt my face heat. "You spoke to his men. Whatever the hell you said to them scared him off. He left minutes—" He slammed his fist into his open hand, and both James and I jumped. "Fucking minutes before we came in! We finally had a real chance to see him, in the flesh. Arrest him and put a stop once and for all to what's going on in that park—but you scared him off!"

"I'm sorry," I said after a few uncomfortable moments when only the clock ticked and Stewart gasped his anger. "I didn't know."

"Damn right you didn't know! Because you are an idiot! A moron! What the hell were you doing there?"

I glanced over at James. Same question Worth had asked, and I hoped James would continue to carry the ball. He didn't let me down.

"She was there to find out what we could about Eddie Hansen's death," James said. He turned and faced Stewart. "For me."

"Brown Eddie?" Stewart asked, and I noticed his breathing slowed. He hadn't been expecting that answer. "Why would you care about the death of a two-bit junkie?"

I froze, expecting an outburst from Eddie, but he said nothing. I glanced in his direction, but could not read his face.

"I am a private investigator," James said, "and I was representing my client. That's all I can tell you."

Stewart stared, his eyes mere slits, as though he was looking through us rather than at us. James had hit an inadvertent bull's-eye.

"Are you talking about Honoria Lowe?" he asked.

James blinked.

"Do you know the name?" Worth asked. "Is that who your client is?"

James didn't answer, but it didn't seem to matter. Stewart stared past us with a thousand-yard stare that chilled me. Then he shook his head, turned on his heel, and marched out of the office without another word.

"Stewart?" Worth asked. "Who is Honoria Lowe?"

The door slammed shut.

"Stewart!" she cried.

The door remained shut.

"Dammit," she muttered.

James and I turned back to her and waited as she straightened her desk, obviously trying to salvage a situation that had spun out of control. The moments stretched to a minute, and then two. She finally looked up at us and frowned.

"So, who is Honoria Lowe?" she asked James. "And why didn't you tell me about her?"

"Because I don't need to tell you who my clients are," James replied, a little snippily. I kept my mouth shut tight and looked back down at my shoes.

"You should tell me everything I want to know," Worth said, just as snippily. "If you want me to keep pulling your fat from the fire."

"I'll take that under advisement," James said.

"Stay away from the park."

"Is Stewart going to raid it again?" James asked.

"That's none of your business."

"Yep," Eddie whispered. "'Cause that's what that bastard does. That's all he does."

"Just stay away from the park," Worth said.

"Okay."

"And get a licence."

"Yes."

"Seventeen days."

"I remember."

"Get out."

She pointed at the door. James and I scrambled up out of our seats and left her office as quickly as we could. Eddie silently followed.

We wound our way through the rabbit's warren of offices and cubicles and finally found our way to the parking garage.

"What was all that about?" I finally asked.

"I don't know," James replied, unlocking the door to the car and holding it open for me.

Eddie slid in the back seat as James walked around the car.

"So what do you think?" I whispered to Eddie.

"I think Stewart will go after the blonde chick now," he said.

"I think you're right. And it has nothing to do with drugs. Did you see that look on his face?"

Eddie shuddered. "It has to do with me. My death."

"I think you're right."

James still wasn't at the driver's door. I peeked out the back window and saw that he'd stopped. He had his cell phone to his ear and was in deep conversation with someone. We still had a minute or two more.

"That son of a bitch will want to know what she knows, and he won't care who finds out. If Sonny and R see the cops going into her building, they might think that she's giving them information," Eddie said.

"How would those guys know if the police were going to talk to Honoria?" I asked. "Even though she does live right across the street from the park, they don't know her."

"But they know about her."

I blinked. "How do they know about her?"

"Because you asked Noreen about her," Eddie said. "Noreen would have told R everything you'd talked about." He smiled. "Including the Honoria chick."

I felt sick. "But she doesn't know anything," I said. "Not about them."

"They don't know that."

"What are we going to do?"

James slid the key into the driver's door and opened it.

"I don't know," Eddie said. "But I'm thinking they will want to find out exactly what it is she knows. So, even if that son of bitch Stewart doesn't do anything to her, Sonny and R will. Bad news for her, either way."

I couldn't answer him. And not just because James was in the car, either. I literally did not know how to respond to him. All I did know was our client was definitely in trouble, and I was the one who had put her there.

"You gotta fix this," Eddie said. "You know that, don't you?"

Then, before I could even nod, he stepped out of the car and disappeared.

"We should get some lunch," James said. "You hungry?"

I shook my head. I didn't think I'd ever be hungry again. "We have to tell Honoria about Stewart. He's going to make real trouble for her. Don't you think?"

"Already done." James put the car into drive and pulled out of the parking lot. "I called her and told her what had happened. She said that she expected us to find her somewhere safe to hide until 'all this foolishness is over.' She said she didn't want to stay at her place. That she doesn't feel safe anymore." He smiled sheepishly. "I told her I'd find her a place to stay until we solve her case."

"Oh." I felt my shoulders relax and then tighten again, maddeningly. I'd been hoping she'd tell us to sod off or something, since all we seemed to be bringing down on her was more and more grief. "Does this mean you've decided to take her case?"

"Well, yeah."

I glanced over at him and saw his face redden. My God, he was blushing!

"Why did you decide that?" I asked, a little more sharply than I probably should have. "I thought you didn't trust her. Thought she was conning us—"

"I feel like we owe her."

"Owe her?"

"Yeah. For the cops. You can bet that Stewart jerk is going to dig into every aspect of her life now that he knows she hired us. And maybe even for the drug dealers hanging around in front of her place. If they figure out she knows something—anything— about Edward's death and that the police are involved, they'll never leave her alone. They might hurt her. Even kill her." He shuddered. "Her life is tough enough, isn't it?"

"Yes, it is."

"So, let's get her out of harm's way."

"Okay."

Even though it was what I wanted for her, I still felt a twinge of something uncomfortable. Was it jealousy?

It couldn't be.

It had better not be.

"She's going to the Chapters on Whyte. We'll pick her up there."

"You better not be thinking of bringing her to the office," I said. I couldn't think of anything worse than having her staring at me, while I tried to work.

"No," he said. "I'll get her a cheap motel room for a couple of days, until we can work out something better." He sighed. "Maybe a couple of days is all we'll need."

"So, we're going to figure out who killed Eddie," I said.

"Yep, I guess we are," James replied.

"And we're being paid for it."

"Yes. It's a real case."

"Is that why you told Sergeant Worth you were keeping the office open? Why you're getting your own licence?"

"Maybe," he said. "Or maybe it's because she pushed me." He smiled at me. "I don't much like being pushed."

"Yeah, I know," I said. "But really? Just because she pushed you?"

"Nah, it wasn't that. Not really. I liked working with my uncle. I did. I realized it was just fear holding me back. So, I decided, what the heck. Right?" He smiled. "So, you jumping with me?"

If there was ever a time that I should have said "No frigging way," it was this one. But I was the one who had originally said yes to Honoria. And I was the one who kept trying to talk him into taking Honoria's case. So I had to say yes.

Didn't I?

"Yes." I leaned back in my seat and felt my shoulders relax. "Yes, I will."

"Excellent." He smiled. "We have a couple of hours before we pick up Honoria, and no matter what you say, you must be hungry. Come on, let's do lunch."

He had it all worked out. Honoria would be safe, and he and I could work together on figuring out who had actually killed Eddie.

A business. He was opening an actual business, and he wanted me involved. This could be good. In fact, it could be great.

"I'd love to," I said.

"Good." He glanced a smile in my direction, then pulled out into traffic.

Now that the pressure was off, I was ravenous. Lunch sounded great.

Eddie:
I Should Get Clean. Really, I Should

I WENT TO the tree.

Don't ask me why, because I wouldn't be able to give you a straight answer. Part of me hoped I'd find a junkie sleeping nearby, because my nerves were starting to jangle something fierce and I knew that soon I wouldn't be good for anything besides lying on the ground and puking my guts out. At least, that's the way it was when I was alive.

Another part of me—the dead part, I'm thinking—didn't want to do that. Didn't want to feel that anymore. Didn't particularly want to go through withdrawals, but really didn't want to get high again. Life's unfair. I got shit on for most of mine, but death? Death really levels the playing field. I was actually starting all over again. All I had to do was decide not to go that route. Get clean and stay that way. Then go on to the next thing. Whatever the hell that was.

There weren't many of my own people around at that hour. Nobody sleeping off a drunk or a high, anyhow. Just civilians in their nice clothes, with their lunches in brown paper sacks clutched in their hands, looking for a place to chow down. They all skittered past the churchyard and the tree, opting for the cement monument known as Churchill Square. Didn't blame them. I could still see blood, dirty brown and flaking away, but still there, on the tree, and the gouges on the branches were still bleeding clear sap. Only a freak would eat at a murder scene.

Yeah, I know, stupid. Seeing that horrible tree freaked me out, and I just wanted to get away from it. So I ran back to the park and waited for Crank to show up. I pretended it was so I could eavesdrop on whatever bit of gossip he was going to spill, but really, it was so I could hook up with one of his early customers and steal a hit. Just to get me over this rough patch.

I'm just as weak dead as I was alive.

Marie:
It Should Have Been the Beginning of a Beautiful Friendship . . . .

JAMES AND I picked up burgers and fries and headed back to the office. I thought we were going to eat together, but James clinked plastic glasses with me, said, "Welcome on board," then grabbed his food and headed for the inner office.

"Where are you going?" I asked.

"I have to set up a safe place for Honoria," he replied. "Just trying to get ahead of the curve for once. You okay out here by yourself?"

"I guess," I said, even though I wasn't. I'd been looking forward to sitting with him, talking to him while we ate. Just spending a little bit of time together that wasn't work-related.

But he walked into his office and shut the door on me. So, as I ate my burger, I decided to do a little more research. About Ambrose Welch, this time.

What I found was exactly nothing.

How could that be? If the police knew him, there had to be something online about him. But there was nothing. It was like he wasn't a real person.

"Maybe because he isn't," I muttered. Ambrose Welch was probably not his real name. But how would I find out his real name? I had no idea and reluctantly put that research aside.

I'd do more checking about Stewart, then. Specifically, more research about his son, Luke.

Luke had died at home, and I still hadn't determined how he'd died. Not really. But I was beginning to lean more toward drug overdose than bad drugs. There were no other newspaper articles about deaths related to bad drugs, anyhow. So I dug deeper.

I found his obituary notice and checked to see where donations in lieu of flowers could be sent, hoping I'd be able to tell from that what had happened to him.

I shouldn't have been surprised to see that good old dad had decided that donations to a cop fund were good enough for his son's memory. No clue about how he died from that.

So why was I trying to figure out how Luke died? Because I thought that maybe—just maybe—if Luke had died from a drug overdose, he might still be where he died, even if it was six months before.

And if Luke died at home, and was still there, he might be able to tell me whether his father had a hand in Eddie's death.

Yes, I was seriously thinking about going to the house of the police officer who had threatened both James and me, to talk to his dead son.

"Did you find something?"

I jumped, then glared at James, who had somehow snuck out of his office without my hearing. "Make more noise, would you?"

"I'm like a panther," he said, grinning. "So what did you find?"

I clicked everything closed. He didn't need to know I was checking out Stewart's son. Not yet. "Nothing much."

I half-expected him to demand to see what I was looking at, but all he did was grab his coat.

"Where are you going?"

"I found a place for Honoria to stay," he said. "I'm going to get her. Wanna come?"

I sure didn't want to be face to face with Honoria again. What if she said something about me? About my "gift." Even in passing. I inwardly shuddered and turned back to the computer. "I have a little more research to do. Mind if I sit this one out?"

"Oh come on," he said. "What, are you afraid that going to a bookstore could infect you or something?" He grinned, and I reluctantly grinned back, and just as reluctantly, reached for my sweater.

"I'm not afraid of going to a bookstore," I said. "Will you buy me a coffee?"

He shook his head. "I was half-hoping you'd want a book."

I shook my head.

"Magazine?"

Another head shake. "Just a coffee."

"You're a cheap date," he said. And then before I could respond to the date thing, he opened the door. "Let's go get our client."

"And a coffee," I said, and scooped up my purse.

He sighed. "And a coffee."

James saw the first tail before we'd gone five blocks.

He glanced into the rearview mirror, frowned, and looked again, more intently.

"Something wrong?" I asked.

"I think we're being followed," he said. He frowned more ferociously. "But I don't think it's the cops. Unless the cops are now driving Escalades."

I felt a jolt of pure fear. "Do you think it could be that Ambrose Welch guy?"

"No idea," he muttered. "Time to lose them, whoever they are."

I blinked. "You can do that?"

"Of course," he scoffed. "Watch me."

He zigzagged through the traffic, and for a while the SUV kept up. I watched it maneuver through the traffic, slewing and squealing its tires as its driver fought to keep it under control. Then I frowned and turned to James.

"I think somebody's following *them*," I whispered.

"What?" James glared into the rearview mirror. "Where?"

"The car behind the SUV. That dark blue one. I swear, it's going everywhere we go."

"Good grief," he muttered.

"Are they following the Escalade—or are they following us, too?" I asked.

James shrugged. "Who knows? Who cares? I'll lose 'em both."

And he did. As soon as we no longer saw either vehicle behind us, James pulled into a long-term parking garage and parked the car. We sat in it, in silence, and listened to the motor tick and ping as it slowly cooled.

"What do we do now?" I finally asked.

"We take a cab," James said. His face looked as tight as his voice sounded. "We have to get Honoria to the safe house, and then we need to figure out why we're being tailed by nearly everyone in the city."

Good grief.

The Chapters bookstore on Whyte Avenue was something to see, I have to admit. I didn't get down to the shabby chic part of the city much and had never even put a foot in the bookstore, though I had been to "Pigs Can Fly" across the street, once, when I was flush and wanted to find quirky cute Christmas gifts for my family units.

The thing that really hit me when James and I first walked in was the amount of stuff for sale that had nothing to do with books.

"What's the deal?" I asked, pointing at the multitude of shelves filled with everything under the sun that was not a book.

"It's a fad," James replied. "Just trying to get people like you in here. Once everybody's hooked on books again, it'll disappear."

I picked up a coffee mug with "Kiss Me I'm a Reader" on it, put it down, and picked up some sort of chocolate-covered candy that I'd never seen anywhere before. "I wouldn't count on it. We nonreaders are pretty set in our ways." I put down the candy and picked up a blanket. "This is pretty, though. And so soft . . ." I put it down, regretfully.

"What about the blanket, instead of a coffee?"

"I'm not buying you a blanket at a bookstore," he said. "Let's find Honoria. She's upstairs."

As we walked further in, James's head was on a swivel.

"Do you see anyone?"

"No." He glanced down at me, and then turned his gaze back to everywhere else. "Looks like we're alone."

"Good." I sighed out my relief. "Where's Honoria?"

"In the washroom at the back of the store."

We walked through what felt like miles of racks of books, to the far wall of the store, and then followed it to the restrooms.

"Go get her," he said, pointing. "She said she'd wait for us in there."

So I did. Much as I didn't want to.

I walked into the washroom and frowned. It appeared empty. I bent down, looking under the line of stall doors, but saw no feet.

"Honoria?" I called, softly. "Are you here?"

I heard noise from the stall furthest from the door. "Is that you, Marie?"

"Yes. James is just outside. We should go."

She opened the stall door and stepped out. She looked around, as though making sure for herself that we were alone, then hitched the big backpack she was carrying a little higher on her shoulder.

"This sure is a mess, isn't it?" she said. "Now I can't even go home."

I knew how that felt, and felt a twinge of sympathy for her.

"It won't be for long," I said.

"Can you guarantee that?" she asked.

I looked into her angry eyes, and then down at the floor. "No."

"Well, you better figure this out, quick," she said. "I'm not going to let my life fall apart. Not again. Fix it, any way you can."

"We're doing our best," I muttered, glancing longingly at the door.

"You better figure out how to do better," she replied. "You know what's at stake, after all."

Then, before I had a chance to even think of anything to say, she pointed to the door.

"Let's get out of here, shall we?"

I stared at her for a long moment, mesmerized by the tremour at the edge of her left eyelid. I should have felt more sympathy for her. Empathy, even. But all I felt was a dull, red anger. She'd threatened me. Again.

"Okay," I said, and held the door open, letting her leave first.

The escape from the bookstore was remarkably uneventful. We stepped out of the washroom, and James walked up to us. His head was back on the swivel again, so that he barely looked at either of us as he jerked his thumb in the direction of the stairs.

Without a word, Honoria and I followed him down the stairs and to the main entrance. The place was full of people, and I had a bad moment or two when I lost him in the stupid bookcases, but Honoria didn't seem to have the same problem, so I trailed along behind her, feeling absolutely like a hanger-on, and a useless one at that.

James got to the front entrance and held his hand up, indicating we should stop. So we did, good soldiers that we were, and I ran my hand over the incredibly soft blanket one last time as we waited for him to let us know it was time to leave.

It only took a moment, and he was back beside us.

"I have a cab," he said. "Let's go."

Honoria didn't even ask about the cab situation. Just followed James out to the crowded sidewalk, stepped into the cab, and settled on the seat with a small sigh.

But I didn't move.

"Come on," James said. "We gotta go."

"I have something I have to do," I said, and pointed down the street, vaguely. "Call me when you have her settled."

I didn't really want to ride in the cab with Honoria. Didn't want to go to her new hideout and sit around drinking herbal tea and chitchatting, or whatever James was going to do to calm down our brand-new client.

He could handle her. I was going to go and find Luke, Stewart's dead son, if he was still on this plane. And I was going to get answers. Finally.

I steeled myself for the inevitable fight and was surprised beyond measure when James said, "No problem." Almost too agreeably, I thought. And then, they were gone.

He hadn't even told me where he was taking her. Like it was a big secret, even from me.

"What? Don't you trust me?" I muttered, then gave my head a shake. Good grief! I was acting like a teenage girl. All he was doing was making certain that our client was safe.

I had to get over myself, get my part of the job done, and then she'd be gone. Out of our lives forever.

Just like I wanted.

I WATCHED THE cab disappear down the congested street, and then turned the other way. I had to get to Stewart's house and talk to Stewart's dead son. He would probably have information about his father—and, if his father was involved at all, he would have information about what happened to Eddie.

Then I could jog Eddie's memory, and get him to see—really see—who had done this to him. I believed this was what was holding him so tightly to this plane. If he knew the answer, that should give him the impetus to move on. It would also tell us who the police should really be investigating, and one way or the other, this would get Honoria out of our lives.

And then, true sleuth that I was, I caught the number eight bus to Stewart's house.

TO TELL YOU the truth, Stewart's place didn't look like a monster's house. It just looked like a nice enough split-level in an older section of north Edmonton, up by the Londonderry Mall. The grass needed to be cut, but it was only one week scruffy, not "call in the City and do something about this nightmare yard." But it still didn't make me like the man.

I walked up the sidewalk slowly, wishing I knew for sure that Stewart was still at work. I did not want to have a confrontation with him on his home turf. He could make my life extremely miserable if he even suspected I was checking up on him.

Mail was still in the mailbox. I hoped he was one of those freaks who felt compelled to empty his mailbox every day and that this was an indication that he was not yet home.

After a quick glance around, I walked up the steps and pressed the doorbell. As I heard it chime inside, I skittered down the steps and hid beside some bushes.

I stiffened as I heard a voice screech, "Nobody's home!" It was hard to tell if it was coming from inside or outside the house. I couldn't see into the big front windows, because the curtains were closed. If I was hearing Stewart, and if he pushed the curtains back to see who was harassing him, great. Just as long as he didn't actually see me, all would be well.

But if it was Luke, that was a different story. He didn't have the capacity to push back the curtains—or anything else. My only hope was, if I bothered him enough, he would want to see who it was. Then, maybe, I could talk him into stepping out on the front step to have a chat with me.

No movement from the curtains, and the yelling had stopped, so I snuck up the stairs and pressed the doorbell again, feeling like I was a kid playing a bad joke on a next-door neighbour. Then I scurried back to the bush and hid.

The screeching started as soon as the doorbell chimed. Whoever it was, he was pissed.

"I said no one's home! Get the hell away!"

Still no movement that I could see. I wondered if maybe whoever was yelling wasn't using the front window to check, but another window in the house. Maybe the one above my head. Now that would have been embarrassing. I scuttled back, still on my haunches, and tried to see into the window on the second floor. Nothing.

I waited a moment more, then squat-ran back to the front step. My legs were starting to cramp, and I thought, as I pressed the doorbell once more, that maybe I should start exercising or something.

"I said there is no one home!" The ghost—I assumed it was Luke—slammed through the front door, wild-eyed and spewing ecto goo everywhere. "Get the hell out of here!"

And then he stepped right into me.

He was cold, and angry. But overlaying all of it was a sadness so profound I almost burst into tears as I scrabbled my way down the stairs, clinging to the bannister to keep from falling. Luke wasn't a drug overdose. He was a suicide. I was definitely dealing with a suicide.

Made sense, actually. Suicides cling to this plane of existence even harder than drug overdoses. I personally think it has something to do with the people around them being so overwhelmingly distraught. It's like they cling to the spirit of the suicide, holding them here. And it makes suicides some of the crankiest spirits to work with, on top of everything else.

My reaction seemed to surprise him. He had been dead for months, and he'd obviously stepped into people before. Probably many, many times. But he'd obviously never had anyone do much more than a little shudder as though they'd been hit with a chill.

"What the hell?" he muttered and, luckily for me, stepped back into the door and away from me.

"Thanks," I said, trying to pull myself together so I could keep the ghost talking and maybe get some information out of him. I snuffled once and wiped the tears from my eyes, because the overwhelming sadness had receded as soon as I had lost contact with him. "That was—thanks."

"Who the hell are you?" He glared at me, his face floating in the door panel like a drowning victim in a lake of glass.

"My name is Marie Jenner," I said. I took one last swipe at my eyes and tried to arrange my features so I seemed friendly and nonthreatening. I had no idea if it worked or not, because Luke's drowning eyes stared at me like they were dead. Which, I guess, they were, but I wasn't used to seeing no emotion on a ghost's face. Not after stepping into him, and knowing, by feel, that he was suffering mightily. "I need to talk to you about your father. And Eddie."

"Eddie?" Finally, emotion touched his eyes. Unfortunately, it was confusion. "What about him?"

Crap. He didn't know about Eddie. As much as I hated telling the living about the passing of a loved one, I hated telling the dead even more. Don't ask me why. Guess it's because it feels like the dead have already been slapped enough.

"I—he died, Luke. I'm sorry."

Luke's eyes closed for a moment, then opened, and he stepped out of the door and into the warm, still air outside. "What happened? Overdose?"

"No." I tried desperately to think of a nice way to say what had to be said, but knew there was no way. "I'm sorry, Luke. He was murdered."

"Oh." Luke's voice stayed completely neutral, as though my words had not registered, but as he spoke that one-syllable sentence, his legs folded under him and he sank to the cement.

"I'm sorry," I said. "I thought your dad would've mentioned it."

Hoped, really, but Luke shook his head.

"It's not like he knows I'm here," he said. "And trust me, he doesn't get any visitors. Not since Mom died."

"Oh."

"Not your fault my dad's an A number one asshole." Then he looked at me with something close to humour on his face. "Is it? It would be nice to have someone else to blame, actually. If this is your fault, let me know. I am getting pretty bored hating him for the train wreck he made of our lives."

"Sorry," I said. "I only met the man a few days ago."

"Hey, I would have been surprised if you had been involved in any way with my father," he replied. "He doesn't care about women, much. Doesn't care about anything human, really. Just the law."

He said "the law" as though it was one of the dirtiest phrases he could think of. I imagined in this house it was.

"I do know Eddie, though," I said. I sat down on the lowest step of the front stairs, carefully staying away from Luke. I didn't want another crying jag. I needed to get information from him, and me blubbering like a fool wouldn't invite trust. Or sharing, I imagined.

"You date him or something?"

"No!" I almost laughed out loud at the idea of dating a ghost. That was almost as bad an idea as dating the living. "I met him after he—passed."

"Oh." He frowned as though trying to wrap his head around this bit of information. "So, what's the deal with you anyhow?"

"I—can see the dead."

"I get that," he replied. He showed impatience at my apparent thickness, and I couldn't really blame him. Talk about stating the obvious. "Is that your whole thing? You can see us, so you get off walking around and talking to us?"

"Not really." Like not at all. "I'm helping Eddie move on. He talked about you—so I thought you might have information about his death that could help him."

"And this information would be about my father, I assume."

Quick study, this one. "Eddie did say your father didn't like him much."

"Hated his guts would be more like it," Luke replied. "Do you really think he would have done that? Killed Eddie?"

"What do you think?"

"I think he's hurt a lot of people in his life. Wouldn't surprise me at all if he killed some of them." He frowned. "How long?"

"How long what?"

"Since Eddie—you know."

"Oh!" Dammit. Why couldn't I be better at this questioning thing? "It's been a few days. Why?"

"Because a while ago, Dad started drinking again. A lot. I thought it was odd."

"Do you think it could have been because of—you?"

Luke snorted humourlessly. "No. He held it together wonderfully well after I died. Got himself a new job and everything. No, it was after that, I think. A couple of months ago. But I could be wrong about that. The days start to bleed together, you know?"

I didn't answer him, because an old guy, walking an even older dog, was staring at me suspiciously. I didn't exactly blame him, because it would have looked like I was sitting on an empty stoop, talking to the closed door.

"We have company," I whispered.

"It's old man Rogers. Watch, he'll let that dog crap on our front lawn. I guarantee it."

I stood as old man Rogers stopped right in front of the house, and his ancient dog hunched and shuddered its way to the middle of the lawn and then did its business.

"See?" Luke yelled. "I told you. Every freaking day!"

The old man didn't respond, of course. But Luke was upset.

"I can't watch that," he said. "I'm leaving."

"Can I come back?" I whispered.

"Yeah," Luke said. "Tell Eddie I'm sorry he's dead. I wish—well, I wish it had worked out differently. For both of us."

I didn't answer him. And I didn't answer old man Rogers when he finally saw me and dragged his dog back on to the sidewalk, growling, "Can I help you?" in his whiny voice. I had to go back to the office and see if I could figure out what had happened that would have pushed Stewart back to drinking.

If his son's death hadn't done it, what could have happened? What did he do?

THE BUS RIDE was quiet, and I got back to the office with a new game plan. I'd found Stewart's son, and something had happened to Stewart a few months before that had pushed him back on the alcoholic train. I'd go back online and see if I could find anything that had happened in the city around that time that could have sent him over the edge.

I knew this didn't have anything to do with Eddie's death, but I was desperate to understand all the players, and Stewart was a big one. I was certain of it. If I could understand him, I could understand the rest of it. I hoped.

James was back, already holed up in his office, doing his version of typing, which was two finger hunting and pecking and a lot of under his breath cursing. He did not acknowledge me when I walked into his office and stood in front of the desk. And I even waited for a second or two.

"So, how did it go?" I finally asked. "Is Honoria all settled in?"

He pressed a couple more buttons before he looked up at me.

"Yes." Then he looked back down at the screen.

What was his damage? "I think I have some new information about Stewart. I just have to check it out online."

He grunted something that could be considered affirmative if a person was feeling open-minded. I was not, but I decided to take the nice route instead of diving right back into nasty. After all, we were officially working together. We'd drunk on it and everything.

"What are you working on?" I asked.

"Registering for a course." He didn't look up. Kept tapping away painfully and squinting as though the type was way too small. He *was* angry. But it couldn't have been anything I'd done. Could it?

"What course?"

He pressed another button and leaned back, gripping his forehead. "I have seventeen days to get my private investigator's licence. Remember?"

"Oh." Right. Sergeant Worth's ultimatum. "You found something online?"

"Yes." He pulled his hands away from his face and stared at the screen. "I'm taking an online certification course."

"Oh. And that's good, right?"

"No, that's not good." He pushed his chair away from the desk long enough to glare at me, then wheeled it back and squinted at the screen again. "That's pathetic. I should be going to a real school, or still learning under my uncle, or off mountain climbing in the Rockies somewhere. I should not be registering for an online course. 'Be a detective in two weeks, guaranteed.' Good grief!"

"You like to mountain climb?" I asked. I never would have guessed it.

"Yes, but that's not the point." He pushed himself away from the desk again, as though the sight of the screen could no longer be tolerated. "I don't even know why I'm bothering with this."

What? What had happened? We'd decided to run this business, together. Hadn't we? We even celebrated with hamburgers. What was I missing?

"Are you all right?" I asked. "Did something happen with Honoria?"

"She's fine," he said shortly. "But I'm no good at this stuff. We haven't had a phone call since all Uncle's old clients found out he died. Well, except for the one today. It's on the machine."

"Another job?" I was really confused now. "Isn't another job a good thing?"

"Go listen to it," he said, acidly. "Actually, there are two messages. The other one's for you."

"Nobody ever calls me here." Basically because I have no friends. "Who was it?"

"Just go listen." He turned back to his computer, sighing hugely.

"It wasn't my mother, was it?" I felt my throat tighten. If something happened to my mother— But James waved his hand dismissively.

"No. It has nothing to do with her."

I walked to my desk and pressed the button that would replay all the voicemail messages. James had been right. We hadn't received many—read any—calls about work since word had gotten out that James the Elder was dead. I suspected from James's demeanor that this was not going to be a big case.

"Hi," a female voice chirped. "I got your name out of the Yellow Pages. I need somebody to find my lost dog. Do you guys do that?"

A lost dog. Great. No wonder James was in the depths of despair. I wrote down the woman's name and phone number. At the very least we needed to call her back, and who knew, maybe it could actually turn into something. I like dogs. Could be a great sideline.

Thinking about finding lost dogs, I missed half of the next message. When I finally came back to reality, all I caught was a man's voice, which I did not recognize, reciting a telephone number.

"Dammit," I muttered, and pressed the replay button.

As the message played again, I understood exactly why James was in such a dark mood.

It was Jerome Leary, of Leary Millworks. He had been terribly impressed with the resume I'd faxed him and wanted to set up an interview as soon as possible.

With fingers that felt frozen, I wrote down the phone number, then deleted both messages. And then I thought, furiously. I hadn't mentioned a thing to James about applying for another job. Had actually forgotten I'd even done it. But now, here it was. On the machine. And he'd heard it.

"It doesn't mean anything," I finally said. He didn't answer.

"I'm not kidding. I just threw my resume in as a lark—just to see if I'd get a bite." That wasn't exactly the truth. I'd sent away my resume because Honoria was blackmailing me about the whole seeing ghosts thing. But I didn't want another job. Not really.

After all, I'd just told James I'd jump. I'd committed to him and his business.

"Are you going to answer me?" I asked.

"What's there to answer?" he replied. "We have exactly one client, and you're looking for another job."

"There's the dog woman," I started, then shut my mouth. Looking for a lost dog would not pay the rent. Anybody's rent.

"See? That's what I mean," he said, and I could hear the self pity oozing through his voice. "What's the point of even trying? I was fooling myself, thinking I could make a go of this. And now, with you leaving—"

"I told you, the resume was just a lark! And what do you mean, you're not built for this? Your uncle didn't leave this business to you because you have the same name as him, no matter what he said. You have a gift for this. You can't just give it up!"

"Back at ya!" he bellowed.

Silence reigned as we both thought about what having a gift for this actually meant. At least, I assumed James was thinking about it. He could have been playing a computer card game for all I knew. I was thinking about it, though. Hard.

I'd convinced James to take the Clairvoyant Honoria job because I had the dead guy and I thought we'd be able to figure out who killed him quickly and quietly. So far, a big fat no to both, and now our client was on the run. James was doing his best to figure out what was really going on, but I wasn't any kind of help. Eddie remembered next to nothing, and even his best friend Luke hadn't been able to give me any good information. The dead could let you down, no doubt about it.

And then there was Honoria. Good old clairvoyant Honoria who'd managed to spook Eddie so much that I knew I'd never be able to talk him into being in the same room with her, even if it was what we needed to bust this case wide open.

Bust this case wide open. Huh. Nothing was going to bust this case wide open. Nothing from my end, anyhow. All I could do was talk to ghosts, and I wasn't even very good at that. Eddie was no closer to remembering anything than he was at the beginning of this adventure. All I could see was this case stretching out before us forever. With Eddie hanging around, getting high and bugging me. Forever.

That thought put my mood right in the toilet.

"I'm no good at this," I snapped. "No matter what you think." Then my stupid throat tightened, and I sniffed.

All I did was lie to him, because of my stupid gift. And I'd probably keep lying to him, until he decided he didn't need a lying liar around him anymore.

He needed to find himself someone who was just a good secretary slash receptionist. And that was all. No goofy gifts that were a gift to no one. No baggage. And no more lies. He didn't need any of it.

I would take my lies and leave.

I picked up the phone, dialed the number to Leary Millworks, and set up an interview for three days from that moment. I knew James could hear me, because I heard him rattling around in that office like he was looking for something big, blunt, and heavy to throw at me, but I didn't care. I was doing this for his own good.

I even told him that. "I'm doing this for your own good, James. You don't need me around mucking up your chances for a happy life."

Yes, I actually said that to him. He was quiet for a few moments. He even stopped rattling around.

"I can't believe you said that to me," he finally muttered. "Sometimes I think you really are crazy, Marie."

Pushed my buttons, big time. So I did the only thing I could think to do. I yelled at him.

"Go straight to hell, James! Straight to hell!"

And then I went to Jasmine's.

I hoped she had more of that scotch left. I felt the need for many, many drinks.

Eddie:
I'm Going to Miss That Girl

ON THE WAY over to the park, I decided to find Noreen and use her to get high. Nasty words, "using her," but that's exactly what I'd decided to do. And it wouldn't be like I hadn't used her before.

I was feeling worse than I had in a while. Since I was dead, actually. Jumpy and unwell. Achy and kind of sick. That was the preamble to withdrawal. Recognized it well enough to know I really didn't want to go down that road again. So, I was looking for my good friend Noreen, so I could use her. One more time.

I walked into the park and looked around, but I didn't see her on the grass or near the benches. This was unusual for her. She always showed up around this time, got high, then went to work. She told me once it was a lot easier to work high, since she had to work longer and longer hours. She figured it was because her looks kind of left. Guess even the dirtbags who are looking for a quick BJ after work are only willing to pay top dollar for somebody pretty. She used to be. But not anymore.

I wandered around the park, but didn't see her, so I checked the alley behind the park. At first I thought it was just the usual suspects back there, but as I wandered into the perpetual gloom of the alley, a ruckus started near the other end.

"Call 911!" somebody cried. "She's dying!"

So, I went to see who had bought it. Don't mean to be cold

about the whole thing, but it happens often enough that the horror of it can wear thin. Guess it's a bit like being a soldier in a war. After a while, the only time you really see how fucked up your life is, is in your dreams. The rest of the time, you just do your job, no matter what it is.

At that moment, my job was going down that alley to see who had died.

I pushed around the people, trying to stay away from touching them too much, because now that I'd made the decision to get high with Noreen, I didn't want to sully it with any of the shit the other fools were taking. I bobbed and weaved until I couldn't help but go through someone, then sort of psychically held my nose as I walked through a couple of them. That actually worked. Didn't get much more than a bit of a jolt of whatever they were on. Almost hooked into a guy I knew who did meth—but he was also HIV positive, and I didn't want to mess with that. Not even dead.

I finally got to the middle of the mob and looked down at the person who had died. I felt something like a punch to the gut when I realized the broken stick figure on the ground was Noreen. Noreen, who had been like a sister to me since I hit the streets.

Her eyes looked like dead glass. The foam slowly leaking from her lips trickled to the pavement. I wasn't the only one who screamed when her arms jerked spasmodically and the foam spewed across her face.

"She's not dead!" somebody—might have been me—cried. "Do something!"

But of course, nobody did. They all knew it was too late. The dead eyes told everybody in the alley that.

"I look like shit, don't I?"

I glanced up, and my heart jumped in my chest—well, not really, but you know what I mean. Noreen was standing beside me, looking down at her own cooling body.

"I always hoped I'd look better when I died," she said. "You know, do one of those go to bed and die in my sleep things, but I guess that doesn't happen for most of us."

"Noreen?"

For a second, staring at her misty spirit standing beside me, I thought I'd been given a chance to actually say good-bye to somebody who mattered. When she didn't react, I felt like crying.

Looked like even that was a no-go.

But then she shifted, as though surprised to hear her own name. Even though everybody in that alley was whispering her name as word of her death passed through the various groups and out into the park. And then she looked at me. Really looked at me.

"Eddie," she said, and smiled, wiping the foam that had gathered on her lips. "You came to see me off. Nice."

"Noreen," I said again, feeling stupid even as I said it. Of course it was Noreen.

"Let's get out in the sun, shall we?" she said. "Doesn't look like I'll be working today. We can talk."

I followed her, through the press of gawkers, out of the alley, and into the park. We walked to an empty bench and sat. She held her face up to the sunlight and sighed contentedly.

"I didn't give myself much of a chance to do this while I was alive," she said. "Guess it won't hurt to do it now, before I move on."

"You—you know about moving on?"

She looked over at me with that look on her face I remembered too well. It was the "what did you think, boy" look. "Of course. Didn't you?"

"But I thought—Marie told me drug addicts have a hard time realizing they are dead." I frowned. "I'm sure that's what she said."

"Small chick? Big eyes? Looks like she's waiting for the next slap to the chops?"

"Could be."

"I seen her at your tree. And here. And I got a strange vibe from her. Like there was more to her than big eyes. So, she can see you, huh?"

She chuckled and wiped more of the foam, of which there seemed to be a never-ending supply, off her chin. "What, you needed to hire somebody to understand what anybody with half a brain should know on their own?"

"I didn't hire her," I protested. "She just showed up. Said she'd help me—"

"Give your head a shake, boy. You should be able to do this on your own. It's like life, man."

"But—"

"No buts, Eddie. You gotta get yourself together, make a decision or two about what you want out of the next bit, and then do it."

"But—"

"What did I tell you about that?"

So I shut my mouth and sat beside her silently as she enjoyed the warm autumn sun.

I couldn't remember the last time I'd just sat in the sun. I started thinking that now that Noreen was dead, and a ghost, we could hang out together. I wouldn't need to be around that wacky Marie chick anymore. I could be back with my own kind. I'd show Noreen how to get high, and then we'd be just fine. Better than before, because we didn't have to do demeaning things like dumpster diving and giving BJs to get cash.

"This is nice," I said. "We should do this every day."

Noreen shook her head. "I'm not sticking around, Eddie."

"But—"

"You back to that again?"

"No. Well, yeah." I shook my head, not understanding at all. "Why won't you stay? This is nice, isn't it?"

"It is, Eddie. No doubt about it." She leaned her head back and closed her eyes, smiling as the warm sun touched her pocked face. "I hope I remember to do this a lot more, the next time around."

"What do you mean?"

She sighed deeply and turned toward me. "You really don't understand any of this, do you? At all."

"Any of what?" I was starting to feel supremely stupid. I should be the one showing her the ropes. After all, I'd been dead a long time, and she—well, her body—hadn't even been picked up off the street yet.

"This is the time to make some decisions, so we move on."

"To what?"

"To whatever." She shook her head, as though disturbed that she couldn't make the retard—that would be me—understand something that was crystal clear to her. "That's what you're supposed to do, now. Look at the way you lived your life, figure out what you'd like to do better, and then move on. To the next place. Or stage, or something."

I was beginning to feel like I was being stubborn in my

stupidity, but I really couldn't wrap my head around what she was saying. Marie had talked about me moving on, but I thought I had to understand how or why I had died. Who had killed me. Yet, here was Noreen, talking about how I lived my life being the key.

"So you're leaving?"

"Absolutely!" She said it so cheerfully, I felt like crying.

"But I can show you how to get high—"

She hushed me with a flick of her hand. "I don't want to hear about it. For God's sake, that shit finally killed me." She motioned to the crowd still hanging around the mouth of the alley. "Why would I want to go back to it, now that I'm free?"

"You're free?" I couldn't believe I was hearing her say that, and I started to feel, around the sadness at her passing, anger at her. "How the hell—"

"Once the body's gone, the only thing holding you to that shit is your mind. If you decide you need it, then you need it. Me? I'm not going that way."

She stood up and stretched, a lazy half-smile on her foaming mouth. "I wasted my life. Let stuff that happened to me when I was growing up rule the way I lived the rest of it. I am not doing that again."

"Again?" I stumbled after her, trying to keep up, but she walked more sure-footedly than I'd ever seen her. "But you're dead."

"You really don't get this, do you?" she said, stopping so suddenly I almost ran into her. I jerked to a stop, suddenly afraid of what I'd find if I walked into her misty form.

"No," I said. "I don't get any of this. It wasn't our fault we ended up here. We *talked* about this!"

I felt frantic. She was my sister, for God's sake. We'd grown up on these streets together. She had to remember. She had to stay.

"Eddie, my dear, we both wasted a lot of time—our lives, to be exact—blaming others for what happened to us. We could have done something good with our lives. Maybe even something noble, but we didn't. We hung out here and got high. Every day. And blamed our fathers. Every fucking day. We never moved on from that moment in time. It's like we were trapped in amber."

She was right about that. We had done that. Blamed our fathers. Even after I'd figured out that mine wasn't that bad—not as bad as hers, anyhow—I'd still played the blame game. Because after the blame game, we got high.

"But this is the next part," she said. "We aren't bound by the rules we made for ourselves anymore. Well, I'm not, anyhow. I promised myself if I ever got out of this mess, I'd do something that meant something. No more blame game, no more waste. No more hurting myself to shut out what happened to me when I was little. I want to live, Eddie. Really live."

"But you're dead, Noreen." I wished I could hold her hand. Wished I could hold her to me, because I could feel her slipping away, even though she was standing right beside me. I even reached out my hand, but pulled back when I saw bright little lights forming around her.

"I know, Eddie. But I've decided to give life another go." She smiled at me, and even with the foam, it was a sweet smile. Finally, there was no anger on her face. She looked ten years younger than she had alive.

Twinkly lights began to buzz around her like fireflies. Most were white, but some were red, and blue, and there were even a couple of black ones. They flitted around her, covering her in sparkle. It was pretty and frightening, all at that same time.

"What's going on?"

"It's time for me to leave."

"But I want you to stay!" I wailed those words, sounding like a fucking kid. And then I did start to cry. I couldn't help myself. "Please stay with me."

"I don't want to," she replied, the number of flitting lights growing and growing, until it was hard to see her in the middle of it all. "And you shouldn't want to stay, either. This part is done. For both of us, Eddie. Just make a decision, and then let the rest of it go."

Her voice was getting as misty as her body, if that makes any sense. It was like she was talking to me from a long way away, even though she was standing right in front of me.

"What do you mean, make a decision!" I cried. "Please! Stay!"

She didn't answer me. As the snowstorm of flickering lights flew around her, she reached her hands up over her head and laughed, delightedly. It was the happiest sound I'd ever heard come out of her mouth the whole time I'd known her. It didn't even sound like her, to be honest.

And then I could no longer see her in the light.

"Noreen!" I screamed.

I ran toward the spot where she'd been, and the bright lights stung me. I waved my arms to drive them away. As I waved, they disbursed, flying up into the still autumn sunlight. Then everything about Noreen was gone, and I was truly, truly alone.

I dropped to my knees, and then onto my face on the dusty grass. A siren announced the arrival of the ambulance finally coming to take away Noreen's body, but I didn't give a shit. I just lay facedown on the grass, and I cried.

AFTER I PULLED myself together, I went back to Marie's office. I had some serious questions for her.

The big problem was, she was gone for the day. And from the way that James guy was banging around, I took it that there'd been a fight. Another one. I didn't quite figure why these two even hung out together.

"Either lay her or move on," I muttered when I heard him hammer on the computer keyboard and curse. "You are letting her wind you up way too much, man."

Of course, he didn't answer me. He couldn't hear me. All he could do was squint at the computer screen, tap away at the keys, and curse a steady stream.

I went to the window and watched the living out doing their thing as the sun slowly set and the black took over.

Noreen had been right. Needing the drugs was definitely all in my head. I had been without a hit for almost a day, but I felt nothing past sadness. I was pretty sure this had a lot more to do with Noreen dying than with me not being high.

So why hadn't Marie told me about this? If she had, I wouldn't have bothered getting high. Maybe. At least I would have known I had a choice about it. Back when I was alive, I never felt like I had a choice. It was either get high or get sick. And nobody wants to get sick.

"You should have told me," I muttered, staring out at the black and listening to James hammer away at the keys, then finally lie down to sleep on that cot in his office. "You should have explained all of this to me."

I had a feeling I was playing that blame game again. All right, so Marie hadn't told me, but someone had, and now I knew. So why didn't I just make a decision about what to do with a brand new life or brand new next stage, or whatever the hell it was that I had, and disappear in a cloud of white lights, just like Noreen had?

Short answer? Because I wanted to give Marie hell. She should have told me what my options were. Told me I even had options. Given me a hint about any of it. I shouldn't have had to wait for my street sister to die to understand what was going on in my own death.

"Bitch," I muttered under my breath as I watched the streets slowly come alive with those of us who inhabited them after the sun went down. "You shoulda warned me about all of this."

Marie:
Maybe Drinking Isn't the Best,
When Life Is Going to Hell

I WOKE UP when the alarm went off, reached over to shut it down, and fell off the couch. I hit the rug with a thunk that rattled my skull and reminded me just how much scotch Jasmine and I had consumed the night before.

"Unhh." My head swam, and I stayed on the floor for a minute, trying to get my bearings. Luckily the alarm—which was actually in Jasmine's bedroom and nowhere near me—was now off. All I heard was softly playing cartoon music, with the occasional "Boinng!" thrown in for good measure.

I opened one eye, and saw Billie, Jasmine's youngest, parked in front of the TV with a big bowl of some sort of cereal, eating enthusiastically.

He glanced over at me, saw my open eye, and smiled. "Can I turn it up now?"

"Sure." I put one hand under me, and then another, and slowly pulled myself more or less upright. "What are you watching?"

He named some cartoon I'd never heard of, and I watched with him for a minute, until I was certain that I could actually navigate to the kitchen without falling down again. Then I got up and shakily walked through the big doorway, holding onto the wall as if it were my best friend on earth. Which, at that moment, it was.

Jasmine was up, drinking coffee and reading the newspaper. She grinned at me wickedly.

"How you feeling?"

"Horrible." I shuffled my way to the cupboard and pulled out a cup. "The coffee smells good, though."

"My special blend." She glanced at the paper, then back at me. "Want something to eat?"

"Nope." I poured a cup and shuffled over to the table. "Quite possibly, never again."

"It was good scotch though, wasn't it?"

I groaned. "Don't remind me."

She laughed as she pushed the cream and sugar in my direction, then went back to her newspaper.

"What are you reading?" I asked.

"There was another death at that park downtown," she replied. "Looks like this one was an overdose, though." She sighed sharply and turned the page. "I don't understand why they don't just close that thing. A waste of prime real estate, if you ask me."

I stirred my coffee, wincing. Even the tinkle of the spoon on ceramic hurt my head. "I may not survive," I muttered.

"You will, girl. You know you will."

"I don't know if I want to," I said. My voice sounded sullen and whiny. "Do you have orange juice? Maybe that will help."

"In the fridge."

The orange juice tasted fabulous, and my headache abated. Not gone completely, but certainly no longer taking off the top of my head. Then I remembered why I'd decided to drink so very much the night before and groaned again.

"James is so mad at me," I said. "What am I going to do?"

"We talked about this last night," Jasmine said, pushing aside the newspaper. "Or don't you remember?"

I thought for a second, and things started oozing their way into my memory. With it came some—actually, a lot—of embarrassment. "Oh, yeah. We *did* talk about him, didn't we?"

"You actually didn't talk about much else," Jasmine said. "Are you ever going to tell him how you really feel about him?"

"Maybe. Someday. When I pull my life together." I sipped the coffee. "Tastes great."

"Yes, I know, and I'm not letting you change the topic, girl. You have to talk to him about how you feel."

"But—"

"I don't want to hear another 'but' out of your mouth. You know that's just you trying to figure out a way to get around talking to him."

"But—" I snapped my mouth shut and tried to figure out how to say the next sentence without starting with a *but*. Couldn't come up with any way to do it, so sipped more coffee.

"Better," Jasmine said.

"Whatever."

Jasmine laughed. "You know you have to do it eventually."

"No I don't," I replied stubbornly. "If we don't get any more work there, I won't even be working with him anymore. I'll move on, he'll move on, and that will be the end of it."

That last comment made me cringe. Even though I knew it would be better for both of us if we didn't pursue anything romantic, the thought of never seeing him again felt really wrong. I buried my face in my cup morosely.

"Well, from what it sounded like, you have at least one more case," Jasmine replied. "And according to you, that could be the beginning of great things."

I frowned, feeling my headache sneaking back. "What other case?"

"Veronica Stafford. You're going to find her dog, Gypsy."

"Who?" Headache screamed back, and I grabbed my head. "I'm going to find her what?"

"That girl who phoned your office and left you a number. You called her last night."

I stared at Jasmine, barely able to comprehend her words. "I called the dog girl?" I finally whispered. "I don't remember that."

"Oh yes, you had a great little chat with her. I did tell you not to, but you wouldn't listen. And you told her you'd be happy to take her case. Said it would be a cake walk."

"A cake walk?" I closed my eyes, certain they were about to begin bleeding. "I actually called that girl and told her I'd find her dog?"

"Yes." Jasmine, evil woman that she is, grinned at me, obviously enjoying the heck out of torturing me. "You did."

"Did I talk about how much I was going to charge her?" I hoped I hadn't, because there was a possible out for me. I'd just call her back and tell her I was going to charge an outrageous sum—

"Oh yeah," Jasmine said, leaning back in her chair and grinning. "Gave her a real deal. Because she sounded like such a nice person."

"Did I actually say that?"

"Yes, you did. I swear, I thought you two were going to be BFFs before the end of that phone call."

"Oh, Jasmine!" I put my poor pounding head down on the table and rocked it back and forth a couple of times, until vertigo kicked in and I stopped, fast. "What am I going to do?"

"You're going to have a shower, pull yourself together, then go find a dog."

"Do I have to?" I knew I sounded like one of her kids, whining that life wasn't fair and all that, but I couldn't stop it. Jasmine pointed at the hallway that led to the bathroom.

"Yes, you do. You told her you would, so you're going. You have to keep your word, don't you?"

"Yeah."

Jasmine laughed and turned back to her paper. "Have fun."

"Kiss my ass," I muttered, glancing around to make sure none of her kids were in hearing range. "And I mean it."

"I'm sure you do," she said distantly, already engrossed in another article. "You wrote down all her particulars on a piece of paper in the living room. Just so you know."

"I mean it," I said, again. "Really."

As I looked over the information I'd gathered, bits of the telephone conversation I'd had with Veronica seeped into my brain. Her high, breathless voice describing Gypsy and how she, like, smiles. Veronica was twelve. I was sure of it.

"Good grief," I muttered, dropped the paper on the coffee table, and then went to take a shower.

"So how does one actually go about finding a lost dog?" I muttered as I worked shampoo into my hair without tipping my head either too far forward or back, because I was still dealing with some pretty bad vertigo, and did not want to find myself on my ass on the floor of the shower, on top of everything else.

First thing was, call the city pound. Then, if they didn't have him—no, her—check to see if she had been turned into the Humane Society. Then, and only then, I would head out to the off-leash area, the place Veronica said she'd been walking the dog when it disappeared.

I was going to need a car—or somebody with a car. The pound was at one end of the city, and the Humane Society at the other. And then the off-leash area was way down in the deep southwest somewhere. Which meant I would have to talk to James. Perfect.

"What have I done?" I muttered as I rinsed the shampoo from my hair.

Made my life way more complicated than it had been the day before. That's what I had done.

"Do you have to sit there and listen?" I asked Jasmine an hour later, after I'd made all the phone calls and ascertained that Gypsy the dog had not been picked up by the pound or been delivered to the Humane Society. Now I had to get out to the off-leash area, and there was no way to do that without getting a ride.

"Yes, I do," she said, a fresh cup of coffee in her hand and a smug look on her face.

"Don't you have to go to work?"

"Not for another hour." She gestured with her cup. "Ignore me! Act like I'm not even here. Just make the call."

"Jesus." I jabbed the buttons so hard, I was amazed I didn't snap a nail. I listened as the phone rang twice, and made to disconnect. "He's obviously not there."

"Give it a minute," Jasmine said. "It's only 8:30 in the morning. Maybe he isn't up yet. You did say he's still staying at the office, didn't you?"

"Yes." I sighed, listening as the phone rang twice more. "Is that enough, Mom?" I asked sarcastically, then jumped nearly out of my skin when James picked up.

"I knew he'd be there," Jasmine said as I stuttered through my hellos and listened to his voice ice considerably when he realized it was me. I slapped my hand over the mouthpiece.

"He's pissed that I'm calling," I snapped. "I'm hanging up."

"Just talk to him!" Jasmine yelled. "It's a case, for heaven's sake!"

"I have a case," I said to James, then rushed through the gist of it without giving him much time to say anything past, "Oh."

He didn't seem surprised that I'd called the lost dog girl or that I'd taken the case. He didn't sound thrilled, either, but at least some of the ice thawed from his voice when he said he'd be there in twenty minutes to pick me up.

I was going to say something about the car, and all the people we had tailing us the day before, but I didn't. He'd handle it, I was sure. Just like he had before.

My hands were shaking when I finally disconnected.

"There," Jasmine said with a smug look on her face. "I told you it wouldn't be so hard."

"Yes it was!" I yelled. "Good grief! And now I have to go out and look for a lost frigging dog. Because I got drunk last night and said I would."

"At least it's not raining," Jasmine said.

"Shut up." I went to find my coat and boots, so I didn't have to look at her anymore. This was all so ridiculous, I could barely believe it.

James showed up with a pretty good attitude, all things considered. He drank coffee and joked with Jasmine as I ran around pulling myself together, and then we left.

Jasmine was right. It was a nice morning, the air crisp and clear. I almost felt like I would survive. Until I saw Eddie skulking in the back seat of the car, looking absolutely furious. Seeing him brought the pounding behind my eyes back.

I glanced up and down the street, looking for vehicles I didn't recognize.

"Don't worry," James said. "I wasn't followed."

"Good," I said.

"Now, are you going to tell me what made you decide to take this case?" James opened the car door for me. "I thought you were leaving."

"I don't know," I replied miserably. "The girl needs her dog. I thought we could help. Stupid, huh?"

"No," he replied, and gave me a real smile. It felt like ages since I'd seen him smile, even though it had only been a day. "It's not stupid. She asked us for help. So we help."

"Thanks," I whispered.

"And who knows?" he continued. "Maybe if it goes well, you can forget that interview and stick with me. Heck, this could be our 'thing.'"

"Like that guy in that movie," I said. "You know the one?"

"Yeah," he replied. "I thought it was pretty funny."

"So did I."

He almost closed the car door, then stopped. "I'm sorry."

"For what?" I asked. If anyone should have apologized, it was me.

"For yelling about you looking for another job. You can take whatever job you want. I was being an ass."

"I don't want the other job." I spoke in a rush, to get all the words out before I did something stupid, again. "I really don't. I'd much rather work with you. If that's all right."

"It's absolutely all right." He smiled, and he pointed at a to-go cup in the holder by my left hand. "I brought you coffee."

Then he shut the door, and I was momentarily alone with furious Eddie.

"Why didn't you tell me about this moving on shit?" he asked. "Why did I have to wait for Noreen to clue me in?"

"Noreen?" I grabbed my coffee and popped the top, breathing in the excellent scent and hoping this wouldn't turn into one of those horrible three-way conversations that never seemed to go my way. I watched James walk slowly around the front of the car and knew we had only moments before he was in. "Can we talk later? Please?"

"Yeah," he said, surprising me a lot. "I want your full attention. Because I need some real answers out of you."

"Thanks," I breathed.

"I'm not doing it for you," he replied shortly. He sat back in the seat with his arms folded over his chest as James opened his door and got in.

"Where are we going?" he asked.

I pulled the sheet of paper out of my pocket and read off the address of the dog park, where Veronica had last seen her dog.

"She said the dog just took off over a hill and never came back," I said. "I'm honestly not sure how we are going to find him. Her."

"We'll start there," James said, pulling the car into traffic. "How's the coffee?"

"Excellent." I smiled at him. "Thanks."

"What breed are we looking for?"

"A lab," I said. "A black lab. Her name is Gypsy." I looked

down at the sheet of paper with my drunken writing scrawled all over it. "She has a red collar, with a heart shaped dog tag. At least, that's what Veronica told me."

"You talked to her last night?"

"Apparently."

"You drinking again?"

I stiffened. Whether I had a couple of drinks was none of his business. "Just a couple. Why?"

"I can smell it on you."

"And?"

"You seem to be doing that a lot, lately."

"And?" I felt my anger build, and behind it, my stupid headache.

"Nothing. Just an observation." He changed lanes, then glanced over at me. "Any particular reason?"

"No." I looked out my side window, so I didn't have to look at him. "Just felt like it."

"All right."

Even though his voice sounded neutral, I was certain I heard judgment in it. God! People judged about everything. I took another sip of coffee and watched the streets blur by. I was tired of always having to explain my every action to everybody. Why couldn't they all just leave me alone?

Because I pulled them into my ridiculous schemes, with my drunk calling and other stuff. That's why. I morosely buried my face in my coffee and tried to bury the nasty thoughts, hoping we'd get to the dog park fast.

Luckily, both the guys in the car left me alone. The dead one because he was super pissed with me for not giving him enough information about moving on, even though I was sure I had. And the live one? I hazarded a glance at him. He didn't look pissed, but he had been the night before.

I hoped we'd find the dog quickly. We seriously needed one in the win column, even if we were working for a twelve-year-old.

Eddie:
Playing at the Dog Park

EVEN THOUGH I was pissed at Marie, that dog thing was something to watch, I must say.

I was going to stay in the car, but there was a bunch of dogs running around, sniffing the air and each other's butts, and looking like they were having such a good time, I decided what the hell and went out into the middle of the field to watch them.

Funny. Didn't know dogs could feel when a ghost is around, but I learned the hard way. Caused a bit of a dog pile as they all rushed over to me, which caused a couple of fights. It wasn't even the big dogs that started snapping and snarling, it was the little guys. A Jack Russell terrier ran up, peed in the general direction of my leg, and hit a big bull mastiff, which ruffled his feathers. Both owners called their animals with angry looks that told everyone there they felt if the other owner had just bothered to teach their dog any manners whatsoever, this unfortunate incident wouldn't have happened.

I moved away from the dog pile as the owners sorted things out. I was looking for Marie, but when I saw that the dogs were following me again, decided what the hell and led them all on a merry chase around the field. Probably looked funny as hell, a pack of dogs chasing absolutely nothing, but it was fun. The sun hit my face, warming me, and the dogs barked and ran behind me, sounding like they were having as much fun as I was. Then they dropped off, one by one, as owners regained control, until I was left alone.

I heard Marie calling "Hey, Gypsy? Come here girl!" over and over again, in a small grove of trees, and jogged in her direction.

Then her voice changed. "Oh, Gypsy," she said, and the sadness oozed through those words until I didn't want to see what she'd found. Thought about turning and walking back to the other dogs, all out running around enjoying the hell out of life, and leaving Marie with her dog and the death that seemed to follow that girl wherever she went.

But I didn't. I walked over to her, even as James smashed through the underbrush from the other direction, calling, "Marie, are you all right?"

My guess was, she wasn't all right. Not at all.

Marie:
Moving On Gypsy

I FOUND GYPSY in the creek that meandered through the trees at the back of the dog park. It looked like she'd drowned. I hoped for a second that it wasn't Gypsy, until I saw the collar. Red, with a heart-shaped ID tag. I'd found Veronica's dog.

I heard soft growling coming from the thick brush by the creek. I glanced over, afraid for a second that I was dealing with another dog, or maybe a wild animal. Then, I saw the aura. And the red collar.

It was Gypsy's spirit, still hanging around her body.

Eddie skittered up to me, and I noticed a half-smile on his face.

"Having fun?" I asked.

"Some," he said. "But you're still not off the hook." He pointed at the carcass in the creek. "Gypsy?"

"Yep." Then I pointed to the bush. "And there's that."

Eddie bent and stared for a long moment at the glowing figure of the dog crouched in the thick underbrush.

"Ghost dog," he said, rather unnecessarily. "Cool. Can I keep her?"

"No," I whispered.

"I'm just kidding," he said. "Mostly. Looks like she doesn't want to have anything to do with me."

He held out his hand to the spirit, as if to prove his point. The dog ignored him completely. She was staring at me, and then she began to creep out of the underbrush, haunches shaking, and the hair on the nape of her neck standing upright.

"She looks scared."

"She is," I said, holding my hand out to the ghost dog. "She doesn't understand what's happened. Do you, girl?"

A ghostly whine from the dog, and a flick of her tail. She took a couple more tentative steps toward me, but stopped just out of my reach. She dropped onto her stomach, right by the creek where her body lay, and huffed out a sigh as she rested her head on her front paws.

James blundered closer, and the ghost dog tensed, looking like she was going to run away.

"It's okay," I said softly. "You're safe."

My voice seemed to calm her, but I was afraid that all the noise James was making as he smashed through the underbrush would scare her off.

"James," I said softly. "I'm over here."

"You all right?" he called.

"I found her."

He stopped. "Is she—?"

"Yes."

"Are you sure?" He started walking toward me again, but much more slowly this time, as if he didn't want to see. I didn't blame him, much. Dead dogs are sad, sad things. Just about as sad as dead people.

"Am I sure she's dead?" I asked.

"No," he replied, finally pushing through the underbrush and out into the small opening where we were. "Are you sure it's Gypsy?"

I glanced over at the spirit of the dog, who had lifted her head and was watching James come toward us. "Pretty sure."

"Darn it."

James walked up beside me, then squatted. The ghost dog didn't move. We all sat, a silent tableau in front of the carcass. The ghost dog put her chin back on her front paws, still waiting.

"I guess you better call Veronica," James said. "Unless you want me to do it."

"Please," I said, keeping my eyes on the spirit of the dog. I didn't know why, but I did not want her to run away before Veronica got there. It was important.

James stood and pulled his cell phone out, flipped it open, then frowned. "No bars."

"We're in a gully," I said. "Try out in the open."

"Should she come and, you know, identify her?"

"Yes."

He disappeared from sight. The dog still hadn't moved.

"So what's going to happen now?" Eddie asked.

"I would imagine Veronica's going to cry a lot," I replied.

"But what about her?" Eddie pointed at the ghost dog, who looked as though she was thinking about going to sleep.

"I don't know."

"Will she go with her master?"

"I don't know, Eddie."

"Well, she can't just stay here." He began pacing back and forth. "That wouldn't be right. You need to do something."

I stared at him. "Like what?"

"Help her move on. You know, to the next area of living or whatever—"

"Next plane of existence." I shook my head. "I don't think I can do that with a dog."

"Well, you can't just leave her here! And there's nobody else who can help her."

The ghost dog lifted her head and cocked one ear, as though she was listening to what we were saying. Eddie pointed at her.

"See?" he said. "Even she thinks you should do something. And she's a dog, for God's sake!"

"Maybe it's like you said, Eddie. Maybe she'll follow Veronica home," I said. Eddie's face spasmed, like I'd slapped him.

"That's not good enough, Marie. She died here. She'll come back. You know that. You need to help her move on."

"Eddie, if I could, I would," I said, glancing in the direction James had gone, to see if he was coming back. The last thing I needed was for him to catch me talking to a dead dog.

This seemed to infuriate Eddie.

"Why the hell don't you clue him in to what you can do?" he cried. The ghost dog shuffled as though she was going to get up, maybe even run away.

"Lie down, Gypsy," I said, keeping my voice as calm as I could, even though absolutely everything Eddie was saying was upsetting as hell. I couldn't let the spirit of the dog run away. "It's okay. Everything's all right."

"No, it's not!" Eddie whispered. "You gotta do the right thing. That dog is dead. Her ghost is going to be trapped in these frigging woods forever if you don't do something. So do it, already. Don't be such a bitch about this stuff."

I blinked. "I'm not trying to be a bitch, Eddie. Really I'm not. I don't know how to move a dog's spirit on. I'm sorry."

"Well, Jesus, can't you even try?" He choked on sudden tears. "What the hell's wrong with you?"

"There's nothing wrong with me," I snapped. "Just leave me alone."

The dog lifted her head and growled, just a tiny note in her throat, but enough to let us both know she was getting upset.

"Help her," Eddie whispered. "Please."

James picked that moment to come back to us. "Got her," he said, holding the cell phone up as though it was a prize. "She's coming down. Should I go meet her?"

"That'd be good," I said.

"What does she look like?"

"No clue, James." I shrugged. "Sorry."

"Oh, yeah," he replied, and shuffled his feet as though embarrassed. Then he took another small step toward me, and the dead dog tensed. "Want to come with? You don't have to stay here. We'll be able to find the spot again."

"Just go get her, James," I said. "I'm not leaving Gypsy alone." He nodded and walked back out into the sunshine, and then he was gone.

"So, what are you gonna do?" Eddie asked.

I sat, staring at the spirit of the dog, and thought. Hard. Could it actually work the same way with an animal? With the spirit of an animal? Would they actually move on, like a human?

I didn't know, but Eddie was right. I had to try to do something. I couldn't leave her here, all by herself. That would be more than cruel. I stood, my knees popping.

"I'll try," I said. "All right, Eddie? I'm not guaranteeing a thing, but I will try. If she lets me get close to her."

I looked over at the ghost dog, wondering if she would let me near her. She'd stopped growling, but was sitting upright, looking as though she was waiting for something—or someone—to walk into the woods.

"I bet she's waiting for Veronica," Eddie said. "Dogs do that, don't they? Wait for their masters?"

"You're right," I said, then turned back to the dog. "Is that it, Gypsy?" I asked. "You waiting for Veronica?"

The dog wagged her tail and cocked one ear, as though she understood what I was saying.

"Wow," Eddie muttered. "You're like a dog ghost whisperer or something."

"Yeah," I replied, back down on my haunches and desperately trying to concentrate. "That's exactly what I am. Can we all just be quiet for a minute, so I can think, please? I have to figure out how to do this—"

"What if she doesn't move on on her own?"

"Then I'll help her," I said, my lips tight. "Though I'd rather not have to do anything in front of Veronica."

"Veronica. Yeah. Right." Eddie shook his head. "I'm thinking it's James you're more worried about. What is the deal between you two, anyhow? Don't you talk?"

"We talk. We talk all the time," I said, wishing Eddie would just shut up. The ghost dog moved restively.

"Yeah, I heard you," Eddie said. "But how come you don't tell him about being able to see us?" He pointed at himself and the ghost dog, who perked up one ear again. "See? Even Gypsy wants to know."

"That is none of your business, Eddie." I snapped a glare at him, to stop the foolishness, then turned my gaze to the dog. "Or yours, either."

IT TOOK TEN more agonizing minutes for Veronica to drive to the dog park. Why was it agonizing? Because Eddie wouldn't shut up about the fact that he thought I should tell James all about my gift.

"Man, if I could do something cool like that, I think I would have yelled it from the rooftops and shit. Not you though. You just sit there, looking pissy, like it's all a big inconvenience."

"Why won't you stop?" I asked. "I do not want—"

Then I saw the ghost dog sit up, both ears cocked as though she heard something really interesting. Then she whined a few times and stood, her tail whipping back and forth in a happy tattoo. She didn't leave her body, but she did stare hard at a spot just out of the trees.

"I bet Veronica's here," Eddie said. "I don't get how dogs know when their master is coming, but they always do."

"She probably heard the vehicle," I replied. I was starting to feel extremely nervous and was trying to figure out how to keep from transferring it to the dog's spirit.

"Or maybe she smells her. I think I read that somewhere. Dogs have really good noses. Can smell a thousand times better than us, or something."

"Whatever. Can you see if they're coming?" I said.

"You're going to do fine," Eddie said.

"Just tell me when they get close,okay? I have to get ready for this."

I watched him walk away from me and the dog and out into the sunlight, and I hoped that the spirit of the dog would see her master and just move on, with no help from me.

"Please," I whispered at the dog's spirit. "Please move on."

She cocked her head again, obviously not understanding a single word I was saying.

Crap.

Eddie:
It Was Something to See

I LEFT MARIE and the dog in the deep shadows of the trees and stepped out into the sunlight. James stood at the top of the hill, with a short blonde beside him. She looked like a soccer mom. James held her arm, gently leading her down the grassy hill toward me. When they got closer, I could hear her crying.

Man, I hoped Marie had her dog. It wouldn't go well for them if she went through all this mourning for nothing.

"We found her over there," I heard James say to her, grabbing her arm to steady her when she tripped over a hummock of grass. "I'm sorry. It looks like she drowned."

"I can't believe this," Veronica said, sniffling into a hand full of tissue. "I was here every day since she ran away. I looked everywhere. Are you sure it's Gypsy?"

"I believe so, but you'll have to make the identification," he replied. "I'm so sorry about this."

"So am I." Veronica stopped and wiped her eyes, sighing heavily. "I really love that dog. She's my best friend."

"I'm sorry." James kept one hand on her shoulder, and the woman seemed to take comfort from it. "We just have to follow that path," he said, pointing at the narrow opening in the solid bank of trees.

"Let's get this over with," Veronica said. She took one more deep breath, in and out, as though to steady herself. Then she walked through the opening, James on her heels.

Long story short, the dog Marie found was hers, and for a while there was a lot of crying on Veronica's part. Marie and James tried to console her, but there is really no consoling someone face to face with death like that.

The saddest part was the ghost dog. She was so happy to see Veronica, she whirled in small circles, then she stopped and jumped at the blonde. She ran a few more of the small tight circles, then came back, head down, ass up, tail wagging like crazy. She looked like she was trying to play.

Veronica didn't say anything to her because, of course, she couldn't see her. I could see the dog getting confused, and then looking hurt as her master continued to ignore her, focusing instead on the dead carcass in the leaf-covered creek in the small forest.

When Veronica threw herself into the creek and grabbed the carcass of the dog, wailing out her grief, the dog joined her at the side of the creek, howling as though her heart was breaking, too.

"Do something," I whispered to Marie.

Marie squatted next to the poor ghost dog, putting her hands near the place where her back fur would have been if she'd still been alive. Neither James or Veronica noticed what she was doing, because James had jumped into the creek to help Veronica get the carcass from the creek to the shore.

"It's okay, girl," Marie whispered to the ghost dog. "You're okay. You're a good dog."

The ghost howl wound down, until only the whine was left. The ghost looked at Marie, and then over at Veronica, who was sitting on the edge of the creek, sobbing, as James gently hoisted the dog's soaked body up to dry ground, and then at Marie again. That's when the small flickers of light started to form around the ghost dog and Marie.

"I've seen that before," I whispered.

Marie ignored me. Kept her eyes closed, and ran her hands through the place where the fur would have been, whispering, "Good dog, you rest now," over and over as the bright white twinkles of light formed and coalesced around the two of them.

The flickering lights became a small blizzard. James, who had been consoling Veronica, looked at Marie, concern splashed all over his face.

"Marie? Are you all right?"

No answer, just the low murmur of her voice saying "good dog" over and over, and her hands moving over the ghost fur as the dog began to relax, slumping further and further down on the ground until she was lying flat, with her chin between her front paws.

James reached out one hand to touch her just as the blizzard of light swirled around and around in a tornado and the ghost dog let out one more whine.

A dog howled somewhere up the hill, followed by another, and another, and James jerked away from Marie without touching her.

"What's going on?" he asked, and walked to the edge of the woods, to see what was happening in the dog park.

What was happening was the other dogs were sending one of their own on. That's what I think.

The blizzard of light was almost gone, and with it the ghost dog. Just a faint outline on the leaf-covered grass and then, as the last of the lights flitted up toward the sky, even that disappeared, and Marie was alone. She sighed once, almost sounded like she was crying, and then slumped over the spot where ghost Gypsy had been.

"You should see this," James said, walking back to Marie. "Those dogs are—" Then he saw her lying on the ground, unmoving.

"Marie!" he cried and ran to her, gathering her in his arms. "Are you all right?"

She moved weakly for a moment, as though recovering her senses, then opened her eyes and smiled up at him.

"Did I do it?" she asked.

"What?"

"Oh." Her smile faded. "Oh. I must have—" She struggled briefly, and he set her back on the ground.

"Sorry," he said. "I thought—"

"I'm all right," she said. She walked away from him and toward Veronica, who was still boohooing over the body of her dead dog, and tripped over a root hidden in the fallen leaves. James stuck out a hand to help keep her upright, and she glared, yanking her arm from his. "I said I'm fine," she snapped.

"Quit being such a bitch. He's just trying to help," I said. But all she did was ignore the shit out of me and walk over to Veronica, putting her arm around her shaking shoulders.

"We should move the body," she said.

Veronica nodded. "I don't know what I'm going to do without her," she whispered. "We've been together every day since she came into my life." She sniffled and pressed her sodden tissue to her face. "This is so hard."

"I know," Marie said, signaling over her shoulder for James. "Go get a blanket or something."

"Will do."

In short order he was back with a rough brown blanket. He quickly wrapped the dog's body, then pulled it up into his arms. He led the way out of the grove of trees, with Veronica and Marie following, arm in arm. Then came me. Last ghost left in the dog park.

James loaded the dog's body in the back of Veronica's Suburban. When he closed the back, Veronica walked up to him, cheque in hand.

"Thank you," she said.

"I wish it could have been a better ending," he replied.

"So do I."

She got in the Suburban and drove away, a funeral procession of one. We watched until the vehicle disappeared over a hill, then turned to James's car.

"Let's get out of here," Marie whispered. "I'm exhausted."

Marie:
One More Glass of Water, and I'll Be Fine . . .

"CAN I HAVE another glass of water?"

I hated the weak whiny sound of my voice, but moving on Gypsy the dog had been as draining as moving on a human, and I didn't have anything more left.

It didn't help that we'd taken the car back to the parking lot, and I had to walk four more blocks to the office. Just made me even more weak and whiny. If that was possible.

James continued to be a gentleman and got me another glass, which I guzzled greedily like I was dying of thirst, which I was, almost. But then he blew it.

"You must have tied one on last night," he said. "You're really dehydrated."

"Let it go, James."

I set the glass down and flicked on the computer so I didn't have to look at him anymore. Then Eddie laughed, and that set me off. He should have known better. He'd actually seen what I did. And why I was so dehydrated.

"Leave me alone!" I roared, insta-anger huge in my chest and pushing to get out. Through my mouth. "I don't need to listen to you! Just leave me the hell alone!"

"Jesus, lighten up, woman," Eddie barked. "Can't you even take a joke?"

James didn't answer me at all. Just stomped off to his office and slammed his door.

"Frigging wonderful." I hammered away at the keys, getting exactly nowhere and pissing myself off further. "Why don't you go away, Eddie? I don't have time for you and your jokes."

I just wanted a little quiet time to pull myself together, maybe have another drink of water and eight hours sleep. That's all I wanted.

What I got was the other guy in my life—the dead guy—losing it on me, too.

"Look," he snapped, all humour gone. "I told you. I'm not leaving until you and I have a talk about that moving on thing. Remember?"

"Yes," I hissed, still staring stubbornly at the computer monitor.

"Well, why haven't you?"

"Haven't I what?"

"Helped me move on? Why would you help a dog, but you won't help me?"

I whirled my chair around so I was looking right at the seething ghost. He was even throwing off a little ecto goo, which I hate. But I ignored it. He had to understand he'd brought most of this on himself.

"You told me you didn't want to move on. When we first met. Do you remember that?"

His forehead wrinkled, and the ecto goo eased as he thought, hard. "Yeah," he finally said. "I remember."

"So what's the problem? You didn't want to move on, so I didn't move you on. I did exactly what you wanted. Then, when you said you wanted to move on, I said I'd help. Remember?"

"Yes."

"Why are you so pissed?"

"Because I didn't understand," he said, anger seeping back into his voice. "I didn't get it. It wasn't until I talked to Noreen—"

It was my turn to wrinkle my forehead with hard thinking. "Oh. The woman at the park. Your friend."

"Yep, that's the one," he replied. "She died and she moved on. All on her own. Hanging around isn't right. Isn't what we're supposed to do. She told me that."

"So?"

"So!" he roared. "So? Are you kidding me? You're supposed to be the leader here! You got the power!"

"I've got the power?" I hammered a key, hard, lost my connection to the internet, and slapped the computer shut. "What frigging power do I have? I can see you. Talk to you. How is that powerful?"

"You know how this stuff is supposed to work," Eddie said again. "Why didn't you tell me? Lead me?"

"Why don't you take responsibility for your own actions?" I barked back, absolutely at the end of my rope. What right did he have to tell me I was the one who was supposed to fix his death? Make sure he followed the rules? He'd never followed the rules in his life. Why was it up to me to make sure he did the right thing dead?

"I didn't want any of this," he said. He backed away from the desk as though my anger frightened him. "I didn't ask for any of this."

"Do you think I did?"

"But you did," he said. "You were the one looking for me. Remember?"

He was right. I had searched him out, and I'd done it so we could solve this stupid case and make some cash.

I was still too angry to admit any wrongdoing on my part, though. So, I acted like an even bigger jerk instead.

"Why don't you hit the road if you hate the way I'm doing things so much?" I snapped. "You are nothing but a pain in my ass, Eddie."

He took another step away from me, a stricken look on his face. "You really *were* just using me, weren't you?"

God, yes I was. "No. Not really. It's just that you told me—"

"You should have explained the rules better."

"I barely understand the frigging rules, Eddie."

"Maybe you should learn them, then," he said. He shook his head and walked back to the window. "Because I don't understand at all. I need some help here, and I think you at least owe me that."

He was right. I did owe him that.

I knew it was better for ghosts to move on than to keep hanging around. And I knew I had the capacity to help him, just like I had with the dog.

"Dogs are easy," I muttered.

"What?" Eddie asked, still staring out the window.

"I said dogs are—"

Then I stopped as the front door flew open and the drug cop Stewart and two of his cronies stormed in, looking mightily pissed. He hammered on my desk with an open fist.

"Where the hell is she?" he bellowed. "I need to talk to her. Now."

Eddie backed away from my desk, looking frightened. I imagined I looked pretty frightened myself.

"I don't know who you're talking about," I said, even though I could guess, and wished James would step through the door and deal with this situation. He didn't.

"Honoria Lowe," Stewart yelled. "She's not at home, and she's not answering her cell. Where is she?"

"I have no idea." I was glad James hadn't told me where he was taking her, because now, at least, I didn't have to lie to a police officer.

"I don't believe you," Stewart said. His buddies both leaned in, looking seriously scary.

"I really don't," I said again, hating how small and frightened my voice sounded. I pulled myself out of my chair and backed to James's office door, eyes still on Stewart. I felt like I was watching a snake about to strike. "Let me get James. He might be able to help you."

I knocked on the door, smiling weakly at the cops. No answer.

"James," I called, knocking again, a little harder this time. "We have company." Still no answer, so I threw open the door and yelled, "James! The cops are here!" as loudly as I could.

James was sitting behind his desk and didn't even jump when the door flew open. "What do they want?"

"Honoria. They can't find her."

"Oh." He looked back down at the computer screen and pressed another button. "So?"

"They think we know where she is."

"Really?"

"Yes." Stewart pushed past me, his cronies following. "I know you two have contact with her. Tell me where she is. Now."

James surprised the heck out of me by picking up the telephone. "No problem," he said. "I'll call her and set up a meeting."

"We called her," Stewart said. "No answer."

"It could be she doesn't want to talk to you," James replied. "She doesn't trust people she doesn't know."

"I'm a cop," Stewart growled.

"So?" James pushed the last button and held the receiver to his ear.

Stewart didn't seem to have a good answer. Just snapped his mouth shut and waited. We could hear the phone ring faintly through the receiver. Three times. Four. As the fifth ring started, James looked concerned.

"She always answers." The sixth ring. James pulled the receiver away from his head and stared at it, then, when the seventh ring started, hung up.

"So, she didn't answer you either," Stewart said, rather unnecessarily.

"No, she didn't." James looked extremely worried, then tried to cover it up by looking nonchalant. It didn't work.

"Do you know where she is?"

"No." I tried not to look at James in surprise. He'd just lied. To the police. "We contact each other by phone."

"So, you got no better idea what's going on with her than I do?"

James stared at the phone as though through sheer force of will, he could get it to ring. "No, sorry."

"Son of a bitch." Stewart pulled out a business card and flipped it onto James's desk. "Call if you hear from her. Find out where she is, and call immediately. You understand?"

"Yes."

Stewart stood over the desk a moment more, staring at James. "So where's your car?" he finally asked. "That old Volvo finally give out on you?"

I blinked, and blinked again, but James didn't. "I found a place to park it," he said, and smiled like butter wouldn't melt in his mouth. "This is a bit of a tough neighbourhood."

"Huh," Stewart said. He glared, but James didn't respond. I was afraid I was responding enough for both of us, if he looked at me.

He didn't. Just turned on his heel after that incredibly uncomfortable moment, and left.

I waited until the door slammed shut before I asked the

obvious question. "So, what do we do now?"

"Go watch Stewart," James said shortly. "Make sure he isn't waiting for us out there. I'll try Honoria again. She should have answered."

He picked up the phone and dialed as I scurried to the window and watched Stewart and his people come out of the building and head for a dark blue sedan parked in front of our building. They got in and sat.

"They're not moving," I said.

"They will," Eddie murmured. "Keep watching."

"I'm still not getting an answer," James said. "We gotta go."

"But Stewart's just sitting there," I said, still staring out the window. I could see the three of them having an animated discussion inside the car and guessed it wasn't about where to go for lunch. I hoped they'd decide we weren't worth their time and move on. "What about you sneaking out the back?"

"Won't work," James replied, as he put down the receiver again and walked into the front office. "He'll follow me to my car. And I don't want that."

"Oh."

"Yeah," James said. "Even he'd be able to follow me, if I left now."

"What are we going to do?" I breathed.

"They'll go," Eddie said. He wasn't even looking out the window anymore. "Trust me. One more minute and they'll leave."

"I don't know, exactly," James said. "They have to leave, or we're stuck here."

"Any second now," Eddie said.

I could see the conversation inside the vehicle had turned decidedly angry. As Stewart punched the steering wheel of the sedan, I could hear short angry blasts from the horn. Then, without warning, the sedan lurched out into the steady stream of traffic. Horns blared as it weaved in and out between the other cars on the road. After a few moments, it was out of my sight.

"They're gone," I said.

"Told you," Eddie said, sounding extremely self-satisfied.

"Good." James ran back into his office, returning with his keys. "Let's go before they decide to come back. We have to find Honoria and make sure she's all right."

"I think I should stay here." The last thing in the world I

wanted to do was have another meeting with Honoria the Clairvoyant, who felt it was important that I let everybody know about my little seeing-ghosts secret. She might forget that she promised not to say anything if we helped her. I didn't think I'd be able to stand that. "You know. Just in case she calls back."

"She has my cell number," James said, then shook his head and headed out the door. "Whatever. Stay. Do what you want."

"Somebody should be here if she calls!" I cried. The door banged shut on my words, and I sat down and held my head in my hands.

"Your headache back?" Eddie asked. "Gee, that's too bad."

"Shut up, Eddie."

Eddie:
All She Has to Do Is Answer a Few Questions. How Hard Can That Be?

MARIE DIDN'T LOOK too good. She sat hunched over with her head on the desk, rocking it back and forth, and occasionally saying, "shit" under her breath.

I wasn't one to let somebody else's bad day get in my way though. I had questions for her. And she was going to answer them.

"You ready?"

"Yes." She didn't lift her head from the desk, but she had answered me. Good enough.

"Do only the messed-up ghosts need help moving on?"

Marie glanced at me like she didn't quite understand the question, so I tried again.

"Like me," I said. "Noreen moved on right after she died. But me, I'm stuck. So, are you like a ghost shrink or something? You help the ghosts who don't get the whole moving-on thing? Is that what you are?"

Marie laughed, but it was not a happy sound. "Sure," she said. "Ghost shrink sounds as good as anything else."

"Cool."

I'd only had one shrink before. Court-appointed, the last time

I'd been caught breaking into a Shell station. They'd decided that no one sane would throw himself through a plate glass window to get at a chocolate bar. Especially since the gas station was open at the time. Looking back on it, I could see why this decision was made, but I hadn't been ready to give up my life of drugs and crime right then, so the shrink got nothing much out of me. Just enough for him to certify me sane but belligerent. I spent a winter behind bars for that.

At least I was warm.

"So how you going to do it?" I asked.

"Do what?"

"Help me move on?"

She stared down at the scarred wooden top of her desk, as though considering all the potential therapies she had at her fingertips. "I dunno," she finally said. "Wanna talk about your childhood or something?"

"Really?" I couldn't quite believe it was going to go this way, but decided to play along. "You want me to lie down on a couch?"

She stared at me, her eyebrows raised incredibly high. "I'd rather you didn't," she finally said.

"Oh."

"Drug use usually stems from childhood trauma. So, let's talk about your childhood. Did your dad beat you?"

"No. Just left."

"Oh." She said the word the same way the prison shrink had.

"Don't read too much into that," I replied. "He did leave, but I got it. It wasn't my fault. It was my mom's fault."

"Oh!" Same sound as the shrink, and I almost laughed. They're always so happy when they think they figure out which parental figure did the most damage. And they all think it's either mommy or daddy issues.

"I'm shitting you." I laughed. "They just couldn't make a go of it. Mom's a bit fucked-up—come on, you met her, you know what I'm talking about—and Dad had a nice little drinking problem. Since it wouldn't go away, he did. Mom blamed herself and decided to make up for it by having the cleanest house on the block."

"But you don't blame her for everything?"

"Nope. I used to, but then I stopped that."

"Why?"

"Because I realized she couldn't help the way she was. You should have met *her* mother!"

"Huh," she muttered. "You're fairly self-aware for—"

"A ghost?"

"No, actually, for a drug addict," she replied. "So, why the drugs? If you get that your parents screwed up, but you felt they did their best at the time—in other words, if you forgave them for your childhood—why did you resort to drugs?"

"I resorted to drugs before I figured out about my parents. By the time I let them off the hook for my shitty little life, I was well and truly hooked. I couldn't figure out how to live my life without them."

"But—"

"But nothing," I said. "I went to crystal meth, baby. Started there, and stayed there my whole, short, and pitiful life. That shit is a gateway drug to hell. Don't let anybody tell you any different."

I sighed, wishing I didn't have to tell her any of this. It sounded so stupid. Which it was.

"After the last time I was picked up by the cops, I decided to do a little research to try and get off the old meth train."

"But you didn't."

"No. I couldn't. Coming off—well, it wasn't just the physical sickness and then the depression, though that was pretty bad. Nope, it was the realization that my life was a big pile of crap. That's what kept pushing me back to drugs. My life was so bad, and I had engineered the whole thing. I couldn't not be on drugs."

"Oh."

"Yeah." The sympathy in her eyes made me feel sick, so I turned away and walked over to the window. At least when I looked out there, I just saw idiots running around looking for the good life. I didn't have to see my failure reflected in the eyes of my ghost shrink.

"I don't understand," Marie finally said, forcing me to turn back to her.

"What?"

"I don't understand why you aren't ready to move on. You should be. You've forgiven your parents, understood that your life was designed by you and that it ended up this way because of decisions you made . . . What's holding you here?"

"I don't know! Jesus, I've confessed all my frigging sins, so why can't you figure this part out? Why do I have to do it all?"

Marie suddenly laughed, and she sounded relieved. I glanced at her, and she looked like she had a clue. Maybe she knew what it was I had to do.

"What?"

"Holy crow," she said. "I'm an idiot! The answer was right in front of my face the whole time. You don't need to forgive anyone. You need to be forgiven. By your mom. Or maybe your friend, Luke."

"Luke Stewart?"

"Yes." She breathed a sigh of relief. "You talked about thinking it was your fault he was dead. Could that be what's holding you here?"

Something thunked in my chest like a big lock suddenly sprang open. "Might be," I whispered.

"You think about that," she replied, her voice more gentle than I'd ever heard it. "Because if it's either your mom or Luke, I might be able to help you make amends."

"How would you do that?" I felt something—hope, or something close—warm my chest.

She smiled, and the warmth grew. I almost believed she could do something for me. Something real.

"Trust me—" she started, then stopped mid-sentence when the frigging phone rang.

"Ignore it!" I barked.

"It'll just take a second," she said, and picked up the receiver.

I could tell by the look on her face it wasn't going to take a second. It was going to take a hell of a lot longer than that. She was talking to James, and he was giving her nothing but bad news.

"What do you mean you can't find her?" she asked. "How can that be?"

She listened for a moment, and her face went back to looking pinched. "Well, that's fantastic," she muttered. "What should I do?" She listened for another minute more, then snapped, "Of course I'm willing to help you! Don't be an ass!"

"I'll go check out her apartment," I said. She ignored me. "I said I'll go check out her apartment," I said, louder this time.

She snapped to attention and hastily put her hand over the receiver. "Would you really? Maybe she went back there—"

"Happy to."

Actually, I wasn't. That blonde chick creeped the hell out of me, but if Marie was going to do something to help me move on, I could afford to be altruistic and shit, and help her.

"Great," she breathed, then pulled the receiver back to her ear. "I'll do what I can from this end. Just keep looking for her. Yes! I'll be here when you get back!"

She slammed down the phone and shook her head. "That guy drives me crazy!" Then she turned to me. "You don't have to do this, you know," she said. "I'm going to help you in any case, Eddie. Really."

"I know," I said, and when I smiled at her, it felt real. "I want to."

"Thanks."

"When I get back—"

"I'll help you move on."

"Cool."

But as I walked out the door, I didn't know if it was so cool. She'd talked about making amends with Luke. But Luke was dead. The only way I could make amends would be through his father, and that son of a bitch deserved to rot in hell for the way he'd treated Luke. And me.

I hoped she knew what she was doing.

Eddie:
Turmoil at Honoria's Place

I ALMOST DIDN'T make it to Honoria's apartment. Took the long route, through the park, and saw a buddy sitting there, high as a kite, and thought, "What the hell, one hit, just for the road."

Yep. Actually thought that. Would have been so easy. Just had to step in, and I would have been there.

It was the thought of going into Honoria's apartment again that had pushed me to the addict thought again. I was sure of it. Man, that chick freaked the hell out of me. Every time I was near her, it felt she was looking right into my soul. Seeing right into my soul. Marie—I didn't get that vibe from her. She could see me, and talk to me, and all that shit. But she did not look directly into my soul. It's more like one person talking to another with her. I could hide what I wanted. Couldn't do that with Honoria. She saw fucking near all.

So I went to the park and thought about taking the edge off. Even though I knew it was only my head talking. Didn't need the drugs anymore. No body, so no physical addiction. But that didn't stop me from going over there and thinking about it. Long and hard.

Then I gave my head a shake. I wanted to follow Noreen, not this pack of assholes. I'd had enough of this life—and this death. It was time to move on. Moving on meant growing up and doing what I said I would do. So I turned my back on the park and headed over to Honoria's apartment.

The place was packed with cops. I had a bad minute or two when I thought I heard Luke's asshole dad, but it was only his voice on a walkie talkie.

I walked through the door and scared the hell out of a police dog who was sniffing around the place. Looked like he'd been looking for drugs before I set his nerves a-jangling. When he leaped for me—crotch-height, what, do they teach those dogs that's the best place to hit?—I jumped back and squealed like a little girl before I remembered I was fucking dead and he couldn't do a damned thing to me.

"Jesus, Fargo!" the cop handling the dog gasped as the dog yanked him all over the small apartment. "Sit! Sit!"

There was no sitting on Fargo's part. Just more leaping around trying to tear me apart, with no luck of course. Finally, the handler lost his temper and pulled the dog up nearly off his feet. Just to get his attention.

"I said stop it right the hell now!" he yelled. The dog finally remembered his training, but by that time, the head cop had had enough.

"Get him out of here," said the big guy parked over by the kitchen sink.

"I'm sorry, sir," the handler said, letting the dog's feet finally touch the floor. "I don't know what came over him."

"Just get him out," the big guy snapped. "We're not going to find drugs in this place." He looked around as the handler pulled the whining dog out the door and down the stairs. "We're not going to find anything in this frigging place."

"What are we looking for exactly?" Another cop, in plainclothes and harried-looking, looked up from the big pile of old mail on the minute kitchen table.

"Anything that would give us a hint where she might be." The big guy shrugged. "In other words, your guess is as good as mine."

"Jesus, I don't know how she could live like this," the other cop muttered and turned back to the pile of mail. "What a shit hole."

I personally thought the cop was being overly critical. All right, the place was pretty small and the furniture was all Sally Ann special, but it was clean, except for the few dirty dishes in the sink. However, the big guy nodded his agreement. Apparently living standards for the police were considerably higher than for people like us.

I glanced over at Honoria's art table and saw the sketches she'd done. One or two of the church, and that godawful tree. And I felt myself slip . . .

And I was back at the tree.

I guess I shouldn't have been surprised to see Honoria sitting on the church steps, drawing on a large sheet of paper lying on the step beside her. Her eyes were closed as her hand holding the charcoal pencil jerked over the page.

I didn't want to go near her because I hated how I felt when I was in her proximity, but I wanted to see what she was drawing. So I crept up behind her and looked over her shoulder.

She was drawing herself. She looked like she was being tortured. Hung up by her arms, her head bent forward, hair in her face, and I could see her mouth was open and screaming. Didn't doubt she'd be screaming. Looked like the torture being used was electricity, thanks to car batteries at her feet. Nasty shit, that. I'd scream too.

Something about the place looked familiar, but I couldn't place it.

"Where is that?" I whispered, half-afraid she'd answer me.

She stiffened, opened her eyes, and looked around, like she'd suddenly felt me whispering to her. Spooky shit.

Then she said, "I had to come here, Eddie. The pictures, they never lie."

God, she was talking to me again. I took a couple of big steps away from her and then, when she turned around and stared at the spot where I'd been, I ran.

I told myself it was so I could get back to Marie and tell her what I'd seen, but it wasn't that. I didn't want to spend another second around the blonde. She creeped me the hell out.

Marie:
Can We Keep It Down, Please?
I Can't Hear the Ghost

I'D NEVER BEEN so glad to see anybody wander into that office as I was when Eddie finally came back. I couldn't say anything to him, of course, because the place was packed to the rafters with angry book club members. But if I could have, I would have given him a big kiss.

"I am trying to explain a few facts of life to you." Queen Bea was sitting in my chair behind my desk, directing traffic and generally getting under my skin in a huge way. "And if you'd just get the rest of us our coffees, I'd be happy to show you the small presentation we've put together."

She pointed at my computer. "Can we run the PowerPoint presentation from here? Where do you keep your projector and screen?"

Eddie stared at the throng of women in my office and shook his head.

"I don't have a projector or a screen," I said to the book club, even though I desperately wanted to find out what Eddie knew. "And I'd appreciate it if you'd go sit in another chair, Bea."

"I need the lumbar support," Bea replied majestically.

"You gotta get them out," Eddie said. "Now."

I rolled my eyes, hoping he'd understand that I meant, "I would if I could, but I don't have a clue how to move them, so I can't."

"I know where Honoria is," he said.

"Where?" I said out loud, before I really thought about what I was doing.

"I'm talking about my back, dear," Bea replied, looking at me like she thought I was anything but dear. "You do understand, don't you?"

"Yes," I muttered, reaching around her for the pad of paper and pen by the phone. I scuttled over to the window, hoping Eddie would follow me.

Of course, every member of the book club shut up and watched me do this. I looked out the window, feeling like an absolute idiot because, of course, Eddie didn't follow me.

So, I turned around and glared at him, and he finally got the hint.

"She's at the churchyard," he said. "Where I was—you know."

Yes, I knew exactly where he meant. Why was she there? What was going on with that woman? Didn't she know everyone in the world, it seemed, was looking for her?

"Is there something we can help you with, dear?" Bea called from my chair.

"No." I walked back into the middle of the room and tried keep the sudden panic out of my voice as I spoke. "I don't want to see a PowerPoint presentation, and I don't have all day to discuss your ideas—"

"Investigation, dear," Bea said haughtily. "We did a thorough investigation."

"Yes, of course. Sorry." I ground my teeth, then tried to smile. "I do have somewhere to be. Do you think perhaps we could set up a time for a meeting when James could be here . . ."

"No, dear, sorry," Bea replied, shaking her head. Then all the rest of them started shaking their heads and clucking until I felt like I was trapped in a chicken coop with a bunch of broody hens, and I fought the sudden scream that pressed against my lips.

"We gotta go," Eddie said. "Now."

I sucked in a quick breath to calm myself. "Give me the gist," I said, grabbing up the pad of paper and pen and making a great show of preparing to write down every damned word they told me. "But I only have a couple of minutes."

"Fine," Bea said. "But you won't get the full effect if we just tell you who it is without telling you how we came to these conclusions. It's really quite fascinating."

"I'm sure it is," I said, pressing the pen point so hard into the pad of paper I was shocked it didn't break off and spray black ink everywhere. "But I honestly don't have the time to listen to everything. Please, just tell me your theory."

"Fine. Even though our journey of discovery is nearly as interesting—no, I would call it captivating—as our conclusions, here it is. We believe—" She stood, ponderously, and held out one hand for effect. I was sure I heard a couple of the book club members suck air through their teeth in anticipation.

I sucked a little air myself, but just to keep my calm.

"Please, just tell me," I said. Begged, really. "Please."

"The killer is Raymond Dunning."

I actually started to write the name, then stopped and stared at the gloating woman. A spatter of applause started somewhere in the back of the room, but I yelled over it.

"Who is Raymond Dunning?"

Bea smiled so patronizingly I felt a sudden urge to slap it off her face. "Didn't do your homework, now did you?"

"What?" I gasped. Eddie started to say something, but Queen Bea rumbled over his words.

"Raymond Dunning deals drugs—among other things." Bea's mouth turned down in a moue of disapproval, and I heard a couple of the other women tsk.

"Thank you for that information," I said, writing the name beside the address on the pad of paper and putting down the pen hopefully. "I'll let you know if you were right. And now—"

"Oh no," Bea said, shaking her head. "You are going to hear all about how we figured this out. Fascinating information, really fascinating."

"I wish I could, but—"

"But nothing!" Bea said sharply. "You will sit and listen. We've put in some long hard hours here, missy. We deserve to be heard."

"We gotta go," Eddie said. "Get 'em out."

"Just give us an hour," Bea said, leaning forward eagerly. "And if you find us that projector, the PowerPoint presentation takes—"

"No!" I bellowed, and they all, finally, shut up. Shock electrified the air, but I steadfastly ignored it. "Look ladies, I'm sure it's all fascinating, but I do not have time for this." I pointed to the door. "You have to leave. Now."

"But—"

"No." I spoke as firmly as I could and kept pointing at the door. "It's time for you to leave."

"But—"

"No."

Bea pushed the chair away from the desk and pulled her considerable bulk from it.

"Fine," she said, dropping an old-fashioned computer disc that evidently held the PowerPoint presentation she so wanted me to see into her purse and snapping it shut. "We'll leave. But if and when you finally do realize that Raymond is the real culprit, you owe us one hour for the presentation, plus a question and answer period after."

"And snacks," another woman said as she stood, clutching her purse to her chest and looking just as peeved as Bea. "Don't forget the snacks."

I said nothing, afraid that if I said a word, they'd take it as a sign I was weakening, and settle back in. More than likely so they could negotiate what snacks should be served.

"Do we have a deal?" Bea asked.

I nodded, but kept my finger pointing at the door.

"Fine," she said again, and walked to it, her entourage following. "Expect to hear from us. Soon."

Finally, they left.

"Get James on the phone," Eddie said. "And tell him where we'll be. We can't waste any time."

I picked up the phone and quickly dialed James's cell number.

"James?" I said, when he answered. "She's at the Holy Trinity Church. Sitting on the front steps."

"How do you know that?" he asked, but before I could think of anything, he said, "Forget it. Doesn't matter. I'll be there in ten minutes."

"I'll meet you." I hung up the phone and turned to Eddie. "Sorry. You'll have to wait a little while longer."

"No problem," Eddie said. "Just go get her somewhere safe."

I stopped, surprised. "Aren't you coming?"

"I'd rather not," he said, prissily. "I hate that place—and I don't much like her."

"Join the club," I muttered, and grabbed my purse.

"Do you want me to come?" he asked.

"If you want." I was surprised. He'd never seemed to care whether I wanted him around or not before.

"Well, maybe I will," he said. Then suddenly light swirled around him and for a brief second before he disappeared, he looked distraught.

I wondered, briefly, where he'd gone. Suspected his disappearance might have had something to do with him talking about the churchyard. But I didn't have time to think about him anymore. I had to find Honoria.

I HEARD EDDIE before I got to the churchyard. It almost sounded like his voice was in my head as much as it was in the air.

"They got her!" he cried, over and over. "They got her!"

"Who got her?" I muttered, hoping against hope he could hear me, too. He didn't respond, but I could see him at the far end of the block, standing in front of the tree where his life had ended.

I ran to him, hoping to get there before James did. But James slewed up in his car at exactly that moment, so it was the three of us standing in front of the tree. Just the three of us. Honoria was nowhere to be seen.

"Where is she?" James asked.

"I—I don't know." I looked around, uselessly. "She was here—"

Wasn't she? Eddie had been the one to tell me she was at this spot, and he had no reason to lie to me. I glanced at him, but he was standing, still as stone, staring at the church steps. So I looked in that direction, too. Hoping against hope that Honoria would somehow appear in a poof of pixie dust or something.

"I saw them. They took her," he muttered. "And that's all that's left."

"Who took her?" I wanted to scream. But I couldn't. James was there, staring at me. And Eddie wouldn't look in my direction. Just kept muttering, "They took her," over and over again, until I wanted to shake him. Hard.

Then I saw something on the church steps and walked closer. It was a sheaf of papers, scattered over the top two stairs.

"Where is she?" James asked again. "I thought you said—"

"I did," I said, and walked to the steps. Picked up one of the pieces of paper and stared at it. It was one of Honoria's sketches. I was certain of it. "But she's gone."

I held out the sketch to James, but spoke to Eddie. "Do you know this place? Do you recognize it at all?"

James looked down at the sketch, gasped, and looked up at me. "Is that Honoria?"

She'd drawn herself this time. Black slashes across the white paper showed her being held. Being tortured.

I picked up another sketch. More of the same. But one sketch, near the bottom, showed the front of a house, two-story and old. And the address. She'd put the address on the bottom of the sketch.

"She's there," I said, pointing with shaking fingers. "They've taken her there."

"Who has?" James asked, grabbing the sketch with a hand that was shaking as badly as my own. "Where is this?"

"I don't know," I said. My mouth felt like dust and I swallowed, hard.

"I do," Eddie whispered. "Ambrose Welch uses this place. Crank and R were the ones who grabbed her. We gotta hurry."

I glanced at Eddie and felt a sudden thrill of horror. His light was almost gone. As though his aura was being extinguished from within.

Eddie, I thought. *Don't go this way. Don't go.*

He didn't answer me. Didn't even look at me. Just stared at the tree and darkened, one lumen at a time.

"We need to go to this house," I said frantically to James. "Ambrose Welch is involved. We need to go right now."

I was expecting him to say something like, "How do you know Ambrose Welch is involved," but he didn't. All he said was, "No," and pulled a business card from his jacket pocket. "We need to call the cops." He held out the card, and I recognized it as the one that Stewart had given him. "These cops."

He pulled out his cell phone, and I grabbed at it. "Don't do that," I said. "Call Sergeant Worth if you have to call one of them. Not him, though."

"We can't do this ourselves," James said, matter-of-factly. "And we don't have time to bring Worth up to speed. Stewart knows these guys, knows this area. If there is any reality to this sketch at all, this has gone way past Honoria not wanting to be accused of Edward Hansen's murder. You get that, don't you?"

"I understand," I said. "But not him, James. He's evil. He really is."

"He might be, but he has more firepower at his disposal than we do. If she's at this house, and she's being—"

"Tortured," Eddie whispered. "She's being tortured. They think she knows something."

"Tortured," I said, almost at the same time, hating the way the word felt in my mouth. "They're torturing her."

"We need the police," he said. And he made the call.

At that moment, my cell beeped and I answered it, shortly. I didn't need to deal with anything else right now. James was bringing one of the bad guys down on us—on Honoria—and I couldn't stop him.

"What?" I barked.

"This is Bea."

Good grief. She and her entourage had just left the office. What could she possibly want?

"I don't have time for this right now," I started, but she ran over my words like a German Panzer.

"Since you weren't willing to listen to our complete presentation," she snapped, "we've decided to do something about it ourselves."

"What?" God, I had to get off the phone. James was about to talk to the nastiest cop I'd ever met, and Eddie looked like he was about to extinguish right in front of me. "What are you talking about?"

"We have the address of a house that Raymond Dunning owns, and we are going there to confront him. You might not care, but Naomi needs closure."

What?

"What's the address?" I asked.

Bea told me, and my blood ran cold. It was the address of Ambrose Welch's drug house, where Honoria was being held. How had they found it?

"Bea, don't do this," I said. "It's too dangerous."

"Girl," Bea snapped, "someone has to."

And then she was gone.

Good God, those women were walking into quite possibly the

most dangerous house in all of Edmonton.

I looked at James and his ferocious frown as he spoke quickly into his phone and then disconnected.

"Voicemail," he said tersely.

"We gotta go there," I said. "Right now."

"Why?" he asked.

So I finally told him about the book club.

ALL THINGS CONSIDERED, he took the information quite well. But Eddie didn't. He looked horrified, absolutely horrified, and darkened until he was barely a smudge of grey.

"Is my mom with them?" he asked.

I nodded.

"Ambrose will kill them," he said. "He'll kill them all if he even suspects they know anything." He sobbed and covered his face with his ripped-up hands. "This is my fault, too."

I finally understood why he was losing his light so quickly. He thought Honoria—and now, his mother—were in danger because of him. More people about to be hurt, because of him.

"James, we have to go there and stop them," I said. "They're going to get hurt if they go anywhere near that house."

James stared down at the phone in his hand, as if hoping it would ring and a miracle would spew from it. No such luck, James.

"Let's go," I said. "Please."

"All right." He glanced at his cell one last time, then tucked it into his pocket. "Let's go."

Eddie:
Dying All Over Again

ALL I COULD think was, "Hurry up hurry up hurry up," as the car slowly—and I mean slowly; James was driving like an old woman!—wound its way north to Ambrose Welch's drug house. I felt like I was barely hanging on. I kept thinking of Honoria's drawing of the basement torture room, and that made me think of the tree where I'd been crucified. Left a taste of copper in my mouth, which surprised me, because I hadn't actually tasted anything since I died.

I saw Honoria's screaming face in my mind's eye, and then, overlaying it, was my face. My scream jumped an octave every time the hammer came down on the spike that pierced my palm.

I felt sick and looked out the side window, hoping the image would leave. It faded a bit, but didn't disappear completely.

"Open the window," I said.

Marie didn't even argue. Just cracked the window and let some air whistle in.

"More," I said. "I feel sick."

She glanced back at me, as though gauging whether or not I was telling the truth. However I looked, I could tell by her reaction it wasn't good. She gasped and rolled the window down completely, then tucked her hair into the collar of her jacket so it didn't turn into a riot of snarls.

"Can't you close that?" James said. "It's cold."

"No, sorry," she said. She snuck another glance in my direction, and her face whitened. "Lie down," she mouthed.

I did so, but felt even worse. Like I was sucking all the bad visions in, like I was drowning in the sight and sound of me being killed.

"Oh my God!" I gasped, and sat up. I felt like I was drowning. Drowning in death. "Help me."

Sparks pushed out through my skin. Could feel them, like small gnat bites all over. Didn't take long before they filled the back seat. None of them were white, like I'd seen with Noreen. None of them. They were yellow and red and black. Lots and lots of black sparks, and through it all, I kept seeing my death, feeling my death as the spikes hammered into my palms and then my feet, and the Donald Duck wielding the hammer grunted with every hammer stroke, and through the mask I could see the face of my father, and then my mother, and then my first grade teacher, and then my girlfriend, the one from ninth grade who dumped me in front of homeroom, and then Santa, and Grandma Jenkins, and on and on. Like I was seeing the faces of everyone who had ever hurt me, had ever given me a push down the bad road, and I started to scream, because the gnat bites were suddenly larger, more painful, and the light popping out of my skin was larger and whirling around me in a cacophony of light and sound, now the sound; moans and screeches and whispered words: "You were never any good," "You don't wear the right kind of clothes," "They call you Brown Eddie because you shit yourself in third grade," "What can you expect? He's got the bad Hansen genes—I warned you. Nothing good ever comes from a Hansen."

And then I heard my mother crying, "Please! Come back!"

"I gotta get out," I grunted, pushing myself through the door of the moving car, feeling like I was drowning in the emotion and the light. "I gotta get out!"

I heard Marie scream as I hit the pavement and rolled, spewing black and red and yellow curds of light around me as I hit the sidewalk, then up onto a scrabbly bit of grass by an apartment building. The curds of light kept vomiting out through my skin, and the horrible feelings rampaged through me and I guess I screamed a couple of times, setting a dog who was walking with his master into a seething, frothing panic attack. It was one of those pit bulls, so it was really something to see.

Then Marie was beside me. I could see blood oozing from a hole in one knee of her jeans.

That pulled me back from the edge. "You're bleeding."

"You have to stay with me, Eddie!" she cried, kneeling beside me with her hands mostly covering her face as though she was fighting through a snowstorm. "You can't go like this!"

"It's all my fault," I whispered. "Honoria. And now, my mom." I shuddered. "I'm so afraid."

Truer fucking words were never spoken.

"I want you to focus on me," Marie said. "Please, Eddie. Look at me. Focus on my voice and my face. You're not ready to do this. You have to come back."

I heard whimpering, and thought for a second it was the dog, but it was me. "Help me."

"Look at me!" Marie's voice was strong. Pulled me away from the edge and to her. I stared at her face and felt a tiny bit of calm in the maelstrom that was me.

"Listen to me!" she cried, and I took in a deep breath, then let it out, trying not to cry when I saw a huge gout of red and black sparks fly out with it. "You need to focus on the here and now. Focus on what's in front of you. Right now."

I coughed up more sparks. The here and now? What the fuck was she talking about?

"What is happening around us now?" she asked.

"Dog's going crazy," I muttered. I could still hear the dog fighting with his master, his high hysterical yips mixing chaotically with the storm of light around me.

"Yes," she answered. "Yes, he is. What else?"

"What else what?"

"Do you hear? See? You need to focus on this moment, Eddie. Focus hard."

"But all the sparks," I said. "I can't see past them."

She flung herself even closer to me, her face right in front of mine. "Can you see me?" she asked. "See my face?"

Through the blizzard, I could see her. She looked scared, but she also looked real. More real than the sparks. "Yes."

"Keep looking at me until the light clears," she said. "Think of nothing but my face and this moment in time. Let the rest of it clear away. Hang on to me."

"It's hell, isn't it?" I whispered, feeling more afraid than I ever had. "I'm supposed to go to—"

"Don't even say that!" she cried, shaking her head. "You don't need to go there. Just focus on me. I'll help you come back."

"Promise?" I reached out a hand, wailing when it went through her arm and her chest. I briefly felt her heart pounding until my hand fell through to the concrete.

"I promise," she said.

So I did as she asked. I stared at her face and thought of nothing but that moment in time. Heard the dog being dragged away, snarling and snapping and definitely destined for more training, by his hysterical owner. Heard James run up and throw himself on the pavement beside Marie, asking over and over if she was all right. Saw the sun on the side of the broken-down old apartment building, and heard a couple more people venture up to the spot where I was. They were there for Marie, I knew that, and only had the courage to come over now that someone was in charge. That would be James.

He grabbed Marie's arm. "Are you hurt?" he cried. "My God, I can't believe you fell out of the car! Are you hurt?"

Marie ignored him, still staring at me. I could see her much more clearly. The sparks were disappearing, one by one. Poof. Then a little more light would get through. Another small piece of the puzzle that was this spot on the pavement at this exact time. Chewed gum. I could see gum ground into the sidewalk, beside Marie's right hand.

One last languid spark popped though my skin, just above my wrist, stinging me as it struggled its way through to the light. It bumbled off, like a half-frozen wasp, then, with a small poof, disappeared.

"Are you here?" Marie asked.

"Yes." I moved my arms, and then my legs, and felt like maybe I was going to hold together.

"Are you going to stay?"

I thought for a minute, then nodded.

"Thank God," she breathed, and sat back on her haunches. "You scared me!"

"I scared you!" James said. "How do you think I feel! I think you need to go to the hospital—"

"I wasn't talking to you," Marie replied, still staring down into my eyes. I could feel strength running from her to me and drank it in.

"Then who—" He stopped, and stared at her. "Did you hit your head or something? Maybe you really do need to go to the hospital."

"I'm fine." She continued to stare at me, and I continued to take her strength. "Do you think you can move?"

I knew she was talking to me, but of course James answered. She snapped at him, and he backed off, looking pissed and scared and most of all, confused. Welcome to my world!

"I think so," I muttered. I struggled briefly, like a turtle on its back, then pulled myself upright, and though I swayed like I was caught in a big wind I managed to keep myself on my feet.

"Can you walk?"

I took a couple of tentative steps. "Looks like."

"Good." Marie turned to James, who was flapping around a few feet from us, looking like he wished he had something to punch. "Where's the car?"

"Around the corner. Do you—need help?"

"No," Marie said. "Just show me where it is."

James took her arm. She tried to slap him away, but he ignored her, holding her protectively as he walked her to the car.

"Are you ever going to tell me what's going on?" he asked.

"Someday," she said. "Not right now, though. All right?"

He didn't answer her, just kept his hand protectively on her arm.

"Thanks for saving my ass," I said as I limped along beside them.

She didn't answer because of James. From the look on his face, I believed she didn't need the facade any more. But she clung to it, not saying another word about what had just happened as he bundled her into the car and headed back out into the congested street.

STAGE THREE

POOF!

Marie:
I Just Want to Save the Book Club . . .

THE DOOR TO that house was metal and painted black. I could see where someone—lots of someones, actually—had tried, unsuccessfully, to bash it in. Not much damage, actually. Scuffs on the paint and teeny little dents. That, and the heavy mesh over the windows, chilled me to the bone. We had a way in, but I couldn't see an easy way out, if things got messy. And knowing us, things were definitely bound to go in that direction.

"This is a fortress," I whispered.

"It is," Eddie said. "Fuckin' fortress of doom."

James didn't say anything. He hadn't spoken a word since we got back in the car. Just drove, his hands so tight on the wheel that his knuckles pushed white against his skin.

He pulled the car into a space two car lengths from the house and shut off the engine. We sat in the silence, each of us staring straight ahead.

"We have to go," I finally said, and reached for the door handle.

"Not yet," James said.

Oh God, he wanted to talk. And that was the last thing in the world I wanted to do. As afraid as I was of going up to the front door of that house, I was even more afraid of talking to James about why I had thrown myself out of his car at twenty klicks an hour down an extremely busy street.

"Honoria," I said. "The book club."

He ignored my words and glanced in the rearview mirror. "Are we alone?"

He turned and stared in the back seat, so I turned and stared, too. At Eddie, who didn't look a lot better than he had before he'd stepped out of the vehicle and nearly moved on to his own form of hell.

James reached back and waved his hand through what should have looked to him like empty air. His hand ran through Eddie, who shuddered and pulled to my side of the vehicle.

"Are we alone?" James asked again. And then he looked me right in the eye. Pinned me to the seat, like a bug or something. "Is there someone else in this car? Someone you can see, but I can't?"

I didn't answer him, just gulped and gaped like a fish that had just been hauled out of the life-giving water and was busily in the process of drowning on air.

"You're like Honoria," he said. "Aren't you? That's why you wanted me to take this case. Because you and she are the same. Aren't you?"

"Looks like he's figured out your big secret," Eddie said, rather unnecessarily, I thought. "Just tell him."

But I couldn't. I broke free of his stare and looked down at my hands. I couldn't say a darned thing, though, because I thought I'd throw up if I opened my mouth. Oh my God. He knew. Not all of it, but enough.

"Tell him!" Eddie yelled.

"Tell me," James said. His voice sounded hard and cold, like iron. "I want the truth. Now."

He knew.

I looked up from my hands and out the windshield. What I saw gave me a moment of relief so pure, I almost sobbed.

"It's the book club," I said, and threw the door open. "We have to stop them before they get to that house."

But as I ran across the street to intercept the women bearing down on the Fortress of Doom, I couldn't think of anything but the fact that James knew my biggest secret.

He knew.

"WHAT ARE YOU doing here?" Queen Bea barked as I ran across the street toward them.

"I told you not to come here, Bea," I said. "This is dangerous. You understand that, don't you?"

"Danger does not concern us, girl." Bea glared at me as only Bea could glare, but she did stop. Her entourage belatedly stopped, too, bumping into her and knocking her hat slightly askew. She whirled and her hat fell off. "Be careful, would you?" she snapped. She reached down, picked up her hat, and rammed it on her head. Then she turned back on me.

"So, are you going to help us or hinder us?"

"Ladies!" It was James, across the street, standing near his car. And he was smiling like everything was just fine. Great, in fact. "How can we help you?"

"Are you the private investigator?" Bea asked, imperiously.

"Yes," he said, and walked across the street. He stopped beside me, close enough to touch me if he wanted. He didn't. "My secretary told you to stay away from this place, didn't she?"

The "secretary" jibe stung, but I didn't say a word. The women were responding to his smile, and his "I'm a big strong man and I'll look after you little ladies" persona. A couple of them tittered, and Bea seemed taken aback enough to glance at her entourage for support.

One woman was not taken in by James and his smile, though. She pushed to the front of the group and stood, gasping as though she'd run ten miles. It was Naomi Hansen, Eddie's mother, looking like she'd aged a decade since I last saw her.

That's when Eddie made his appearance, in a swirl of grey blue light.

"It's my mom," he said. He sounded like he was about to cry, and then he did. Bawling like a little kid, great luminescent tears running down his face to his dirty white tee shirt. "Get her out of here, Marie. Please!"

"Mrs. Hansen," I said, doing my best to keep my voice calm, even though my heart was beating a million miles an hour, at least. "Please. You have to leave."

"No," she said. She was still gasping, and I realized it was from fear more than anything else. I didn't blame her for being afraid. I was terrified. "That drug fiend is in there. The one who came to my house." She gasped. "The one who killed my boy. He has to pay."

Who was she talking about? I tried desperately to remember what she'd screamed at me, the first time we met.

She'd accused me of being a drug fiend. Like Luke Stewart. Then I blinked. She'd said, "You're looking for money, like the others."

"Who?" I asked. "Who came to your house besides Luke, looking for Eddie?"

"Why, Raymond Dunning," she said. And then she pointed at something—someone—behind me. "There he is," she said, her voice suddenly as hard and cold as stainless steel. "And he killed my boy, too. I'd bet my life on it."

I turned, slowly. All right, I don't think I actually turned slowly, but it certainly felt like it. I watched James whirl, looking down the sidewalk, and then I heard Eddie scream.

"Not you!" he cried. "It can't be you. You were—my friend." He sobbed again, his voice breaking. "I thought you were my friend."

Finally, I saw who Naomi Hansen had pointed to. It was Crank, but he didn't look relaxed like he had when I met him at Needle Park. No, he looked horrified and angry. And the knife he held in his hand looked lethal.

Not quite as lethal as the huge man standing behind him, of course. But lethal enough.

"We have to leave," I said to the crowd of women. "Now."

"Are we gonna have a problem here?" James said, walking up to Crank menacingly.

"You!" Naomi cried. "Raymond! Raymond Dunning! What did you do to my son?"

Then I watched the angry mountain behind Crank reach over with his huge, angry hand and grab Crank by the shoulder. "Why does she know that name?" he asked.

Crank didn't have a chance to answer, because the angry mountain clenched his fist and I heard something break in Crank. He screamed and crumpled to his knees. "Please, R!" he cried. "I didn't do anything!"

One of the book club members cried, "Let the poor boy go!" and Naomi turned, her face a mask of hatred.

"He's not a poor boy!" she cried. "He's the son of a bitch who was responsible for the death of my son." Then she turned back to R, the huge angry mountain of a man who was still standing over Crank as he cried and writhed on the sidewalk. "Kill him," she said. "He deserves to die for what he did."

"Go for it, Mom," Eddie said.

James, surprisingly enough, did nothing but slowly raise his hands. "Just put the gun down, mister," he said.

Gun? I hadn't seen a gun. Then James shifted, and there it was, in R's hand. Pointing at James. Pointing at us all.

"We'll all leave, I swear," James said. "Just put the gun down, please."

"Too late," the mountain said. "Everybody, move. Now."

A couple of the book club members cried out, but didn't try to run. No one did. The gun R was holding was huge, and there was no one on the street besides us.

"Into the house," R said. He waved the gun at us and then grabbed Crank by the collar of his shirt, forcing a scream of agony from him. "All of you. Now."

You wouldn't think that one man with one gun could manage to keep all of us under control, but he did. Quite handily. I kept hoping for someone—anyone—to show up, but the street remained completely deserted. Of course.

When that big black door boomed shut behind us, R made us all sit on the dirty floor of the entrance. I felt like maybe, just maybe, we weren't going to get out of this one.

"Oh my God, you have to let us go," one of the book club members cried. I barely recognized Bea's voice, she sounded so frightened. For just a moment, I felt sorry for her. "You just have to!" Then she did a foolish thing. She opened her purse.

"What the hell do you think you're doing?" R growled. He pointed the gun directly at her and she froze.

"I'm—I'm getting my cell phone." Bea's voice cracked. "I was—"

"Just give me your purse," R said. He waved the gun over our heads, and a couple of the women wailed. "Everybody. Purses to the front." He glanced at James, who was sitting with the rest of us, but did not look like he was cowed in the least. "And cell phones. All of them. Now."

I handed my cell phone to James and tried to catch his eye. I was hoping for some miracle, like he'd somehow magically communicated with Stewart and the police were on their way.

Even Stewart would be better than this.

But he didn't look at me. Just took my phone and passed it forward to R with the rest of the useless junk we'd carried into this horrible place.

R tossed our cells into one of the purses and hung them all from one arm. Then he pulled out his own cell and made a call.

"We got a problem at the house," he said. He looked over at all of us. "A big problem. You gotta come."

I suspected he'd called Ambrose Welch. Looked like we were about to meet him. Lucky us.

R kept us on the ground for the ten minutes it took Ambrose Welch to get to us. He came in from the back and stood beside R, staring at all of us as though he couldn't quite wrap his head around all the sudden visitors.

Crank groaned, holding his hurt arm in front of him. I suspected R had broken his collarbone. He shrank as R looked over at him.

"This is his fault," R said. "He went to her house." He pointed at Eddie's mother, who was staring steadfastly at her hands, clasped in front of her like she was praying. "To get the money Brown Eddie owed. And he used the name Raymond Dunning."

Ambrose's face stilled. "He what?"

"He—"

"I heard you." Ambrose looked down at Crank. "You did that?"

"I had to get the money, Ambrose." Crank's voice sounded young. And frightened. Very, very frightened. "You told me I had to get the money."

"Yes." Ambrose sighed and shook his head. "I did, didn't I?"

Crank scrambled to his feet, still holding his arm to his chest. "Yeah, I was just trying to do what you told me to do. That's all."

He grinned and for a horrible second, he reminded me of a dog grinning grotesquely in an effort to appease its master.

"I get that," Ambrose said. "But why did you have to use the name of the man who owns this house, Crank? Why did you do that?"

Before Crank could answer, Ambrose pointed at the doorway through which he'd so recently appeared. "You want to go and wait for me downstairs," he said.

Crank's face stilled. "But, Ambrose—"

"Now." Ambrose Welch's voice sounded calm, relaxed. "I'll be right down."

"But, Ambrose," Crank said again. "I didn't do nothing wrong."

"Now," Ambrose said again.

Crank sobbed but turned, obediently enough. He took one shambling step down the hallway and then another. Then he ran.

Ambrose sighed as we all listened to Crank blunder down the stairs, sobbing and crying out when he bumped his hurt arm.

"Take care of him, R."

R nodded once, dropped his armload of purses to the floor, handed Ambrose the huge gun, and walked to the back of the house. As he disappeared through the doorway, I thought I saw him pull something—maybe another, smaller gun—from his pocket. Then the door boomed shut, and we all sat in silence for a few moments.

"He's done for," Eddie said. And he smiled, a ghastly thing on his white, drawn face. "Good."

The gunshots didn't sound like anything more than a couple of soft pop-pops. Could have been firecrackers in the backyard, but we all jumped as though we had been the ones who had been shot. One of the women moaned and slumped over in a faint, but no one reached out to help her. We all kept our eyes on Ambrose Welch.

He didn't even blink. Just kept the big gun nonchalantly trained above our heads as he waited for R to come back. I had no doubt that he'd use it on all of us if we did anything. Anything at all.

Trust Bea to decide to use this moment to leap into action.

Well, she didn't really leap. She growled something unintelligible and scrambled to her hands and knees.

"Are you crazy, woman?" Ambrose said. He almost looked amused as he pulled the gun down until the business end was pointed at Bea's enraged face. "Sit back down."

"I will not," she said, and pushed herself to standing. She grabbed the head of one of the other women from the book club to steady herself, and the woman screamed as though Bea was somehow killing her. Another and another started wailing as Bea flailed around, still getting her footing.

Ambrose rolled his eyes. "I said sit down," he said. And then he struck Bea hard with his free hand, knocking her back to her knees.

Bea cried out and grabbed her face where he'd hit her. She was bleeding, and the rage on her face leaked away, leaving only fear. But she couldn't stop herself and said, "You have to let us go, young man. People know we're here."

"Who?" Ambrose asked and lifted the barrel of the gun until it was pointed at her face. "Tell me who, right now!"

"I'm not telling you anything," she said. A tired dignity came over her, and she sank back down to the floor. "Not another word."

"Leave her alone," James said. His voice sounded amazingly calm, even when the barrel of the gun swung in his direction. "She's just an old woman playing detective. They all are. Please don't tell me you have been spooked by a bunch of women?"

"I have not been spooked!" Ambrose bellowed, sounding as frightened as I'd ever heard a man sound. "You better shut your mouth now," he said, trying desperately to regain some of his lost dignity, and failing, miserably. "I'll have no problem kicking the crap out of you." He glanced at the rest of us. "Just to teach you all a lesson."

I heard someone stumbling up the stairs at the back of the house, sniveling and crying softly. Well, I didn't really hear him stumbling up the stairs, but I did hear the sniveling and crying. I glanced around me and no one else was reacting to the noise. No one but Eddie.

"He's baack!" he singsonged. "I can see his light from here."

And then I could too. It was Crank's spirit, looking very much the worse for wear.

"What the hell?" he muttered as he floundered into the entryway. "What the—" Then he stopped and stared at Eddie. If I could have worked up the courage, I would have laughed. He looked so scared. Like he was seeing a ghost. Which, of course, he was.

"Eddie?" he whispered. "What are you doing here? I thought—"

"Yeah," Eddie said. "I'm dead."

Crank stumbled back a step, looking even more distraught, if that was possible. Eddie followed him.

"And so are you," he hissed.

"But— No—" Crank said. He stumbled back to the wall and fell through it with a small, wild yip. As he disappeared from view, Eddie laughed.

"Serves you right, you son of a bitch," he said. And then he made a move as though he was going to follow him.

He had to stop. No matter what Crank had done to him in his former life, Eddie had to stop what he was doing. Now.

"Don't!" I cried. "Don't do that!"

Both Eddie and Ambrose turned to me, and when the big gun swung in my direction, my mouth went dust dry.

"What, do all of you have a death wish?" Ambrose said. "I said shut the hell up."

"Why shouldn't I?" Eddie said at the same time. "You know what he did to me. You know!"

"I know," I whispered. "Just don't."

"Holy shit, girl, I've had it with you," Ambrose's voice suddenly hit the stratosphere, and I wished I had the courage to put my hands over my ears. "R! Get up here now!"

"Be quiet, Marie." James's voice sounded urgent, and I knew he was right. But I had to make certain that Eddie understood. He had to stay away from Crank's spirit. Better if he could forgive him, but I couldn't see that happening in a matter of moments. And I was pretty sure that was all the time I had to convince him. No matter what Ambrose Welch did to me.

If Eddie confronted Crank's spirit and Crank decided that he needed to go to hell for what he'd done—he could pull Eddie down with him. The two spirits could become entangled, if Eddie wanted badly enough to make Crank pay for what he did. Then Eddie would pay, too.

"Stay away from him," I said, looking past Ambrose to Eddie. "You have to. Or you'll go to hell."

I didn't even see the barrel of the gun swing in my direction, but I did see stars when he hit me with it. And, as I blacked out, I heard James cry, "No!"

That was all I heard. The horror and rage in James's voice as I slithered down a cold dark hallway to absolute black.

Eddie:
Not Going to Hell. Not Me. Not Today

AS I WATCHED Ambrose Welch smash Marie in the face, knocking her to the floor, I thought about everything that had brought me to this point in time. A teeny bit of that "seeing your life flash in front of your eyes thing," I suppose. Mom. Dad. Luke. Luke's frightening father. Even Noreen had led me right to this moment in time. But none of them were to blame. I'd done all this myself. Every decision, ultimately, had been mine. But Crank? That was a different kettle of fish. My life had ended because Crank had decided he wanted to get ahead in Ambrose Welch's organization. And Crank needed to pay.

All I'd been trying to do was carve out a little piece of the Canadian Dream for myself in that churchyard, and he'd killed me. Not just killed me, but hung me up like a grotesque scarecrow as a warning to all the other wannabe businessmen.

I always thought he was a friend of mine. I stared at the spot on the wall where his spirit had fallen through for a long time, wondering how I could have been so unbelievably wrong about him. Sure, I was a frigging addict and didn't have the best instincts, but still. You'd think I would have been able to see that someone who I thought was an honest-to-God friend would have the capacity to kill me.

James said something, and when I looked back, I saw he had Marie's unconscious body in his arms, and he looked like he wanted to kill someone. Specifically, Ambrose Welch. Marie moaned, and I should have gone over to make sure she was all right, but then I heard Crank crying and wailing somewhere down in the basement. And I had to look him in the eye, no matter that Marie had told me to stay away from him.

I walked down the steps one at a time and enjoyed the hell out of listening to Crank gasp and gibber and cry out when he saw me.

"Yep," I whispered. "Vengeful spirit here. Hope you like the idea of hell, my friend. Because that's exactly where you're going. And I'm going to put you there."

Marie:
I Wish I'd Stayed Knocked Out, to Be Honest

THE BLACK WENT grey and then white. That scared me for a second, I have to tell you, but my face hurt so much, I was pretty sure I wasn't dead. Not yet, anyhow.

My vision cleared enough to see that James had me in his arms. He was glaring at Ambrose Welch like he wanted to kill him or something. And Ambrose looked back at him, looking just as angry.

"Let me go," I said. My words sounded garbled, like my mouth was full of marbles. James glanced down at me and then back up at Welch. "I have to find him," I said, and struggled to sit up, wishing I didn't feel so weak and wishing that James didn't look like he was absolutely capable of murder.

Finally, he looked back to me, but his eyes were still ice. He set me on the filthy floor, carefully. "You can't go anywhere," he said to me. "Not yet."

Then he turned to Welch. "What happens now?"

Welch didn't answer him. Just called out to R again, and finally I heard him bumbling up the stairs, talking to himself distractedly.

I looked around. No Eddie, which frightened me. Where was he? The women were quiet, for the most part, though a couple of them were crying softly. Bea looked like a battered queen, a

269

trickle of blood running down her cheek where Welch had smacked her. She reached over and patted my hand, absently, as if to say "everything will be fine."

Not so much, Bea.

I turned my head back so I could see Welch. "What are you going to do to us?" I asked.

Welch ignored me, which was probably for the best, because when I tried to sit up, my head swam, and the world briefly turned grey again.

When my head cleared, R was standing beside Welch. How long had I been out?

"Only for a second," James said.

I blinked at him, wondering if he could read my mind. He shook his head, and said, "Don't talk anymore."

Oh. My internal voice had gone external. Not good. I clamped my lips shut and tried to figure out what the heck was going on.

"All of them?" R said.

"All of them." Welch's face was stone, and I clutched for James's hand.

"But—"

"They walked into my house, R. My house. I don't care who they are, they are going to be put down. Got me?"

"Yeah," R whispered. "I understand."

James squeezed my fingers once, reassuringly, but when I glanced at him, he still looked like he could easily kill someone.

"Take them to the basement," Welch said. "We'll deal with the bodies later."

The word "bodies" threw the book club into a frenzy, and for a horrible moment, I was afraid Welch was going to shoot us all right there, just to shut them up. But James came to the rescue.

"Please, ladies," he said. "Be quiet. Everything will be just fine. I promise."

One by one, the women quieted.

"Get them up," Welch said. R waved his gun in our direction, and the women stood. I clutched at James's arm, pulling his head close to mine. I couldn't move yet, because I was certain when I tried, I'd black out again.

"What are we going to do?" I mouthed, and was shocked when he smiled. It was an easy, sunny smile. Like we were out for a Sunday stroll or something.

"Don't worry," he said. "We're going to be fine."

Oh my God, he had a plan. He actually had a plan! Relief ran through me like cool spring water, and I would have cried if I'd had the time.

I didn't though, because R was waving his gun at us. "It's time," he said. "Move."

Eddie:
Watching Crank Go Poof

CRANK HAD TAKEN a bullet to the brain pan, and the bits of skull and brain were scattered all over the floor and far wall of the basement. Kinda made me feel sick, seeing it. But Crank acted like it wasn't even there.

"You gotta help me," he said. It was the third time he'd said it, and I was getting tired of hearing his voice.

"Go to hell," I said and then laughed at my pathetic excuse for a joke. A black light bee popped out of Crank's skin, right next to the bullet hole, and he flinched as it bit.

"What's going on?" he said, touching his fingers to his face. "Why does it hurt?"

"Because you got shot," I said. "Maybe?"

"No. It's like a hornet or a wasp," he said. Then he stopped and stared. "R shot me." A tear seeped from his last good eye and hung, glowing, on his lower lashes. That bullet had done a crapload of damage. "He shot me."

"Yeah." Suddenly, I didn't feel so vengeful anymore. Crank looked so scared. So hurt.

He sniffled. "I'm sorry," he said. "I wish things had turned out different. You know?"

Another black wasp of light popped through his skin. He flinched and then watched it bumble around him, as though it

273

was looking for a place to light.

"I hate wasps," he said. "I'm allergic. You know?"

I distantly heard yelling coming from upstairs, and then the crying and wailing of women. My mom was up there somewhere, and I knew I should be more worried about her, but I wasn't.

A third wasp light bled through his skin. Also black.

"You can decide, you know," I said. "Where you go."

"How do you know that?" Crank watched a fourth and then a fifth black light pop out of his skin, barely flinching this time.

"Noreen told me," I said. "And Marie."

He snorted tired laughter. "You shouldn't listen to a couple of skanks," he said. "They don't know what they're talking about."

The black lights were popping out of him in multitudes now. I could barely see his form in the blizzard, and I took a step back.

"I think they do," I said. "Just choose something else. Anything else."

"And what?" he asked. "Clean slate?"

"I guess."

"No," he said, and one more tear, this one blood red, slipped down his ruined face. "I'll go with my boys. I'd rather be in hell with them than anywhere with you. You were always just a tourist, you know? Just a junkie tourist. You didn't commit to the life. Not like me. I'll pick my boys every time."

The black blizzard took him, and I only felt a tiny pull. Like feeling a tornado from a mile away.

I wasn't going with him. I was going somewhere else. And Marie was going to help me get there.

If she got out of here alive.

Marie:
Face to Face With Evil,
and He's as Confused as Me

"MOVE." R'S VOICE crashed over us like frozen river gravel. One of the women cried out, a long, low wail that didn't stop. I wondered, distantly, how she could keep it up so long without breathing.

"Shut up," R said, and the noise stopped as though the woman had lost her vocal cords. I watched Bea reach a hand to the woman, patting her shoulder.

"Come on, dear," she said. "We mustn't do anything to antagonize him further."

The woman, her hand still pressed to her mouth to stop her wail, clutched Bea's hand as though it were a life preserver. Then she looked at me. They all looked at me. I was the only one still sitting on the floor.

"All right." I sighed. "I'll get up."

Easier said than done, I must say. It took James and Bea both to pull me upright. My head hurt, and I could still see flashes of light at the corners of my eyes. A concussion, I bet. How the heck had James recovered so quickly?

I glanced at him, but he still had that sunny, happy-go-lucky smile on his face. "Can you walk?" he asked.

I nodded, hoping I wasn't lying to him.

"On your own?"

I nodded again, then stopped when I felt my brain sloshing. "I think so," I said.

"Good."

He stepped away from me and walked among the women, whispering words of encouragement. I noticed that R wasn't telling him to shut up or anything. Was probably glad of the help, because Ambrose Welch had disappeared down the short hallway and through a door.

"I can't see this," he said. "Plausible deniability and all that."

"I understand." R pointed at the other doorway. The one we were to walk through. "Go," he said. "Now."

I tried taking a step, stumbled sideways, and ran into one of the women. Naomi, Eddie's mom.

"I'm sorry," I whispered, and straightened.

"I guess I should have left this to the police," Naomi replied. Her lips were white, and she kept licking them as though it would help somehow.

"I guess we all should have," I said. I clutched the sleeve of her coat, and we stumbled together through the doorway into a small, filthy, old-fashioned kitchen. In the far wall was another doorway, leading down, presumably, to the basement.

James was at the front of the line of women, urging them forward and asking them to keep calm, please keep calm. He sounded like a flight attendant trying to get hysterical passengers off a burning plane, but his calm voice was working. The women were filing down the stairs, quietly and one at a time.

James looked past us to R, who was bringing up the rear. Then he turned and pushed his way through the line of women and down the stairs and out of sight.

R pushed at Naomi and me, and I could feel the cold steel of the gun barrel in my back.

"Please," I said. "Not so fast. I feel sick."

"I don't care," he replied.

"I'll help her," Naomi said. "I will."

R didn't answer. But he kept the gun in my back as we stumbled down the stairs and into the basement proper.

The women milled about near the stairs. One—the one who had been wailing earlier—was staring at the far wall and sobbing uncontrollably. I glanced and saw gore splashed liberally all over the far wall.

It looked fresh. It was probably Crank's. Then I frowned. Even though R had obviously hidden the body somewhere, I should have been able to see his spirit. Where was he? And Eddie? Why couldn't I see Eddie?

"Oh my God," I gasped and picked up my pace. My head was spinning so terribly, I was certain I was going to fall, was going to black out, but I had to find Eddie. I had to save him. "Where is he?"

"He's dead!" the wailing woman screamed.

"He's dead," R said in his ice-cold, gravelly voice.

"Of course he's dead," I muttered. Then I realized he was probably talking about Crank.

"And he's gone." Eddie's voice wafted in from somewhere, more in my head than in the room, and I looked around frantically.

I could have cried in relief when I saw him swirl through a small door at the far end of the room. He was clear and looked oddly calm, as though nothing that was happening on this plane of existence was having any effect on him at all any longer.

I shambled two more steps toward him, and I felt the cold ring that was the barrel of the gun pressing into my back disappear. R had stopped walking forward. I was free.

"She's there," Eddie said, pointing at the door. "Honoria. She's in there."

I didn't know why R had stopped. To assess the situation, to check that he had enough bullets to kill us all. I didn't know why he stopped, but he had.

"Duck," Eddie said.

So I did, and a bullet slapped into the cement wall just above me. Behind me, I heard a fleshy clap and a grunt, and the women started to scream.

James and R were on the floor, fighting for the gun. R was huge and looked like he was built entirely of rock-hard muscle, which should have given him an advantage, but it wasn't working out that way. James had caught him off-guard and had him pinned to the ground as he grappled for the hand that still held the gun.

R's finger on the trigger. I could see it and tried to yell,

"Down!" even as R fired the gun into the cement wall by the stairs, spewing concrete chunks everywhere and causing the women to scream at an even higher register.

James grabbed and pulled the gun down, toward them both, and I was so afraid he'd be killed I almost threw myself on top of them, but someone grabbed me from behind and held me.

"He'll win," Bea grunted into my ear as she worked at holding my arms. "Don't need you to get hurt, too."

Another shot, this time into the ceiling by the stairs, and James said something—something I couldn't make out—and then suddenly he had the gun. He slapped R with it twice. And then, when stupid R still insisted on grabbing at the gun, once more.

I'd never seen a pistol whipping before and truth be told, I don't want to see it happen again. When James was through with R, his head was bleeding profusely and his eyes were rolling in his head as though he was on the verge of blacking out.

"Stay down," James said, and stood.

At that moment, the door through which Eddie had materialized opened and a man walked through it, into the main room.

"What the hell—" he started, then pulled himself back as quickly as he could. Not quickly enough, of course, because James had the gun. He snapped off a shot without even seeming to aim and caught the man in the shoulder. The man disappeared, and the door slammed shut, but we could all hear him screaming.

"Watch that one," James said to the room at large and strode to the closed door. Bea picked up a length of two-by-four lying on the floor and planted herself by the now-unconscious R. She waved the board menacingly, as if daring the man to try anything. Anything at all.

James threw the door open and caught the man within still flailing in pain and trying, without any luck, to disengage his gun from his outsized pants.

"That gangster look is so last year," I muttered as James quickly disarmed the man.

"Get her down," James said, pointing to Honoria in the corner of the dirty, musty room.

She was hanging from a link of chain that was hammered into the exposed ceiling beams, her toes barely touching the floor. She looked so much like her sketch that it stopped me in my tracks. Even the car batteries, sitting beside her, just like the picture she'd drawn.

"Jesus," I muttered. Then I tottered up to her and did my best to free her.

My best was not good, but luckily Eddie's mother, Naomi, came into the room and helped me. Meaning she did most of the freeing while I flailed around like I had a concussion or something. Which I did.

Soon Honoria was sitting on the floor, still mostly unconscious, with Naomi's arm around her protectively. "You poor dear," she said, over and over. "You poor poor dear."

Honoria groaned.

"Is she going to be all right?" It was Eddie's voice in my head. He materialized by his mother, as clear as glass. So ready to move on, it seemed that a small breeze would push him through to the next phase of existence.

"Yes," I said and smiled at him, even though his mother thought I was speaking to her. "I hope so."

"Good," he said. "Even though she still freaks me the hell out."

Me too, Eddie. Me too.

WE MOVED BACK out into the main area of the basement and James checked R. Still unconscious, with Bea still standing over him with her length of two-by-four at the ready.

"He's not going anywhere," she said. "Not while I still have breath in my body."

"Let's just tie him up," James said. He pulled a length of wire from somewhere and quickly hogtied the huge man, who groaned once and then fell silent and still.

"That's a good boy," James muttered and patted R's unconscious face. Then he stood and looked around the room. "We need to get out of here," he said. "Any ideas?"

The rest of the women looked at the walls with three small, high, wood-covered windows. One of them, the wailer I thought, ran up to one of the windows and attempted to pull down the wood. No luck, and she turned back to James and shrugged.

"Maybe you can get it down?"

I didn't pay any more attention to the women or the windows. I looked at Eddie.

"Maybe you can use the tunnel," he said.

"Tunnel?" I asked, thinking I had probably heard him wrong. A bad knock on the head could do that to you.

"Tunnel?" James said, and I shut my eyes briefly. Internal had gone external again, and he was staring at me as though I was some kind of a freak. "What tunnel?"

Screw it. I was too tired and hurt to cover up anymore. I turned to Eddie. "What tunnel?"

"It's over there, somewhere." Eddie pointed to the wall opposite the stairs, covered with shelves and junk. He sighed. "Crank told me somebody told him about it."

"There's a tunnel," I said, pointing at the shelves and junk. "Behind that."

One of the women, Naomi I thought, said, "How does she know that?" and I could tell they all had that frightened look on their faces I'd lived with most of my life.

"Just check," I said. I didn't look at James. I couldn't stand seeing that look on his face too.

"Yeah, check." Honoria's voice sounded small and hurt, like she'd been tortured. Which she had. "I really want to get out of here."

James walked up to the shelves and stared, without touching them. Then he smiled and pointed at the floor, where we all could now see scrape marks on the cement. Those shelves had been pulled away from the wall, and more than once.

"I told you so," Eddie said.

James grabbed the far edge of the shelves and gave a pull. The wood squealed and shuddered across the cement floor and all of us stared up at the ceiling, afraid that somehow Ambrose Welch would hear and come downstairs to investigate.

"Maybe he's gone," someone, probably Bea, said.

"We don't have that kind of luck." That was me. I recognized my voice and wondered why the hell I couldn't stop speaking out loud.

"It's probably the concussion," Bea replied, and I groaned. This was getting ridiculous.

James pulled the shelves back as far as he could and then we all stared at the black rough-cut hole jackhammered into the wall. "Looks like a tunnel to me," James finally said. "Let's check it out."

Then he glanced over at me. "Any idea where this goes?"

"To the garage at the back of the property," Eddie said. "That's what Crank said, anyhow."

"There's a garage. At the back of the property." I couldn't keep eye contact with James and looked down at my hands. "We should be able to get out from there."

A boom echoed through the house, and we all looked up.

"Was that a gunshot?" Bea asked.

Another boom, and cracking. Like wood cracking. Like the wood of a doorjamb cracking.

"It's the cops," I muttered. "We called them." I pointed at James. "He called them."

"I'll go see what's up," Eddie said and disappeared in his usual poof of blue and silver.

"So we're saved," one of the women said.

"That would be nice," I muttered.

"Not yet," Honoria said, and I heard her struggling to get up from the floor. "We gotta go. Now."

That's when we all heard the footsteps clattering across the floor above our heads.

"They're here to save us!" one of the women cried, and headed for the stairs leading to the main floor.

"We gotta go," Honoria said urgently. She tottered up to James, who was still standing by the tunnel entrance, glaring into the inky blackness like he could light it with his anger or something. "Let's go."

"All right," James said. "Everybody into the tunnel. Now."

I grabbed the woman who had run to the stairs. It was the wailer, I was pretty sure of that. She flinched away from me, as though I had suddenly become more dangerous in her eyes than the crazy men who had kidnapped us.

Typical. Try to save someone and they look at you like you're crazy.

Whatever.

"Let's go." I yanked her away from the steps and toward the tunnel. "Now."

Then I heard Eddie's voice, in my head and upstairs, all at the same time.

"Run!" his voice screamed. "He's coming! Oh my God, he's coming!"

And so I ran, dragging the wailer with me.
"We gotta get out of here now!" I cried.
But I was too late. Of course.

Eddie:
I Tried to Warn You. I Really Did.

AMBROSE WELCH HADN'T gone anywhere. He'd been sitting in a back bedroom, playing Grand Theft Auto as he waited for R to finish getting rid of all the problems in his crappy little life. He jumped when he heard the cops hit his fortified front door with their battering ram and put his controller down on the unmade bed. Then he picked up the big gun R had given him, clicked off the safety, and ran to the front room.

The door held, even as the battering ram hit it again. He smiled and ran into the kitchen, heading for the stairs to the basement.

So I ran down the stairs myself. I don't know what I thought I was going to do, maybe scare the son of a bitch to death, but I ran through him to Marie.

Running through Ambrose Welch was like running through a racing horse. His heart rate was so high, it felt like a high-pitched thrum. Then I ran into Marie. Her heart was beating a mile a minute too, and the fear ran through her like quicksilver. Not as bad as Ambrose, but bad enough.

"Get out!" she cried and shuddered. Full body shake. But all I could do was burst through her and blunder into the rest of the book club. Jesus, this was like a nightmare. And then I was running through Honoria, who gasped and grabbed her chest as though she was having a heart attack.

"He's here," she said. "I feel him. He's here."

"Who?" That was James, who had disappeared up the tunnel.

"Brown Eddie!" Honoria wailed.

I flailed out of her and stepped into James as he ran back to the basement. He had taken out R—no small feat—and was now going to take care of Ambrose Welch. His heart rate? I bet if I'd had the time to check it, it would have been no more than 70. It was like the guy was sitting watching TV or something. Who the hell was this guy, anyhow?

I stepped away from him and watched as he maneuvered between the women and finally burst out of the tunnel. Just in time to see Ambrose Welch grab Marie and hold the huge gun just under her chin.

I'm thinking James's heart rate spiked right then. Through the roof.

"Back off," Ambrose said. He scanned the room frantically, and his eyes widened when he saw R trussed up and unconscious on the floor. "I'm leaving, and I'm taking her with me."

Another boom and more wood cracking. Why the hell couldn't those idiots get through the front door?

Marie needed to be saved. Right now.

Marie:
I'd Never Been in an Escalade Before

AMBROSE CAME UP behind me and grabbed me before I could do anything more than grunt my surprise. He rammed the business end of the barrel of his amazingly big gun under my chin so hard my teeth clashed together and I bit my lip.

"Please don't hurt me," I said, tasting blood. "Please."

He ignored me and glared at James, who was walking toward us, the gun he was holding at the ready. "Let me through or I kill her," Ambrose said. "I shit you not."

"I can't let you do that," James said.

Ambrose laughed, roughly, and pulled me tighter to his chest. The barrel of his gun ground against the tender skin under my chin, and I groaned. "Looks like you're expendable."

I looked over at James, who still held the gun out, pointing at Ambrose and me. I saw something in his eyes. He had a plan. Another one. All I had to do was somehow get out of the way and he'd stop this madman in his tracks.

I smiled at James to let him know that I understood, and then I flew into action. Well, really, what I tried to do was drop to my knees in an effort to break Ambrose's grip on me, but it didn't work quite the way I saw it in my poor concussed head. He had me too tight, see, and so when I unlocked my knees and tried to drop to the floor, he simply gripped me even tighter.

Luckily, my head flipped back when I tried my move. Even more luckily, the barrel of the gun momentarily pointed at the ceiling, and not my chin, because Ambrose's stupid finger was on the stupid trigger and bullets burped into the ceiling, leaving a trail of destruction in their wake.

"Stop!" James cried. At least I think that's what he said. The stupid gun had gone off right beside my ear, and all I could hear was a high-pitched squeal, but I was pretty sure he said, "Stop." And then he put his gun down and pointed at the tunnel. "Just don't hurt her," I thought he said. Hoped he said.

Ambrose walked me up to the gun James had dropped. "Pick it up." He was on my good side, so I could hear him just fine. I picked up the gun by the barrel and handed it to him, wishing I was braver, wishing I had the guts to try another move, but not wanting to die.

He dragged me to the tunnel and into the screaming blackness within.

The screaming was the book club and Honoria. Ambrose pushed his way through, using me as a battering ram. Soon they were behind us, and we were alone.

"Please don't kill me," I whimpered. "Just go. I can't stop you. No one can."

He continued to ignore me, which was starting to tick me off. He whirled us both around and used me as a shield as he backed both of us the rest of the way through the tunnel.

"Up," he said when we finally stopped.

"Where?" I could see nothing in the thick darkness and felt for a moment like I was drowning.

"Up," he said again and pushed me against a rough wooden ladder.

So I looked up and finally could see something. Sunlight, or something like it, leaking around the small door that covered an opening into what I assumed was the garage.

I quickly climbed the ladder, hoping against hope he'd have to loosen his grip on me, so I could kick him or something. But his grip never loosened, even for a second.

I pushed the door, hoping it was locked, but it popped open easily and in a moment, he and I were both through it and standing in the small, musty garage. Taking most of the space was a huge SUV. An Escalade, black. Looked like it had just been polished to within an inch of its life. He kicked the door closed and pointed to a large tool chest.

"Pull that over the door," he said. "Now."

I grabbed it and pulled, hard. I'd been expecting real resistance, but the thing was on wheels, and I nearly pulled it on top of me. Ambrose pushed me back to upright when I fell against him, then grabbed me by the hair.

"Let's go."

He pulled me to the Escalade, to the driver's side.

"I can't drive," I said, hoping he'd believe me.

"Do your best," he said. "Because you're getting me out of here."

He clambered into the vehicle, keeping one hand on me and another on that big gun, and pulled me in after him.

"Now you get your first lesson," he said and laughed. He sounded crazy, and I shuddered when he pressed that gun against my head, next to my ear. "You better be a quick study."

Eddie:
I Never Thought I'd Be Happy to See Stewart.
I Was Right

JAMES DIDN'T EVEN try to follow Ambrose and Marie. He clambered up the stairs and to the front door of the house, which the cops were still trying to knock in.

"Stop!" he yelled. "I'll let you in. Just stop!"

The banging stopped, and James quickly worked the locks. As he turned the last one, the door burst open, and there was some flailing around, mostly on James's part, until Stewart came through the door.

"Where is he?" he asked, grabbing James and pulling him upright.

"Out the back," James said. "There's a tunnel to the garage. You can stop him if you hurry. But be careful. He has Marie."

Stewart sneered. "Marie. Yeah, gotta make sure she stays safe." He grabbed his walkie-talkie and spoke into it urgently, then signaled for the rest of the men to leave.

"No," James said. "There are people still here. People that have to be saved."

"Where?" Stewart barked.

James pointed at the hallway. "Through the kitchen and down the stairs. Don't hurt them. They have nothing to do with any of this." Then he shrugged. "Well, the ones who are tied up are involved. Just not anyone else down there."

Stewart considered James for a long moment, then shrugged himself. "Take them all," he said to one of his men. "But don't hurt them." He pointed at James. "Including him."

"No," James said and pulled away from them all. "Not a chance."

He disappeared out the front door, and Stewart cursed.

"Should we go after him, sir?" one of his men said.

"No," Stewart replied. "I'll take care of him myself."

He disappeared out the front door after James. And then all hell broke loose.

Marie:
The Driving Lesson Didn't Go Quite as Planned

I MANAGED TO act really stupid about driving for approximately a microsecond, until Ambrose pressed that big gun even harder into my head and screamed, "R! You idiot! Put the little needle on R, not N!"

"Oh," I said and put my shaking hand back on the gear shift. "I was sure you said N."

I put the vehicle into reverse, but didn't touch the gas. The Escalade crawled backward at about a single mile an hour and then stopped when it touched the big double doors at the back.

"What now?" I asked, my heart positively pounding itself silly and my mouth as dry as dust.

"Hit the gas!"

"This one?" I touched the brake with my foot, and I thought he was going to lose it right there.

"No one's that stupid!" he screamed and rammed the gun against my head. I saw stars again and knew I could no longer play the fool. I'd run out of time. I was going to have to make a run for it with a maniac.

"Buckle up," I muttered and hit the gas. Hard.

Eddie:
All I Can Say Is Wow

THE ESCALADE BURST out of the small garage into the back alley, into the Tactical van and an absolute crapload of police with guns.

Chunks of plywood garage door flew everywhere when they backed out of the garage. They rammed the police car blocking the other side of the alley, and it took Stewart no time at all to scream, "Fire!"

The Escalade lit up like a Christmas tree as all the bullets hit it, but it was soon apparent, the bullets were not penetrating.

Stewart cursed a blue streak and pointed to one of the black-garbed Tactical team members, who scurried to the van and pulled out the biggest baddest looking gun I've ever seen in my life.

"Stop!" James cried. "Marie's in there!"

The Escalade leapt forward, back into the garage and then through it, blowing boards and window glass all over the unkempt backyard of the drug house. The Tactical Unit ran to intercept as the vehicle fishtailed, spraying grass and dirt on what was left of the garage as it aimed for the fence of the house next to it.

"He's going around!" Stewart barked. "Take him out!"

The member with the rifle settled himself as the Escalade

began to find purchase on what little grass was left and skittered toward the old bowed fence that ran down the property line between the drug house and the one next to it.

"Now! Now!" Stewart screamed. The gunman took aim at the Escalade. The Escalade leaped forward a few more feet, then, over the scream of its motor, we all heard wood cracking.

"Huh," James said, almost smiling. "Idiot forgot about the tunnel."

The earth opened up with a small scream and a huge plume of dust as the Escalade's front end buried itself windshield-deep in the escape tunnel. The engine roared, but did nothing more than push it further into the ground. Then, even that stopped and for a moment, there was no noise from anywhere.

The sharpshooter walked up to the driver's side door with his weapon trained on whoever had been driving. A small red dot of light reflected off the tinted side window, but no one moved inside the vehicle. Soon a multitude of red dots swarmed over it as the rest of the Tactical unit aimed their weapons at the Escalade.

"Hands out the windows," the marksman barked. "Now."

The windows slowly opened and Marie, who'd been driving, obediently did what she was told. "Don't shoot," she said. "I'm unarmed."

"And you!" The marksman pointed his weapon at Ambrose Welch, semi-conscious in the passenger's seat, and the tiny red dot touched his forehead. "Hands out, now!"

A small runnel of blood ran down from Ambrose's hairline into one eye. But I could see the other eye, very clearly. That was definitely the eye of a guy who realized his luck had run out.

"Yeah, yeah," he said. But before he could move, Stewart was beside him, pressing a revolver to his head just above his ear.

"You son of a bitch," Stewart hissed. Ambrose flinched as the muzzle bit into the tender skin of his head. "I finally got you."

"Just arrest me," Ambrose said, keeping his hands up and open so everyone there could see he did not have a weapon. "I'm not talking until I see my lawyer."

"Oh really?" Stewart growled. He pulled the revolver away from his head and pulled the trigger. Both Ambrose and Marie screamed and flailed, and the marksman who had had his weapon trained on Ambrose jumped back, doing some outraged growling of his own. Stewart ignored everything and put the muzzle of his gun back to Ambrose's head. "You ready to talk now?"

"You son of a bitch!" Ambrose yelled. "I'm not armed!" He looked past Stewart to the police on the other side of the vehicle. "I don't have a weapon!"

"Stewart!" James yelled. "Stop."

Stewart ignored him, pressing the gun barrel harder into Ambrose Welch's head. "Talk. Now. Why did you kidnap that woman and torture her?"

The police standing around the vehicle looked shocked. And no one moved. Stewart ground the muzzle of his gun into the side of Ambrose's head. "Tell me. Right now."

"Word was she knew who offed Brown Eddie," Ambrose finally said. "We wanted to know what she knew—what she'd told you."

"And why would you care who killed that piece of shit?" Stewart rasped.

All right, I must admit, even though I knew the guy hated me on principle, the "piece of shit" remark stung. But at least he was trying to figure out who'd killed me.

Ambrose Welch, blood streaming down his face, relaxed and smiled. A terrible smile. "You aren't going to be able to use anything I tell you, you know. I already asked for my lawyer."

"I don't care! Tell me everything," Stewart said, and his eyes went wild. "Everything! Who else have you killed? Who else? Who else?"

"I'm telling you nothing more," Ambrose said. "I want my frigging lawyer."

And then he slowly reached for Stewart's gun.

That's when Marie started to scream her head off.

Marie:
No Way I'm Dealing With a Dead Ambrose Welch. No Way

I HAD NEVER been so afraid in my whole life.

"Don't shoot him!" I yelled. "Please, don't shoot him!"

Stewart wasn't listening, and Ambrose Welch was still moving his hands up, toward Stewart's gun. If I didn't do something, Stewart would kill him.

And then I'd have to deal with him.

I'd never met anyone so evil before. It came off him in crazy-making waves and I knew that dealing with his spirit would be nothing I could handle. My mom, maybe, but not me. Not me!

Neither of the men was listening to me. Stewart had taken a step back as he belatedly realized what Ambrose Welch was attempting, but it looked like he wasn't going to be quick enough. Welch was going to touch that gun and then—then everybody with a weapon was going to use every bit of force at their disposal to stop him.

Suicide by cop.

So I reached over and rammed my thumb in his eye. Hard. Yelling, "Don't shoot him, don't shoot him!" over and over as I felt his eyeball compress and then give. And then he screamed, high and tight, and forgot all about Stewart's gun. Forgot about everything but his eye and my thumb.

Finally, Stewart did the right thing and backed away. The rest of the cops swarmed the vehicle, pulling Ambrose Welch from it and throwing him to the ground as he screamed and clawed at his wrecked eye.

They pulled me out and tossed me on the ground, too. I pressed my face into the torn-up grass and let them do whatever they wanted to me. I didn't care at that moment. I'd stopped Ambrose from killing himself. Thank God.

I MUST HAVE blacked out, because the next thing I heard was Stewart saying, "Take them away, boys."

Seriously. "Take them away, boys." Who did he think he was, John frigging Wayne?

I rolled onto my back and groaned. I hurt absolutely everywhere. "Don't move," someone said. I opened my eyes, and there was James, looking worried.

Not angry or suspicious. Just worried.

"Did we get them?" I asked.

"Yep." He almost smiled. "Can you stand?"

"I don't know." I tried moving my arms. Had some luck, so tried my legs. More luck, so I slowly sat up, and then, with James's help, I stood. Shaky, like a newborn foal, but I did stand.

I heard a spatter of applause from somewhere behind the mostly destroyed garage. "What's that?" I asked.

"I think it's the book club ladies," James said. "Showing their appreciation."

"Huh." I grabbed his arm and hobbled a few steps, then stopped and really looked around. Ambrose Welch was gone. So was Stewart.

"Where are they? The bad guys?"

"Stewart took them to the cop shop. For a little more interrogation."

I shook my head. "I don't think he's going to get any more out of that guy."

James shrugged. "I don't care, to be honest. Welch as much as confessed to killing Brown Eddie, and that gets Honoria off the hook."

"Honoria," I gasped. For a brief moment my head spun, and James grabbed my arm, helping me stay upright. "Where is she?"

"On her way to the hospital."

"Is she—is she going to be all right?"

James's face froze. "She took a lot."

"Jesus, James. They tortured her." I couldn't believe that anyone could do that to another human being.

"I know." James put his arm around my shoulders and gave me a quick, hard hug. "I think the book club ladies want to talk to you."

"Right." I sighed. "None of them actually got hurt, did they? Queen Bea will never forgive me."

"Queen Bea," James half-smiled. "That's funny. No. Nobody hurt. I'd appreciate it if you handle them, though. I really don't know what they expect of me."

"I think they expect a job," I muttered, looking around. "Where are they?"

"Over there." He pointed somewhere past the wrecked garage. "Want me to help you?"

"No," I said. "I think I can do it under my own power."

I hobbled away from James's protective arms and past the cops milling around the crime scene, stretching out the oh-so-familiar yellow and black tape that would soon keep everyone from muddling the scene further.

I got to the tape and attempted to bend over, to scoot under it, and stumbled. A police officer ran up and pulled the tape high enough for me to walk more or less upright.

"Thanks," I said.

"Good job with the driving," he said and pointed at the Escalade, still buried nose-deep in Ambrose Welch's escape tunnel.

Oh yeah, like I meant to do that. "Thank you."

"And taking Welch out. That was really something to see."

"Thanks."

"Maybe we can go out for a drink or something, and you can tell me all about it."

Good grief.

I smiled at him, said something terrifically noncommittal, and hobbled away before he could press the offer of a drink.

I managed to get past the garage and saw a police car blocking the alley. Behind it, I could see Bea and the rest of the women on the grass of someone's backyard. Bea put a china cup to her lips and sipped.

Trust Bea to be able to find tea in the middle of a crime scene. "How are you?"

"Fine," she said and took another sip from the china cup.

"Where did you get that?"

"From her." She pointed over to an ancient woman who was hobbling among the book club women with a huge teapot. "She lives in that house." Bea pointed at the house on the corner. "And she was good enough to give us a cuppa something."

"Nice."

"Yes," she said. "Some people know how to treat us."

I chuckled. Looked like the moment of appreciation was over. "Hey, we got you out of there," I said. "Wasn't that good enough?"

"We will discuss this at another time," she said imperiously and turned her back on me.

"Oh come on, Bea," I started, but she held up a hand, palm out, without turning around.

"At another time."

Hey, I tried.

I caught a glimpse of Eddie's mother, and my heart jumped. I hadn't seen Eddie since we escaped the tunnel. Had he moved on in the middle of that bedlam? I hoped not. He'd been so close to going to his version of hell. I was afraid if he'd slipped over, he'd still let himself go there. He didn't deserve that.

She was sipping tea over by a weeping birch tree, and she looked up and smiled at me faintly as I walked over to her. Then I saw Eddie, standing in amongst the branches of the tree, watching her.

"Hi," I said, to both of them.

"Hi," Eddie said, and a second later his mother said hello.

"How are you?"

"I'm fine," Eddie's mother said. Eddie didn't answer, so I glanced in his direction. He was crying.

"I hurt her so bad," he whispered. "How can I ever make up for that?"

"I'll be back in a second," I said, and without looking at his mother again, walked over to Eddie. "You can't, Eddie," I whispered. "I'm sorry, but you can't."

"I know," he said. "But she came here because of me. Jesus, even after I'm dead I'm causing her grief! Nearly got her killed!

You tell me why I don't deserve to go straight to hell for that."

"Because she decided to do this, Eddie. Not you. Her."

"Yeah but—"

"But nothing."

"Who are you talking to?"

I could tell by the look on Eddie's face that his mother had followed me and was now watching me argue with what looked like nothing.

I was going to turn and give her some song and dance about seeing a cat or some such foolishness, I really was, but then something snapped. I was tired of the lies and the hiding. Just this once, I decided to tell the truth. Screw it.

"I'm talking to your son. To the spirit of your son."

Eddie's mother's face blanked, then tightened, and she took a small step away from me. "I don't think that's very funny, young lady," she snapped.

"See?" I said, turning back to Eddie. "They think I'm a liar or crazy. *That's* why I never tell."

"Tell her I'm sorry," he whispered.

"She doesn't believe I'm even talking to you."

"Stop that," Eddie's mother said and took another scuffling half step back.

"I'm telling you the truth," I said hopelessly. She was never going to believe me.

"Prove it," she snapped.

"How?"

"Oh God, just tell her I'm sorry," Eddie said, on the verge of tears again. His voice sounded weak, and I glanced back at him, almost ready to see those Godawful black and red sparkling lights around him again, but they weren't. He just looked immeasurably tired.

"What did I get him for his fourteenth birthday?"

"What?" I turned back to his mother and stared at her. She glared back.

"If I'm supposed to believe you, you should be able to answer that simple question," she said. Her chin began to quiver. "What did I get him for his fourteenth birthday?"

I looked at Eddie, but he just looked confused, so I turned back to his mother. "Why his fourteenth?"

"That was the last time I bought him a birthday gift that didn't have anything to do with the streets and drugs," she said, her voice small. "The very last time."

"Oh." I looked back at Eddie, and he had the saddest smile I'd ever seen on a ghost's face. And that is going some.

"She bought me a hamster," he whispered.

"A hamster?" I asked, but didn't need to see his nod to know I had passed his mother's test. Her half-scream and the crash of breaking china hitting hard-packed earth told me everything.

"Tell her I'm sorry," Eddie said.

"Please, please tell him I'm sorry," Eddie's mother cried. "I'm so sorry! If I'd just been a better mother, maybe none of this would have happened!"

"No," Eddie said. "That's not right. I was making my own choices. She was my excuse for doing what I did. She doesn't need to apologize. I do."

"Please tell him," she whispered. "I am so sorry for everything."

"He can hear you," I said. "He thinks it was all his fault."

She laughed, sounding heartbroken. "No," she said, shaking her head. "If I'd been better, somehow, this wouldn't have happened."

"She's wrong," Eddie said. "You know that, don't you?"

We had hit a bizarre impasse. Eddie desperately needed his mother's forgiveness, or he would push himself to that hell he'd built for himself. And I had this horrible feeling that if Eddie didn't forgive his mother, the same thing would happen to her. I couldn't allow that to happen. Not on my watch.

"Just forgive each other—and yourselves. Please?"

I jumped when I saw a couple of vans pull up beside the police car blocking the alley entrance. "They're going to take us all away," I said to Eddie's mother. "Please. Forgive him, so he can move on."

Her lips quivered, and her eyes filled with tears. "I forgive you. Do you forgive me? Please say you forgive me!"

"I—I forgive you," Eddie whispered. "I love you, Mom."

I told her what he'd said, and she threw herself into my arms and sobbed. I felt Eddie's cold steal over me as he reached through me to touch his mother, and for a moment, before the police hauled us all away, our three hearts beat as one.

But Eddie didn't move on. He really did need Luke, just as I suspected.

Dammit, anyhow.

THE POLICE GRABBED everybody to take us down to the police station, and I obediently followed along until I felt someone's hand on my elbow, pulling me out of the line.

I turned and saw it was James. "You can ride with me," he said. "If you want."

For a second, I thought about saying, "No, it's all right, I'll ride with the book club ladies," but I didn't. I just nodded silently and followed him to the car.

It was time for our talk, whether I wanted it or not.

But here's the thing. He helped me into the car, ever the gentleman, and pulled away from the old house with the black door without saying a word. When I said, "I suppose you want to talk now," all he did was shake his head.

"Not now," he said. "Let's do what we need to do first. We can talk later."

So we drove to the cop shop in total silence. He seemed calm. Almost at peace. But I was neither. I felt nearly as scared as I had in the Escalade, moments before Ambrose Welch's attempted suicide by cop, because I was absolutely certain that when our talk was over, we'd be over, too.

WE WALKED INTO the front entrance of the cop shop and were immediately buzzed in and herded through to the interview rooms at the back. I saw that the book club had beaten us there, as had Eddie. He was standing with his mother, still looking as clear as glass.

After we collected our cell phones, we stepped into line behind the women. Eddie walked up to me and stood solemnly.

"Thanks, Marie. I know that was hard for you, putting yourself out there like that."

I wouldn't answer him, because James was standing beside me, but Eddie didn't seem to care. Just wandered back to his mother, who I hoped would keep her mouth shut. She'd said she would, but I'd learned the hard way not to trust people when they say they'll keep a secret.

His mother looked surprisingly good. She was comforting a couple of the other book club members who had decided that since things were now relatively quiet and they were out of danger, they could afford to have small meltdowns. She looked at me over the head of the woman sobbing all over her and smiled as though her biggest burden had been lifted. Maybe it had.

I looked at Eddie. He had the same look on his face. Maybe I'd helped them both. Not a bad day's work, if I had.

A cop walked past, then stopped and looked at James and me.

"You're not supposed to be here," he said and hooked his finger at us, indicating we needed to follow him, ASAP. But before I could follow, Eddie's mother reached out and grabbed my sleeve. I turned and tried to plaster a smile on my face.

"I just wanted to thank you for what you did for me," she said.

"You're welcome," I whispered, pointing to the line of women moving away from us. "You have to go."

"I know." She smiled. "You gave me something I never thought I'd get."

"I'm glad."

She leaned forward. "Did he—move on?" she mouthed.

I glanced over at Eddie, who was still standing beside her. "No. Not yet."

"I hope he finds what he needs."

"So do I."

I turned and scurried after James. We turned a corner and then both the book club and Eddie were out of my sight.

"That was Eddie's mother, wasn't it?" James asked. "What did she want?"

"Just wanted to thank me." I pointed to the impatient police officer waiting to escort us to wherever we were going. "Why aren't we going with the others, do you think?"

"I imagine Sergeant Worth wants to have words," James replied. "And then you'll have to tell me what you did to help her."

"Yeah," I said and walked away from him to the cop. "We're ready to go."

I didn't really want to go talk to Sergeant Worth. She was going to be angry, and that was never good for us. But it would be much better than talking to James about Eddie's mother. Or about Eddie.

I WAS RIGHT about Sergeant Worth. She was mad. I only felt a teeny bit better when I realized she was more mad at Stewart than she was at us.

"I told you to stay away from that place, James. You could have been killed." She glared at him over the top of some very old-fashioned looking reading glasses, then ripped them off and slammed them down on the mountain of paper on her desk.

"I know," James mumbled, doing his best "I'm a bad boy" routine. I didn't think she was buying it. "But we felt that time was of the essence—"

Worth's face tightened, and she slammed her hand down on the desk top—and her glasses. I heard one of the arms snap off and stared down at my shoes.

"Time—essence?" she yelled. "And what if one of those women had been killed. How would you have felt then?"

"Not good," James mumbled, then looked up. "But we went there to stop them, you know. And no one was hurt—"

"Not because of you, but in spite of you!" Worth bellowed. James finally stopped trying to make things better, which, as far as I was concerned, made things better almost immediately.

"Now, which one of you is going to tell me what happened while the arrests were being made?" she asked. She swept the broken glasses into the trash and squinted at the open file in front of her.

James and I glanced at each other. I was the one who had seen everything, and James had burned his bridge. Much as I hated talking to the woman, it would be me. I put up my hand, tentatively, like I was in sixth grade, about to answer a question I wasn't exactly sure of, to a teacher I didn't like at all.

"Speak," Worth said. "Succinctly, if you can."

"I'll do my best," I said and stared back down at my shoes. It was easier to pretend I wasn't in danger that way. I quickly went through events after Welch's attempt to break out of his own backyard and Stewart's brutal impromptu interrogation after that. To give Worth her due, she didn't stop me once. She even waited for a beat or two after I'd stopped talking.

"Did you see this?" she asked, looking at James. "Can you corroborate what she saw?"

"No. I was with our client. But the rest of the police saw."

"What was going on there?" she muttered, scribbling down notes and frowning furiously.

"He was trying to get Welch to confess to Brown Eddie's

murder," I said. "And somebody else's, I think." I didn't know if I was being helpful or stupid, but I did know for sure that someone had to do something about what had happened there.

"Whose?" Worth said.

"No idea. But if I had to guess, I'd bet it had to do with his son, Luke."

"Hmm." Worth leaned back and shook her head. "We thought he was all right after Luke died. Thought him wanting to get back to work was a good sign."

"Looks like it wasn't," I muttered, hoping this would all stop soon. I desperately wanted to get out of here, have a three-hour shower, and then a drink or two. Or three. Jeez, maybe James was right. Maybe I was leaning a bit hard on alcohol to get me through.

I only jumped a bit when Eddie oozed through the closed door and sidled up to me. "When can we get outta here? You promised me you'd move me on." His voice shook. "I really need to do that, soon. Hearing Luke's old man losing it out there is really taking it out of me, man."

I tried to look at him without acting like I was really looking at him. Didn't work out quite as well as I'd hoped.

"You got a problem, Marie?" Worth asked.

"I—I need to use the washroom," I said. Fast thinker, me, but a quick bathroom run was actually not a bad idea. I could talk to Eddie about Stewart, actually use the washroom, and—

"Hold it," Worth said shortly. "We're not done here."

"He's not here now," Eddie said. "He left. Bet he's gone to the hospital, to find out who else Ambrose killed."

I didn't even pretend not to react. "What?"

"I said hold it," Worth replied.

"I said he's probably at the hospital losing his mind on Ambrose Welch." Eddie sighed. "Why?"

I'd finally remembered something Mom had taught me, years before. It was when she'd first realized I had the "gift" and was determined to make me just like her.

She had told me that spirits trapped in our plane of existence can have an effect on the living around them. Usually, the effect wasn't good.

I realized that Luke was doing that to his father. Making him crazy, just by being around him. Making it so that his father could not move on with his life, just like Luke couldn't move on with his death.

"Can we go soon?" I asked. Worth rolled her eyes.

"I still have a few more questions for you. Just wait!"

So I suffered through the rest of her questions, letting James take the bulk of them and get back on her good side.

Stewart wasn't acting crazy because he was a nasty man. He was acting crazy because Luke was haunting him.

We just had to get out of here. I wriggled on my chair. Man, now I did have to pee!

Eddie:
I Haven't Seen You in a Long Time, My Friend

THE CHICK COP kept Marie and James answering questions for another hour and a half, just to be a bitch, I think. It looked like poor old Marie's back teeth were floating, the way she beat it to the restroom.

I followed her there, thinking we were going to talk, but she told me to bugger off. So me and James stood outside the door and waited.

She sure took her own sweet time. I almost went in a couple of times to see if maybe she'd fallen in or something, but I didn't. Did the gentleman thing and didn't feel like I deserved her glower when she finally pushed the door open.

Apparently she'd been waiting in there for me. Hey, how was I supposed to know?

"Let's go to the hospital," James said. "We need to check on Honoria. Make sure she's all right. And you have to get your head checked."

"No," Marie said. "I have to go somewhere else first." She looked up at him with those big eyes of hers, and I watched James melt. Man, the guy had it bad.

"Where do you need to go?"

"To Angus Stewart's house."

James opened his mouth and then snapped it shut. "Why?" he

asked, his voice tight and high, like he already knew the answer, just needed her to confirm it.

"Trust me," she said. "It's the only way to save Stewart."

"We were just in Sergeant Worth's office!" James exclaimed, scurrying after her. "If he needs saving, why didn't you tell her to do it?"

"Because she can't do what he needs, James." Marie smiled over her shoulder at him and even I melted a little bit. "But I can."

"And we need to go to his house?"

"Yes. Because his son's still there."

"But Luke's dead," James said.

She looked down at her feet. "Yes."

"And you think he's still—there." James's voice had gone flat, like he was trying his best to work out a difficult algebra problem in his head and was failing.

But I understood. I understood absolutely.

"We gotta go," I said. "We gotta go, now."

"Yes," Marie said. Her voice was quavering like she was terrified. Which she probably was. "Please, can we go? I'll explain everything as soon as I do this."

"Promise?" He stopped and grabbed her by the hand, forcing her to stop, too.

She stared into his eyes for a long time, then slowly nodded her head. "I promise," she whispered.

I hoped she would. The guy deserved to know the truth about the woman he was absolutely head over heels in love with.

I knew for a fact that she didn't realize how he felt about her, and I wasn't even sure he knew how he felt himself. But I could feel it coming off them in waves and felt a brief spurt of envy.

I'd screwed up my life, no doubt about it. I hadn't even fallen in love, but the regret about that felt like a distant ache. It was probably better that I'd never been in love, or had kids. Looking at the way I'd lived, I should probably be relieved that I hadn't procreated. I hadn't had the chance to screw up the next generation.

No, the one thing that I really, truly regretted was not being able to say goodbye to Luke. That boy had been my best friend, no doubt about it. And I'd let him down terribly at the end. If I could have had one wish, it would have been to have a do-over where he was concerned.

It looked like I was going to get my final wish.

At last.

IT WAS A pretty quiet drive to Stewart's house, I must say. I think Marie was regretting what she'd promised James, and I think James was regretting going along with Marie about going to Stewart's place without any evidence as far as he could see. I didn't really blame him—I wouldn't have bought it either. Being dead, well, that kind of changes a person's perspective on things, but I could get where he was coming from.

"We're here," Marie whispered, pointing at Stewart's house. "Just pull up front and wait. I'll be back soon."

"What—" James started, then shut his mouth, and shook his head. "Right. I get all the answers after you're done. Right?"

"Right." Marie didn't actually look like she believed her own words. "Do me a favour though. If you see Stewart pull up to the house or whatever, please let me know." She twittered anxious laughter. "I don't want him to catch me in there."

"I will," he said. "Be careful."

She got out, and I followed her.

"You want to know how to get in the house?" I asked.

"Not yet," she muttered.

I looked back at James, who was watching her progress up the walk. "Why not? You're going to tell him all about me when we're done here anyhow. What's the deal?"

"I haven't decided yet how much to tell him," she said stiffly.

"Oh come on!" I barked. "You promised the guy!"

"I know!" she cried. "Can we talk about this in the house?"

"Fine."

"Do you know where a key is? Please say under a rock by the front step!"

"Under a rock by the front step."

She stopped and stared at me. "Are you kidding?"

"Yeah, I am," I replied. "Last time I was here, there was one in the mailbox."

"What cop leaves the key to his house in the mailbox?"

"I guess the one who knows nobody would be stupid enough to steal from him." I shook my head. "I wasn't, anyhow."

"Really?" She walked up the steps and pulled open the mailbox, then ran her fingers across the bottom.

"Really," I replied. "He's got guns. Lots of them."

"Oh." She pulled her hand from the box and opened it, smiling triumphantly. On her palm sat a house key.

"Told you."

She put the key in the lock and turned it, then blanched when we heard someone inside yelling.

She turned to me, her face ashen. "Prepare yourself," she whispered.

"Prepare myself? What do you mean—"

But by that time, she'd swung the door open, and I was face to face with Luke.

He looked at me and almost faded from sight.

"Eddie," he whispered. "What are you doing here?"

"I don't know," I whispered back. Then everything went black.

LONG STORY SHORT, I fainted. Yeah, yeah, a ghost fainting, how pathetic can a guy get, right? I came to with Marie leaning over me.

"Are you all right?" she asked.

I didn't bother answering her. I needed Luke. "Where is he?"

"He's—hiding," she said. "I'm sorry. I should have warned both of you it would be a bit of a shock."

"Damned straight you should have." I struggled to sit up, then gave up and stayed on the floor. "He's been stuck here the whole time?"

"Yes."

"By himself?"

"Yes."

"That's brutal." I turned my head and looked down the hallway, and thought I could see a hint of light from around the corner that led to the kitchen. Man, she wasn't kidding. He *was* hiding.

"Luke, bro!" I called. "Come here!"

He stuck his head around the corner, and I almost laughed. He was as bright as Casper in those stupid cartoons.

"Man, you scared the shit outta me, dropping like that," he replied. "If you weren't already dead, I woulda swore—"

"Yeah, well, nothing that dramatic." I hoped I couldn't blush. That whole fainting thing was pretty embarrassing, and I didn't want to dwell on it.

"Eddie," Marie said. "It's almost time."

"I know," I said. "Just give me a minute."

"But—"

"Just one minute," I snapped. I turned away from her and looked at Luke.

"Man, it's been an age since I've been in this house," I said.

"We used to have some good times here, didn't we?" Luke asked. He slid to the floor beside me and stared up at the dusty light fixture above our heads.

"We did have some," I said, even though it wasn't exactly the truth. His father never let him have any fun at all. But hey, whatever. He could remember the place any way he wanted. His death.

"You should stay," he said. "We can hang out. Just like the old days."

I turned my head and looked at his translucent profile. He wasn't glowing as brightly as he had before. Didn't know what that meant and couldn't work up the energy to care. I was so tired.

"I don't think so, Luke. She's going to help me leave."

"But you just got here." He didn't turn his head. Just stared hard at the light above our heads like it was the only thing that mattered anymore.

"Not here," I said and waved my arms. "I gotta leave all of this. She told me. I don't have to just hang around, Luke. I got a choice about that." I blinked. "I bet you do, too."

"Really?" He flopped his head to the side and stared into my eyes. "You think so?"

"Really."

"How?"

"I have a gift," Marie said. "I'll help him."

Luke glanced at her. "Will you help me, too?"

"You think you're ready to leave this house and go to the next plane of existence?"

"I sure am tired of being stuck in here." He looked at me and his face creased in concern. "Is something wrong?" he asked. "You're—disappearing."

"He's right," Marie said. "I can barely see you."

"Is that good?" I felt light. Like I was barely attached to this world any longer.

313

"It is if you're ready," she said.

"Take me with you!" Luke cried, struggling to roll over on his side. "I don't want to stay here alone anymore."

"Can I take him with me?" I asked Marie, and then I laughed. I sounded like Luke was a dog in the pound or something.

"You can help me help him," she said. "If you want."

"I want."

Marie walked between us and put her hands where our chests would have been if we had been alive. Her touch soothed me until I felt that the only thing holding me to the earth was her hand and then her voice.

She talked about letting all that was earthly go. Luke asked her some question, and even though I was right beside him, I could barely hear his voice. I don't know if it was because he was speaking so low, or because I just wasn't hearing anything of this earth any longer. Whatever it was, she leaned over him, looked him in the eye, and answered him.

"No," she said. "It won't hurt."

Good, I thought. *He's had enough of that.*

I felt warmth under her hand and then saw the light begin to swirl around her.

"Make your choice," she said, her voice calm, soothing. "Make your choice and move on. You have nothing more to learn. You can move on."

The light from my chest moved up her arm. Wound around and around, and then began to intertwine with light winding up her other arm. Light from Luke. I could feel his strength in that light, even as I offered him mine.

"Come on, buddy," I mumbled. "This is going to be great."

Then I saw the light. And by fuck, it was beautiful.

Marie:
So *That's* What Getting Hit by a Mack Truck Feels Like!

I LAY ON the floor for a while after Luke and Eddie moved on, wishing there was someone I could convince to get me a big drink of water and a nice warm blanket. I felt like I'd been run over, and I didn't want to move.

But I did. We had a client to go see, and an office to look after, and a prickly police sergeant to deal with. I dragged myself out of that house, locked the door, rubbed my fingerprints off of the knob, walked down the stairs, remembered the key, which was still in my hand, wanted to cry but didn't have the liquid reserves to do that, so just tossed the key in the general direction of the mailbox, and floundered back to the car.

James was properly shocked at my appearance and made me sit through a rather thorough check for bullet holes. Apparently, he had decided that I looked like I'd been shot.

"Are you sure you're all right?" he asked when he got tired of looking for blood.

"Yes. Let's go see Honoria," I muttered, pushing his hands away from me and trying, without success, to do up my seatbelt.

"What happened in that house?"

I was going to say "I did a double," but was pretty sure he'd misunderstand, so I didn't say anything. I just flailed away with the seat belt, then fell back against the seat with a sigh that sounded more like a groan of pain than relief when I finally heard the dry click as the two pieces connected and I was finally safe.

"I want you to get checked out when we get to the hospital," he said as he put the car into gear and moved out into traffic.

"I'm fine. Just fine," I mumbled. At least I thought I said that. I fell asleep so quickly, I can't actually be sure of anything.

I OPENED MY eyes when somebody touched my face and was rewarded with a bright white light boring into one eye. It hurt, so I did what anyone would do in that situation. I struck out. Hard.

"What the hell?" Whoever was on the other end of the little flashlight apparently didn't like being punched, but at least the light was out of my eyes.

"Leave me alone," I yelled and tried to roll over. Seat belt had me trapped good, though, and I fought it, too.

"Is she drunk?" I assumed that was whoever had been wielding the flashlight.

"No, she's not. I think she's been hurt." James sounded pretty panicky. That was never good.

"I think she's drunk." Definite judgement in the other voice, so I pried open an eye to see who it was.

An angry-looking nurse stood beside the open door of James's car. He'd obviously been trying to examine me.

"James, I don't need help!" I jerked ineffectually at the seatbelt a couple more times, then gave it up. "I'm just tired, that's all."

"No. You should have seen her. She looked like—I don't know!" James sounded nearly beside himself. "Please look her over."

"I'm fine, James." I finally got the stupid seatbelt open and shakily pulled myself to my feet beside the nurse. "Really. He shouldn't have bothered you. I'm all right."

"You're sure?" the nurse said, flicking the flashlight in the general direction of my eyes again before turning to James. "Sorry, bud. She says she's fine." He walked away, leaving me with James, who did not look pleased at all.

"You should be checked out," he said. "There's something wrong. You look terrible."

"Thanks," I said sarcastically. "I'm sure."

"You know what I mean," he said. "God, you drive me crazy sometimes! Can't you just let a doctor look you over?"

"No." I shook my head, and even though it gave me such a bad case of vertigo that I thought I was going to vomit again for a second, I continued to do it. He had to understand. I make the choices about my health.

"Maybe you should sit down," he said acidly. "You've gone green."

"Fine." I sat down on the car seat, then briefly put my head between my knees. "I'll be all right in a second. Just leave me alone, all right?"

"I don't understand why you won't let me take care of you when you need it," he said. When I lifted my head, warily, afraid the vertigo would return, I could see he'd gone from angry to sad. Man, I didn't need that either. I was so tired.

"I just need to sleep, James."

"Are you sure?" I couldn't look in his puppy dog eyes any longer, so I pulled myself back into the car, and reclined the seat.

"Yes. Really. That's all it is. Go see Honoria and make sure she's all right. I just need to close my eyes for a few more minutes. Really."

"All right." He walked a few steps away from the car, then turned back to me. "I wish you could trust me," he said, then turned on his heel and marched into the hospital.

I wanted to follow him and tell him that I mostly trusted him—and that the lack of trust had nothing to do with him and everything to do with me. I really did. But I was so tired, I fell asleep again before he was even out of sight.

I wish now I had.

I WOKE UP when the sun broke over the horizon and filled the inside of the car with light. I moved my head and my neck screamed holy hell, apparently because I hadn't moved it in over six hours.

"What the hell?"

I pulled the seat to upright and yanked at the jacket that wrapped me. Why was I wrapped in a jacket? James's jacket. The one he'd been wearing when he'd headed into the hospital the last time I saw him. When had he come back? Why wasn't he here?

What was going on?

I looked around, trying to get my bearings. The doors were all locked. I hadn't done that. And the keys were in the ignition. I was sure he'd taken them with him when he'd left.

I shook my head, trying to clear my poor overwhelmed brain. There was a bottle of water in the cup holder, so I grabbed it and drained it. That helped.

I reached over and touched the keys.

"He must still be in the hospital," I whispered. "But why would he leave the keys with me?"

Nothing was making sense. I ran my hands through my hair, wishing I had another bottle of water. I was still parched.

"I could go in and buy one," I muttered and rammed one hand into the pocket of James's jacket, looking for change. I knew I didn't have a cent to my name. There was nothing in the pocket, though. Not even lint.

"This is bad," I muttered, then decided to man up a bit and go into the hospital, and find out what the heck was going on.

I'd only walked halfway across the deserted parking lot when I saw a small woman, her arm in a sling, walk out through the big double doors. It looked like Honoria, but I knew I had to be wrong. She would be in the hospital a lot longer than just one night.

"Hey!" The small woman waved her good arm energetically. "Marie! Hey girl! Did you sleep well?"

I picked up speed slightly, going from a limp to a hobble. Sleeping in a car, not my best choice.

"Honoria?" I called back. "What are you doing? I thought—"

"Not ready for the undertaker yet!" Honoria called. She looked remarkably well. I touched my black eye ruefully. Probably better than me, for heaven's sake. "You ready to take me to the bus depot?"

"What?"

"The bus depot. It's time for me to get out of Dodge. James said you'd do it—you're okay with that, aren't you?"

I decided to hobble right up to her before finishing the conversation because I was pretty sure I wasn't hearing her right. She met me way more than halfway, moving much more easily than I was. And she'd been tortured, for heaven's sake.

"You look like crap, girl. I think you should have spent the night in the hospital instead of me," Honoria said, tapping me lightly on the cheek, just below my blackened eye. I decided to ignore that.

"So James told you I'd take you to the bus depot?"

"Yes. You'll do it. Right?"

"I guess." I looked around, as though I thought—hoped, really—that he'd leap out from behind another parked car or something. "Where is he?"

"He said he had to go," Honoria said, and reached with her good hand into the pocket of her coat. "He left this for you. Said it would explain everything."

In her hand was an envelope, with my name written across the front in James's bold handwriting.

I didn't want to take that envelope from her hand. Not at all. Envelopes from men never held anything good.

"When did you last see him?" I asked.

"He left about three hours ago. He and I had a good old talk and then he said he had some things he had to figure out for himself."

I looked at her sharply. I did not want a clairvoyant telling my James things about me. Not at all.

She laughed when she saw my look. "Don't worry," she said. "I didn't spill your secrets. I told you I wouldn't."

"He already knows," I said, miserably.

"Oh." She smiled. "So the hard part's over."

"Yeah, sure." Not believing that for a second, sister.

"I want to thank you," she said. "For saving me. And for saving Eddie." She sighed. "Finally, he's at peace, which means I will be, for a while, anyhow."

I didn't know what to say, so I didn't say a thing. She waved the envelope at me. "Take it."

I opened the envelope carefully, like I was afraid something horrible was going to jump out at me. Actually, that's exactly the way I felt, if I was going to be honest about the whole thing. I'd never had what you'd call a happy surprise when I opened an envelope from a man. Never.

Inside I found five one hundred dollar bills and a note. I stared at the money for a long time before I dared open that note. And by the time I did, I *knew* I didn't want to read it. Money plus a note always means disaster.

I was angry to see my hands were shaking. Come on, I thought. Woman up. You knew he wouldn't stick around. They never do.

I read the note quickly and started crying before I got halfway through.

Marie—

I have some stuff I have to work out, so I'm hitting the road.

The money and the car are yours. Call it payment for wages owed.

Leave the key to the office under the welcome mat, if you're going to take that other job, please. I hope you don't, but I wouldn't blame you if you do.

I'll find you when I come back. We still need to talk.

Love,

James

"Where did he go?" I asked, ramming the money and the note back into the envelope. "Why didn't he talk to me? Why did he leave?"

"I don't know, Marie. He didn't tell me any of that. Just assured me you'd drive me to the bus depot. You will, won't you?"

"Yes, I will." I walked around to the driver's side door, tried to open it, nearly snapping a nail because it was still locked.

I knew he'd leave, if he found out my secret. I just knew it.

How could he do that to me?

Honoria reached over and popped the lock open, but before I could grab the handle, my cell phone buzzed.

"James," I muttered, flailing around in my pockets. "If this is you, I'm killing you! Dead!"

I found the phone, and barked, "James?" before I even got it to my ear.

It wasn't James. Not even close.

"Hey there, girl," my mother singsonged, as my heart dove for the soles of my feet. I did not want to talk to my mother. Not now. "I am definitely not James! But maybe you can tell me why he'd be calling me?"

"What?"

"I said why is James coming up to visit me?" she said. "He says we have to talk. Did you two fight?"

"He's coming up to see you?" My knees unlocked so that I

nearly fell to the pavement. I clawed the car door open and dropped into the driver's seat, keeping the cell phone glued to my ear so I didn't miss a word.

"That's what he says, dear. Aren't you coming with him? What's this all about?"

An excellent question. One I would definitely ask him, when I saw him again.

"I'm not sure, but I will be there. Yes, I will. Give me eight hours," I said.

"It sounds to me like you're going on a road trip," Honoria said. "What, did James decide it was time to meet your parents?"

"I guess so," I said, and threw the car into gear. "And he will definitely pay, when I catch up with him."

Oh yes. That man is going to pay.

About the Author

E.C.Bell (also known as Eileen Bell) has had short fiction published in magazines and several anthologies, including the double Aurora Award winning Women of the Apocalypse and the Aurora winning "Bourbon and Eggnog." When she's not writing, she's in Edmonton, Alberta, living a fine life in her round house (that is in a perpetual state of renovation) with her husband, her two dogs, and her ever hungry goldfish.

CPSIA information can be obtained at www.ICGtesting.com
Printed in the USA
LVOW10s0752181115

463036LV00001B/97/P